MW01596278

辜鸿铭 英译经典 —— 中英双语评述本

论语

辜鸿铭 英译

王京涛 评述

The Discourses and Sayings
of Confucius

中华书局

图书在版编目(CIP)数据

辜鸿铭英译经典:论语:中英双语评述本/辜鸿铭英译;王京涛
评述. —北京:中华书局,2017.1
ISBN 978-7-101-11774-5

Ⅰ.辜…　Ⅱ.①辜…②王…　Ⅲ.①儒家-汉、英②《论语》-
汉、英　Ⅳ.B222.21

中国版本图书馆 CIP 数据核字(2016)第 090872 号

书　　名	辜鸿铭英译经典:论语(中英双语评述本)
英 译 者	辜鸿铭
评 述 者	王京涛
责任编辑	王　芳　万　骏
出版发行	中华书局
	(北京市丰台区太平桥西里 38 号　100073)
	http://www.zhbc.com.cn
	E-mail:zhbc@zhbc.com.cn
印　　刷	北京瑞古冠中印刷厂
版　　次	2017 年 1 月北京第 1 版
	2017 年 1 月北京第 1 次印刷
规　　格	开本/880×1230 毫米　1/32
	印张 14½　插页 2　字数 330 千字
印　　数	1-6000 册
国际书号	ISBN 978-7-101-11774-5
定　　价	56.00 元

出 版 说 明

　　《论语》是儒家经典，其英译本是西方读者了解中国思想文化的重要途径之一。自1809年英国传教士马士曼(Joshua Marshman，1768—1837)出版第一部直接译自中文的《论语》英译本(实际上是半部，只含《论语》前十篇的翻译)，到1861年英国传教士、汉学家理雅各(James Legge，1815—1897)出版译著《中国经典》(*Chinese Classic*)第一卷(包括《大学》《中庸》《论语》)，一直以来儒家经典的英译工作都是西方传教士垄断的，直至辜鸿铭的《论语》英译本出现。

　　辜鸿铭(1857—1928)是中国近代著名学者，学贯中西，精通英、法、德等多种西文，他是第一个独立完成《大学》《中庸》《论语》三部儒家经典英译的中国人。不同于理雅各等传教士，辜鸿铭翻译儒家经典的目的是要向西方传播中国文明和儒家思想。尽管精通西方文化，但辜鸿铭并不认为西方文化优于中国文化。他希望他的译介工作，能够改变西方对中国文化的不公正态度，重新认识中国。正如其《论语》英译本(1898)序言中所说："希望那些不辞劳烦阅读我们这个译本的、受过教育、拥有思想的英国人，能够重新修正他们迄今为止对中国人的看法。而且，这样做不仅能让他们重新定义对中国人的看法，也能从个人及国家层面改变对中国人及中国的态度。"他的译本不仅面向学者，也面向广大不懂中文、对中国文化感到陌生的一般西方读者，行文努力按照一个受过教育的普通英国人的思维方式来表达，尽量去掉那些中国的专有名词，多用他们熟悉的名物，如以"gentlemen"、"art"、"God"来对译"君子"、"礼"、"天"，以"古罗马"与"意大利"的关系来比喻"殷"与"宋"的传承，以"古代中国的法兰西"来称呼齐国，以1878年的柏林会议来说明齐桓公"九合诸侯"的意义，以摩西比作周公，以俾斯麦比作管仲等，故颇合西方大众口味，一直以来很受欢迎，流传甚广。

此次出版的辜鸿铭的《论语》英译本，以中英双语形式呈现，包括英译文、《论语》原文、中文今译三部分。英译文采自其1898年初版，《论语》原文采自《四书章句集注·论语》(中华书局，1983)，中文今译则回译自辜鸿铭的《论语》英译文。另外，每个章节的最后附以回译者的评述，让读者更好了解辜鸿铭对《论语》独到的理解与译法。

中华书局编辑部

2016年4月

目　录

THE DISCOURSES AND SAYINGS

OF

CONFUCIUS

论语^①

---

① 辜鸿铭译《论语》书名为"孔子的话语与格言"(The Discourses and Sayings of Confucius)，并称其英译《论语》是一种征引了歌德等作家的话作为注释的、新的特殊翻译。

PREFACE

IT is now forty years since Dr. LEGGE began the publication of the first instalment of his translation of the "Chinese Classics". Any one now, even without any acquaintance with the Chinese language, who will take the trouble to turn over the pages of Dr. LEGGE's translation, cannot help feeling how unsatisfactory the translation really is. For Dr. LEGGE, from his raw literary training when he began his work, and the utter want of critical insight and literary perception he showed to the end, was really nothing more than a great sinologue, that is to say, a pundit with a very learned but dead knowledge of Chinese books. But in justice to the memory of the great sinologue who, we regret to hear, has just recently died, it must be said that notwithstanding the extremely hard and narrow limits of his mind, which was the result of temperament, he was, as far as his insight allowed him, thoroughly conscientious in his work.

To an earnest student who can bring his own philosophical and literary acumen to study into those ponderous volumes know as Dr. LEGGE's translation of the "Chinese Classics", no doubt some insight into the moral culture, or what is called the civilization of the Chinese people, will reveal itself. But to the generality of the English reading people we cannot but think the intellectual and moral outfit

序　言

　　距离理雅各博士出版他的第一部"中国经典"，迄今已经四十年了。而在今天，即使是任何一个不具备丝毫汉语知识的人，当他不辞劳烦地翻阅理雅各博士的译文时，也会禁不住感到，他的翻译是多么差强人意。对于理雅各来说，从他开始翻译这些书所表现出的文学训练的欠缺，到最后表现出的在批判性洞察力与文学观念上的彻底匮乏，说明他仅仅是一位伟大的汉学家而已。换言之，他仅仅是一位拥有关于中国典籍的死知识的博学之人。但为了公正地看待这位伟大的汉学家（我们遗憾地闻悉他最近刚刚逝世），我们必须指出，尽管他的思想受限于极端的艰涩与狭隘，但这只是他自身气质的结果，在他的洞察力所及的范围内，他在书中完全是认真负责的。

　　对于一个热心的学生来讲，如果他能将他的哲学与文学方面的聪颖，运用于研究理雅各博士所翻译的"中国经典"那些呆板的书卷中，毫无疑问，其中对于道德文化或所谓的中国文明的某种洞察力，将会展现出来。然而，对于大多数英文读者来说，我们将不由得想到，理雅各博士在翻译中所表现出的中国人的智力与道德装备，在普通英国人眼中，就像所见到的中国人的服装与外表一样奇怪与

of the Chinaman as presented by Dr. LEGGE in his translation of the Chinese books, must appear as strange and grotesque as to an ordinary Englishman's eyes, unaccustomed to it, the Chinaman's costume and outward appearance.

The attempt is therefore hear made to render this little book, which, of all books written in the Chinese language, we believe, is *the* book which gives to the Chinaman his intellectual and moral outfit, accessible to the general English reader. With this object in view, we have tried to make Confucius and his disciples speak in the same way as an educated Englishman would speak had he to express the same thoughts which the Chinese worthies had to express. In order further to take away as much as possible the sense of strangeness and peculiarity for the English readers, we have, whenever it is possible to do so, eliminated all Chinese proper names. Lastly, with the hope of bringing home, so to speak, the significance of the thought in the text, we have added as notes quotations from well known European authors, which, by calling up the train of thought already familiar, may perhaps appeal to readers acquainted with those authors.

We take the opportunity here of paying our tribute of respect to the memory of an Englishman, Sir CHALONER ALABASTER, who has at different periods published masterful translations of many portions of this book. When in Canton ten years ago, we urged upon him to seriously undertake the translation of the Chinese sacred books, with Dr. LEGGE's translations of which we were both dissatisfied. But he was very conscientious. He said that his knowledge of Chinese books and literature was too limited; besides, that he was not a "literary man". He in turn advised us to undertake the work. Now, after ten years, just as we

4

荒诞。

因此，我们尝试让这本完全用中文写就的小书，在表达上能让普通英文读者容易理解，我们确信，这本书给中国人提供了智力与道德的装备。为了达到这个目的，我们尝试了让孔子及其学生们如同受过教育的英国人那样去说话，而表达的则是与中国先贤们相同的思想。为了尽可能地消除英国读者的陌生和古怪感，只要有可能，我们都删去了书中所有特定的中文名称。最后，为了让这本书的思想展示得到家，我们也从著名的欧洲作家那里引用了一些话，作为注解而添加其中，通过唤起已经熟悉的相关思想，或许能吸引熟知这些作家们的读者。

在此，我们也借此机会向一位英国人致敬，并把此书献给他，他就是查洛纳·阿拉伯斯特爵士。他曾在不同时期发表过对这本书的许多部分的娴熟的译文。十年前在广州时，我们曾敦促他认真着手对中国经典的翻译，因为我们对理雅各博士的译本普遍感到不满意。但他极认真负责，他说他对于中国典籍与文学的知识太有限，另外，他也并非一个"文人"。他反而建议我们去做这项工作。如今，十年过去了，当我们在他的建议之下，完成第一次尝试后，噩耗传来，这个对我们的小书有些兴趣的人，却已离我们而去了。

在前文我们说过，这本包含了孔子及其学生的话语与格言摘要的小书，给中国人提供了智力与道德的装备。在马修·阿诺德先生的极小的范畴里，他将之称为"生活评论"。对于这些装备的本质与价值，我们并不打算发表看法。我们仅想表示的是，希望那些不辞劳烦阅读我们这个译本的、受过教育、拥有思想的英国人，能够重新修

finish this first attempt to follow his advice, the melancholy news comes that he, to whom our little work would have been of some interest, has passed away from among living men.

We have said that this little book, which contains the digested saying and discourses of Confucius and his disciples — presenting in a very small compass what the late Mr. MATTHEW ARNOLD would call a "criticism of life", — is the book which gives to the Chinaman his intellectual and moral outfit. Of the nature and value of that outfit we do not feel ourselves called upon here to express an opinion. We will only here express the hope that educated and thinking Englishmen who will take the trouble to read this translation of ours, may, after reading it, be led to reconsider their hitherto foregone conceptions of the Chinese people, and in so doing be enabled not only to modify their preconceptions of the Chinese people, but also to change the attitude of their personal and national relations with the Chinese as individuals and as a nation.

KU HUNG-MING.

Viceroy's Yamen,
Wuchang,
1st August 1898.

正他们迄今为止对中国人的看法。而且，这样做不仅能让他们重新定义对中国人的看法，也能从个人及国家层面改变对中国人及中国的态度。

辜鸿铭

总督衙门

武昌

1898年8月1日

CHAPTER I
学而第一^①

---

① 辜鸿铭的翻译略去了每章篇名，这里是译者所加，下同。

1. Confucius remarked, "It is indeed a pleasure to acquire knowledge and, as you go on acquiring, to put into practice what you have acquired. A greater pleasure still it is when friends of congenial minds come from afar to seek you because of your attainments. But he is truly a wise and good man who feels no discomposure even when he is not noticed of men."

2. A disciple of Confucius remarked, "A man who is a good son and a good citizen will seldom be found to be a man disposed to quarrel with those in authority over him; and man who are not disposed to quarrel with those in authority will never be found to disturb the peace and order of the State."

   "A wise man devotes his attention to what is essential in the foundation of life.When the foundation is laid, wisdom will come. Now, to be a good son and a good citizen — do not these form the foundation of a moral life?"

3. Confucius remarked, "With plausible speech and fine manners will seldom be found moral character."

4. A disciple of Confucius remarked, "I daily examine into my personal conduct on three points: — First, whether in carrying out the duties entrusted to me by others, I have not failed in conscientiousness; Secondly, whether in intercourse with friends, I have not failed in sincerity and trustworthiness; Thirdly, whether I have not failed to practice what I profess in my teaching."

1. 子曰："学而时习之，不亦说乎？有朋自远方来，不亦乐乎？人不知而不愠，不亦君子乎？"

孔子说："去获取学问，并在不断获取的同时，又运用于实践之中，的确是件快乐的事；更快乐的事，是意气相投的朋友因你的成就而从远方来拜访你。一个人，即使在没有被人们注意到时，也并不感到烦乱不安，他就真的是一个明智而良善的人。"

2. 有子曰："其为人也孝弟，而好犯上者，鲜矣；不好犯上，而好作乱者，未之有也。君子务本，本立而道生。孝弟也者，其为仁之本与！"

孔子的一位学生说："一个作为好儿子与好公民的人，你很少会发现他喜欢与权威高于他的人争吵；而不喜欢与有权威的人争吵的人，你就绝不会发现他去扰乱国家的和平与秩序。

一个明智的人会把注意力集中在生活基础的关键问题上。这个基础确立后，智慧随之而来。现在，去做一个好儿子和好公民吧——这些不就是形成道德生活的基础吗？"

3. 子曰："巧言令色，鲜矣仁！"

孔子说："具有貌似合理的言语和伪善态度的人，你很少会发现他具备道德品质。"

4. 曾子曰："吾日三省吾身：为人谋而不忠乎？与朋友交而不信乎？传不习乎？"

孔子的一位学生说："我每天都在这三方面审查我的个人言行：第一，在执行那些别人委托给我的职责时，我是否没有丧失良心；第二，在与朋友们的交往中，我是否没有失掉真诚与可靠；第三，我是否没有践行我在教学中所宣称的东西。"

5. Confucius remarked, "When directing the affairs of a great nation, a man must be serious in attention to business and faithful and punctual in his engagements.He must study economy in the public expenditure, and love the welfare of the people.He must employ the people at the proper time of the year."

6. Confucius remarked, "A young man, when at home, should be a good son; when out in the world, a good citizen.He should be circumspect and truthful.He should be in sympathy with all men, but intimate with men of moral character.If he has time and opportunity to spare, after the performance of those duties, he should then employ them in literary pursuits."

7. A disciple of Confucius remarked: "A man who can love worthiness in man as he loves beauty in woman; who in his duties to his parents is ready to do his utmost, and in the service of his prince is ready to give up his life; who in intercourse with friends is found trustworthy in what he says, — such a man, although men may say of him that he is an uneducated man, I must consider him to be really an educated man."

8. Confucius remarked, "A wise man who is not serious will not inspire respect; what he learns will not remain permanent."
   "Make conscientiousness and sincerity your first principles.
   "Have no friends who are not as yourself.
   "When you have bad habits do not hesitate to change them."

5. 子曰："道千乘之国，敬事而信，节用而爱人，使民以时。"

　　孔子说："当管理一个大国的事务时，一个人必须严肃认真地做事，并在自己的契约中忠诚、守时。他必须在财政支出中留心节俭，并热爱人民的福祉。他必须在一年中恰当的时机使役人民。"

6. 子曰："弟子入则孝，出则弟，谨而信，泛爱众，而亲仁。行有余力，则以学文。"

　　孔子说："一个年轻人，在家应该做个好儿子；在社会上应该做个好公民。他为人应该谨慎而诚实。他应该怜悯所有的人并亲近有道德品质的人。如果在履行这些义务之后，他有额外的时间与机会，那么，他应该追求文学。"

7. 子夏曰："贤贤易色；事父母能竭其力，事君能致其身，与朋友交言而有信。虽曰未学，吾必谓之学矣。"

　　孔子的一位学生说："一个人能够热爱人的美德就像他热爱女人的美貌；在为父母尽义务时，准备做到最好，而在为国君服务时，准备献出自己的生命；与朋友交往时，他说的话总是被认为值得信任——这样一个人，尽管人们会说他是未受教育的人，但我一定会把他视为一个真正受过教育的人。"

8. 子曰："君子不重则不威，学则不固。主忠信。无友不如己者。过则勿惮改。"

　　孔子说："一个明智的人，如果他不严肃庄重，就不会受人尊敬；他所学的，也就不会保持牢固。

　　"把良心与真诚作为你的首要原则。

　　"没有与你自己不同的朋友。

　　"当你有了坏习惯，要毫不犹豫地改正它们。"

9. A disciple of Confucius remarked: "By cultivating respect for the dead, and carrying the memory back to the distant past, the moral feeling of the people will waken and grow in depth."

10. A man once asked a disciple of Confucius, saying, "How was it that whenever the Master came into a country he was always informed of the actual state and policy of its government? Did he seek for the information or was it given to him?"

    "The Master," replied the disciple, "was gracious, simple, earnest, modest and courteous; therefore he could obtain what information he wanted.The Master's way of obtaining information — well, it was different from other people's ways."

11. Confucius remarked, "When a man's father is living the son should have regard to what his father would have him do; when the father is dead, to what his father has done.A son who for three years after his father's death does not in his own life change his father's principles, may be said to be a good son."

12. A disciple of Confucius remarked, "In the practice of art, what is valuable is natural spontaneity.According to the rules of art held by the ancient kings it was this quality in a work of art which constituted its excellence; in great as well as in small things they were guided by this principle.

    "But in the being natural there is something not permitted.To

9. 曾子曰:"慎终追远,民德归厚矣。"

　　孔子的一位学生说:"通过培养对逝者的敬意,并追忆那遥远的过去,人们的道德情感就会觉醒并趋于醇厚。"

10. 子禽问于子贡曰:"夫子至于是邦也,必闻其政,求之与? 抑与之与?"子贡曰:"夫子温、良、恭、俭、让以得之。夫子之求之也,其诸异乎人之求之与?"

　　有一次,有人问孔子的一位学生:"老师每到一个国家,总能获悉其政治的实际状态与政策,这是怎么回事呢? 信息是他寻求来的,还是别人给他的?"

　　"我们的老师,"那位学生回答,"是和蔼、简朴、诚挚、谦逊而又恭敬有礼的,因此,他总是能获得他想知道的信息。老师获取信息的方式——是啊,与其他人的方式是不同的。"

11. 子曰:"父在,观其志;父没,观其行;三年无改于父之道,可谓孝矣。"

　　孔子说:"一个人,当他的父亲健在时,他应该注意到他父亲想要他做什么;在他父亲去世后,他应该注意到他父亲做过什么。如果一个儿子在他父亲去世后三年以内,他在自己的生活中没有改变他父亲的原则,那么,他就可以被称作是个好儿子。"

12. 有子曰:"礼之用,和为贵。先王之道斯为美,小大由之。有所不行,知和而和,不以礼节之,亦不可行也。"

　　孔子的一个学生说:"艺术实践中的价值,是天然的自发性。通过古代国王们持有的艺术法则来看,正是艺术品中所蕴含的这种特质,形成了它的卓越性;无论是重大的还是细微的事情,它们都被这种原则所引导着。

know that it is necessary to be natural without restraining the impulse to be natural by the strict principle of art, — that is something not permitted."

13. A disciple of Confucius remarked, "If you make promises within the bounds of what is right, you will be able to keep your word. If you confine earnestness within the bounds of judgment and good taste, you will keep out of discomfiture and insult.If you make friends of those with whom you ought to, you will be able to depend upon them."

14. Confucius remarked, "A wise and good man, in matters of food, should never seek to indulge his appetite; in lodging, he should not be too solicitous of comfort.He should be diligent in business and careful in speech.He should seek for the company of men of virtue and learning, in order to profit by their lessons and example.In this way he may become a man of real culture."

15. A disciple of Confucius said to him, "To be poor and yet not to be servile; to be rich and yet not to be proud, what do you say to that?"

"It is good," replied Confucius, "but better still it is to be poor and yet contented; to be rich and yet know how to be courteous."

"I understand," answered the disciple:

"We must cut, we must file,

Must chisel and must grind."

"That is what you mean, is it not?"

"但在自然而发时，也有些东西是不被允许的。没有通过严格的艺术原则来抑制冲动的自然而发，就是不被允许的，这个需要搞清楚。"

13. 有子曰："信近于义，言可复也；恭近于礼，远耻辱也；因不失其亲，亦可宗也。"

    孔子的一位学生说："假如你在正义范围之内作出承诺，你就能够遵守诺言。假如你把热诚限制于判断力与良好品位的范围之内，你将免于挫败与羞辱。假如你与那些值得交朋友的人相交，你将能够依靠他们。"

14. 子曰："君子食无求饱，居无求安，敏于事而慎于言，就有道而正焉，可谓好学也已。"

    孔子说："一个明智而良善的人，在饮食上绝不应追求放纵他的食欲；在住宿上不应过于渴望安逸舒适。他应该做事勤勉，言语谨慎。为了能够从别人的经验与榜样中获益，他应该寻找具有美德与学问的人为伴。这样，他就会成为一个真正有教养的人。"

15. 子贡曰："贫而无谄，富而无骄，何如？"子曰："可也。未若贫而乐，富而好礼者也。"子贡曰："《诗》云：'如切如磋，如琢如磨。'其斯之谓与？"子曰："赐也，始可与言《诗》已矣！告诸往而知来者。"

    孔子的一位学生问他："贫穷但并不奴颜婢膝，富有但并不妄自尊大，您认为怎么样？"

    "这很好，"孔子回答说，"但比之更好的，是贫穷但知足安乐，富有但恭敬有礼。"

    "我懂了，"那位学生回答说：

    我们必须切而又切，磋而又磋，

"My friend," replied Confucius, "now I can begin to speak of poetry to you. I see you understand how to apply the moral."

16. Confucius remarked, "One should not be concerned not to be understood of men; one should be concerned not to understand men."

又须凿刻碾磨。

"这就是您的意思,不是吗?"

"我的朋友,"孔子回答说,"现在,我可以开始给你谈论诗了。我想你已懂得了如何去致力于道德修养。"

16. 子曰:"不患人之不己知,患不知人也。"

孔子说:"一个人不应该担心不被他人理解;而应该担心对他人不理解。"

【评述】

1. 在这里，"君子"译为"a wise and good man"，即"明智而良善的人"（通俗的译法是"一个聪明的好人"）。

2. 这一节中，辜鸿铭略去了"有子"的名字。在对《论语》的英译中，辜鸿铭略去了大部分人名、地名、国名，甚至普通器物的名称，把《论语》变成一部比较单纯的思想对话录。他之所以这样做，是"为了尽可能地消除英国读者的陌生和古怪感"（序言语），但对于后文中一些关键的人物及其他名称，他还是作了保留的，比如"仲由"、"颜回"、"管仲"、"尧"、"舜"、"禹"等人的名字。"孝弟"是本节的关键词。"孝"，辜鸿铭译为"be a good son"，"做一个好儿子"；"弟"译为"be a good citizen"，"做一个好公民"。"孝弟也者，其为仁之本与"一句，"仁"译为"a moral life"，"道德的生活"；"本"译为"what is essential in the foundation of life"，"生活基础的本质或关键问题"。本节说的是，"孝"（做一个好儿子）与"弟"（做一个好公民）是道德生活的本质。

3. "巧言令色"，辜鸿铭译为"with plausible speech and fine manners"，"具有貌似合理的言语和伪善态度"。这里的"仁"，译为"moral character"，"道德品质"。本节指判断一个人的道德品质，绝不能仅仅依据于他外在的言辞与态度。

4. "为人谋而不忠乎"一句，"忠"，辜鸿铭译为"not fail in conscientiousness"，"没有丧失掉良心或责任心"。辜鸿铭在多数情况下都是将"忠"译为"conscientiousness"，即良心或责任心，指做事尽责。

5. 这一节是孔子关于治国的讨论。"道"，辜鸿铭译为"direct"，即指导，管理。"千乘之国"，译为"a great nation"，"一个大国"，此处省略了"千乘"的具体含义。

"敬事而信"一句，"信"，译为"faithful and punctual in his engagements"，"在契约中忠诚守时"。在《半部〈论语〉》一文中，辜鸿铭又将"信"解为"有恒"："朱子解'敬事而信'曰：'敬其事而信于民。'余谓'信'当作'有恒'解。如唐诗'早知潮有信，嫁与弄潮儿'。"（汪堂家编译，《乱世奇文·张文襄幕府纪闻》，上海人民出版社，2002，第399页）

"使民以时"一句，"时"辜鸿铭译为"the proper time of the year"，即"一年中恰当的时候"，指在恰当的时候让人民承担劳役。辜鸿铭注释说：

> 在古代中国，人民具有较轻的征税负担，但在战争时期却对国家肩负劳役和兵役的义务。

6. 辜鸿铭把"弟子"译为"a young man"，即年轻人；把"孝弟"分别译为"be a good son"和"be a good citizen"，即"做一个好儿子"和"做一个好公民"。在此可以看出，儒学中对人的"出"与"入"两个方面的不同要求，构成了传统中国人为人处世的两个维度。

"泛爱"译为"in sympathy with"，"同情、怜悯、体谅"之意。这也是辜鸿铭对"爱"的独特解读，他认为，泛爱众即指对大众要有怜悯、同情之心。这里的"仁"，译为"men of moral character"，此处并非指品德，而是指具有道德品质的人。

"行有余力，则以学文"一句，辜鸿铭将"学文"译为"literary pursuits"，即追求文学之意。辜鸿铭一贯看重文学作品对于人的道德品性的影响。他在《中国人的精神（在北京东方学会上所宣讲的论文）》一文中认为："学校——中国国教中的教堂，教人以诗文，培养人美好的感情，使之服从道德行为规范。事实上，正如我曾说过的那样，所有伟大的文学作品都能像宗教一样使人受到感动。马太·阿诺德在谈及荷马及其《史诗》时说：'《史诗》那高尚的思想内容，可以令读者变换气质、受到陶冶。'实质上，在学校——中国国教的教堂里，一切文雅、有价值的美好东西都得到了传授。学校让学生不断想着这些美好的事物，自然激发出人之向善的情感，从而自觉地遵守道德规范。"（夏丹等选编，《辜鸿铭作品精选·中国人的精神》，长江文艺出版社，2004，第59页）

7. 在辜鸿铭看来，这一节讲的才算是真正的教育。他将"未学"译为"uneducated"，即没受过教育的；"学矣"，则译为"really educated"，即真正受过教育的。他认为，教育的真正意义并不是知识，而是人格的培养。即使没有专门受过教育，但在生活中形成了良好的道德品质，那他就是个真正受过教育的人。

文中，"贤贤易色"，他将第一个"贤"译为"love"，"热爱"；第二个"贤"译为"worthiness"，"美德"；"色"译为"beauty"，"美丽，美貌"。这句是指希望人们能够像喜爱"女人的美丽"那样天然地喜爱美德。

8. 文中，辜鸿铭将"主"译为"make ... first principles"，即"将之作为第一原则"，也就是人应将"忠信"（conscientiousness and sincerity，良心与真诚）当作做人的首要原则。"无友不如己者"，译为"have no friends who are not as yourself"，"没有与你自己不同的朋友"，"如"译为"as"，相同、相似之意。

9. "慎终追远"，辜鸿铭译为"cultivating respect for the dead, and carrying the memory back to the distant past"，"培养对逝者的敬意，并追忆那遥远的过去"。他注释说：

我追思往昔，默念我心中永恒的岁月。

"民德归厚"译为"the moral feeling of the people will waken and grow in depth","人们的道德情感就会觉醒并趋于醇厚",指对祖先及历史的追述对人民的道德具有醇远的影响。

10. 本节重点在于阐述怎样的人才能获得尊重与信任。简言之,就是要"温、良、恭、俭、让"的品质。辜鸿铭译为"gracious, simple, earnest, modest and courteous",实则在翻译中变换了顺序,"温、俭、良、恭、让",即"和蔼的、简朴的、诚挚的、谦逊的、有礼的"。做到如此,自然可以获得尊重与信任。"政",他译为"the actual state and policy of its government",即该国政治的实际状态与政策。

11. "三年无改于父之道"的"道"字,译为"principles","原则",指父亲的做事原则。指通过对父亲生前的了解,于其去世之后继承其志愿。这节表达了父子之间要有一种精神层面的传承关系。

12. 本节的核心是对"礼"的阐释,而辜鸿铭极为特殊地解读了"礼":将"礼"译为"art",即艺术。他首先对"礼"(art)添加了大段注释:

理雅各博士认为,我们在此将汉字"礼"译成"art"的这个词,很难用另外一种语言来描绘。张伯伦先生在他的《日本事物志》(*Things Japanese*)一书中也认为,与汉语具有相同书面语言的日语中,也没有固有的词来对应"art"。

如果我们没搞错的话,英语词汇"art"常在多种多样的运用中去展现其含义:第一,艺术作品(a work of art);第二,艺术实践(the practice of art);第三,与"天然的"(natural)相对的"人工的"(artificial);第四,与本质(nature)的原理相对的技巧(art)的原理;第五,严格的艺术的原理(the strict principle of art)。在这里的最后一项所要表达的英文词汇"art"的意思,即理雅各博士评论我们在上面提及的那个汉语词汇时所说的,在万物关联中"什么才是恰当的与合适的"的见解。

对那些对此话题可能有兴趣的人,我们需要在此处强调,现代日语中用来对应"art"的*bijutsu*美术(美丽的戏法)一词,并不是个恰当的词汇。在汉语中对应"艺术作品"的术语应该是"文物";对应"艺术实践"的是"艺"。实际上,日语词汇"艺师"的表面意思是指一位艺人。同样的,对"art"这一术语在"人工的"(artificial)——用来对应"天然的"某物——的运用中,庄子这位哲学家用的是"人"(human)和"天"(divine)。

然后,在"技巧的原理"(the principle of art)作为"本质的原理"(the principle of nature)的对立面讲时,应该用汉语中的"文"来对应"技巧","质"来对应"本质"。

举例子来说，歌德在"技巧被称作技巧（art），是因为它不是本质（nature）"一句中具有同样的主张。翻译成汉语或日语即"文之所以谓之文，为非质也"。中国的艺术评论家也用"化工"来表示创造性的艺术，而"画工"则表示模仿性的艺术。最后，我们需要附加说明的是，汉语中用来表达机械式的艺术及其实践的术语是"技艺"。

也就是说，一般情况下，辜鸿铭在《论语》中谈"礼"这个问题时，很多情况下就是谈"艺术"问题。他甚至将中国人的礼节也理解为"艺术"，是一种行为的艺术。但在整部《论语》中，辜鸿铭对"礼"的翻译还是比较多样的，会根据不同的语境而进行不同的翻译，在接下来的篇章中我们会遇到。

在将"礼"解读为"艺术"的基础上，辜鸿铭将"和"译为"natural spontaneity"，即天然的自发性。因为将"礼"理解为"艺术"，所以，他将"先王之道"的"道"译为"the rules of art"，即艺术的法则。"美"，译为"constituted its excellence"，即卓越的。也即，这种遵循天然的自发性的艺术原则，使得艺术品变得优秀卓越。但在强调"天然的自发性（和）"的同时，文中还指出"不以礼节之，亦不可行也"，辜鸿铭译为"To know that it is necessary to be natural without restraining the impulse to be natural by the strict principle of art, — that is something not permitted"，"没有通过严格的艺术原则来抑制冲动的自然而发，就是不被允许的"。

13. "自由率性"与"社会约束"这对矛盾在辜鸿铭的思想中占有很重要的位置，也是他认识儒学的一个重要方面。本节中，"恭"与"礼"同样是这对矛盾的体现。"恭"，译为"earnestness"（热诚，发自内心的热情、诚挚），"礼"译为"judgment and good taste"（判断力与良好的品位，即人的理性与修养）。"恭近于礼，远耻辱也"即指在"判断力与良好的品位"的约束之下来表达自己的热诚，就会免于"discomfiture and insult"（挫败与羞辱）。

14. 本节说的是一个"君子"合理的生活方式与行为方式。其中，"敏于事而慎于言，就有道而正焉"是指行为方式。这里的"有道"，译为"men of virtue and learning"，"有美德与学问的人"。"正"，译为"profit by their lessons and example"，"从他们的经验与榜样中获益"。这句话就是指人们应从那些有德之人身上汲取生活的修养、品德，来完善、修正自己的品格。而如果能达到以上行为标准，他就是"好学"的。"学"译为"of real culture"，即"具有真正的教养"。

15. 本节包含着一种递进的逻辑，即从"贫而无谄，富而无骄"到"贫而乐，富而好礼"的递进，而文中引自《诗经·卫风·淇奥》的那句诗也表达了这样的含义。

"贫而无谄，富而无骄"一句，"谄"译为"servile"，"过分屈从的，奴性的，逢迎的"。"骄"译为"proud"，"傲慢，妄自尊大"，指虽然贫穷，但坚持自己的自主性与尊严，即使富有也不会妄自尊大。再进一步，到"贫而乐，富而好礼"。辜鸿铭将"乐"译为"contented"，"满足的，安心的"，即不会仅仅因为贫穷而心生不满。"好礼"，译为"know how to be courteous"，"恭敬有礼"。即在同样贫穷或富有的条件下，从"不奴颜婢膝、不妄自尊大"的消极姿态，递进为更理想的"知足安乐、恭敬有礼"的积极姿态。

　　"始可与言诗已矣"一句中的"诗"，学者多理解为《诗经》一书，辜鸿铭则将之翻译为"诗歌"，泛指诗这种文学形式。辜鸿铭对文学的看法见本章第6节的评述。辜鸿铭将下一句的"告诸往而知来者"译为"understand how to apply the moral"，"我想你已懂得了如何去致力于道德修养"，是一种意译，指子贡已经懂得了精益求精（递进）地致力于道德修养的方法。

　　16. 文中，"知"，辜鸿铭译为"understand"，"理解"之意。"己知"即他人理解自己；"知人"指自己对他人的理解，这里反映的是自己与他人之间的关系。指人应该担心自己不理解别人，而不是担心别人不理解自己。在《照相》一文中，辜鸿铭曾引述其老师（英国思想家托马斯·卡莱尔）的话表达了类似的看法："凡贵人欲观人者也……贱者欲取观于人者也……。"（汪堂家编译，《乱世奇文·张文襄幕府纪闻》，第416页）这可以概括为"贵者观人，贱者受观"的思想。

CHAPTER II
为政第二

1. Confucius remarked, "He who rules the people, depending upon the moral sentiment, is like the Pole-star, which keeps its place while all the other stars revolve round it."

2. Confucius remarked, "The Book of Ballads, Songs and Psalms contains three hundred pieces.The moral of them all may be summed up in one sentence:'Have no evil thoughts.' "

3. Confucius remarked, "If in government you depend upon laws, and maintain order by enforcing those laws by punishments, you can also make the people keep away from wrong-doing, but they will lose the sense of shame for wrong-doing. If, on the other hand, in government you depend upon the moral sentiment, and maintain order by encouraging education and good manners, the people will have a sense of shame for wrong-doing and, moreover, will emulate what is good."

4. Confucius remarked, "At fifteen I had made up my mind to give myself up to serious studies. At thirty I had formed my opinions and judgment. At forty I had no more doubts. At fifty I understood the truth in religion. At sixty I could understand whatever I heard without exertion.At seventy I could follow whatever my heart desired without transgressing the law."

5. A noble of the Court in Confucius' native State asked him what constituted the duty of a good son. Confucius answered, "Do not fail in what is required of you."

1. 子曰:"为政以德,譬如北辰,居其所而众星共之。"

　　孔子说:"用道德情感来统治人民的人,就像北极星,它保持在那个位置上不动,而其他所有的星辰却都围绕它旋转。"

2. 子曰:"《诗》三百,一言以蔽之,曰'思无邪'。"

　　孔子说:"那本关于民谣、诗歌与赞美诗的文学典籍,包含三百篇作品。它们的寓意可以用一句话来概括:'没有邪恶的思想。'"

3. 子曰:"道之以政,齐之以刑,民免而无耻;道之以德,齐之以礼,有耻且格。"

　　孔子说:"如果你在统治中依赖律法,并通过刑罚强制实施那些律法来维持秩序,你也可以使人民免于犯罪,但他们将丧失犯罪的羞耻感。另一方面,如果你在统治中依靠道德情感,并通过促进教育与良好的礼仪来维持秩序,那么人民就会有犯罪的羞耻感,而且,他们还会达到符合道德的标准。"

4. 子曰:"吾十有五而志于学,三十而立,四十而不惑,五十而知天命,六十而耳顺,七十而从心所欲,不逾矩。"

　　孔子说:"十五岁时,我已下决心投身于认真严肃的学习研究。三十岁时,我已形成了自己的观点和判断力。四十岁时,我已经不再有疑惑。五十岁时,我明白了宗教中的真理。六十岁时,我能够懂得任何我所听到的事情,而毫不费力。七十岁时,我能够遵从任何我心中所欲求的,而不超越律法。"

5. 孟懿子问孝。子曰:"无违。"樊迟御,子告之曰:"孟孙问孝于我,我对曰'无违'。"樊迟曰:"何谓也?"子曰:"生,事之以礼;死,葬之以礼,祭之以礼。"

Afterwards, as a disciple was driving him in his carriage, Confucius told the disciple, saying, "My Lord M — asked me what constituted the duty of a good son, and I answered, 'Do not fail in what is required of you.'"

"What did you mean by that?"asked the disciple.

"I meant," replied Confucius, "when his parents are living, a good son should do his duties to them according to the usage prescribed by propriety; when they are dead, he should bury them and honour their memory according to the rites prescribed by propriety."

6. A son of the noble mentioned above put the same question to Confucius as his father did.Confucius answered, "Think how anxious your parents are when you are sick, and you will know your duty towards them."

7. A disciple of Confucius asked him the same question as the above. Confucius answered, "The duty of a good son nowadays means only to be able to support his parents.But you also keep your dogs and horses alive.If there is no feeling of love and respect, where is the difference?"

8. Another disciple asked the same question.Confucius answered, "The difficulty is with the expression of your look.That merely when anything is to be done the young people do it, and when there is food and wine the old folk are allowed to enjoy it, — do you think that is the whole duty of a good son?"

孔子故国王室的一位贵族问他，什么才是一个好儿子的义务。孔子回答说："不要违背所要求你做的。"

后来，当一位学生为他驾驶马车时，孔子告诉那位学生："孟大人问过我什么才是一个好儿子的义务，我回答说，'不要违背所要求你做的。'"

"您是指的什么意思呢？"那位学生问。

"我是说，"孔子回答，"当他父母在世时，一个好儿子应该按照礼节规定的方式来为他们尽义务；父母去世后，他应该按照礼节规定的仪式来安葬和纪念他的父母。"

6. 孟武伯问孝。子曰："父母唯其疾之忧。"

上面提到的那位贵族的一位儿子，像他父亲一样，问孔子同样的问题。孔子回答："想想当你生病的时候你父母是多么焦急，你就会明白你对他们的义务了。"

7. 子游问孝。子曰："今之孝者，是谓能养。至于犬马，皆能有养；不敬，何以别乎？"

孔子的一位学生问他上面提到的同样问题。孔子回答说："今天，一个好儿子的义务，仅仅是指能够赡养他的父母。但你同样也养活了你的狗和马。如果没有热爱与尊敬的情感，区别在哪儿呢？"

8. 子夏问孝。子曰："色难。有事弟子服其劳，有酒食先生馔，曾是以为孝乎？"

孔子的另一个学生问及同一个问题。孔子回答说："困难在于你脸色的表达。当有任何事需要做时，年轻人去做；当有食物和美酒时，让长辈去享用，仅仅这样——你认为这是一个好儿子的全部义务吗？"

9. Confucius, speaking of a favourite disciple whose name was Yen Hui, remarked, "I have talked with him for one whole day, during which he has never once raised one single objection to what I have said, as if he were dull of understanding. But when he has retired, on examining into his life and conversation I find he has been able to profit by what I have said to him. No — he is not a man dull of understanding."

10. Confucius remarked, "You look at how a man acts; consider his motives; find out his tastes. How can a man hide himself; how can he hide himself from you?"

11. Confucius remarked, "If a man will constantly go over what he has acquired and keep continually adding to it new acquirements, he may become a teacher of men."

12. Confucius remarked, "A wise man will not make himself into a mere machine fit only to do one kind of work."

13. A disciple enquired what constituted a wise and good man. Confucius answered, "A wise and good man is one who acts before he speaks, and afterwards speaks according to his actions."

14. Confucius remarked, "A wise man is impartial, not neutral. A fool is neutral but not impartial."

9. 子曰:"吾与回言终日,不违如愚。退而省其私,亦足以发。回也不愚。"

   孔子谈到一个他最喜爱的名叫颜回的学生,说:"我曾一整天和他谈话,过程中他从来没有对我所说的话提出异议,哪怕一次,就像是他理解力迟钝一样。但当他离开之后,通过查看他的生活和人际交往,我发现他已经能够从我对他所说的话中受益了。不——他并不是个理解力迟钝的人。"

10. 子曰:"视其所以,观其所由,察其所安。人焉廋哉?人焉廋哉?"

   孔子说:"你审视一个人如何处事;注意他的动机;找出他的旨趣所在。这样,他怎么能够掩饰得了他自己呢;他怎么能够对你掩饰得了他自己呢?"

11. 子曰:"温故而知新,可以为师矣。"

   孔子说:"如果一个人能够不断地温习他已经获得的学问,并不断地用新学问去补充它,他就可以成为人们的老师。"

12. 子曰:"君子不器。"

   孔子说:"明智的人将不会让自己变成一台可怜的机器,只适合做一种工作。"

13. 子贡问君子。子曰:"先行其言而后从之。"

   一位学生询问怎样才算是一个明智而良善的人。孔子回答说:"一个明智而良善的人,就是一个先做而后说,然后,又按照行动来说话的人。"

14. 子曰:"君子周而不比,小人比而不周。"

   孔子说:"明智的人,是公正而非中立的。愚蠢的人则是中立而非公正的。"

15. Confucius remarked, "Study without thinking is labour lost. Thinking without study is perilous."

16. Confucius remarked, "To give oneself up to the study of metaphysical theories — that is very injurious indeed."

17. Confucius said to a disciple, "Shall I teach you what is understanding? To know what it is that you know, and to know what it is that you do not know, — that is understanding."

18. A disciple was studying with a view to preferment. Confucius said to him, "Read and learn everything, but suspend your judgment on anything of which you are in doubt; for the rest, be careful in what you say: in that way you will give few occasions for men to criticise what you say. Mix with the world and see everything, but keep away and do not meddle with anything which may bring you into trouble; for the rest, be careful in what you do: in that way you will have few occasions for self-reproach."

    "Now if in your conversation you give few occasions for men to criticise you, and in your conduct you have few occasions for self-reproach, you cannot help getting preferment, even if you would not."

19. The reigning prince of his native State asked Confucius what should be done to secure the submission of the people. Confucius answered, "Uphold the cause of the just and put down every cause that is unjust, and the people will submit. But uphold the cause of the unjust and put down every cause that is just, then the people will not submit."

15. 子曰："学而不思则罔,思而不学则殆。"

    孔子说:"学习而不思考,是徒劳的。思考而不学习,则是危险的。"

16. 子曰："攻乎异端,斯害也已!"

    孔子说:"使自己沉湎于形而上学理论的研究之中——那的确是非常有害的。"

17. 子曰："由!诲女知之乎? 知之为知之,不知为不知,是知也。"

    孔子对一个学生说:"让我告诉你什么是聪明吧? 要知道什么东西是你所知道的,也要知道什么东西是你所不知道的——这就是聪明。"

18. 子张学干禄。子曰："多闻阙疑,慎言其余,则寡尤;多见阙殆,慎行其余,则寡悔。言寡尤,行寡悔,禄在其中矣。"

    一位学生为了晋升而在学习。孔子对他说:"研究与学习每件事情时,要停止判断任何你所心存疑惑的事情;至于其他事情,谈论时要谨慎:这样,你将很少给人们机会去非难你所说的话。与世人相处并经历每件事情时,要远离而且不参与任何能给你带来麻烦的事情;至于其他事情,做事时要谨慎:这样,你就很少有机会去自责。

    "如果你在谈话中给人们很少的机会去非难你,在行为上很少有机会去自责,你自然就会获得晋升,即使你不想。"

19. 哀公问曰："何为则民服?"孔子对曰："举直错诸枉,则民服;举枉错诸直,则民不服。"

    孔子故国的执政国君问他,应该怎么做才能获得民众的服从。孔子回答说:"支持公正的主张而取缔任何不公正的主张,人民就会服从。支持不公正的主张而取缔任何公正的主张,人民就不会服从。"

20. A noble who was the minister in power in the government in Confucius' native State asked him what should be done to inspire a feeling of respect and loyalty in the people, in order to make them exert themselves for the good of the country. Confucius answered, "Treat them with seriousness and they will respect you. Let them see that you honour your parents and your prince, and are considerate for the welfare of those under you, and the people will be loyal to you. Advance those who excel in anything and educate the ignorant, and the people will exert themselves."

21. Somebody asked Confucius, saying, "Why are you not taking part in the government of the country?"

Confucius answered, "What does the 'Book of Records' say of the duties of a good son?

"'Be dutiful to your parents; be brotherly to your brothers; discharge your duties in the government of your family.'These, then , are also duties of government. Why then must one take part in the government of the country in order to discharge the duties of government?"

22. Confucius remarked, "I do not know how men get along without good faith. A cart without a yoke and a carriage without harness — how could they go?"

23. A disciple asked Confucius whether ten generations after their time the state of the civilisation of the world could be known.

20. 季康子问:"使民敬、忠以劝,如之何?"子曰:"临之以庄则敬,孝慈则忠,举善而教不能则劝。"

    孔子故国政府中一位身为当权大臣的贵族问他,要在人民中激发起尊敬与忠诚的情感,以便让人民能为国家的利益而努力,应该如何去做。孔子回答说:"严肃认真地对待他们,他们就会尊敬你。让他们看到你敬重你的父母和国君,并关怀那些地位比你低的人的福利,人民就会忠诚于你。晋升那些在任何方面有所擅长的人,并对那些缺乏知识的人提供教育,人民就会努力。"

21. 或谓孔子曰:"子奚不为政?"子曰:"《书》云:'孝乎惟孝、友于兄弟,施于有政。'是亦为政,奚其为为政?"

    有人问孔子,说:"你为什么不参与国家的政治呢?"

    孔子回答:"《尚书》中是怎么谈论一个好儿子的义务的?

    "'对父母要恭顺,对兄弟要友爱,在家政中要履行你的义务。'那么,这也是政治的义务啊。一个人如果要履行政治的义务,为什么非要参与国家的政治呢?"

22. 子曰:"人而无信,不知其可也。大车无輗,小车无軏,其何以行之哉?"

    孔子说:"我不知道一个人如果没有诚信会怎样生活下去。一驾大车没有套牲口的曲木,一辆小车没有马具——它们怎么行驶呢?"

23. 子张问:"十世可知也?"子曰:"殷因于夏礼,所损益,可知也;周因于殷礼,所损益,可知也;其或继周者,虽百世可知也。"

    一位学生问孔子,他们十代之后的世界文明的情况能否知晓。

Confucius answered, "The House of Yin adopted the civilisation of the Hsia dynasty; what modifications they made is known. The present Chou dynasty adopted the civilisation of the House of Yin; what modifications this last dynasty made are also known. Perhaps some other may hereafter take the place of the present Chou dynasty; but should that happen a hundred generations after this, the state of the civilisation of the world then, can be known."

24. Confucius remarked, "To worship a spirit to whom one is not bound by a real feeling of duty or respect is idolatry; to see what is right and to act against one's judgment shows a want of courage."

孔子回答说:"殷王朝继承了夏朝的文明;他们所做的一些修改是知道的。当前的周朝继承了殷王朝的文明,它所做的一些修改,也是知道的。也许,此后其他朝代会替代现在的周朝;但即使是在百代之后发生,那时世界文明的情况也是可以知道的。"

24. 子曰:"非其鬼而祭之,谄也。见义不为,无勇也。"

孔子说:"崇拜一个你对其并没有真正的义务与敬意的神灵,就是盲目崇拜;看到了正义,却在行为上与你的判断相悖,这显示出你勇气的缺失。"

【评述】

1. 本节讲的是"德治"的政治理念。"德",辜鸿铭译为"the moral sentiment","道德情感"。"以",译为"depend upon","依靠"之意。在辜鸿铭看来,"道德情感"是一种政治统治应该依靠的精神力量,因为他不仅强调了"道德",他也强调了那是一种"情感"。他在《雅各宾主义的中国》一文中说:"那个成功地变作最高统治者的人,必须具备能激发憧憬并赢得全民族尊敬的卓越的道德品质。"(夏丹等选编,《辜鸿铭作品精选·中国牛津运动故事》,第209页)

2. 文中,"诗"也即《诗经》,辜鸿铭译为"The Book of Ballads, Songs and Psalms","关于民谣、诗歌与赞美诗的文学典籍"。这一翻译体现了《诗经》的内容构成:分别用"Ballads"对应"风",即民谣,民歌;用"Songs"对应"雅",泛指诗歌;用"Psalms"对应"颂",即宗庙祭祀的诗篇。他在此注释说:

> 现在被称作"精品诗集",即在"中国圣经"中被称作"五经"中的一部。

下文中"思无邪"一句,辜鸿铭译为"have no evil thoughts","没有邪恶的思想"。他将"思"译为"thoughts","思想",即《诗经》所蕴含的寓意、所表达的思想"之意。

3. 本节与本章第1节讲的都是以德治国的政治理念,而本节的关键则在于"耻"字。"耻",辜鸿铭译为"the sense of shame",即"廉耻感"。在辜鸿铭看来,人类的"廉耻感"是社会与文明的最根本的基础,而且是社会得以运转所必需的。他在《中国人的精神(在北京东方学会上所宣讲的论文)》中说:"孔子在国教中教导人们,君子之道、人的廉耻感不仅是一个国家,而且是所有社会和文明的合理的、永久的、绝对的基础,除此之外,别无其他。……为了使社会的每一部分都得以运转,廉耻感不仅是重要的,而且是绝对必需的。……实际上,人没有了廉耻感,社会就只能依靠暴力来维持一段短暂的时间。但我可以证明,暴力无法使一个社会长治久安。警察靠暴力迫使商人履行合同。但法官、政府官员或共和国总统又是如何使警察恪尽职守的呢? 当然不再是暴力。那么又是什么呢? 或是靠警察的廉耻感,或是利用欺骗。"(夏丹等选编,《辜鸿铭作品精选·中国人的精神》,第41—42页)

另外,此节的"礼"字,辜鸿铭译为"education and good manners","教育与良好的礼仪"。"格",译为"emulate what is good","达到符合道德的标准"。他意在表达的是,道德统治的目的,其实并不在于"统治",而在于"自治",即激发人民自身的道德情感,使他们养成自觉的道德素养,从而使外在的统治变得多余。辜鸿铭在著作中多次表达这样的思想,并称之为这是传统中国社会中理性的民主。他在《孔教研究之二》中说:"中国人民今天是世界上唯一民主的民族。……首先，和平、秩序与安宁乃至国家本身的存在，不是依赖于法律和宪法，而是仰赖于中国的每个臣民都尽自己最大的努力，去过一种真正虔诚的生活，或时髦地说，一种道德的生活；其次，孝弟应作为道德生活或虔诚生活之本；再次，良民宗教的秘密是人们尽义务而不是争权利。人们不对权威表现出不信任和怀疑，而表现出对它的尊崇。"(黄兴涛编译，《辜鸿铭文集·上卷·呐喊》，海南出版社，1996，第545—546页)辜鸿铭认为，所谓"道之以德，齐之以礼"的德治所要达到的效果，正是这样的一种理性的民主。

4. 文中，孔子讲述了自己的人生成长阶段与演进过程。"三十而立"的"立"，辜鸿铭译为"formed my opinions and judgment"，"形成自己的观点与判断力"，指三十岁时能形成自己的比较成熟与稳定的价值观和世界观。

"天命"，译为"the truth in religion"，"宗教中的真理"。他将此处的"天"理解为"宗教"。此外，他还经常将"天"译为"God"，即"上帝"，如他在英译《中庸》的开篇，即把"天命"译为"the ordinance of God"，"上帝的训令"。其实，对于辜鸿铭而言，无论是他将"天"译为"宗教"还是"上帝"，都有着同样的含义，那就是代指宇宙的根本规律。对此，他曾在《中国人的精神（在北京东方学会上所宣讲的论文）》一书中明确阐述："所有伟人，所有富有智慧的人们，通常都信仰上帝。孔子也信奉上帝，虽然他很少提及它。……然而，富于智慧的人们，其心中的上帝有别于常人。他们对上帝的信仰，就是斯宾诺莎所说的对神圣的宇宙秩序的信仰。孔子曾说过：'五十而知天命'。——懂得神圣的宇宙秩序。富于智慧的人们为这种宇宙秩序起了不同的名称。德国哲学家费希特称之神圣的宇宙观。在中国的哲学语言中，它被称之为'道'。但是无论被赋予了什么名字，它只是一种关于神圣的宇宙秩序的知识。这种知识使富于智慧的人们认识到，道德规范或'道'属于宇宙秩序的一部分，所以必须遵守。"(夏丹等选编，《辜鸿铭作品精选·中国人的精神》，第49页)所以，他将"天命"译为"上帝的训令"，其实是一种"神圣的宇宙秩序"。

5. 辜鸿铭此节的翻译有两点值得注意：
（1）他将"孝"译为"the duty of a good son"，"一个好儿子的义务"。辜鸿铭认为，孔子并非在谈论"什么是"孝，而是在讲"如何做"才算孝。换言之，辜鸿铭认为文中所讲的三点（"生事之以礼，死葬之以礼，祭之以礼"），即构成了孝子的三个义务。
（2）他将"礼"分别译为"the usage prescribed by propriety"、"the rites prescribed by propriety"，分别是指"礼节规定的习惯、习俗"与"礼节规定的仪式"。这里讲的是世俗生活中的"礼"。

6. 文中，"父母唯其疾之忧"，译为"think how anxious your parents are when you are

sick, and you will know your duty towards them"，"想想当你生病的时候你父母是多么焦急，你就会明白你对他们的义务了"，指从父母对自己的关心中，来反思自己对父母的责任和义务。

7. 文中，"至于犬马，皆能有养；不敬，何以别乎？"一句，辜鸿铭对句中前后两个"养"做了不同的翻译，第一个对父母而言，译为"support"，供养；第二个对犬马而言，译为"keep alive"，饲养。这句指人作为子女不应像饲养动物那样供养父母，父母需要的不仅仅是"活着"，更需要子女的敬爱。

8. 本节仍然是论述何为"孝"。其中，"色难"二字，辜鸿铭译为"the difficulty is with the expression of your look"，"困难在于脸色的表达"。在《一个大汉学家》中，辜鸿铭曾专门论述过对"色难"的翻译与理解，他认为，真正的孝，"重要的不在于你对你的父母履行什么义务，而在于——以什么方式和态度，你在履行这些义务时，以一种什么精神面貌"。（夏丹等选编，《辜鸿铭作品精选·中国人的精神》，第103—104页）接着，他在文中指出，孔子的这种论述，显示了他作为"宗教导师"的特质，而非单纯的"道德学家"。

9. 在本节中，辜鸿铭添加了一条注释，表达了他对颜回这个历史人物的看法，以及为何在书中保留"颜回"的名字：

> 儒家福音中的圣·约翰———一位纯粹、英勇而理想的人物，是夫子所喜爱的那个学生。因为这个学生的名字在全书中出现得很频繁，所以我们在此处打破了省略那些固有中文名字的通例。此后也会经常地用他的名字来介绍他。

在此，辜鸿铭通过将"颜回"比作基督教中的"圣·约翰"，而将儒家与基督教作了联系。他认为，儒家与基督教的本质并无不同。而根据人的道德品质，他其实只将信仰者分为两类人——"基督徒、文明人"与"乱臣贼子、市侩、异教徒、暴君、野兽"。这种分类与具体哪种宗教无关。他在《中国札记之三》中说："子曰：'人能弘道，非道弘人。'通俗地说就是，'你的品质造就了你的宗教，而不是你的宗教造就了你的品质'。只要你无私和仁慈，你就是一个基督徒，一个文明人——不管你是犹太人、中国人还是德国人，也不管你是商人、传教士、军人、外交官还是苦力。假如你自私自利、冷酷无情，即便你当上了世界的皇帝，你也不过是乱臣贼子、市侩、异教徒、暴君和野兽。"（汪堂家编译，《乱世奇文·尊王篇》，第85—86页）这是辜鸿铭对宗教精神的总体看法。

文中还讨论了颜回"愚"与"不愚"。辜鸿铭将"愚"译为"dull of understanding"，"理解力迟钝"，是就理解力而言的。而在很多地方，他通常将"小人"译为"fool"，"愚人，蠢人"。这可做一对比。本节还意在表达，与口舌之快相比，生活实践更加重要，这也是儒家所倡导的一种精神，比如接下来的章节中所提到的"仁者其言也讱"、"先行其言而后从之"等说法也在表达这个意思。

10. 在本节中，孔子认为观人要看三项，即"所以"、"所由"、"所安"，辜鸿铭分别译为"how a man acts"、"his motives"、"his tastes"，即"一个人如何处事"、"他的动机"和"他的旨趣所在"，只要看清一个人的这三项特点，他就无所掩饰了。

11. 文中，"知"，辜鸿铭译为"add to it"，即"补充"的意思，指不断用新学问补充旧学问。这是一个人做学问的方法，懂得这个方法就可以做别人的老师。

12. 文中"不器"一词，辜鸿铭译为"not make himself into a mere machine fit only to do one kind of work"，"不让自己成为一台可怜的机器，只适合做一种工作"。辜鸿铭一贯反对人在社会中仅变成适合某项职业的职业人，而应该是具有道德素养的并懂得生活的人。

13. 文中，"先行其言"，辜鸿铭译为"acts before he speaks"，"先做而后说"。"而后从之"译为"afterwards speaks according to his actions"，"然后，又按照行动来说话"。这节指君子做事应谨言慎行，并言行一致。

14. 文中，"周"，辜鸿铭译为"impartial"，"公正的，公平的"，指站在"正义"或"道义"一方，即公正、公平；"比"，译为"neutral"，"中立的，无倾向性的"。按照辜鸿铭的翻译，这句话中包含着一种对于虽表象客观但实际违背是非的"比"（即"中立"）的一种批判。

15. 文中，"罔"，辜鸿铭译为"labour lost"，"徒劳的"，意思是，如果只"学习"而不"思考"的话，将不会真正从中受益，不会得到真正的学问并取得进步，与"不学"一样，所以是徒劳的。"殆"，译为"perilous"，"危险的，冒险的"，指如果没有学问的积累只是凭空去"思"是危险的。

16. 本节仍然是对"学"的探讨。但关于本节的解释，用《论语集释》撰者程树德的话说，"此章诸说纷纭，莫衷一是"。我们看看辜鸿铭的理解。"攻"，译为"to give oneself up to the study"，"沉湎于研究之中"（皇侃、朱熹等也作如此解释）。"异端"，译为"metaphysical theories"，"玄学的、形而上学的理论"。"斯害也已"，译为"that is very injurious indeed"，"那的确是非常有害的"。

事实上，很多时候，辜鸿铭认为孔子所称的"异端"，是指老庄学说。他认为，儒学是一种世俗哲学（他称之为"良民宗教"）。他在《孔教研究之二》中说，儒教的教徒并不是仅仅"静思其灵魂状态和对上帝之义务"的僧侣或基督徒，而是"纳税、付房租的平民百姓"，这些百姓作为"孔教的弟子"，"不仅要思索其灵魂状态和对上帝的义务，还要考虑对人类的义务"。（黄兴涛编译，《辜鸿铭文集·上卷·呐喊》，第541页）所以，如果仅仅"沉湎于形而上学理论的研究之中"而忽略正常生活的学问及义务，是有害的。这也就是孔子说的"未知生焉知死"，"未能事人焉能事鬼"之意。

17. 本节一连出现6个"知"字，辜鸿铭认为，第一个与最后一个"知"字意思相同，均译为"understanding"，"了解，明白，通达"，也即"聪明"之意。他将中间4个"知"译为"know"，"知道"。连起来意思是"知道什么是自己知道的，也要知道什么是自己所不知道的"，即人应有自知。

18. 文中"学干禄"一词，辜鸿铭译为"study with a view to preferment"，"为了晋升而学习"。也就是说，本节孔子讲的是人在世俗生活中获得晋升所需备的精神条件。从整句话来看，指对存有疑问的事情停止判断，而且在谈论其他事情时要谨慎，这样就不会遭到别人的非难（criticise），即"尤"；对能带来麻烦的事情不参与，而且做其他事情时要谨慎，这样就不会自责（self-reproach），即"悔"。

19. 文中，"直"，辜鸿铭译为"the cause of the just"，"公正的主张"；"枉"译为"every cause that is unjust"，"任何不公正的主张"。另外，辜鸿铭将"举"译为"uphold"，"支持"之意，也有"举起"之意；将"错"译为"put down"，"取缔"之意，也有"放下"之意。他采用这两个英文词与汉语原词一样，都是双关语。本节强调的是要建立良好的统治，统治者首先应做到坚持"公正"（the cause of the just）。

20. 在对本节的翻译中，辜鸿铭将"敬、忠"译为"a feeling of respect and loyalty"，"人民的尊敬与忠诚的情感"，辜鸿铭用了"feeling"（情感）一词，意思不仅仅是指"尊敬与忠诚"的态度，更是一种在人们心中激发出的这类情感。这是辜鸿铭的思想中"感性特征"的一个体现。另外，他将"孝"译为"honour your parents and your prince"，"敬重你的父母与国君"，比他通常的"be a good son and a good citizen"（做一个好儿子与好公民）的翻译更具体些。他将"慈"译为"considerate for the welfare of those under you"，"关怀那些地位比你低的人的福利"。这一翻译，可以说对"慈"的含义做出了具体解释，即从现实角度，关注人民的福利。

21. 文中，辜鸿铭将问者的"为政"译为"take part in the government of the country"，

"参与国家的政治",即从政;将孔子所说的"为政"译为"discharge your duties in the government","履行政治中的义务"。也就是说,问者问的是为政的形式,而孔子答的则是为政的义务。

辜鸿铭认为,"为政"是一种履行义务的事情,无论是在家庭中,还是在国家政治中。这是他对"政"的理解,同时也体现了辜鸿铭思想中一个很大的特点:强调人的"义务"、"牺牲"这些"付出型"的美德。他在《中国妇女》一文中认为,中国的女人和男人,都是在作出"牺牲"的,女人为了父亲、丈夫、孩子而牺牲自我;同样,男人为了家庭、国家而牺牲自我。他说:"在中国,理想女性并不要求一个男人终其一生去拥抱她和崇拜她,而恰恰是她自己要纯粹地、无私地为丈夫活着……在中国,那些辛辛苦苦支撑家庭的丈夫们,尤其当他是一个士人的时候,他不仅要对他的家庭尽责,还要对他的国王和国家尽责,甚至在对国王和国家服务的过程中,有时还要献出生命……"(夏丹等选编,《辜鸿铭作品精选·中国人的精神》,第68页)

另外,辜鸿铭将文中提到的《尚书》翻译为"Book of Records","记录之书"。这一翻译说明了《尚书》作为一部"史书"的性质。

22. 文中,"信",辜鸿铭译为"good faith","诚信";"可"译为"get along","生活下去",也即生存。这节指诚信是生存的必要条件。

23. 文中,"十世",辜鸿铭译为"ten generations after their time the state of the civilisation of the world","十代之后的世界文明的情况",并注释说:

> 这里的"world""即中国"。

下文中"礼"字,辜鸿铭译为"the civilisation","文明"。这是辜鸿铭对"礼"的又一种翻译,指这里讨论的是孔子对于中国文明演进的整体看法。

另外,辜鸿铭在本段的翻译中保留了"夏"、"殷"、"周"的名称,对于三者之间的关系,他注释说:

> 夏朝(公元前2205—前1818年)之于中国的孔子时代的人,就如同希腊历史之于今天的欧洲人。同样的,殷朝(公元前1766—前1154年)之于孔子时代的人,就如同罗马历史之于今天的人。

24. 文中的"谄"字,辜鸿铭译为"idolatry","盲目崇拜"。他对此字注释说:

字面意思是"过分屈从的奴性"。(对于好人来说,他们的怯懦是一种不幸。——伏尔泰)

文中的"鬼"字,辜鸿铭译为"spirit","神灵",一种泛指,是指任何文化或宗教中人们的崇拜对象。"非其鬼而祭之",译为"to worship ... not bound by a real feeling of duty or respect","崇拜一个对其并没有真正的义务与敬意的神灵",即对方虽是神,但并不是统属他的神,也去崇拜。

在下文中,他将"见义不为,无勇也"译为"看到了正义,却在行为上与你的判断相悖,这显示出你勇气的缺失"。这也是强调一种对正义的坚持的勇气。

CHAPTER Ⅲ
八佾第三

1. The head of a powerful family of nobles in Confucius' native State employed eight sets of choristers [an Imperial prerogative] in their family chapel. Confucius, remarking on this, was heard to say, "If this is allowed to pass, what may not be allowed?"

2. The members of the same powerful family mentioned above concluded the service in their chapel by chanting the hymn used only on occasions of Imperial worship. Confucius remarked on it, saying:

   "The words of the hymn begin —

   Surrounded by his nobles and princes,

   August the Son of Heaven looks."

   "Now what is there in the chapel of this noble family to which those words of the hymn can be applied?"

3. Confucius remarked, "If a man is without moral character, what good can the use of the fine arts do him? If a man is without moral character, what good can the use of music do him?"

4. A disciple asked what constituted the fundamental principle of art.

   "That is a very great question," replied Confucius, "but in the art used in social usages it is better to be simple than to be expensive; in rituals for the dead, it is better that there should be heartfelt grief than minute attention to observances."

1. 孔子谓季氏:"八佾舞于庭,是可忍也,孰不可忍也?"

　　孔子故国一个有权势的贵族家族的当家人,在他们家族祠堂里使用八队唱诗班歌手(一种帝王特权)。有人听到孔子这样评论这件事:"如果这是可以容忍的,那还有什么是不可容忍的?"

2. 三家者以《雍》彻。子曰:"'相维辟公,天子穆穆',奚取于三家之堂?"

　　上面提到的那个有权势的家族的人,通过吟诵仅用于帝王祭拜仪式的颂歌来结束他们在祠堂举行的礼仪活动。孔子评论这件事说:"那些辞句开始是——

　　　　'他的贵族、诸侯围绕身边,

　　　　上天之子看上去多么威严'。"

　　"那么,在那家贵族的祠堂里,怎么能用得上颂歌里的这些辞句呢?"

3. 子曰:"人而不仁,如礼何? 人而不仁,如乐何?"

　　孔子说:"如果一个人没有道德品质的话,优秀艺术的运用对他还有什么益处呢? 如果一个人没有道德品质的话,音乐的运用对他还有什么好处呢?"

4. 林放问礼之本。子曰:"大哉问! 礼,与其奢也,宁俭;丧,与其易也,宁戚。"

　　一个学生问到什么才是艺术的根本原则。

　　"这是一个非常重大的问题,"孔子回答说,"用于各种社会习俗的艺术,简朴要好于奢华;在为逝者举办的仪式中,发自内心的悲痛要好于对礼仪的密切关注。"

5. Confucius remarked, "The heathen hordes of the North and East, even, acknowledge the authority of their chiefs, whereas now in China respect for authority no longer exists anywhere."

6. The head of the powerful family of nobles mentioned in section 1 of this chapter was going to offer sacrifice on the top of the Great T'ai Mountain [an Imperial prerogative].Confucius then said to a disciple who was in the service of the noble, "Can you not do anything to save him from this?" "No," replied the disciple, "I cannot." "Ah, then," answered Confucius, "it is useless to say anything more. But, really, do you think that the Spirit of the Great Mountain is not as Lin-fang?"

7. Confucius remarked, "A gentleman never *competes*[①] in anything he does, — except perhaps in archery. But even then, when he wins he courteously makes his bow before he advances to take his place among the winners; and when he has lost he walks down and drinks his cup of forfeit. Thus, even in this case of competition, he shows himself to be a gentleman."

8. A disciple asked Confucius for the meaning of the following verse:
> Her coquettish smiles,
>> How dimpling they are;
> Her beautiful eyes,
>> How beaming they are;
> O fairest is she,

---

① 斜体为辜鸿铭所设,回译文对应处译者加以着重号,下同。

5. 子曰:"夷狄之有君,不如诸夏之亡也。"

　　孔子说:"即使是生活在北方与东方的野蛮部落,也是承认他们酋长的权威的,然而现在的中国,对权威的尊崇已经几乎不存在了。"

6. 季氏旅于泰山。子谓冉有曰:"女弗能救与?"对曰:"不能。"子曰:"呜呼! 曾谓泰山,不如林放乎?"

　　在本章第1节中提到的那个有权势的贵族家族的当家人,将要去泰山之巅献祭(一种帝王特权)。孔子就向一位在这个贵族家族中任职的学生说:"你难道不能阻止他这样做吗?""是的,"那位学生回答说,"我不能。""唉,那么,"孔子回答说,"说什么都没有用了。但是,你认为泰山之神不像林放一样吗?"

7. 子曰:"君子无所争,必也射乎! 揖让而升,下而饮,其争也君子。"

　　孔子说:"一个绅士从不在任何事情上与人竞争——或许射箭除外。但即使那时,如果获胜,他也会在取代其他获胜者而晋级下轮比赛前礼貌地鞠躬示意;而如果输了,他会走下来喝掉罚酒。这样,即使在这种竞争情况下,他仍会显示出自己是个绅士。"

8. 子夏问曰:"'巧笑倩兮,美目盼兮,素以为绚兮。' 何谓也?"子曰:"绘事后素。"曰:"礼后乎?"子曰:"起予者商也! 始可与言《诗》已矣。"

　　一位学生问孔子下面这些诗句的意思:

　　　　她迷人的笑容,

　　　　　酒窝浅浅;

　　　　她美丽的眼睛,

　　　　　欢悦扑闪;

　　　　噢,她是最美的,

Who is simple and plain.

"In painting," answered Confucius, "ornamentation and colour are matters of secondary importance compared with the groundwork."

"Then art itself," said the disciple, "is a matter of 'secondary' consideration?"

"My friend," replied Confucius, "You have given me an idea. Now I can talk of poetry with you."

9. Confucius remarked to a disciple, "I can tell you of the state of the arts and civilisation during the Hsia dynasty [say the Greek civilisation]; but the modern State of Ts'i (say modern Greece) cannot furnish sufficient evidence to prove what I say.I can tell you of the state of the arts and civilisation during the Yin dynasty (say Roman civilisation); but the modern state of Sung (say Italy) cannot furnish sufficient evidence to prove what I say. The reason is because the literary monuments extant are too meagre, — otherwise I could prove to you what I say."

10. Confucius remarked, "At the service of the great Ti sacrifice (the 'Mass' in ancient China), I always make it a point to leave as soon as the pouring of the libation on the ground is over."

11. Somebody asked Confucius for the meaning of the great Ti sacrifice mentioned above.

"I do not know," answered Confucius, "One who understands its significance will find it as easy to rule the world as to look at this — thus." pointing to the palm of his hand.

朴素而简单。

"在绘画中，"孔子回答说，"与它的本质相比，装饰和色彩是次要的。"

"那么，艺术本身，"这位学生说，"也是个应被看做'次要'的东西吧？"

"我的朋友，"孔子回答说，"你启发了我。现在我可以和你谈论诗了。"

9. 子曰："夏礼吾能言之，杞不足征也；殷礼吾能言之，宋不足征也。文献不足故也，足则吾能征之矣。"

　　孔子对一位学生说："我能够告诉你夏朝时艺术与文明的情况（好比希腊文明）；但现在的杞国（好比现在的希腊）并不能提供足够的证据来证明我的话。我能够告诉你殷朝时艺术与文明的情况（好比罗马文明）；但现在的宋国（好比意大利）并不能提供足够的证据来证明我的话。原因是现存的文学遗产太贫乏了——否则，我可以给你证明我所说的。"

10. 子曰："禘自既灌而往者，吾不欲观之矣。"

　　孔子说："在重大的禘祭仪式（古代中国的"弥撒"）上，只要把祭酒洒于地上的环节一结束，我就故意离开。"

11. 或问禘之说。子曰："不知也。知其说者之于天下也，其如示诸斯乎！"指其掌。

　　有人问孔子上面提到的禘祭的意思。

　　"我不知道，"孔子回答说，"明白它意义的人，将会发现，统治这个世界就像看这个一样容易——这样。"他指着自己的手掌。

12. Confucius worshipped the dead as if he actually felt the presence of the departed ones.He worshipped the Spiritual Powers as if he actually felt the presence of the Powers.

He once remarked, "If I cannot give up heart and soul when I am worshipping, I always consider as if I have not worshipped."

13. An officer in a certain State asked Confucius, saying, "What is meant by the common saying 'It is better to pray to the God of the Hearth than to the God of the House'?"

"Not so," replied Confucius, "a man who has sinned against God, — it is useless for him to pray anywhere at all."

14. Confucius remarked, "The civilisation of the present Chou dynasty is founded on the civilisations of the two preceding dynasties. How splendidly rich it is in all the arts!I prefer the present Chou civilisation."

15. When Confucius first attended the service at the State Cathedral (Ancestral Temple of the reigning prince), he enquired as to what he should do at every stage of the service. Somebody thereupon remarked, "Who tells me that the son of the plebeian of Ts'ow is a man who knows the correct forms?"

When Confucius heard of the remark, he said, "*That* is the correct form."

12. 祭如在,祭神如神在。子曰:"吾不与祭,如不祭。"

　　孔子祭拜死者时,就像他真的感觉到那些逝者的存在。他祭拜神灵时,就像他真的感觉到神灵的存在。

　　他曾说:"如果我在祭拜时不能献出我的真心和灵魂,我总是觉得好像未曾祭拜似的。"

13. 王孙贾问曰:"与其媚于奥,宁媚于灶,何谓也?"子曰:"不然,获罪于天,无所祷也。"

　　某国的一位官员问孔子:"那句俗语'向灶台之神祷告,比向房屋之神祷告要好',是什么意思?"

　　"不是这样的,"孔子回答说,"一个犯了违逆上帝之罪的人——无论他怎么祷告都是没用的。"

14. 子曰:"周监于二代,郁郁乎文哉! 吾从周。"

　　孔子说:"现在周朝的文明,是基于之前两个朝代的文明之上而建立的。在所有的人类艺术中,它是多么辉煌而华美啊! 我更愿选择现在周的文明。"

15. 子入大庙,每事问。或曰:"孰谓鄹人之子知礼乎? 入大庙,每事问。"子闻之曰:"是礼也。"

　　孔子第一次在国家总庙(执政国君的祖庙)参加祭拜仪式时,他在礼仪的每个环节都要询问应该怎么做。于是,有人就说:"是谁告诉我,鄹地那个庶民的儿子是个懂得正确举止的人?"

　　孔子听说了这句话之后,说:"那就是正确的举止啊。"

16. Confucius remarked, "In archery, putting the arrow *through* the target should not count as points, because the competitors cannot all be expected to be equal in mere physical strength. At least, that was the old rule."

17. A disciple wanted to dispense with the sheep offered in sacrifice in the religious ceremony held at the beginning of every month.

    "What *you* would save," said Confucius to him, "is the cost of the sheep; what *I* would save is the principle of the rite. "

18. Confucius remarked, "Men now account it servile to pay to their prince all the honours due to him."

19. The reigning prince of Confucius' native State asked Confucius how a prince should treat his public servant and how a public servant should behave to his prince.

    "Let the prince," answered Confucius, "treat his public servant with honour. The public servant must serve the prince, his master, with loyalty."

20. Confucius remarked, "The first ballad in the Book of Ballads and Songs expresses the emotions of love. It is passionate, but not sensual; it is melancholy, but not morbid."

16. 子曰:"射不主皮,为力不同科,古之道也。"

孔子说:"在射箭比赛中,用箭射穿靶子是不应算作分数而计入得分的,因为并不能要求每位比赛者在体力上都是相同的。至少,这是古制。"

17. 子贡欲去告朔之饩羊。子曰:"赐也,尔爱其羊,我爱其礼。"

一个学生想要免除在每月初举行的宗教仪式上献祭的羊。

"你想要节省的,"孔子对他说,"是羊的成本;而我想要保留的,是仪式的原则。"

18. 子曰:"事君尽礼,人以为谄也。"

孔子说:"现在,人们认为对他们的国君献上应有的完全的敬重,是奴性的。"

19. 定公问:"君使臣,臣事君,如之何?"孔子对曰:"君使臣以礼,臣事君以忠。"

孔子故国的一位执政国君问孔子,一位国君应该如何对待他的公务人员,而一个公务人员对他的国君又应如何表现。

"让国君,"孔子回答说,"以尊敬之心对待他的公务人员。而公务人员则必须以忠诚来服务于他的国君,他的主人。"

20. 子曰:"《关雎》,乐而不淫,哀而不伤。"

孔子说:"那本有关民谣与诗歌的文学典籍的第一篇民谣,表达了爱的情感。它是多情的,而不是淫秽的;它是忧思悲哀的,而不是病态痛苦的。"

21. The reigning prince of Confucius' native State asked a disciple of Confucius about the emblems used on the altars to the Titular Genius of the land.

The disciple answered, "The sovereigns of the House of Hsia planted the pine tree; the people of the Yin dynasty adopted the cypress; and the people of the present Chou dynasty has chosen the *li* (chestnut) tree as a symbol of awe (*li*) to the population."

When Confucius afterwards heard of what the disciple said, he remarked, "It is useless to speak of a thing that is done; to change a course that is begun; or to blame what is past and gone."

22. Confucius, speaking of a famous statesman (the Bismarck of the time), remarked, "Kuan Chung was by no means a great-minded man!"

"But," said somebody, "Kuan Chung was simple in his life: was he not?"

"Why," replied Confucius, "Kuan Chung had that magnificent Sansouci Pleasaunce of his. Besides, he had a special officer appointed to every function in his household. How can one say that he was simple in his life?"

"Well," rejoined the enquirer, "but still, Kuan Chung was a man of taste who observed the correct forms; was he not?"

"No," answered Confucius, "The reigning princes have walls built before their palace gates. Kuan Chung also had a wall built before his door.When two reigning princes meet, each has a special *buffet*. Kuan Chung also had his special buffet.If you say Kuan Chung was a man of taste, who is not a man of taste?"

21. 哀公问社于宰我。宰我对曰："夏后氏以松,殷人以柏,周人以栗,曰使民战栗。"子闻之曰："成事不说,遂事不谏,既往不咎。"

　　孔子故国的执政国君,询问孔子的一位学生有关土地守护神的祭坛上所使用的象征。

　　那位学生回答说："夏朝的君主们栽种的是松树;殷朝的人采用的是柏树;而现在周朝的人选择了'栗'树(栗树)作为让人民畏惧(栗)的象征。"

　　孔子后来听到了这位学生说的话,说："去谈论已经完成的事情,去试图改变已经开始的事情,或者去指责已经过去或消逝的事情,是没用的呀。"

22. 子曰："管仲之器小哉!"或曰："管仲俭乎?"曰："管氏有三归,官事不摄,焉得俭?""然则管仲知礼乎?"曰："邦君树塞门,管氏亦树塞门;邦君为两君之好,有反坫,管氏亦有反坫。管氏而知礼,孰不知礼?"

　　孔子在谈到一位著名的政治家(那时的俾斯麦)时,说："管仲绝不是个思想伟大的人!"

　　"但是,"有人说,"管仲在生活中是很简朴的,不是吗?"

　　"那为什么,"孔子回答说,"管仲有他自己华丽的无忧宫乐园呢?另外,他还任命了一个专门的官员负责他家族中的每项职责。怎么能说他在生活中是简朴的呢?"

　　"那么,"那人又说,"管仲至少是个遵守正确礼仪、举止得体的人吧,不是吗?"

　　"不,"孔子回答说,"执政的国君们在官殿大门前会建墙。管仲在他的家门前也建墙。当两位执政国君会面时,每人都有一个专门的餐台。管仲也有自己专门的餐台。如果你说管仲是个行为得体的人,那谁不是呢?"

23. Confucius remarked to the Grand Kapel Meister of his native State, "I think I know the way in which a piece should be played with a full orchestra.At first, the full volume of sound in the piece should be heard. Then, as you proceed, you must pay attention to and bring out each note of the piece, distinct and clear, but flowing, as it were, without break or interval, — thus to the end."

24. An officer in command of a certain Pass on the frontier where Confucius on his travels was passing, asked for the permission to be presented to him; saying, "Whenever a wise man passes this way, I have always had the honour to wait upon him."Confucius' disciples accordingly presented him.

When the officer came out of the interview he said to the disciples, "Gentlemen, why should you be concerned at your present want of official position! The world has long been without the order and justice of good government; now God is going to make use of your Teacher as a tocsin to awaken the world."

25. Confucius, speaking of a famous piece of music (the most ancient then known in China), remarked, "It has all the excellence of the physical beauty of harmony; it has also all the excellence of moral grandeur."Speaking of another piece, of a more recent date, Confucius remarked, "It has all the excellence of the physical beauty of harmony; but it has not all the excellence of moral grandeur."

26. Confucius remarked, "Possession of power without generosity; courtesy without seriousness; mourning without grief, — I have no desire to look at such a state of things."

23. 子语鲁大师乐。曰："乐其可知也：始作，翕如也；从之，纯如也，
皦如也，绎如也，以成。"

孔子对其故国的那位最高乐队的师傅说："我想我知道一个完整的乐
队演奏一首乐曲的正确方式了。首先，必须能让人听到乐曲的最大音量。
然后，在演奏过程中，你必须注意到并准确而清晰地演绎出乐曲的每个音
符，但同时，要让它流畅而不会出现中断或间隔——这样直到结束。"

24. 仪封人请见。曰："君子之至于斯也，吾未尝不得见也。"从者见
之。出曰："二三子，何患于丧乎？ 天下之无道也久矣，天将以夫
子为木铎。"

孔子在旅途中经过边境时，一位负责管辖某个关口的官员请求见
他，说："每当明智的人经过这里时，我通常都会有幸谒见。"

当这位官员拜访结束出来时，他向那些学生说："先生们，为什么你
们还因目前没有官职而担忧呢！这个世界没有善政的秩序与正义已经
很久了；现在上天要以你们的老师为一个警钟，来唤醒世界。"

25. 子谓《韶》："尽美矣，又尽善也。"谓《武》："尽美矣，未尽善也。"

孔子谈到一首非常著名的乐曲（那时所知中国最古老的），说："它
拥有外在和谐之美方面的所有优点，它同样拥有道德的伟大方面的所
有优点。"论及另外一首年代更近些的乐曲，孔子说："它拥有外在和谐
之美方面的所有优点，但它并不具有道德的伟大方面的所有优点。"

26. 子曰："居上不宽，为礼不敬，临丧不哀，吾何以观之哉？"

孔子说："拥有权力却没有宽容；殷勤有礼却不严肃庄重；服丧时不
悲痛——对于这样的事情，我一眼都不想看。"

【评述】

1. 文中，"佾"译为"chorister"，借用的是基督教会中的唱诗班歌手的概念。这一翻译既有利于西方读者理解文意，其实也包含了与西方宗教进行类比的含义；"庭"，译为"family chapel"，即"家中教堂"（"家族祠堂"）。

辜鸿铭的这些翻译表现了他的"儒学即国教"的观念。他认为，不仅在理论上，而且在实际的"组织构架"中，儒学都是一种"国教"，尽管在宗教含义上与西方不同。他在《中国人的精神（在北京东方学会上所宣讲的论文）》一文中说："儒教是中国的国教，相当于其他国家的教堂宗教。儒教也利用一种相当于教堂的组织来使人服从道德规范。在中国的儒教里，这个组织就是学校。在中国，学校就是孔子国家宗教里的教堂。"（夏丹等选编，《辜鸿铭作品精选·中国人的精神》，第57页）在此，他首先指出学校就是中国的教堂。他分析说，宗教与教育都用一个"教"字，"正如教堂在中国就是学校一样，中国的宗教也就意味着教育"。（同上，第57页）接下来，他进一步指出："但是更准确地说，在中国的国教里，相当于其他国家宗教的教堂是——家庭。在中国，孔子国家宗教的真正教堂是家庭，学校只是它的附庸之物。有着祖先牌位的家庭，在每个村庄或城镇散布着的有祖先祠堂或庙宇的家庭，才是国教的真正教堂。"（同上，第59页）也就是说，中国的真正的教堂，是"有祖先祠堂或庙宇的"家庭。他继续分析说，在中国的家庭中，一些仪式与规范培养了人们对父母和祖先的爱，这正与基督教教堂培养教徒对上帝的爱是相对应的。

2. "三家者"，辜鸿铭译为"The members of the same powerful family mentioned above"，"上面提到的那个有权势的家族的人"，即，"三家"就是上一段中提到的"季氏"。"彻"，译为"concluded the service"，"结束祭礼"。

在文中，辜鸿铭还对出自《诗经·周颂·雍》的诗句"相维辟公，天子穆穆"一句进行了翻译："Surrounded by his nobles and princes / August the Son of Heaven looks"，"他的贵族、诸侯围绕身边，/上天之子看上去多么威严"。他认为，这句诗是用来描述和称颂天子的，而不是称颂"三家"他们自己的祖先，所以，下一句话孔子说："奚取于三家之堂"，"在那家贵族的祠堂里，怎么能用得上颂歌里的这些辞句呢?"

3. 文中，"仁"，辜鸿铭译为"moral character"，"道德品质"，即人的道德之心或美好的人性；"礼"，译为"art"，"艺术"；"乐"，译为"music"，"音乐"。礼、乐，辜鸿铭认为指一般意义上的艺术与音乐。整句话的意思就是，人如果没有道德品质（或说道德之心或美好的人性），那么，艺术与音乐对他来说是没有任何意义的。

4. 本节中的"礼"字，辜鸿铭仍译为"art"，"艺术"。"本"，译为"the fundamental principle"，"根本原则"。辜鸿铭认为，这段话所讨论的是艺术的根本原则问题。而在孔子的回答中，他将"礼"译为"the art used in social usages"，即"用于各种社会习俗的艺术"。他在《中国文明的历史发展》中说："所谓'礼'就是艺术，它不仅仅限于西方人通常所理解的艺术只包括绘画、雕刻一类，还包括行为的艺术，活动的艺术。"（黄兴涛编译，《辜鸿铭文集·下卷·辜鸿铭论集》，第296页）这节文字所讨论的"礼"，其实就是指人们的生活习俗。

那么，下文"礼，与其奢也，宁俭；丧，与其易也，宁戚"就是孔子对前面"礼之本"的阐述。"奢"，译为"expensive"，"奢华"；"俭"译为"simple"，"简朴"；"易"，译为"minute attention to observances"，"对礼仪的严密、细心的关注与留意"；"戚"译为"heartfelt grief"，"发自内心的悲痛"。在世俗的礼节上，与其在形式上奢华隆重，不如形式简朴而情感真挚。

5. 在本节的翻译中，辜鸿铭将"夷狄"译为"The heathen hordes of the North and East"，"生活于北方与东方的野蛮部落"。另外，他将"有君"译为"acknowledge the authority of their chiefs"，"承认他们酋长的权威"。

这里，通过对比"野蛮部落"与"文明国家"对"权威"的不同态度，辜鸿铭意在表现如今人们已经失去了对权威的尊崇的意识。在《中国牛津运动故事·自序》中，他认为，"权威"是确实存在的，他称之为"理性和上帝意志"，也可以理解为"绝对真理"，而尊重权威则是人类文明秩序的保证。他说："实际上，无论是中国还是欧洲，当前的危险，……在于他们根本不相信有理性和上帝的意志这种东西存在。……不相信这些东西，世上就没有文明可言，只可能有无政府混乱状态。"（夏丹等选编，《辜鸿铭作品精选》，第200—202页）

另外，在本节末尾，辜鸿铭还对这种尊崇权威的含义注释说：

> 中国骑士精神（Chinese chivalry）的口号是"尊王攘夷"（尊崇国家君主而打破野蛮势力）。对这四个汉字的真正含义的理解，而不是通俗的意义，塑造了今天的现代日本。丁尼生用欧洲语言对欧洲骑士精神的阐述，成为了他作为一位骑士的精神誓言："去敬爱国君，就如同他是他们的良心，他们的良心也如同国君。打破野蛮势力，维护基督的教义。"

6. "旅"，传统学者多认为是一种"祭名"。辜鸿铭译为"offer sacrifice"，泛指"献祭"。"救"，译为"save him from this"，即阻止他这样做，辜鸿铭认为季氏僭礼，而冉有却没能阻止他。而对于最后一句话中提到"林放"，辜鸿铭诚实地注释说：

> 在本章第4节提问的那位学生的名字。在最后一句话提及这位学生的目的：我们承认，我们也不理解。

7. 辜鸿铭在不同的场合对"君子"做了不同的解释，此处，他译为"gentleman"，"绅士"，凸显的是绅士的风度或气质，不同于他之前"a good and wise man"的翻译。

文中"compete"一词，用了斜体。他意在表现，具有绅士风度的人，在任何事情上都是不会去竞争的，除了一件事，那就是射箭。但即使是在竞争时，君子也会保持自己的绅士风度。

下文"揖让而升，下而饮"一句中，"升"辜鸿铭译为"advances to take his place among the winners"，"晋级下轮比赛"；"下"，译为"lose"，"输掉比赛"。所以，"下而饮"的"饮"，自然就译为"drinks his cup of forfeit"，"喝掉罚酒"。这是绅士在射箭竞争时的风度。

8. 文中诗句，前二句出自《诗经·卫风·硕人》之二章，最后一句为逸诗，是形容一位美丽女子的，辜鸿铭进行了精彩的翻译。"倩"，译为"dimpling"，"泛着酒窝"；"盼"，译为"beaming"，"明亮的，愉悦的"；"素"，译为"simple and plain"，"朴素而简单"；"绚"，译为"fairest"，"最美的"。连起来看，意思就是，一位美人之所以美，并不是她的装束，而是她的简单和朴素。而子夏所不明白的是，为什么朴素才是美。所以，下文中，孔子谈了"绘事"，即绘画艺术。在辜鸿铭看来，这一段是讨论艺术与美的。对于诗句所传达的含义，辜鸿铭注释说：

> 未装饰的美，其实已被最好地装饰了；最后那行诗，可以说是对霍勒斯"简而雅"（simplex munditiis）的一个精确翻译。英国的研究者在此可能会记起汤姆·莫尔的这两句诗："莱丝比尔愉悦地看了一眼，/但没人知道那是对谁浅笑。"

下文中，辜鸿铭将"绘事后素"的"后"译为"of secondary"，"次要的"；将"素"译为"the groundwork"，"根本，本质"。按他的理解，绘画作为一种艺术，无论具有怎样的外在表现（即装饰与色彩），都必须要围绕其本质进行。这就是主次的关系。

对于"礼后乎"一句，辜鸿铭译为"艺术本身也是次要的东西"，意思是说，对于人生而言，艺术本身就像绘画中的"装饰与色彩"，相对于人生的价值、意义来说，同样处于次要位置。

9. 本节中的"礼"字，辜鸿铭译为"the state of the civilisation and arts"，"文明与艺术的状态"，与前面第二章第23节"殷因于夏礼"一句的翻译相近。辜鸿铭认为，这里所说的"礼"，是指整个朝代或社会的文明与艺术状态。

文中杞、宋分别是夏、殷的后代诸侯国。辜鸿铭用了比拟的手法，来帮助西方人理解，即，将"杞"与"夏"的关系比喻为"现代希腊"与"古希腊"的关系；将"宋"与"殷"的关系比喻为"意大利"与"古罗马"的关系。

10. 本节有一个问题最值得注意,就是辜鸿铭对"禘"的理解。辜鸿铭认为,此处的"禘"是所有祭祀中最重要的一种,因此,他将之比拟为"Mass","弥撒",即天主教中纪念耶稣牺牲的最崇高的祭礼。这是拿中西文明中各自两个最大的祭礼做类比。他始终将儒学视为古代中国的"国教","国教"中很大一个表现就是"祖先崇拜",而他认为"禘"是祖先崇拜的最高仪式。

11. 文中,"说",辜鸿铭先后译为"meaning"与"significance",按这一翻译,问者重在问禘的"意思",而孔子所答,重在回答它的"意义"。

12. 文中,"祭如在,祭神如神在"一句,有学者认为,指祭拜时因对神的畏惧而不敢不敬。辜鸿铭则一直对这种带有"功利"色彩的祭拜或崇拜持批判态度。他在《中国札记之四》中指出:"乱臣基督徒之所以想当基督徒是出于对地狱之火的恐惧。贼子基督徒之所以想当基督徒是因为他渴望进入天堂,与天使们饮茶吟诗。"(汪堂家编译,《乱世奇文·尊王篇》,第99页)他引用19世纪英国作家罗斯金的话说:"我不仅相信有地狱,我还知道这种地方在哪儿;我也明白,一旦人们相信行善只是出于对地狱的恐惧,他们已经进了地狱。"(同上,第99页)他认为,人们信仰宗教的原因不应是出于对地狱的恐惧与对天堂的向往。对于真正的原因,他在《中国人的精神(在北京东方学会上所宣讲的论文)》中说:"请允许我首先指出你们有一个极大的误解,即认为使人们遵从道德规范的约束力是来自于上帝的权威。……但我说这只是一个表面现象……使人们遵从道德规范的真正权威,是人们的道德感、是君子之道。"(夏丹等选编,《辜鸿铭作品精选·中国人的精神》,第48—49页)人们自身的廉耻感、道德感、君子之道,这就是他给出的答案。

文中"与"字,辜鸿铭译为"give up heart and soul","献出真心与灵魂"。

13. 文中,"奥",《说文解字》解释为"室之西南隅",泛指室内深处。此处指房屋之神。"灶",灶台,此处指灶神。这句话是古时谚语,所以,辜鸿铭翻译时用"the common saying"作了说明。辜鸿铭认为,这是王孙贾向孔子请教一个有关"信仰"的问题。

对于文中的"天"与"祷",辜鸿铭从宗教信仰的角度来解释,将"天"译为"God"、"上帝";"获罪于天"译为"sinned against God","犯了违逆上帝之罪",即违背了上帝的原则。这里指如果一个人自己明明违背着上帝的原则,不去改正,而只知道向神祷告,是无用的。

14. 辜鸿铭认为,"监于二代",指周代是建于夏、商两个朝代文明的基础之上的。"从周",则是指更倾向于选择周代的文明。在《中国文明的历史发展》中,辜鸿铭认为,"中国文明开始于夏代,发展于商代,全盛于周代",他说:"在西方,与中国夏文明对应的是古埃

63

及文明。与中国商朝相对应的是犹太文明；在中国周朝的文化达到最高潮的时候，欧洲也相应盛开了古希腊文明之花。中国文明开始于夏代，发展于商代，全盛于周代。据我的研究，中国的夏代，像西方的古埃及一样，是物质文明发展的时期。……在商代，中国文明在道德以及心的方面，在形而上学的方面得到了相当的发展。周朝主要发展知的方面。"（黄兴涛编译，《辜鸿铭文集·下卷·辜鸿铭论集》，第295页）他进而认为："……周文化同古希腊文明是对应的。我以前曾说，现代欧洲文明所以庸俗丑陋，是因为荒废了古希腊文化的修养。"（同上，第295页）换言之，他认为周文明对于今天来讲仍具有重大意义。

15. 文中的"大庙"，指鲁国的周公庙，辜鸿铭译为"the State Cathedral"，"国家总庙"，并注以"Ancestral Temple of the reigning prince"，"执政国君的祖庙"，译出了"大庙"的地位，并解释了鲁国与周公的关系：鲁国国君是周公之后。

在本节中，辜鸿铭将"孰谓鄹人之子知礼乎"的"礼"字译为"the correct forms"，"正确的举止"。这是他对"礼"字的又一新的解释，指孔子"每事问"的这一做法是正确的。

他在"鄹"字处注释说：

> 地名，孔子的父亲曾在那里担任主要行政官。

值得注意的是，他将文中"鄹人"译为"the plebeian of Ts'ow"，"鄹地的庶民"，而"plebeian"含有"下等人"、"粗俗的人"等贬义，他的翻译，表现出文中"或曰"中所表达的对孔子的鄙夷态度。

16. 文中，"主皮"，辜鸿铭译为"putting the arrow through the target"，"用箭射穿靶子"；"力"，译为"physical strength"，"体力"；"同科"，译为"be equal"，"相等"。这节的意思是，因为每个人的体力不同，不应要求每射必须要射穿靶子，能射中即可，并不是仗着体力强穿靶子为优。这是孔子对射箭规则的描述。

接下来，孔子指出这是"古之道"，辜鸿铭译为"the old rule"，"古时的规则"。他开头用了"at least"，"至少"，意思是，即使很多人可能仍坚持"用射穿靶子判优劣"的做法，但至少古制不是这样的。从语态上判断，孔子是用"古制"来为自己论证射箭的规则。

17. "告朔"，周代礼仪。辜鸿铭遵循一贯的翻译原则，略去了"告朔"的名称，简单地译为"每月初举办的宗教仪式"。

文中两个"爱"字，辜鸿铭译为"save"，表现了原句中的双关语意。"羊"译为"the cost of the sheep"，"羊的价值"；"礼"译为"the principle of the rite"，"仪式的原则"。

依辜鸿铭的翻译,第一个"爱"(save)当是"节省"之意,即省下一只羊的花费。第二个"爱"(save)当是"保留"之意,即保留仪式的原则。按子贡的说法,尽管可以节省下一只羊的成本,却破坏了这一仪式的原则。

18. 文中,"礼",辜鸿铭译为"the honours due to him","本应属于国君的敬重",后面的"谄"译为"servile","奴性的,过分屈从的"。这节的意思是指本来敬重国君是理所当然的事情,是一种修养与文明的表现,但被人们误认为是一种"奴性"。他认为,人们已经失去了敬重国君的道德感。对比节,他注释说"见本章第5小节的注释"(见本书第61页第5节评述中所引辜鸿铭注释),他认为,本节同样意在表达"中国骑士精神"(Chinese chivalry),也即"尊王攘夷"(尊崇国家君主而打破野蛮势力)。

19. 文中"礼",辜鸿铭译为"honour","尊敬";"使",译为"treat","对待";"事",译为"servant","服务"。"君使臣以礼,臣事君以忠",指君主应该用尊敬之心来对待大臣,大臣应该忠诚地服务君主。辜鸿铭认为,孔子所修《春秋》表达的,就是"忠诚之道"。他在《中国人的精神(在北京东方学会上所宣讲的论文)》中说:"在这部书中,孔子首次确立了忠诚之道,称之为春秋名分大义,或简称为春秋大义。孔子的这部传授忠诚之道的著作,就是中华民族的大宪章。它使全中国人民和整个国家绝对地效忠于皇帝。这种神圣的契约、这部名誉法典,不仅是中国的政府,而且是中国文明的唯一——部真实的宪法。"(夏丹等选编,《辜鸿铭作品精选·中国人的精神》,第47页)他还在《中国人的精神·导论》中说:"良民宗教告诫人们,正义的法则就是要真实、可信、忠诚;每个妇人必须无私地绝对地忠诚其丈夫,每个男人必须无私地绝对忠诚地忠诚其君主、国王或皇帝。……这种良民宗教的最高责任,就是忠诚之责任。"(同上,第23页)"良民宗教"(The Religion of Good-citizenship,译"好公民宗教"更佳),即他所认为的"儒教"。

20. 在翻译《关雎》之名后,辜鸿铭自己添加了一句话:"expresses the emotions of love","表达了爱的情感"。在他看来,这一节表达的则是对爱情的认识。

文中"乐"、"淫"、"哀"、"伤"是关键词。"乐",辜鸿铭译为"passionate","多情的";"淫",译为"sensual","耽于肉欲的、荒淫的、色情的";"哀",译为"melancholy","忧愁的";"伤",译为"morbid","病态的"。连起来就是,这首诗是多情的、忧愁的——这些都是正常的情绪;而不是淫秽的、病态痛苦的——这些都是情绪的变态或极端化。

21. 文中,"社",辜鸿铭译为"emblem used on the altars to the Titular Genius of the land","土地之神祭坛上使用的象征"。并注释说:

在古代中国,这些象征的采用,就像现在"玫瑰花"(Rose)之于英国,以及"莺尾花"(Fleur de lys)之于法国波旁王朝作为现代象征的采用。

22. 本节孔子表达了对管仲的看法。辜鸿铭一贯将辅佐齐桓公取得霸主地位的管仲比作统一了德意志帝国的政治家俾斯麦。他注释说:

> 奇妙的是,管仲这位古代中国的俾斯麦,在政治上也恪守着与那位著名的现代德意志帝国的奠基者同样的箴言:"Do, ut des",汉语是"欲取之故与之"。

孔子称管仲"器小",辜鸿铭译为"Kuan Chung was by no means a great-minded man","管仲绝不是个思想伟大的人",指管仲的思想与品德修养而言。

"三归",是管仲修筑的"三归之台",辜鸿铭译为"Sansouci Pleasaunce","无忧宫乐园",是比作18世纪普鲁士国王腓特烈二世模仿法国凡尔赛宫而建的"无忧宫",位于德国波茨坦市北郊,被称为德国建筑精华之作。

"官事不摄",辜鸿铭译为"he had a special officer appointed to every function in his household","他任命一个专门的官员负责他家族中的每项职责"。"树塞门",辜鸿铭译为"have walls built before their palace gates","在宫殿大门前建墙","树"译为"built","塞门"译为"wall"。"反坫",译为"buffet",宴会、酒会用的餐台。以上,都表现了管仲生活的奢靡与违礼之处。

最后,"知礼"译为"a man of taste who observed the correct forms","遵守正确礼仪、举止得体"。此处他用"taste"与"observe the correct forms"来解释"礼"字,即指人行为得体并遵守正确的礼仪,而管仲没有做到。

23. 文中,"大师",辜鸿铭译为"the Grand Kapel Meister","最高乐队的领班";"乐",辜鸿铭根据下文的内容认为,并非指一般的音乐,而是特指乐队的演奏。所以,孔子说"乐其可知",即是说自己懂得"the way in which a piece should be played with a full orchestra",即"一个完整的乐队演奏一首乐曲的正确方式"。

下面的文字即辜鸿铭所说的"一个完整的乐队演奏一首乐曲的正确方式"。

24. "仪封人",辜鸿铭译为"an officer in command of a certain Pass","负责管辖某个关口的官员",也即疆吏之意。三国时何晏《论语集解》引东汉郑玄注:"仪,盖卫邑。封人,官名。"

文中,"丧"译为"your present want of official position","你们目前没有官职",指孔子的学生们目前尚无官职。"无道",译为"without the order and justice of good government",

"没有善政下的秩序与正义"。那么,"道"自然就是有秩序与正义的善政。这是辜鸿铭在政治概念上对"道"的解释。

"以夫子为木铎"一句,辜鸿铭译为"make use of your Teacher as a tocsin to awaken the world","以你们的老师为一个警钟,来唤醒世界"。辜鸿铭认为,孔子生活的时代,社会秩序发生根本性混乱,而孔子则为未来的文明奠定了基础。他在《中国人的精神(在北京东方学会上所宣讲的论文)》中说:"孔子生活在中国历史上的春秋时期——那时封建时代已进入末期。半宗法式的社会秩序和统治方式必须扩建和重建。这种巨大的变化不仅必然带来了世界的无序,而且造成了人们思想的混乱。……中国人在二千五百年前的觉醒,探寻事件的因果,这无异于欧洲所谓的现代精神——自由主义精神,追寻事物因果的探索精神。有着这种现代精神的中国人,认识到传统的社会秩序和文明与现实生活已不甚相符,他们不仅要建立新的社会秩序和文明,而且还要为之寻找一个基础。但是在中国,为这个新秩序和文明寻找基础的尝试均告失败。……"(夏丹等选编,《辜鸿铭作品精选·中国人的精神》,第36—37页)

那么,孔子是如何解决这一问题的呢? 辜鸿铭又说:"实际上孔子毕生都致力于为社会和文明规定一个正确的发展方向,给它一个真实的基础,并阻止文明的毁灭。……当孔子看到中国文明这一建筑已不可避免地趋于毁灭时,他自认只能抢救出一些图纸。这些被抢救出来的东西现在被保存在中国古老的经书中——即著名的五经之中。因此我认为孔子对中华民族的一大贡献,在于他抢救出了中国文明的蓝图。"(同上,第37—38页)他进一步说:"孔子的最大贡献是按照文明的蓝图做了新的综合与阐发。经过他的阐发,中国人民拥有了一个真正的国家观念——为国家奠定了一个真实的、合理的、永久的、绝对的基础。"(同上,第38页)

25. "美"与"善"是本节的关键词。"美"辜鸿铭译为"the physical beauty of harmony","外在的和谐之美";"善",译为"moral grandeur","道德的伟大"。据此可以说,乐曲外在之"美"以和谐为标准,而内在之"善"则以道德为标准。"尽",译为"have all the excellence of",即"拥有……方面的全部的优点或杰出性",也即完全、彻底之意。

26. 文中,"居上",辜鸿铭译为"possession of power","掌权者",可以指处于任何管理职位的人。"居上不宽"指拥有权力而不懂宽容,这是孔子所不想看到的。

"为礼"译为"courtesy","殷勤有礼",指"殷勤有礼"的态度;"敬",译为"seriousness","严肃,庄重"。"为礼不敬"指表现得"殷勤有礼"的姿态,然而却不严肃庄重。这也是孔子所不想看到的。

"临丧",译为"mourning","服丧"。"临丧不哀"指服丧时并不悲痛。孔子同样不愿看到。

CHAPTER IV
里仁第四

1. Confucius remarked, "It is the moral life of a neighbourhood which constitutes its excellence. He is not an intelligent man, who, in choosing his residence, does not select a place with a moral surrounding."

2. Confucius remarked, "A man without moral character cannot long put up with adversity, nor can he long enjoy prosperity."

   "Men of moral character find themselves at home in being moral; men of intelligence find it advantageous to be moral."

3. Confucius remarked, "It is only men of moral character who know how to love men or to hate men."

4. Confucius remarked, "If you fix your mind upon a moral life, you will be free from evil."

5. Confucius remarked, "Riches and honours are objects of men's desire; but if I cannot have them without leaving the path of duty, I would not have them. Poverty and a low position in life are objects of men's dislike; but if I cannot leave them without departing from the path of duty, I would not leave them.

   "A wise man who leaves his moral character is no longer entitled to the name of a wise man. A wise man never for one single moment in his life loses sight of a moral life; in moments of haste and hurry, as in moments of danger and peril, he always clings to it."

1. 子曰:"里仁为美。择不处仁,焉得知?"

   孔子说:"一个地区要有道德的生活才算好。如果一个人在选择居住地时,不挑选一个拥有道德环境的地方,他就算不上是个有智慧的人。"

2. 子曰:"不仁者不可以久处约,不可以长处乐。仁者安仁,知者利仁。"

   孔子说:"一个不具备道德品质的人,无法长久地忍受困境,也无法长久地享受幸福。

   "具备道德品质的人,往往会发现自己处于道德之中而安逸自在;而有智慧的人会发现他们的智慧有助于让自己变得道德。"

3. 子曰:"唯仁者能好人,能恶人。"

   孔子说:"只有具备道德品质的人,才懂得如何去关爱及憎恨他人。"

4. 子曰:"苟志于仁矣,无恶也。"

   孔子说:"如果你专心于道德的生活,你就会免于邪恶。"

5. 子曰:"富与贵是人之所欲也,不以其道得之,不处也;贫与贱是人之所恶也,不以其道得之,不去也。君子去仁,恶乎成名?君子无终食之间违仁,造次必于是,颠沛必于是。"

   孔子说:"财富与荣誉是人们所渴望的,但如果我除了远离责任之路外不能拥有它们,那我将不会去拥有。贫穷与卑贱是人们所厌恶的,但如果我除了离开责任之路而不能摈弃它们,那我将不去摈弃。

   "一个聪明人如果丢掉了道德品质,就不再有资格享有聪明人的名声了。一个聪明人在生活中绝不会忽略道德的生活,哪怕只是瞬息片刻;在匆忙与仓促的时刻,以及在危险与危难的时刻,他都会坚持它。"

6. Confucius remarked, "I do not now see a man who really loves a moral life; or one who really hates an immoral life.One who really loves a moral life would esteem nothing above it.One who really hates an immoral life would be a moral man who would not allow anything the least immoral in his life.

"Nevertheless, if a man were really to exert himself for one single day to live a moral life, I do not believe he will find that he has not the strength to do it.At least I have never heard of such a case."

7. Confucius remarked, "Men's faults are characteristic. By observing a man's failings you can judge of his moral character."

8. Confucius remarked, "When a man has learnt wisdom in the morning, he may be content to die in the evening before the sun sets."

9. Confucius remarked, "It is useless to speak to a gentleman who wants to give himself up to serious studies and who yet is ashamed because of his poor food or bad clothes."

10. Confucius remarked, "A wise man in his judgment of the world, has no predilections nor prejudices; he is on the side of what is right."

6. 子曰："我未见好仁者，恶不仁者。好仁者，无以尚之；恶不仁者，其为仁矣，不使不仁者加乎其身。有能一日用其力于仁矣乎？我未见力不足者。盖有之矣，我未之见也。"

　　孔子说："我现在还没见到真正热爱道德生活的人，或真正厌恶不道德的生活的人。一个真正热爱道德生活的人，将不会更珍视其他东西。一个真正厌恶不道德的生活的人，将是一个有德之人，他不会允许在生活中有丝毫不道德的东西。

　　"不过，如果一个人真的要努力过一天道德的生活，我不相信他会发现他没有力量去做。至少，我还没有听说过有这种事情。"

7. 子曰："人之过也，各于其党。观过，斯知仁矣。"

　　孔子说："人们的过错都是个性化的。通过观察一个人的缺点，你就能判断他的道德品质。"

8. 子曰："朝闻道，夕死可矣。"

　　孔子说："当一个人早晨时即已学到了智慧，他可能甘愿在太阳落山之前的傍晚死去。"

9. 子曰："士志于道，而耻恶衣恶食者，未足与议也。"

　　孔子说："与一个既已致力于严肃的学问研究，却又因自己粗劣的食物与衣服而感到羞耻的绅士谈话，是毫无意义的。"

10. 子曰："君子之于天下也，无适也，无莫也，义之与比。"

　　孔子说："一个明智的人在他对世界的判断中，没有偏袒，也没有偏见；他只是站在正义的一边罢了。"

11. Confucius remarked, "A wise man regards the moral worth of a man; a fool, only his position. A wise man expects justice; a fool, only expects favours."

12. Confucius remarked, "If you always look only to your own advantage you will be sure to make many enemies."

13. Confucius remarked, "He who can rule a country by real courtesy and good manners that are in him, will find no difficulty in doing it. But a ruler who has no real courtesy and good manners in him, what can the mere rules of etiquette and formality avail him."

14. Confucius remarked, "Be not concerned for want of a position; be concerned how to fit yourself for a position; Be not concerned that you are not known, but seek to do something to deserve a reputation."

15. Confucius remarked to a disciple, "In all my life and teaching there is one underlying connected principle." "Even so," answered the disciple.

Afterwards, when Confucius had left, the other disciples asked the disciple who was above spoken to, "What did the master mean by what he said just now?" "The principle in the master's life and teaching," answered the disciple, "is comprised in the two words: conscientiousness and charity."

11. 子曰:"君子怀德,小人怀土;君子怀刑,小人怀惠。"

　　孔子说:"明智的人关注的是一个人的道德品质;蠢人只关注他自己的社会地位。明智的人期待公正,蠢人只期待庇护。"

12. 子曰:"放于利而行,多怨。"

　　孔子说:"如果你总是只顾及自己的利益,就一定会树立很多敌人。"

13. 子曰:"能以礼让为国乎? 何有? 不能以礼让为国,如礼何?"

　　孔子说:"一个能够通过其自身真正的谦恭与良好态度来统治国家的人,将发现那样做并不困难。但如果一个统治者其自身并没有真正的谦恭与良好态度,那些仅有的礼法与礼节,对他又有什么用处呢?"

14. 子曰:"不患无位,患所以立;不患莫己知,求为可知也。"

　　孔子说:"不要为没有地位而担忧,要担忧的是如何让自己适合某个地位。不要为自己并不知名而担忧,而要寻求着去做些事情让自己值得某个声望。"

15. 子曰:"参乎! 吾道一以贯之。"曾子曰:"唯。"子出,门人问曰:"何谓也?"曾子曰:"夫子之道,忠恕而已矣。"

　　孔子对一个学生说:"在我所有的生活与学说中,有一个贯穿始终的根本原则。""正是如此。"那位学生回答说。

　　后来,孔子离开之后,其他学生问上面那位孔子与之说话的学生:"老师刚才说的话是什么意思?""老师的生活与学说中的那个原则,"那位学生回答说,"蕴含在这两个词中:良心与博爱。"

16. Confucius remarked, "A wise man sees what is right in a question; a fool, what is advantageous to himself."

17. Confucius remarked, "When we meet with men of worth, we should think how we may equal them; When we meet with worthless men, we should turn into ourselves and find out if we do not resemble them."

18. Confucius remarked, "In serving his parents a son should seldom remonstrate with them; but if he was obliged to do so, and should find that they will not listen, he should yet not fail in respect nor disregard their wishes; however much trouble they may give him, he should never complain."

19. Confucius remarked, "While his parents are living, a son should not go far abroad; if he does, he should let them know where he goes."

20. Confucius remarked, "A son who for three years after his father's death does not, in his own life, change his father's principles, may be considered to be a good son."

21. Confucius remarked, "A son should always keep in mind the age of his parents, as a matter for thankfulness as well as for anxiety."

16. 子曰:"君子喻于义,小人喻于利。"

　　孔子说:"聪明人在一个问题中看到的是正义,而蠢人看到的则是自己的私利。"

17. 子曰:"见贤思齐焉,见不贤而内自省也。"

　　孔子说:"当我们遇到高尚的人时,应该考虑如何才能与他们一样。而碰到卑劣的人时,应该反观自己,并搞清楚我们是否与他们是不一样的。"

18. 子曰:"事父母几谏。见志不从,又敬不违,劳而不怨。"

　　孔子说:"儿子在照顾他的父母时,不应该经常劝谏他们;但如果不得不这样做,而又发现他们不会听从时,他也不应该不尊重他们以及忽视他们的愿望;无论他们给他带来多少麻烦,他都应该毫无怨言。"

19. 子曰:"父母在,不远游。游必有方。"

　　孔子说:"当他的父母都还在世时,儿子不应远走他方。如果他这样做,就应该让父母知道他去哪儿。"

20. 子曰:"三年无改于父之道,可谓孝矣。"

　　孔子说:"如果在他父亲过世三年之内,儿子在自己的生活中没有改变他父亲的原则,他就可以被视为一个好儿子。"

21. 子曰:"父母之年,不可不知也。一则以喜,一则以惧。"

　　孔子说:"儿子应时常牢记他父母的年龄,作为一件让他感激也让他担忧的事情。"

22. Confucius remarked, "Men of old kept silence for fear lest what they said should not come up to what they did."

23. Confucius remarked, "He who wants little seldom goes wrong."

24. Confucius remarked, "A wise man wants to be slow in speech and diligent in conduct."

25. Confucius remarked, "Moral worth is never left alone; society is sure to grow round him."

26. A disciple of Confucius remarked, "In the service of your prince, if you keep constantly pointing out his errors it will lead to your disgrace; if you act in the same way to your friends it will estrange them."

22. 子曰:"古者言之不出,耻躬之不逮也。"

　　孔子说:"古代的人不太讲话,是因为他们生怕所说的话不符合他们所做的事情。"

23. 子曰:"以约失之者鲜矣。"

　　孔子说:"需求微少的人,很少犯错。"

24. 子曰:"君子欲讷于言而敏于行。"

　　孔子说:"一个聪明人,总想在言辞上是笨拙的,而在行为上是勤勉的。"

25. 子曰:"德不孤,必有邻。"

　　孔子说:"有道德品质的人从不会被孤立,友伴必会围绕于他。"

26. 子游曰:"事君数,斯辱矣,朋友数,斯疏矣。"

　　孔子的一个学生说:"服务你的国君时,如果你总是不断地指出他的过失,这将会给你带来耻辱;如果你以同样的方式对待你的朋友,这将会疏远他们。"

【评述】

1. 文中，"里"字，辜鸿铭译为"a neighbourhood"，"某地"，指由邻里构成的一个地区，这种翻译带有一丝乡土气息。第一个"仁"，译为"the moral life"，"道德生活"。第二个"仁"，辜鸿铭译为"a place with a moral surrounding"，"一个具有道德环境的地方"，是代名词，指选择具有道德环境的地方居住。"美"，译为"excellence"，"杰出、卓越、优点"之意。"里仁为美"指居民拥有道德生活的地方，才是好的，可以来选择居住的。

2. 本节讲的是道德品质与一个人生活状态的关系。第一句上半句，"约"，辜鸿铭译为"adversity"，"困境，逆境"；"处"，译为"put up with"，"忍受"，他强调的是，不具备道德品质的人忍受不了困境。第一句下半句，"乐"，译为"prosperity"，"幸福，繁荣，成功"之意，他强调的是人所处的积极发展或成功的状态；"处"，译为"enjoy"，"享受"，指不具备道德品质的人，甚至连幸福或成功都不可能长期享有或保持。

"安仁"，辜鸿铭译为"at home in being moral"，"在道德中安逸自在"。是一种超脱功利的道德观。即有道德品质的人，对于道德是自然流露且感到舒适快乐的。"利仁"，译为"advantageous to be moral"，"有利于[让自己]变得道德"。意思是，"智慧"本身对他道德的养成有帮助作用。

3. 文中，"仁者"，辜鸿铭译为"men of moral character"，"具备道德品质的人"；"能"，译为"know how to"，"懂得如何去做"，指只有具有道德品质的人，才懂得如何去热爱别人与憎恨别人。

4. 文中，"恶"，辜鸿铭译为"evil"，"罪恶"；"无"，译为"be free from"，"远离，免于"，指致力于道德的修养，就会远离或免于罪恶或邪恶，指人性而言。

5. 文中，"贵"，辜鸿铭译为"honours"，"荣誉"；"道"，译为"the path of duty"，"责任之路"，指财富、荣誉都是人们追求的；贫穷与卑贱是人们所厌恶的，然而都要合乎"责任"或"义务"之道。

6. 辜鸿铭将"好仁者"、"恶不仁者"视为两种人，即"真正热爱道德生活的人"与"真正憎恨不道德生活的人"。"仁"，译为"moral life"，"道德的生活"。在辜鸿铭看来，"真正热爱道德生活的人"与"真正厌恶不道德生活的人"，是同样的意思，是从正、反两个方面来表达君子对道德生活的追求。当然，以上两种人只是理想中的人物。而在现实中，但凡人们"用其力于仁"，"to exert himself to live a moral life"，"努力过一种道德的生活"，其实并不难实现，只是人们没有这样做而已。

7. 文中，"党"，辜鸿铭译为"characteristic"，"个性化的"，他强调的是人的性格特征，即人的过错都是由其不同的性格造成的；"知仁"，译为"you can judge of his moral character"，"能够判断他的道德品质"，此处的"仁"译为"moral character"，"道德品质"。指通过人的错误就能看出他的道德品质的真实状况。

8. 文中，"道"，译为"wisdom"，"智慧"；"可"，译为"may be content to"，"可能甘愿"。"夕死可矣"指如果学到智慧，他可能甘愿死去。

9. 文中，"道"，译为"serious studies"，"严肃的学问研究"。"志于道"，即致身于严肃的学问研究。这句话是说，既然已经致身于某项严肃的学问，就应该具有真诚的、纯粹的心境，而不应再耽于物质的享受。

10. 文中，"适"，辜鸿铭译为"predilection"，"偏袒"；"莫"，译为"prejudice"，"偏见"；"比"，译为"on the side of"，"站在……的一边"。本节的意思是，君子对待事物或人，不应有事先的偏袒与偏见，而是应坚持"义"的原则。

11. 在对本节的翻译中，辜鸿铭首先认为"小人怀土"的"土"字是一种书写错误，他注释说：

> 我们在此冒险地认为，原文中的"土"，earth，很明显的是"位"字的书写错误，迄今为止，这一点一直未被中国的注释家们所注意到。这两个字在古老的篆书写法中是完全相同的，因此导致了这种书写错误。

在此基础上，他将"土"译为"his position"，"地位"。

文中，前两个"怀"，译为"regard"，"关注"之意；"德"，译为"moral worth"，"道德品质"，"怀德"，即君子关注的是自己的道德，并由此而获得自己的人格价值；而"怀土"则指小人只关注自己的社会地位（利益）。后两个"怀"译为"expect"，"期待"。"刑"，译为"justice"，"公正"。"惠"，译为"favour"，"庇护"。很显然，后面这两点，都是指法律而言。君子与小人的不同在于，君子期盼的是公正；而小人则期盼能受到特殊的庇护，是自己的私利。

12. 文中，辜鸿铭将"放"字译为"look only to"，"只顾及"的意思；"利"译为"your own advantage"，"自己的利益"；"怨"为"make enemies"，"树敌"。本节指人在社会交往中，不能只顾自身利益。

13. 文中两个"礼让",第一个"礼让"译为"real courtesy and good manners that are in him","他内心真正的谦恭与良好的态度",强调的是人内心的本性。第二个"礼让"译为"the mere rules of etiquette and formality","仅有的礼法与礼节的规则",即外在的礼节。很显然,辜鸿铭是将"礼"分成了内、外两部分,内部所指就是前面所说的"内心真正的谦恭与良好的态度",是指人心而言;外部所指,只是一些规则、礼节、形式。如果人没有内在的"礼"而只有外在的"礼节",那么,这外在的"礼节",就只能是形同虚设了。

14. 文中,"位",辜鸿铭译为"position","地位,身份",也有"职位"之意;"立",译为"fit yourself for a position","让自己适合某个地位或职位"。辜鸿铭对两个"知"做了不同的翻译:将第一个译为"known","闻名";将第二处的"可知"译为"deserve a reputation","值得某个声望"。这节可以泛指一个人的社会属性的表现,对于个人来说,最重要的并非获得某种成就,而是具备这样的素质与品质。每个个体是完善的、处于恰当位置的,这个社会才是完善的。

15. 本节是对孔子"一以贯之"的"道"的阐述。"道",辜鸿铭译为"underlying ... principle ... in all my life and teaching",即"全部生活与学说中的根本原则",也就是说,孔子的"道"是指导全部的生活与学说的,孔子的生活与学说是统一的,即内心与行为是同一的;"贯",译为"connected",即"连贯的,或连在一起的",结合整句来看,即"贯穿始终"之意。"一以贯之"即"贯穿始终的根本原则"。这一原则,是孔子生活与学说共同的基础。

最后一句中的"忠恕"是孔子一以贯之的道。"忠",辜鸿铭译为"conscientiousness","良心,或责任心",这是他对"忠"一贯的译法;"恕",译为"charity","博爱、慈悲"。从这个翻译可以看出,辜鸿铭将"良心"与"博爱"视为孔子学说的根本原则。

16. 文中,"喻"辜鸿铭译为"see","看到",且句中还有"in a question"一语,"在某一个问题中"。这句话说的是君子小人看待问题的不同表现。"义",译为"what is right","正义",这也是他的一贯译法;"利"译为"what is advantageous to himself","对他有利的东西,私利"。整句话的意思是,君子与小人看一个问题,君子看到的是这件事正义与否;小人看到的则是这件事对自己是否有利。辜鸿铭最后在注释中引用了另外一种相近的翻译:

阿查利爵士是这样翻译的:"绅士关注什么是正义的,而粗鄙无礼的人则关注将得到什么好处。"

17. 文中,"贤",辜鸿铭译为"men of worth","高尚的人";"不贤"译为"worthless

men", "卑劣的人", 都是偏重指道德品质。"齐", 译为 "equal them", "与他们一样"; "内自省", 译为 "turn into ourselves and find out if we do not resemble them", "反观自己, 并搞清楚是否与他们是不一样的", 与朱熹在《四书章句集注》中的解释 "恐己亦有是恶" 相近 (见朱熹撰,《四书章句集注》, 中华书局, 1983, 第73页)。本节是教人在生活、修养、学习等各方面要善于反思, 不断完善自己。

18. 本节说的是子女与父母的相处方式。

19. 本节是说, 父母在世时, 子女不应离他们太远。

20. 本节已见第一章第11节。

21. 文中, 辜鸿铭将 "喜" 译为 "for thankfulness", "感激"; 将 "惧" 译为 "for anxiety", "担忧"。本节意思是, 知道父母的年龄, 子女会因父母养育自己这许多年而心存感激; 同时, 又为父母年事渐高而担忧。

22. 文中, "古", 辜鸿铭译为 "old", "古代"; "言之不出", 译为 "kept silence", "保持沉默" 或 "不太说话", 指的是言语谨慎。"逮" 字表达的是 "言" 与 "行" 的关系, 辜鸿铭译为 "what they said should not come up to what they did", "所说的话不符合所做的事"。本节表达的也是孔子重行而轻言、且言行一致的主张。

23. 对于 "约" 字, 辜鸿铭注释说:

> 或许这样翻译更好: 限制自己欲望程度的人。"你将发现, 一般来说, 乡村的经济师要比城镇少, 而小城镇的又比大城市少。为什么? 是有限的环境让人们这样考虑的。"(歌德)

而在翻译中, 他译为 "wants little", "需求微少", 他强调的是人内心对各种欲望的限制。辜鸿铭认为, 人内心的欲望, 是对人类自身破坏性最大的力量。在《中国人的精神·导论》中, 他说:"一切文明都起源于对自然的征服, 即, 通过征服和控制自然界可怕的物质力量, 使人类免受其害。……但是, 在这个世界上, 除了自然力, 还存有一种较自然力更可怕的力量, 那就是蕴藏于人心的情欲。……毫无疑问, 如果这一力量——人类情欲——不予以调控的话, 那么不仅无所谓文明存在之可言, 而且人类的生存也是不可能的。"(夏丹等选编《辜鸿铭作品精选》, 第17页)

24. 文中，"讷"，辜鸿铭译为"slow"，"笨拙，迟钝"；"敏"译为"diligent"，"勤勉，勤奋"，意思是，人更应该致力于自己的行为，而不是言辞。这同样表达了孔子重行而轻言的思想。

25. 文中，"不孤"，辜鸿铭译为"never left alone"，"永不会被孤立"，不仅仅指居住而言；"有邻"，译为"society is sure to grow round him"，"友伴必会围绕于他"，其中，"society"还有交际、交往、友谊的意思。本节是说，真正有道德的人，总会有朋友愿意与他交往，即使不受没有道德的人的欢迎。

26. 文中，辜鸿铭将"数"译为"keep constantly pointing out his errors"，"不停地指出他的过失"。"辱"译为"disgrace"，除耻辱的意思外，还指失宠，即被君主厌恶，这对于朋友也是如此，频繁指出对方过失，会导致双方关系的疏远。

CHAPTER V
公冶长第五

1. Confucius remarked of a disciple, saying, "No man need hesitate to give his daughter to such a man to wife. It is true he has been in prison, but it was through no crime of his."

   Confucius accordingly gave him his own daughter to wife.

   Confucius remarked of another disciple, saying, "When there is order and justice in the government of the country, he will not be neglected. But should there be no order and justice in the government of the country, he will escape persecution."

   Confucius accordingly gave his niece to him to wife.

2. Confucius then went on to remark of another disciple, saying, "What a wise and good man he is! I wonder if there were no wise and good men in the country, how that man could have acquired the character he has."

3. Another disciple who heard the above remarks said then to Confucius, "And I, what do you say of me?" "Yes are," answered Confucius, "a work of art." "What work of art?"asked the other."A rich jewelled work of art."was the reply.

4. Somebody remarked of a disciple of Confucius, saying, "He is a good moral man, but he is not a man of ready wit."

   When Confucius heard the remark, he said, "What is the good of a ready wit? A man who is always ready with his tongue to others will only often make enemies.I do not know if he is a moral man, but I do not see the good of having a ready wit."

1. 子谓公冶长，"可妻也。虽在缧绁之中，非其罪也"。以其子妻之。子谓南容，"邦有道，不废；邦无道，免于刑戮"。以其兄之子妻之。

孔子谈到一个学生时，说："把自己的女儿嫁给这样的一个人做妻子，谁都用不着犹豫。他确实身陷牢狱之中，但从始至终他都没有罪过。"

于是，孔子将他自己的女儿嫁给了他做妻子。

孔子又谈到另外一个学生时，说："当国家的政治中有秩序与正义时，他不会被忽视。而当国家的政治中没有秩序与正义时，他又会免遭迫害。"

孔子于是把自己的侄女嫁给了他做妻子。

2. 子谓子贱，"君子哉若人！鲁无君子者，斯焉取斯"？

孔子继续谈到他的另外一个学生，说："他是多么明智而良善的一个人啊！我想知道，如果说这个国家没有明智而良善的人，那么这个人又是怎么获取他所拥有的品格的呢？"

3. 子贡问曰："赐也何如？"子曰："女器也。"曰："何器也？"曰："瑚琏也。"

另一个学生在听到上面的评论后，对孔子说："那我呢，您对我有什么看法？""你是，"孔子回答说，"一件艺术品。""什么艺术品？"另外一个学生问。"一件嵌有宝石的昂贵的艺术品。"孔子回答道。

4. 或曰："雍也仁而不佞。"子曰："焉用佞？御人以口给，屡憎于人。不知其仁，焉用佞？"

有人谈到孔子的一位学生，说："他是个有良好道德品质的人，但他不是个机智善辩的人。"

孔子听到这个评论后，说："机智善辩有什么好处呢？一个总是对别人口齿伶俐的人，将只会经常树敌。我不知道他是否是个有道德的人，但我看不到机智善辩的好处。"

5. Confucius on one occasion wanted a disciple to enter public life."No," answered the disciple, "I have not yet confidence in myself."Thereupon Confucius commended him.

6. Confucius on one occasion remarked, "There is no order and justice now in the government in China. I will betake me to a ship and sail over the sea to seek for it in other countries.If I take anybody with me, I will take Yu, "referring to a disciple.

    The disciple referred to, when he heard of what Confucius said, was glad, and offered to go.

    "My friend," said Confucius then to him, "You have certainly more courage than I have; only you do not exercise judgment when using it."

7. A member of a powerful family of nobles in Confucius' native State asked Confucius if his disciple, the above mentioned Chung Yu, was a moral character."I cannot say," answered Confucius. But on being pressed, Confucius said, "In the government of a State of even the first-rate power the man could be entrusted with the organisation of the army. I cannot say if he could be called a moral character."

    The noble then put the same question with regard to another disciple. Confucius answered, "In the government of a large town or in the direction of affairs in a small principality, the man could be entrusted with the chief authority. I cannot say if he could be called a moral character."

    The noble went on to put the same question with regard to another disciple. Confucius answered, "At court, in a gala-dress reception, he could be entrusted with the duty of entertaining the visitors. I cannot say if he could be called a moral character."

5. 子使漆雕开仕。对曰:"吾斯之未能信。"子说。

   孔子有一次希望一个学生进入政界。"不,"那个学生说,"我自己还没信心呢。"于是,孔子称赞了他。

6. 子曰:"道不行,乘桴浮于海。从我者其由与?"子路闻之喜。子曰:"由也好勇过我,无所取材。"

   有一次,孔子说:"现在中国的政治中并没有秩序与正义。我将要乘船渡海到其他国家去寻求它。如果我要带什么人和我一起的话,我将带上由。"提到一个学生。

   那位被提到的学生在听说了孔子的话之后非常高兴,主动提出出发。

   "我的朋友,"孔子对他说,"你确实比我更有勇气,只是,你在使用它的时候并没有运用判断力。"

7. 孟武伯问:"子路仁乎?"子曰:"不知也。"又问。子曰:"由也,千乘之国,可使治其赋也,不知其仁也。""求也何如?"子曰:"求也,千室之邑,百乘之家,可使为之宰也,不知其仁也。""赤也何如?"子曰:"赤也,束带立于朝,可使与宾客言也,不知其仁也。"

   孔子故国的一位有权势的贵族家族的成员问孔子,他的学生,上面提到的仲由是否是个有道德的人。"我不能确定,"孔子回答说。一再追问之下,孔子说:"即使是在一个一流国家的政治中,他也能够被委托以军事机构的事务。但我不能确定他是否可以被称作一个有道德的人。"

   那位贵族于是询问关于另一个学生同样的问题。孔子回答说:"在一个大型城镇的政治中,或者在一个小型公国的事务管理中,那个人可以被委任以最高职权。但我不能确定他是否可以被称作是一个有道德的人。"

   那位贵族继续询问有关另外一个学生同样的问题。孔子回答说:"在朝廷的盛装接待会上,他可以被委任以招待宾客的职责。但我不能确定他是否可以被称为是一个有道德的人。"

8. Confucius once said to a disciple, "You and Hui (the favourite Yen Hui), who is the abler man?"

The disciple answered, "How should I dare compare myself with him. When he has learnt one thing he immediately understands its application to all cases; whereas I, when I have learnt one thing I can only follow out its bearing and applications to one or two particular cases."

9. A disciple of Confucius spent the best hours of the day in sleep. Confucius, remarking on it, said, "You cannot carve anything out of rotten wood nor plaster up a wall built up of rubbish. What is the use of rebuke in such a case?"

Confucius then went on to say, "At one time, when I wanted to judge of a man, I listened to what he said, and I knew for certain what he would do in his life. But now, when I want to judge of a man, I have to look at what he does in his life as well as listen to what he says. It is, perhaps, men like this young man who have made me change my method of judging men."

10. Confucius once remarked, "I do not now see a man of strong character." "There is So-and-so," said somebody. "No," replied Confucius, "he is a man of strong passions; he is not a man of strong character."

8. 子谓子贡曰："女与回也孰愈？"对曰："赐也何敢望回。回也闻一以知十，赐也闻一以知二。"子曰："弗如也！吾与女弗如也。"①

有一次，孔子向他的一位学生说："你和回（最受喜爱的颜回），谁是更有才华的人？"

那位学生回答说："我怎敢拿我自己和他比呢。他每学会一件事情，立刻就会明白它在所有情况之下的用途；而我呢，每学会一件事情，只能在一两种特定的情况之下运用它。"

9. 宰予昼寝。子曰："朽木不可雕也，粪土之墙不可杇也，于予与何诛？"子曰："始吾于人也，听其言而信其行；今吾于人也，听其言而观其行。于予与改是。"

孔子的一位学生在睡觉中打发一天中最好的时间。孔子对此评论说："你无法把一块腐朽的木头雕琢成任何东西，也无法涂饰一堵由垃圾堆砌的墙。在这样的情况下，责怪还有什么用呢？"

孔子接着说："以前，每当我想判断一个人的时候，我听到他说什么，就会确定地认为他在生活中将会做什么。但是现在，当我想判断一个人的时候，我不得不审视他在生活中做什么，也要去听他说什么。或许，是那些像这位年轻人一样的人，让我改变了判断人的方法。"

10. 子曰："吾未见刚者。"或对曰："申枨。"子曰："枨也欲，焉得刚？"

有一次，孔子说："我至今还没见到过性格刚强的人。""某某人就是啊。"有人说。"不，"孔子回答说，"他只是个欲望强盛的人，而不是个性格刚强的人。"

---

① 最后一句话，辜鸿铭未译。

11. A disciple said to Confucius, "What I do not wish that others should not do unto me, I also do not wish that I should do unto them." "My friend," answered Confucius, "You have not yet attained to that."

12. A disciple of Confucius remarked, "You will often hear the master speak on the subjects of art and literature, but you will never hear him speak on the subjects of metaphysics or theology."

13. When Confucius' disciple, the intrepid Chung Yu, had learnt anything which he was not yet able to carry out into practice, he was afraid to learn anything new.

14. A disciple, speaking of an ancient worthy of the time, enquired of Confucius saying, "How was it that he had the title of 'Beau-clerc' added as an honour to his name after his death?"

"He was," answered Confucius, "a man of great industry, who applied himself to self-culture; he was not ashamed to seek for information from others more ignorant than himself. For that reason he has had the title of 'Beau-clerc' added as an honour to his name after his death."

15. Confucius remarked of a famous statesman (the Colbert of the time), saying, "He showed himself to be a good and wise man in four ways. In his conduct of himself he was earnest, and in serving

11. 子贡曰："我不欲人之加诸我也,吾亦欲无加诸人也。"子曰："赐也,
   非尔所及也。"

   　　一位学生对孔子说："那些我所不希望的、别人不应对我做的事,我
   也不希望我会对他们做。""我的朋友,"孔子回答说,"你还没达到那种
   程度啊。"

12. 子贡曰："夫子之文章,可得而闻也;夫子之言性与天道,不可得
   而闻也。"

   　　孔子的一位学生说,"你将经常听到老师谈论艺术与文学的话题,
   却绝不会听到他谈论玄学与神学的话题。"

13. 子路有闻,未之能行,唯恐有闻。

   　　当孔子的学生,那位刚勇的仲由,学到什么东西还不能付诸实践的
   时候,他就害怕再学到任何新东西。

14. 子贡问曰："孔文子何以谓之文也?"子曰："敏而好学,不耻下
   问,是以谓之文也。"

   　　一个学生在谈到那时的一位名士时,问孔子:"为什么在他死后,他
   的名字上加上了'优秀的学者'这一称号作为一种荣誉呢?"

   　　孔子回答说:"他是一个非常勤奋的人,总是让自己专注于自我修
   养;从知识不及他的人那里寻求学问,他并不感到耻辱。所以,在他死
   后,他的名字中加上了'优秀的学者'这一称号作为一种荣誉。"

15. 子谓子产,"有君子之道四焉:其行己也恭,其事上也敬,其养民
   也惠,其使民也义。"

   　　孔子评论一位著名的政治家(那时的柯尔贝尔),说:"他通过四种

the interests of his prince he was serious. In providing for the wants of the people, he was generous, and in dealing with them he was just."

16. Confucius remarked of another famous statesman (the Sir William Temple of the time), saying, "He knew how to observe the true relations in friendship. However long-standing his acquaintance with a man might be, he always maintained throughout the same invariable careful respect."

17. Confucius remarked of an eccentric character of the time, saying, "The man actually built a chapel elaborate with carvings for a large tortoise which he kept. What can one say of the intellect of a man like that."

18. A disciple of Confucius asked him to give his opinion of a public character of the time, saying, "In his public life three times he was made Prime Minister, and yet on none of these occasions did he show the least signs of elation. Three times he was dismissed from office, and also on none of these occasions did he show the least signs of disappointment. He was careful every time, when giving up office, to explain to his successor the line of policy which the Government under him hitherto had been pursuing."

"Now," asked the disciple, "what do you think of him?"

"He was," answered Confucius, "a conscientious man." "But," asked the disciple, "could he be called a moral character?" "I cannot say," replied Confucius, "if he could be called a moral character."

方式表现出他是一位良善而明智的人。在他自身的行为举止方面,他认真诚挚;在为国君的利益服务方面,他严肃庄重。在为人民提供需求方面,他慷慨大度;而对待他们时,他公平正义。"

16. 子曰:"晏平仲善与人交,久而敬之。"

　　孔子评论另一位著名的政治家(那时的威廉·坦普尔),说:"他懂得如何保持真正的友谊关系。无论他与一个人结识多久,他总是会始终保持同样一成不变的谨慎的尊敬。"

17. 子曰:"臧文仲居蔡,山节藻棁,何如其知也?"

　　孔子评论那时的一个性情古怪的人,说:"那人居然为他养的一只大龟建了一个饰有雕刻的小屋子。对于像这样一个人的智力,还能说什么呢?"

18. 子张问曰:"令尹子文三仕为令尹,无喜色;三已之,无愠色。旧令尹之政,必以告新令尹。何如?"子曰:"忠矣。"曰:"仁矣乎?"曰:"未知,焉得仁?""崔子弑齐君,陈文子有马十乘,弃而违之。至于他邦,则曰:'犹吾大夫崔子也。'违之。之一邦,则又曰:'犹吾大夫崔子也。'违之。何如?"子曰:"清矣。"曰:"仁矣乎?"曰:"未知。焉得仁?"

　　孔子的一位学生请他评价那时的一位公众人物,说:"在他的政界生涯中,他三次被任命为首要大臣,但一次也没表现出丝毫得意的样子。他三次被免职,一次也没有表现出丝毫沮丧的样子。每次在移交职务的时候,他总是非常认真地向他的继任者解释迄今为止他领导下的政府正在实施的政策方针。"

　　"那么,"那位学生问,"您对他有什么看法?"

The disciple then went on to ask about another public character ,
saying, "When the Prime Minister in his native State murdered the
prince, his master, that worthy had large possessions in the country,
but he threw them all away and quitted the country. Arriving at
another State, he remarked, 'I see here they are all patricides, the
same as our patricide minister at home; 'and immediately again
quitted that country. Thus he went on from one State to another,
making the same observation. Now, what do you think of this
man?"

"He was," replied Confucius, "a pure, high-minded man."

"But," asked the disciple, "could he be called a moral character?"

"I cannot say," answered Confucius, "if he could be called a moral
character."

19. It was remarked of a public character of the time that he always
reflected thrice over every time before he acted. When Confucius
heard of the remark, he observed, "Think *twice* — that is
sufficient."

20. Confucius remarked of a public character of the time, saying,
"He was a man who, when there was order and justice in the
government of the country, acted as a man of great understanding.
But when there was no order and justice in the government, he
acted as if he was a man of no understanding. It is easy to act like
him as a man of understanding, but it is not easy to imitate him in
the way he showed how to act as a man of no understanding."

"他是,"孔子回答说,"一个有良知的人。""但是,"那位学生问,"他能够被称作一个有道德的人吗?""我不能确定,"孔子回答说,"他是否能够被称作一个有道德的人。"

接着,那位学生继续询问另外一位公众人物,说:"当他故国的首相谋杀了国君——他的主人时,那位名士虽然在那个国家拥有大量财产,但他还是全部丢弃了它们并逃离了那个国家。到达另外一个国家后,他说:'我看到这里的人都是弑父者,就像国内我们的弑君大臣一样。'他马上又逃离了那个国家。这样,他继续从一个国家到另一个国家,做同样的观察。那么,您对这个人有什么看法?"

"他是,"孔子回答说,"一个纯粹的、高洁的人。""但是,"那位学生问,"他能够被称作一个有道德的人吗?""我不能确定,"孔子回答说,"他是否能够被称作一个有道德的人。"

19. 季文子三思而后行。子闻之,曰:"再,斯可矣。"

那时的一位公众人物被谈论到总是在做事之前仔细思考三次以上。孔子听说后,评论说:"思考两次——那就足够了。"

20. 子曰:"甯武子邦有道则知,邦无道则愚。其知可及也,其愚不可及也。"

孔子评论那时的一位公众人物,说:"他是一个这样的人,当国家的政治中有秩序与正义时,他像一个智力杰出的人那样去做事。但当国家的政治中没有秩序与正义时,他又像个没有智力的人。像他那样去作为一个有智力的人做事是容易的,但要模仿他像个没有智力的人去做事则是不容易的。"

21. When Confucius in the last days of his travels abroad was in a certain State he was heard to say, "I must think of going home. I must really think of going home. My young people at home are all high-spirited and independent; they are, besides, accomplished in all the arts; but they have no judgment."

22. Confucius, remarking of two ancient worthies, famous for the purity and saintliness of their lives and character, said, "They forgave old wrongs: therefore they had little to complain of the world."

23. Confucius remarked of a character of the time, "Who says that the man is an honest man? When somebody begged him for some household necessary, he went and begged of his neighbours for it and gave it as his own."

24. Confucius remarked, "Plausible speech, fine manners and studied earnestness are things of which a friend of mine was ashamed; I am also ashamed of such things. To conceal resentment against a person and to make friends with him: that is also something of which my same friend was ashamed; I am also ashamed to do such a thing."

25. On one occasion, when two of his disciples, the favourite Yen Hui and Chung Yu the intrepid, were in attendance on him, Confucius said to them, "Now tell me, each of you, your aim in the conduct of life."

21. 子在陈曰:"归与! 归与! 吾党之小子狂简,斐然成章,不知所以裁之。"

　　孔子在周游列国最后的那段时间在某个国家,人们听到他这样说:"我必须要考虑回国了。我必须真的要考虑回国了。家乡的我的孩子们都是朝气勃勃而自由独立的,另外,他们精通所有的艺术,但他们还没有判断力。"

22. 子曰:"伯夷、叔齐不念旧恶,怨是用希。"

　　孔子评论两位因生活与人格的纯粹与圣洁而闻名的古代名士,说:"他们宽恕了以前的罪恶,因此,他们对这个世界很少有抱怨。"

23. 子曰:"孰谓微生高直? 或乞醯焉,乞诸其邻而与之。"

　　孔子评论当时的一个人:"谁说那人是个诚实的人? 当有人向他讨要一些家用必需品时,他竟去向他的邻居讨要,却作为自己的东西送出。"

24. 子曰:"巧言、令色、足恭,左丘明耻之,丘亦耻之。匿怨而友其人,左丘明耻之,丘亦耻之。"

　　孔子说:"貌似合理的言语、伪善的态度、故作姿态的真诚,都是我的一位朋友以为羞耻的东西,我同样以这样的事情为羞耻。隐藏起对一个人的愤恨并与他交朋友,这同样是我那位朋友感到羞耻的,我也耻于去做这样的事情。"

25. 颜渊、季路侍。子曰:"盍各言尔志?" 子路曰:"愿车马、衣轻裘,与朋友共。敝之而无憾。" 颜渊曰:"愿无伐善,无施劳。" 子路曰:"愿闻子之志。" 子曰:"老者安之,朋友信之,少者怀之。"

　　有一次,孔子的两位学生,最受喜爱的颜回与刚勇的仲由,在旁侍奉他,孔子问他们:"现在,告诉我,你们各自生活品行的目标是什么?"

"I would like," answered the intrepid Chung Yu, "If I had carriages and horses and clothings of costly furs to share them with my friends, to be able to consider such things as much belonging to them as belonging to me."

"And I," answered the favourite, Yen Hui, "I would like to be able not to boast of my ability and to be able to be humble in my estimate of what I have done for others."

"Now," said the intrepid Chung Yu then to Confucius, "We would like to hear *your* aim, sir, in the conduct of life."

"My aim," replied Confucius, "would be to be a comfort to my old folk at home; to be sincere, and to be found trustworthy by my friends; and to love and care for my young people at home."

26. Confucius was once heard to say, "Alas! I do not see now a man who can see his own failing or is willing to bring a suit against himself before his own conscience."

27. Confucius once remarked, "Even in a very small town there must be men who are as conscientious and honest as myself: only they have not tried to cultivate themselves as I have done."

"我希望,"刚勇的仲由回答说,"如果我有马车、骏马和昂贵毛皮的衣服,去与我的朋友们分享,能够把这些东西看做是属于朋友们的,就像属于我的一样。"

"那么,我,"那位最受喜爱的颜回说,"我希望能够不夸耀自己的才能,在看待为别人所做过的事情时能够谦逊。"

"现在,"那位刚勇的仲由接着对孔子说:"我们想听听您生活品行的目标,先生。"

"我的目标,"孔子回答说,"就是能够成为一个让家乡的老人们感到安慰的人;能够真诚并让我的朋友们感到我值得信赖;能够去爱护和关怀我家乡的年轻人。"

26. 子曰:"已矣乎! 吾未见能见其过而内自讼者也。"

人们有一次听到孔子说:"算了吧! 我现在见不到能够发现他自己的缺陷,或愿意在自己的良心面前控告自己的人。"

27. 子曰:"十室之邑,必有忠信如丘者焉,不如丘之好学也。"

孔子有一次说:"即使是在一个非常小的城镇,也必定会有像我自己这样有良知并诚实正直的人:只是他们没有像我一样试着去自我修养。"

【评述】

1. 本节是孔子对两个人处世方式的评论和肯定。"虽在缧绁之中, 非其罪也" 译为 "It is true he has been in prison, but it was through no crime of his", "他确实身陷牢狱之中, 但从始至终他都没有罪过", 指的是他对德性的坚持。"邦有道", 译为 "there is order and justice in the government of the country", "国家政治中有秩序与正义", 此处 "道" 是政治概念, 指秩序与正义; "不废", 译为 "not be neglected", "不被忽视"; "免于刑戮", 译为 "escape persecution", "免遭迫害"。这是指他在坚持德性时又能保全自身。

2. 文中, "君子", 辜鸿铭译为 "a wise and good man", "明智而良善的人"。这是辜鸿铭对君子的最常见的译法。后文 "取斯" 译为 "acquired the character he has", "获得他所拥有的品格"。本节是说, 子贱能在鲁国形成君子的品格, 说明鲁国是有君子的。

3. 文中, "瑚琏" 一词, 传统学者均解释为一种礼器。朱熹注释说: "夏曰瑚, 商曰琏, 周曰簠簋, 皆宗庙盛黍稷之器而饰以玉, 器之贵重而华美者也。"(《四书章句集注》, 第76页)辜鸿铭先是在前面孔子的答话中将 "器" 译为 "a work of art", "一件艺术品", 后面他将 "瑚琏" 译为 "a rich jewelled work of art", "一件镶嵌宝石的昂贵的艺术品"。

4. 文中, "仁", 辜鸿铭译为 "good moral", "良好的道德"; "佞", 译为 "ready wit", "机智善辩"; "焉用", 辜鸿铭译为 "What is the good of", 即 "有什么好处呢?"

"御人以口给" 一句, 人们多解释为好辩之意, 朱熹注释说: "御, 当也, 犹应答也。给, 辨也。"(《四书章句集注》, 第76页)即应答别人时好辩, 辜鸿铭译为 "ready with his tongue to others", "对别人口齿伶俐"; "憎于人", 译为 "make enemies", "树敌"。

本节表达的也是孔子重行轻言的思想主张。

5. 文中, "仕", 辜鸿铭译为 "enter public life", "进入政界"; "未能信", 译为 "not yet confidence in myself", "自己还没有信心"; "子说", 辜鸿铭译为 "Confucius commended him", "孔子称赞了他"。本节表达的含义与第四章第14节 "不患无位, 患所以立" 相同, 都是指做某事之前首先要具备所需的素质。

6. 本节表达了孔子对仲由的评价。对这个人物, 辜鸿铭注释说:

> 孔教福音中的圣彼得, 一个勇敢、刚毅、鲁莽、侠义的人物。他的名字是 "仲由", "子路" 是他的敬称。如同在第二章第9节提到的颜回的情况一样, 对于我们的原则而言, 我们对他的情况做了例外处理。

102

文中，"道不行"，辜鸿铭译为"there is no order and justice now in the government in China"，"现在中国的政治中并没有秩序与正义"。在《中国文明的历史发展》中，辜鸿铭也说："为了校正中国文明过于向知和礼仪方面发展的偏向，为了挽救中国文明，孔子想了不少办法，但都没有能成功。就如同住了不知多少代的破旧的、即将倾覆的房子一样，无论怎样修补也无济于事。"（黄兴涛编译，《辜鸿铭文集·下卷·辜鸿铭论集》，第297页）辜鸿铭的这段话可以算作孔子"浮海之叹"的注脚了。

7. 文中，"千乘之国"，辜鸿铭略去了具体的历史背景知识，译为"a State of the first-rate power"，"一流实力的国家"；"治其赋"，译为"could be entrusted with the organisation of the army"，"被委托以军事机构的事务"。本节中，辜鸿铭仍将"仁"译为"moral"，"道德"，强调的是人的道德性。

下文中，"千室之邑"，译为"a large town"，"一个大型城镇"；"百乘之家"，译为"a small principality"，"一个小型公国"（传统学者理解为"卿大夫之家"）；"为之宰"，译为"be entrusted with the chief authority"，"被委任以最高职权"（传统学者多将之理解为"家臣"）。"束带立于朝"，译为"in a gala-dress reception"，"在盛装的接待会上"。

这些都是谈的学生们的才能，但孔子认为这些才能与"仁"无关。

8. 文中，"愈"，辜鸿铭译为"abler"，"更有才华"，泛指人的才华、才能；"望"，译为"compare myself with him"，即比较之意。对于本节中"一"、"十"、"二"这些数字，辜鸿铭的翻译是："一"，译为"one thing"，"一件事情"；"十"译为"all cases"，"所有情况下"；"二"译为"one or two particular cases"，"一两种特殊的情况下"。这里的"知"，译为"immediately understands its application"，"马上懂得它的应用"，表达的是子贡与颜回的差距。

9. 文中，"昼寝"，辜鸿铭译为"spent the best hours of the day in sleep"，"用睡觉来打发一天中最好的时光"；"粪土"，译为"rubbish"，"废物，垃圾"；"杇"，译为"plaster up"，"填塞，涂饰"。整句是指，如果一个人的内在品质本身存在问题，那么，只做外在的修饰是无法使他更有价值的。后面的文字，"于人"，辜鸿铭译为"judge of a man"，即判断一个人。这个学生的表现使孔子改变了判断一个人的方式，从"听其言而信其行"到"听其言而观其行"。

10. 文中，"刚"字，辜鸿铭译为"strong character"，"刚强的性格"，指的是真正内心力量的强大；"欲"，译为"strong passions"，"强烈的情欲"，指欲望。两者表面相似实则不同。

11. 文中，"加"，辜鸿铭译为"do unto"，"对……做"，指对别人的态度与行为。这句话表达了"己所不欲，勿施于人"同样的含义，但孔子认为子贡没有达到这一程度。

12. 本节主要表现的是对孔子的"文章"与"性与天道"的对比。"文章"，辜鸿铭译为"the subjects of art and literature"，"艺术与文学的话题"，指的是艺术与文学这种陶冶性情与道德的文化；"性与天道"，译为"subjects of metaphysics or theology"，"玄学或神学的话题"，指的是玄学（或形而上学）与神学这种抽象的文化或思想。据辜鸿铭的翻译，这句话所表达思想的与孔子"未知生焉知死；未能事人焉能事鬼"的思想是一致的。关注现实生活而远离纯粹的抽象思考，也是辜鸿铭一贯主张的思想。辜鸿铭认为，儒学是传统中国的"国教"，就在于教人如何作为社会人而过日常生活。

13. 文中，"闻"，辜鸿铭译为"had learnt anything"，"学到东西"；"行"，译为"carry out into practice"，"付诸实践"之意。这一节同样说明了儒学教人注重生活实践的思想。

14. 本节的"文"字，辜鸿铭译为"Beau-clerc"，"优秀的学者"，孔子谈的是"孔文子"何以被称为"优秀的学者"；"敏而好学"中的"学"，译为"self-culture"，指完善自我，促成优秀人格的养成；"不耻下问"的"下"字，译为"others more ignorant than himself"，即"比他知识更匮乏的人"，从知识的多寡上而论，指并不耻于向比自己知识更匮乏的人请教。

15. 文中，辜鸿铭略去了"子产"的名字，译为a famous statesman，作为对他的介绍。括号中，他将子产比喻为法国历史上以财政擅长并对法国贡献巨大的政治家让-巴普蒂斯特·柯尔贝尔（Jean-Baptiste Colbert, 1619—1683）。
辜鸿铭认为，"其行己也恭，其事上也敬，其养民也惠，其使民也义"这句话列出了子产的四种君子表现，分别是"恭"、"敬"、"惠"、"义"。"恭"，译为"earnest"，"认真的，诚挚的"，意思是，他个人的言行很真诚，是对其个人生活而言的，可以活泼、率性。"敬"，译为"serious"，"严肃的，庄重的"，同时，将"事上"译为"in serving the interests of his prince"，"为君主的利益服务"，意思是，在政治或公务生活中，他会十分严肃、庄重、认真。"惠"，译为"generous"，"慷慨"，同时，将"养民"译为"in providing for the wants of the people"，"为人民提供需求"，意思是，在给人民提供服务、福利时，非常慷慨，心系民生。"义"，译为"just"，"公平，公正"，同时，将"使民"译为"in dealing with them"，"对待他们时"，指的是他对人民的态度。通过辜鸿铭的翻译，我们能清晰地看到一个真诚活泼又严肃庄重、心系民生又公平公正的政治家。

16. 辜鸿铭略去了"晏平仲"的名字，但将他比作英国政治家和外交家威廉·坦普尔

（Sir William Temple, 1628—1699），威廉·坦普尔在英国历史上还是一位散文大师，在其作品中对孔子与中国赞扬有加。

文中，"善与人交"的"交"字，辜鸿铭译为"the true relations in friendship"，"真正的友谊关系"，指晏平仲懂得与人建立真正的友谊；"久而敬之"，译为"maintained throughout the same invariable careful respect"，"始终保持同样的谨慎的尊敬"。本节表达了他是如何能长久地维护友谊的。

17. 本节提到的"臧文仲"，辜鸿铭翻译中称他"an eccentric character"，即性情古怪的人；"蔡"，译为"a large tortoise"，"大龟"；"居蔡"，译为"built a chapel for"，"为……建小屋子"。即建小屋饲养之意；"山节藻棁"，译为"elaborate with carvings"，"用雕刻做装饰"，指的是用雕刻来装饰大龟的小屋子。这指孔子对这样的人无话可说。

辜鸿铭一贯反对华而不实的浮华的文明。他在《中国妇女》一文中，曾借批判现代妇女的浮华而阐明这一思想："……在所有译成中文的欧洲文学作品中，小仲马的这部将污秽堕落的女人视作超级理想女性的小说，在目前赶时髦的现代式中国最为卖座，获得了极大的成功，这本法国小说的中文译名，名叫《茶花女》，它甚至已被改编为戏剧，风行于中国大江南北的各剧院舞台。现在，如果你将闪米特种族的古代理想女性，那为了丈夫不怕雪冻、一心只要丈夫穿得体面的女性，同今日欧洲印欧种族的理想女性，那个没有丈夫、因而用不着关心丈夫的衣着，而自己却打扮得华贵体面，且最后胸前放一朵茶花腐烂而终的茶花女相比，那么你就会懂得什么是真实的，什么是虚伪的和华而不实的文明。"（夏丹等选编，《辜鸿铭作品精选·中国人的精神》，第65页）

18. 本节讨论的核心话题仍是"仁"。孔子认为，文中所提到的人物都表现出了"忠"与"清"，但都未达到"仁"，"moral"，"道德"。其中，"忠"字，辜鸿铭译为"conscientious"，"有良心的，有责任心的"，这是他对"忠"字比较固定的译法，他所理解的"忠"，指的是人的良知、良心。"清"，译为"pure, high-minded"，"纯粹的，高洁的"，意在强调陈文子执着于追求理想的特征，他为了心中理想，完全忽略了现实世界的累赘。

19. 文中，"三"，辜鸿铭译为"thrice over"，"超过三次以上"；"再"，译为"twice"，"两次"，而且用了斜体，即强调"再"是"两次"的意思。

20. 文中，"道"，辜鸿铭译为"there was order and justice in the government"，"政治中有秩序与正义"。辜鸿铭常以"正义"、"道义"、"秩序"等来评论一个国家政治、社会或文明的优劣。"知"，译为"of great understanding"，"杰出的智力"；"愚"，译为"of no understanding"，"没有智力"。这句话指甯武子分别表现出的聪明与愚蠢的样子。

对于文中两个"及"字，辜鸿铭进行了不同的翻译：第一个译为"act like him"，"像他那样去做"；第二个译为"imitate him in the way he showed"，"按照他表现的方式去模仿他"。孔子认为，在智慧或智力上可以赶得上甯武子，却无法像他那样去装傻。

21. 文中，"吾党之小子"，辜鸿铭译为"my young people at home"，"家乡的我的孩子们"。这样翻译，大概是旨在说明当时鲁国年轻人的精神状态，"狂简"、"斐然成章"都是形容那些年轻人的。

22. 对文中所提"伯夷、叔齐"二人，辜鸿铭翻译时略去了他们的名字，但给他们作了详细注释：

> 这两个人的名字是"伯夷"和"叔齐"，一位小型封国国君的儿子。他们都将王位的继承权转让给他们的弟弟，并从世上隐退。当旧朝被替换掉以后，他们拒绝吃新朝的粮食，最后饿死在了一座孤山脚下。

并引用了这段文字：

> 你可以轻蔑地对待大地的伤害，这是小事一桩；正像希腊古人芝诺训练你的那样：大地伤害你，甚至因为大地伤害，你也能热爱大地。世界需要有一个比芝诺更伟大的人，而这个人也被派来了。（译文引自［英］托马斯·卡莱尔，《拼凑的裁缝》，马秋武、冯卉等译，广西师范大学出版社，2004，第179页）

23. 文中，"直"，辜鸿铭译为"honest"，"正直，诚实"之意；"醯"，即醋，辜鸿铭意译为"household necessary"，"家用必需品"，也是略去了"醯"的具体名称。按辜鸿铭的翻译，微生高这样做不是"直"的表现，即不诚实、正直。

24. 文中，"巧言"，辜鸿铭译为"plausible speech"，"貌似合理的言语"；"令色"，译为"fine manners"，"伪善的态度"；"足恭"，译为"studied earnestness"，"故作姿态的真诚"。本节是说，如果行为是不真诚的，不是发自本心的，左丘明、孔子认为这种事情是可耻的。

25. 本节阐明了孔子的"志"，辜鸿铭译为"aim in the conduct of life"，"生活品行的目标"。指在生活中达到如何的德行。辜鸿铭认为，"老者安之，朋友信之，少者怀之"即孔子生活品行的目标。

26. 文中，"见其过"的"过"字，辜鸿铭译为"failing"，"缺点，不足"之意；"内自讼"，译为"bring a suit against himself before his own conscience"，"控告自己来受到良心的审判"，即审视自己的良心良知。

27. 文中，"忠"，辜鸿铭译为"conscientious"，"有良心的，有良知的"；"信"，译为"honest"，"诚实"之意；"好学"的"学"字，辜鸿铭译为"cultivate themselves"，"教化自己"，即脱离低俗的本性，进行文化的自我修养。这一节的意思是，那些人虽然与孔子一样，可能天生是有良知并且诚实的，但他们没有像孔子那样致力于自我修养，进一步提升自己。

CHAPTER VI
雍也第六

1. Confucius, once expressing admiration for a disciple, remarked, "There is Yung — he should be made a prince."

    On another occasion, when that disciple asked Confucius' opinion of a certain public character of the time, Confucius answered, "He is a good man: he is independent."

    "But," replied the disciple, "when a man in his private life is serious with himself, he may, in his public life, be independent in dealing with the people. But to be independent with himself in his private life as well as independent in his public life, — is there not too much independence in that?" "Yes," answered Confucius, "you are right."

2. The reigning prince of Confucius' native State asked him which one of his disciples he considered a man of real culture.

    Confucius answered, "There was Yen Hui. He never made others suffer for his own annoyances. He never did a wrong thing twice. But unfortunately he died in the prime of his life. Now there is no one, none who can be said to be a man of real culture."

3. On one occasion when a disciple of Confucius was sent on a public mission to a foreign State, he left his mother at home unprovided for. Another disciple then asked Confucius to provide her with grain."Give her," said Confucius, "so much," naming a certain quantity. The disciple asked for more. Confucius then named a larger quantity. Finally the disciple gave her a larger quantity than the quantity which Confucius named.

    When Confucius came to know of it, he remarked, "When that woman's son left on his mission he drove in a carriage with fine

1. 子曰："雍也可使南面。"仲弓问子桑伯子，子曰："可也简。"仲弓曰："居敬而行简，以临其民，不亦可乎？居简而行简，无乃大简乎？"子曰："雍之言然。"

   有一次，孔子表达对一个学生的赞赏，说："雍啊——他应该做一名君主。"

   另外一次，当那位学生询问孔子对那时某位公众人物的看法时，孔子回答说："他是个好人：他自由无束。"

   "但是，"那位学生回答说，"如果一个人在他的私人生活中对待自己严肃认真，那么在公务生活中，他对待人民时可以自由无束。但他在私人生活中对待自己自由无束，在公务生活中也自由无束——这难道不是过于自由了吗？""是的，"孔子回答说，"你是对的。"

2. 哀公问："弟子孰为好学？"孔子对曰："有颜回者好学，不迁怒，不贰过。不幸短命死矣！今也则亡，未闻好学者也。"

   孔子故国的执政国君问他，他认为他的学生中哪一个是有真正教养的人。

   孔子回答说："是颜回。他从来不会让别人为了他自己的恼怒而承受痛苦。他从来不会重复做错一件事。但不幸的是，他在盛年的时候死了。现在，没人可以说是一个有真正教养的人了。"

3. 子华使于齐，冉子为其母请粟。子曰："与之釜。"请益。曰："与之庾。"冉子与之粟五秉。子曰："赤之适齐也，乘肥马，衣轻裘。吾闻之也，君子周急不继富。"原思为之宰，与之粟九百，辞。子曰："毋！以与尔邻里乡党乎！"

   有一次，当孔子的一个学生因公务被派往国外，他留下母亲在家无人供给。另外一个学生于是要求孔子为她提供粮食。"给她，"孔子说，"这么多吧。"孔子指定了某个数量。那位学生要求再多些。孔子于是指定了一个更大些的量。最后，那位学生给了她比孔子指定的更大的量。

   当孔子知道之后，评论说："那位妇人的儿子出差外出的时候，乘坐

111

horses and was clothed with costly furs. Now I believe a wise and good man reserves his charity for the really needy; he does not help the well-to-do and rich."

On another occasion, when another disciple was appointed the chief magistrate of a town, Confucius appointed his salary at nine hundred measures of grain. The disciple declined it as being too much.

"Do not decline it," said Confucius to him, "If that is more than necessary for your own wants, cannot you share what you do not want with your relatives and neighbours at home?"

4. Confucius remarked of a disciple whose father was a notoriously bad man, saying: "The calf of a brindled cow, provided it be well conditioned, although men may hesitate to use it in sacrifice, is yet not unacceptable to the Spirits of the land."

5. A minister who was in power in Confucius' native State asked him if his disciple, the intrepid Chung Yu, could be made a minister under the government."He is a man of decision," answered Confucius, "What is there in being a minister under the government that he should find any difficulty in it?"The minister then put the same question with regard to another disciple."He is a man of great penetration," answered Confucius, "What is there in being a minister that he should find any difficulty in it?"

The minister then went on to ask the same question about another disciple."He is a man of many accomplishments," answered Confucius, "What is there in being a minister that he should find any difficulty in it?"

着骏马拉着的马车，穿着昂贵的毛皮衣服。现在我相信，一个明智而良善的人会保留他的赈济品给真正穷困的人；而不会去帮助宽裕与富有的人。"

又一次，当另一个学生被指派到一个乡镇做主要行政官的时候，孔子指定他的薪水为九百计量的粮食。那位学生因为太多而谢绝。

"不要拒绝，"孔子对他说，"如果这超过了你自己的需要，难道你不能与你家乡的亲戚和邻里分享那些你不需要的吗？"

4. 子谓仲弓曰："犁牛之子骍且角，虽欲勿用，山川其舍诸？"

　　孔子评论一位有个声名狼藉的不道德父亲的学生，说："长有斑纹的母牛的牛犊，如果具备很好的条件，尽管人们仍然会犹豫把它用作祭品，然而土地之神未必不接受它。"

5. 季康子问："仲由可使从政也与？"子曰："由也果，于从政乎何有？"曰："赐也，可使从政也与？"曰："赐也达，于从政乎何有？"曰："求也，可使从政也与？"曰："求也艺，于从政乎何有？"①

　　在孔子故国当权的一位大臣问他，是否他的学生，那位刚勇的仲由，能够在政府中被任命为大臣。"他是一个果断的人，"孔子回答说，"对于他来说，在政府中做一个大臣能有什么困难呢？"那位大臣于是问关于另一个学生的同一个问题。"他是一个有杰出洞察力的人，"孔子回答说，"对于他来说，做一个大臣能有什么困难呢？"

　　那位大臣然后继续问关于另外一个学生的同一个问题。"他是一个多才多艺的人，"孔子回答说，"对于他来说，做一个大臣能有什么困难呢？"

---

① 辜鸿铭将原文中的 5、6 节进行了调换。

6. Confucius remarked of his disciple, the favourite Yen Hui, saying, "For months he could live without deviating from a pure moral life in thought as in deed. With other people, the utmost is a question of a day or a month."

7. A minister in power in Confucius' native State sent for a disciple of Confucius to make him the chief magistrate of an important town.

   "Politely decline the offer for me," said the disciple to the messenger sent to him, "and if your master again should send for me, I shall have to leave the country altogether."

8. On one occasion, when a disciple was sick with an infectious disease, Confucius went to see him. Confucius, however, did not enter the house, but, taking the sick man's hands from outside the window, made him his last adieus. Confucius was then heard to say, "We shall lose him. But God's will be done!"At the same time he went on repeating, "Ah! That such a man should die of such a sickness. Ah! That such a man should die of such a sickness!"

9. Confucius remarked of his disciple, the favourite Yen Hui, saying, "How much heroism is in that man! Living on one single meal a day, with water for his drink, and living in the lowest hovels of the city, — no man could have stood such hardships, yet he — he did not lose his cheerfulness. How much heroism is in that man!"

6. 子曰:"回也,其心三月不违仁,其余则日月至焉而已矣。"

   孔子评论他的学生,那位他最喜爱的颜回,说:"他能够好几个月都不违背纯粹的道德生活,不管是在思想上还是行为上。对于其他人来说,顶多就是一天或者一个月的问题。"

7. 季氏使闵子骞为费宰。闵子骞曰:"善为我辞焉。如有复我者,则吾必在汶上矣。"

   孔子故国的一位当权大臣派人去请孔子的一位学生,任命他到一个重要的城镇担任主要行政官。

   "替我礼貌地谢绝这个提议,"那位学生对派来的使者说,"如果你的主人再派人来请我,那么我只好彻底离开这个国家了。"

8. 伯牛有疾,子问之,自牖执其手,曰:"亡之,命矣夫! 斯人也而有斯疾也! 斯人也而有斯疾也!"

   有一次,孔子的一个学生得了一种传染病,孔子去看望他。尽管孔子没有走进屋子,却握住病人从窗口伸出来的手,向他作最后的告别。就听到孔子说:"我们将要失去他了。但上帝的意愿要实现啊!"同时,孔子不断地说:"哎! 这样一个人竟然要死于这样的疾病。哎! 这样一个人竟然要死于这样的疾病!"

9. 子曰:"贤哉,回也! 一箪食,一瓢饮,在陋巷。人不堪其忧,回也不改其乐。贤哉,回也!"

   孔子评论他的学生,那位他最喜爱的颜回,说:"那个人多么具有英雄气概啊! 一天以一顿饭为食,再喝点水,并且住在城里最低矮的简陋小屋里——没人能够忍受这样的艰难,然而他——他却没有失去他的快乐。那个人多么具有英雄气概啊!"

10. A disciple once said to Confucius, "It is not because I do not believe in your teaching, but I want the strength to carry it out into practice."

"Those," answered Confucius, "who only want the necessary strength, show it when they are on the way. But you — you stick at it from the outset altogether."

11. Confucius said to a disciple, "Be a good and wise man while you try to be an encyclopaedic man of culture; be not a fool while you try to be an encyclopaedic man of culture."

12. On one occasion , when a disciple was appointed chief magistrate of an important town, Confucius said to him, "Have you succeeded in getting a good man under you?"

"Yes," answered the disciple, "I have now a man who would never act upon expediency. He never comes to see me in my house except when there is urgent public business to be done."

13. Confucius remarked of a chivalrous public character of the time, saying, "He was a man who never would boast. On one occasion, when the troops among whom he was, took to fight, he slowly brought up the rear; and when they had approached the city gate to which they were retreating, he whipped his horse and was the last man to enter the gate, remarking, simply, 'It was not courage which kept me behind. But you see — my horse would not go!' "

10.　冉求曰："非不说子之道，力不足也。"子曰："力不足者，中道而废。今女画。"

　　　有一次，一个学生对孔子说："不是我不信奉您的教诲，而是我缺乏去将它付诸实践的能力。"

　　　"那些，"孔子回答说，"仅仅缺乏必要的能力的人，在过程中就表现出来了。但是你——你从一开始就完全坚持了下来。"

11.　子谓子夏曰："女为君子儒，无为小人儒。"

　　　孔子对一个学生说："当你试着想成为一个博学于文化的人时，要做一个良善和明智的人；当你试着想成为一个博学于文化的人时，不要做一个蠢人。"

12.　子游为武城宰。子曰："女得人焉尔乎？"曰："有澹台灭明者，行不由径。非公事，未尝至于偃之室也。"

　　　有一次，一位学生被任命为一个重要城镇的主要行政官，孔子对他说："你是否已成功找到一个合适的人做你的下属了？"

　　　"是的，"那位学生回答说，"我现在有一个从来不奉私利而行的人。除非有紧急的公务要办，他也从不到我的住宅来看我。"

13.　子曰："孟之反不伐，奔而殿。将入门，策其马，曰：'非敢后也，马不进也。'"

　　　孔子评论那时一位有骑士风范的公众人物，说："他是一个从来都不吹嘘的人。有一次，当敌军包围了他们的军队时，他渐渐落在了队伍的最后面，当他们接近了要撤到的那个城门时，他抽打着他的马，成了最后一个进城门的人，他简单地说：'让我留在后面的不是勇气。而是你们看——是我的马不走！'"

14. Confucius, referring to two noted characters of his time, remarked, "A man who has not the wit of that person (the Sydney Smith of the time) and the fine appearance of that noble lord (the Lord Chesterfield of the time), will never get on in society now."

15. Confucius remarked, "Who can get out of the house except through the door. How is it that men do not know that one cannot live except through the Way?"

16. Confucius remarked, "When the natural qualities of men get the better of the result of education, they are rude men. When the results of education get the better of their natural qualities, they become *literati*. It is only when the natural qualities and the results of education are properly blended, that we have the truly wise and good man."

17. Confucius remarked, "Man is born to be upright; when a man ceases to be that, it is by the merest chance that he can keep himself alive."

18. Confucius remarked, "Those who know it are not as those who love it; those who love it are not as those who find their joy in it."

19. Confucius remarked, "You may speak of high things to those who in natural qualities of mind are above average men. You may not speak to those who in natural qualities of mind are below average men."

14. 子曰："不有祝鮀之佞而有宋朝之美,难乎免于今之世矣!"

　　孔子提及他那个时代两个知名的人物,说:"一个没有那个人(那时的西德尼·史密斯)的辩才,以及那位贵族阁下(那时的查斯特菲尔德爵士)漂亮的外表的人,如今将无法在社会上生存啊。"

15. 子曰："谁能出不由户? 何莫由斯道也?"

　　孔子说:"谁能出屋子而不经过门呢? 为什么人们就不知道除了通过'道'外,就无法生活呢?"

16. 子曰："质胜文则野,文胜质则史。文质彬彬,然后君子。"

　　孔子说:"当人的天性胜过教育的效果,他们就是粗人。当教育的效果胜过他们的天性,他们就会成为文人。只有当人的天性与教育的效果恰当地融合起来,我们才会拥有真正明智而良善的人。"

17. 子曰："人之生也直,罔之生也幸而免。"

　　孔子说:"人生来是正直高洁的,如果一个人不再如此,他能让自己活下来完全是侥幸的。"

18. 子曰："知之者不如好之者,好之者不如乐之者。"

　　孔子说:"那些懂得它的人,不如热爱它的人;而那些热爱它的人,则不如那些从它那里发现乐趣的人。"

19. 子曰："中人以上,可以语上也;中人以下,不可以语上也。"

　　孔子说:"你可以和那些智力天性在一般人之上的人谈论高深的事情。但不可以和那些智力天性在一般人之下的人去谈论那些。"

20. A disciple enquired what constituted understanding.

Confucius answered, "To know the essential duties of man living in a society of men, and to hold in awe and fear the Spiritual Powers of the Universe, while keeping aloof from irreverent familiarity with them; that may be considered as understanding."

The disciple then asked what constituted a moral life.

Confucius answered, "A man who wants to live a moral life must first be conscious within himself of a difficulty and has struggled to overcome the difficulty: that is the definition or test of a moral life."

21. Confucius remarked, "Men of intellectual character delight in water scenery; men of moral character delight in mountain scenery. Intellectual men are active; moral men are calm. Intellectual men enjoy life, moral men live long."

22. Confucius, referring to the state of government in his native State and that in a neighbouring State, remarked, "If Ts'i would only reform, she would have as good a government as Lu (Confucius' native State), and if Lu would only reform she would have a perfect government."

23. Confucius was once heard to exclaim, "A goblet that is not globular: why call it a goblet; why call it a goblet?"

20. 樊迟问知。子曰："务民之义,敬鬼神而远之,可谓知矣。"问仁。
曰："仁者先难而后获,可谓仁矣。"

   一位学生询问什么是明理。

   孔子回答说:"去了解作为一个生活在人类社会中的人的基本义
务;在避免与世上神明无礼亲近的时候,要保持对他们的敬畏;这可以
被看做是明理的。"

   那位学生又问什么才是道德生活。

   孔子回答说:"一个想要过道德生活的人,首先必须意识到他心中
有个困难,并已经在努力去克服这个困难:这就是道德生活的界定或
考验。"

21. 子曰:"知者乐水,仁者乐山;知者动,仁者静;知者乐,仁者寿。"

   孔子说:"理智型性格的人喜爱水的景观;道德型性格的人喜爱山
的景观。有理智的人活泼热情;有道德的人冷静沉着。有理智的人享
受生活;有道德的人寿命长久。"

22. 子曰:"齐一变,至于鲁;鲁一变,至于道。"

   孔子提及他的国家与邻国的统治状态,说:"只要齐进行变革,她将
拥有一个像鲁(孔子故国)一样好的政治,而只要鲁进行变革,她将拥
有一个完美的政治。"

23. 子曰:"觚不觚,觚哉! 觚哉!"

   有一次,有人听到孔子这样感叹:"一只并非球状的'觚':为什么
还叫它'觚'呢? 为什么还叫它'觚'呢?"

24. A disciple of Confucius once said to him, "A moral man, — if somebody told him that there was a man fallen into a well, I suppose he would immediately follow into the well?"

"Why should he?"replied Confucius, "A good and wise man might be led to hurry to the scene, but not to plunge into the well. He could be imposed upon, but not made a fool of."

25. Confucius remarked, "A good man who studies extensively into the arts and literature, and directs his studies with judgment and taste, is not likely to get into a wrong track."

26. On one occasion when Confucius allowed himself to be presented to a princess of a State who was notorious for the irregularities of her life, his disciple, the intrepid Chung Yu, was vexed.

Confucius then swore an oath, saying, "If I have had an unworthy motive in doing that, may God forsake me — may God forsake me for ever!"

27. Confucius remarked, "The use of the moral sentiment, well balanced and kept in perfect equilibrium, — that is the true state of human perfection. It is seldom found long so kept up amongst man."

28. A disciple once said to Confucius, "If there is a man who carries out extensively good works for the welfare of the people and is really able to benefit the multitude, what would you say of such a man: could he be called a moral character?"

24. 宰我问曰:"仁者,虽告之曰:'井有仁焉。'其从之也?"子曰:"何为其然也?君子可逝也,不可陷也;可欺也,不可罔也。"

   孔子的一位学生有一次对他说:"一个有道德的人——如果有人告诉他,有个人掉到井里了,我猜他会立刻跟着跳到井里去的吧?"

   "他为什么要这样?"孔子回答说,"一个良善而明智的人,可以被诱导着急迫地赶到现场,却不会被诱导着跳到井里。他可以被欺骗,却不可以被愚弄。"

25. 子曰:"君子博学于文,约之以礼,亦可以弗畔矣夫!"

   孔子说:"一个广博地研究艺术与文学,并用判断力和鉴赏力来指导他的研究的良善之人,不太可能误入歧途。"

26. 子见南子,子路不说。夫子矢之曰:"予所否者,天厌之! 天厌之!"

   有一次,孔子允许自己去会见一个国家的一位因生活不检点而声名狼藉的王妃,他的学生,那位刚勇的仲由,非常气恼。

   孔子于是发誓说:"如果我在见她时有一丝卑劣的动机,那么让上天厌弃我吧——让上天永远厌弃我!"

27. 子曰:"中庸之为德也,其至矣乎! 民鲜久矣。"

   孔子说:"运用道德情感时,保持良好的平衡与完美的平静——这就是人类真正的完美状态。但它很少会被发现长久地在人们之间这样保持。"

28. 子贡曰:"如有博施于民而能济众,何如? 可谓仁乎?"子曰:"何事于仁,必也圣乎! 尧舜其犹病诸!"

   有一次,一位学生对孔子说:"如果有一个人,他为了人民的福祉而广施善举,并且确实能使民众受益,那么您对这样一个人有何看法:他可以被称为一个有道德的人吗?"

"Why call him only a moral character," answered Confucius, "if one must call such a man by a name, one would call him a holy or sainted man. For, judged by the works of which you speak, even the ancient Emperors Yao and Shun felt their shortcomings."

29. Confucius remarked, "A moral man in forming his character forms the character of others; in enlightening himself he enlightening others. It is a good method in attaining a moral life, if one is able to consider how one would see things and act if placed in the position of others."

"为什么仅仅称他是个有道德的人呢?"孔子回答说,"如果必须要称呼这样一个人的话,应该称他为一个神圣或圣洁的人。因为,从你所说的工作来看,即使是尧舜这两个古代帝王,也会感到他们的不足。"

29. "夫仁者,己欲立而立人,己欲达而达人。能近取譬,可谓仁之方也已。"①

孔子说:"一个有道德的人,在培养自己品格的时候,也会培养他人的品格;在启发自己的时候,也启发他人。如果一个人能够考虑站在别人的立场看待问题与做事的话,这就是达到道德生活的一个好方法。"

---

① 此句文字与第28节文字在原文中为一段,辜鸿铭将其分为两段来讲。

【评述】

1. 文中，"简"字，辜鸿铭译为"independent"，"独立自主的、无约束的"。下文中"居敬而行简"的"居敬"一词，辜鸿铭译为"in his private life is serious with himself"，指在私人生活中对自己严肃认真。意思是，严肃的生活习惯和态度，能够使自己养成较高的道德修养。所以，后面说可以"居敬而行简"，而不能"居简而行简"，即只有在日常生活中认真严肃，才能够养成必需的道德修养，才能在公务生活中自由独立时游刃有余。可见，自由独立是必须要以高度的道德修养为基础的。在本节，辜鸿铭还对子桑伯子注释说：

> 根据对这个人的记载来看，他习惯脱光衣服，就像现在很多中国人夏天时那样，孔子由此说："这就是导致人们忘记一个人与一只野兽的区别的途径。"

2. 本节讨论的是"好学"，辜鸿铭译为"of real culture"，"真正有教养"。将"学"偏重理解为"教养"的含义，指的是人格的修养。"不迁怒"，译为"never made others suffer for his own annoyances"，即"不让别人因自己的愤怒而感到痛苦"。辜鸿铭认为，本节以颜回为例表达了何谓真正有教养。

3. 本节主要阐述了"君子周急不继富"的道理。"周"，辜鸿铭译为"reserves his charity for"，"救济，赈济"之意；"急"，"the really needy"，"真正穷困的人"；"继"，"help"，"帮助"；"富"，"the well-to-do and rich"，"宽裕与富有的人"。这句话的意思是，要救济那些真正需要帮助的人，而不是帮助那些本来就富有的人。

4. 学者多认为，由于仲弓的父亲品行恶劣，孔子用"犁牛"来比喻其父。辜鸿铭略去了"仲弓"的名字，译为"a disciple whose father was a notoriously bad man"，"一位有个声名狼藉的不道德父亲的学生"。这一节指人们不应根据一些外在或旧有因素而武断地否定某人或某事，不能用一成不变的眼光看问题，事情本身的价值未必等同于我们的经验判断。

5. 本节是孔子对几个学生的评价。"果"，辜鸿铭译为"of decision"，"果断的、坚决的"；"达"，译为"of great penetration"，"有杰出洞察力的"；"艺"译为"of many accomplishments"，"多才多艺"。孔子认为，具备这些能力的这几个学生都可以从政。

6. 本节说的是颜回在"仁"上达到常人难以企及的境界，同时也指出了常人在达到"仁"的程度时的难度。"仁"，辜鸿铭译为"a pure moral life"，"纯粹的道德生活"。同时，他还强调了"仁"是"in thought as in deed"（思想上与行动上），指颜回能够长期坚持按照纯粹的道德的要求来生活。

7. 在本节的翻译中，辜鸿铭相继略去了人名、地名及官职名。"汶"，学者多主张指齐鲁边界之汶河，"汶上"则指的是汶水之北，即齐国。"吾必在汶上矣"，辜鸿铭译为"I shall have to leave the country altogether"，"彻底离开这个国家"。辜鸿铭所侧重表现的是，就像前面第五章第18节中的"陈文子"一样，闵子骞宁可逃离这个国家，也会保持自己的道德情操。

8. "有疾"，学者多解释为"癞"或"恶疾"，指一种皮肤病，辜鸿铭译为"was sick with an infectious disease"，"患有一种传染病"；"自牖执其手"，译为"taking the sick man's hands from outside the window, made him his last adieus"，即从窗口抓住病人的手，做最后诀别，这描述了孔子看望病危学生时的情景；"命"，学者多理解为"天命"。"命矣夫"，辜鸿铭译为"God's will be done"，"但愿上帝的意愿要实现"，"命"即"上帝的意愿"。这是孔子看望伯牛时所作的感叹。

9. "贤"，辜鸿铭译为"heroism"，"英雄气概的，英勇品质的"。他认为，本节所说的颜回能够忍耐异常艰苦的环境，并能够保持快乐，类似英雄不畏强敌并保持乐观一样，是同样性质的高贵品质。因此，这表现了颜回一种乐观的英雄气概。

10. 文中，"子之道"，辜鸿铭译为"your teaching"，"您的学说"，指孔子的学说、思想；"说"，译为"believe"，"相信，信奉"；"力不足"，辜鸿铭译为"want the strength to carry it out into practice"，"缺乏去将它付诸实践的能力"，即没有力量付诸实践；"画"，译为"you stick at it from the outset altogether"，"你从一开始就完全坚持了下来"。本节最后的意思是，孔子反问冉求："你明明已经坚持下来了，怎么又说力不足呢？"

11. 对于"儒"，辜鸿铭译为"encyclopaedic man of culture"，"博学于文化的人"。同时，他在注释中解释这个字的含义说：

> 照字面的意思是"人文学者"，这一术语今天被用于儒家学者及儒教。

辜鸿铭认为，这段话反映了孔子在要求学生成为一个"儒"时，要做一名君子式的"儒"，而不是小人式的"儒"。他认为这是一种教育目标的体现。辜鸿铭还在注释中引用夸美纽斯（Johann. Amos. Comenius, 1592—1670, 17世纪捷克教育家）的话，进一步说明教育的真谛：

> "教育的目的，"夸美纽斯说，"是去教给他能够使他达到作为一个人所能达到程

度的所有必要的东西。"

12. 辜鸿铭认为，这一段反映了子游对澹台灭明行为方式的肯定。"行不由径"，译为"never act upon expediency"，"从不奉行私利"，指澹台灭明为人处世不贪图便宜小利。"非公事，未尝至于偃之室"中，辜鸿铭将"公事"译为"there is urgent public business to be done"，"需要办理的紧急公事"，意思是，只有在非常紧急、非来不可的时候，澹台灭明才会来。

13. 在本节，第一句的翻译中，辜鸿铭就指出"孟之反"具有骑士风范。他认为，后面孔子的论述就是其骑士风范的注脚。"伐"，译为"boast"，"吹嘘、矜夸"，"不伐"即强调其诚实的性格，不仅不夸功，在任何事上都不会自夸。他认为，谦逊诚实是骑士风范的必备特质。

14. 文中，"佞"，辜鸿铭译为"wit"，辩才之意，也有"才智、机智"之意；"美"，译为"fine appearance"，"漂亮的外表"；"难乎免于今之世"，译为"will never get on in society now"，"如今将无法在社会上生存"。这里表达的是孔子对当时秩序崩溃、世道混乱的感叹。另外，文中"宋朝"，指当时的宋国公子朝。辜鸿铭将他比喻为英国著名政治家、外交家及文学家查斯特菲尔德（1694—1773），据说他风流倜傥，是英国讲究礼仪的典范，以其著作《致儿子的信》闻名于世。辜鸿铭还将"祝鮀"比喻为英国海军上将西德尼·史密斯（1764—1840），据说此人一生传奇，拿破仑晚年曾说，"那个人让我想起了我的命运"。

15. 文中，"道"字，辜鸿铭译为"the Way"，用了大写的 W，是一种对哲学意义的"道"的特指。辜鸿铭对此还注释说：

> 离开了道，就无法生存（Sine via, non itur）。

16. 辜鸿铭认为，本节讨论的是如何处理教育与人的天性的关系问题。其中，"文"译为"the result of education"，"教育的效果"；"质"译为"the natural qualities of men"，"人的天性"。文质相对，而"史"（译为"literati"，即"文人"）与"野"（译为"rude"，即"粗野"）则为文质相胜之结果。在辜鸿铭看来，君子要做到"文质彬彬"，就是要做到"properly blended"，即将文与质"恰当地融合起来"，既不失本性，又不失修养。这是人的教育效果的理想状态。这里的君子，是辜鸿铭的一般译法："the truly wise and good man"，即"真正明智而良善的人"。

17. "直"，辜鸿铭译为"upright"，"正直的，诚实的"。这句话的意思是，正直是人的普遍天性,如果丢掉这种天性,则会很危险,连保全生命都不能,除非侥幸。

18. 对于本句中“知之”、“好之”、“乐之”的不同表现,辜鸿铭注释认为:

这就是一个道德学家、一个哲学家与一位真正的宗教信仰者的不同之处。

在《一个大汉学家》一文中,辜鸿铭曾专门论述过“道德家”与“宗教导师”之间的区别。他说:“孔子的道德教义的伟大和真正有效处,正在于翟理斯博士所理解错了的这一点上——他错认为只是在名义上履行道德义务。其实,孔子的主张是,重要的不在于做什么,而在于怎么做。这两种不同就是所谓伦理道德和宗教之间的区别,也就是只作为道德家的准则与伟大的真正的宗教导师之生动教义之间的区别。道德家只告诉你什么行为是道德的,什么行为是不道德的。而真正的宗教导师则不仅仅告知这一点。真正的宗教导师不仅谆谆教诲外在要如何行事,而且还主张重要的更在于行为之态度,那种行为的内在。”(夏丹等选编,《辜鸿铭作品精选·中国人的精神》,第10页)

19. 在本节中,孔子认为,谈论不同深度的事情,要考虑到对方在智力天性方面的接受程度。

20. 文中,“知”,辜鸿铭译为“understanding”,“聪明的、明理的”。樊迟首先问的,是如何才能在生活中做一个明理的人。接着他又问“仁”,这里译为“a moral life”,“道德生活”。

21. 文中,“知者”,辜鸿铭译为“men of intellectual character”,“理智型性格的人”;“水”,译为“water scenery”,“水的景观”。“知者乐水”,指理智型性格的人喜欢观赏水景。“仁者”,译为“men of moral character”,“道德型性格的人”,指为人行事偏重道德准则的人;“山”,译为“mountain scenery”,“山的景观”。“仁者乐山”指道德型性格的人,喜欢观赏山景。

22. 辜鸿铭认为,孔子这句话是在讨论两个国家的政治状态。对于这个问题,他首先进行了注释说明,并认为当时齐国正沉湎在“虚伪的自由主义”之中:

在一位英国人看来,应该称为古代封建中国的法兰西:因人民品质中的骑士精神、公正无私与富于爱心的理念而闻名;但在孔子时代却深深地沉湎在了虚伪的自由主义之中。鲁(孔子故国)或许可称为古代中国的英格兰或大不列颠:因人民品质中对道义的热爱和普世的理智而闻名，但这与那些让他们在政治与统治中日趋功利的理念不相适宜。这两个国家都在现在的山东省，位于东海岸。

23. "觚"，辜鸿铭译为"goblet"，该英文词也常为高脚酒杯、酒杯、卮、樽、觞、觯等的对译，指酒器无疑。"不觚"，译为"that is not globular"，"不是球形的"，用来形容前面的"觚"字，指觚并不像只觚固有的样子。对于本节的主旨，辜鸿铭注释说：

> 提到的是那时一件日常用品被错误地命名，也涉及很多事物，尤其是"某某主义"（-isms）及"某某性质"（-ities）的一类事物在孔子的时代也被错误地命名了。

24. "井有仁焉"辜鸿铭译为"a man fallen into a well"，指的是有人坠入井中。"仁"，此处同"人"。辜鸿铭认为，这段话表明，你可以在事实上欺骗一位君子，但决无法在智力及人格上愚弄他。

25. "文"，大多传统学者认为指"六艺"，即礼、乐、射、御、书、数的知识技能。辜鸿铭译为"arts and literature"，"艺术与文学"。他认为，艺术与文学是最能陶冶性情的。"礼"，辜鸿铭译为"judgment and taste"，"判断力与鉴赏力"；"畔"，译为"get into a wrong track"，"走上错误的方向"，"误入歧途"之意。辜鸿铭认为，这一节强调，君子不仅要广泛研究艺术与文学，而且要有判断力和鉴赏力，否则会误入歧途。

26. 文中，辜鸿铭在翻译时略去了"南子"的名字，但指出她是一位因生活不检点而声名狼藉的王妃，用以说明下文子路为何"不说"，而孔子"矢之"。"矢"，译为"swore an oath"，"发誓"。后面两句话即孔子的誓语："予所否者"的"否"，辜鸿铭译为"have had an unworthy motive"，"有一丝卑劣可耻的动机"；"厌"，译为"forsake"，"厌弃，抛弃"；"天"，译为"God"，"上天，上帝"。这里的意思是，尽管南子行为不检点，但如果我见南子时有一丝不良动机，那么，就让上帝厌弃我。

27. 文中，"中庸"一词，辜鸿铭译为"well balanced and kept in perfect equilibrium"，"保持良好的平衡与完美的平静"；"至"，译为"the true state of human perfection"，"人类真正的完美状态"，完美状态，也即理想状态。辜鸿铭认为，良好的平衡与完美的平静是人类最理想的心灵状态。

28. 本节提及的"尧舜"，辜鸿铭有注释说明，认为他们在中国文明中的地位，就像《旧约》中描述的亚伯拉罕与以撒。他说：

中国历史上氏族时代的亚伯拉罕与以撒。在用这些名字诠释自己的教义时，孟子说："一个人每天早晨早起，并且坚持不懈地工作一天，为了什么呢？如果是为了正义，那么他就是亚伯拉罕（舜）之子。另一个人，同样每天早晨早起，并且坚持不懈地工作一天，为了什么呢？为了获利，那么，他就是盗贼巴拉巴式之子（盗跖）。"

29. 文中，"立"，辜鸿铭译为 "form one's character"，"养成品格"；"达"，译为 "enlighten someone"，"启发某人"；"能近取譬"，译为 "consider how one would see things and act if placed in the position of others"，"站在别人的立场看待问题并做事"。这是对上一句"己欲立而立人，己欲达而达人"的另一种说法，即推己及人。"方"，译为 "a good method"，"好方法"。辜鸿铭认为，站在别人的立场看待问题并做事，是实现道德生活的好方法。

CHAPTER VII
述而第七

1. Confucius remarked, "I transmit the old truth and do not originate any new theory. I am well acquainted and love the study of Antiquity. In this respect I may venture to compare myself with our old Worthy Pang."

2. Confucius then went on to say, "To meditate in silence; patiently to acquire knowledge; and to be indefatigable in teaching it to others: which one of these things can I say that I have done?"

3. Lastly, Confucius said, "Neglect of godliness; study without understanding; failure to act up to what I believe to be right; and inability to change bad habits: these are things which cause me constant solicitude."

4. But notwithstanding what he said above, Confucius in his disengaged hours was always serene and cheerful.

5. Only once in his old age Confucius was heard to say: "How my mental powers have decayed! For a long time now I have not dreamt, as I was wont to do, of our Lord of Chou."

6. Confucius said to his disciple: "Seek for wisdom; hold fast to godliness; live a moral life; and enjoy the pleasures derived from the pursuit of the polite arts."

1. 子曰："述而不作，信而好古，窃比于我老彭。"

   孔子说："我传承古老的真理而不发明任何新的理论。我精通并且热爱对古代的研究。就此而言，我可以冒昧地把我自己与我们那位杰出的老彭相比较了。"

2. 子曰："默而识之，学而不厌，诲人不倦，何有于我哉？"

   孔子接着说："在静默中沉思；耐心地获取学问；并毫不疲倦地把它教给别人：这些事情中，我能说我做到哪一件了呢？"

3. 子曰："德之不修，学之不讲，闻义不能徙，不善不能改，是吾忧也。"

   最后，孔子说："忽视虔敬；研究而不理解；不能遵循我所认为正确的事情；并无力改掉坏习惯：这是些让我经常焦虑的事情。"

4. 子之燕居，申申如也，夭夭如也。

   尽管孔子说了上面的话，在他空闲的时间里，他总是宁静祥和与活泼快乐的。

5. 子曰："甚矣吾衰也！久矣吾不复梦见周公。"

   只有一次在年老的时候，有人听到孔子说："我的意志力已经多么衰退了啊！现在，已经很长时间没有像往常那样梦到我们的周公了。"

6. 子曰："志于道，据于德，依于仁，游于艺。"

   孔子对他的学生们说："要寻求智慧，坚持虔敬之心，过道德的生活，并享受来自追求高雅艺术的快乐。"

7. Confucius remarked, "In teaching men, I make no difference between the rich and the poor. I have taught men who could just afford to bring me the barest presentation gift in the same way as I have taught others."

8. Confucius then went on to say: "In my method of teaching, I always wait for my student to make an effort himself to find his way through a difficulty, before I show him the way myself. I also make him find his own illustrations before I give him one of my own. When I have pointed out the bearing of a subject in one direction and found that my student cannot himself see its bearings into other directions, I do not then repeat my lesson."

9. When Confucius dined in a house of mourning he never ate much. On the same day in which he had occasion to mourn for the death of a friend, the sound of music was never heard in his house.

10. Confucius once said to his disciple, the favourite Yen Hui, "To act when called upon to act, in public life, and, when neglected, to be content to lead out a private life: — that is what you and I — we both have made up our minds upon."

   When his other disciple , the intrepid Chung Yu, heard the remark, he said to Confucius: "But if you were in command of an army, whom would you have with you?"

   "I would not have him," replied Confucius, "who is ready to seize a live tiger with his bare arms, or jump into the sea, without fear of death.The man I would have with me would be a man who is conscious of the difficulties of any task set before him, and who, only after mature deliberation, proceeds to accomplish it."

7. 子曰："自行束修以上,吾未尝无诲焉。"

　　孔子说："在教授别人的时候,富者和贫者在我眼中没有区别。我教授那些仅能够负担得起给我最起码的晋见之礼的人,像教授其他人一样。"

8. 子曰："不愤不启,不悱不发,举一隅不以三隅反,则不复也。"

　　孔子然后继续说："在我的教学方式中,在教给他我的方法之前,我总是等我的学生努力地寻找他自己的方法渡过难关。在教给他我的一个解释之前,我总是让他找出他自己的解释。如果我从一个角度指出了一个课题的意义,却发现我的学生无法自己从其他角度见到它的意义,我就不再重复了。"

9. 子食于有丧者之侧,未尝饱也。子于是日哭,则不歌。

　　孔子在服丧的人家用餐时,从来吃不多。在吊唁朋友之死的同一天,在他屋子里从不会听到有音乐声。

10. 子谓颜渊曰："用之则行,舍之则藏,唯我与尔有是夫!"子路曰："子行三军,则谁与?"子曰："暴虎冯河,死而无悔者,吾不与也。必也临事而惧,好谋而成者也。"

　　有一次,孔子对他的一个学生,那位他最喜爱的颜回,说:"在公务生活中,要求去做事时就去做事,当被忽视时,又甘愿去开始一种私人生活。——这就是你和我——我们两个人共同决定去做的事情。"

　　当他的另一个学生,那位刚勇的仲由,听到这句话之后,对孔子说:"但是如果您统帅一支军队,您将会带谁和您一起?"

　　"我将不会带一个,"孔子回答说,"准备徒手捕捉老虎或跳入海中而不怕死的人。我将要带的人,将会是一个能够意识到摆在他面前的任何一项任务的困难,并且只有在深思熟虑之后才会去完成它的人。"

11. Confucius once remarked, "If there is a sure way of getting rich, even though one had to be a groom and keep horses, I would be willing to be one.But as there is really no sure way of getting rich, I prefer to follow the pursuits congenial to me."

12. There were three cases in life in which Confucius considered a man was called upon to exercise the most mature deliberation: in case of worship, of war and of sickness.

13. When Confucius on his travels was in a certain State he, for the first time, heard played a piece of ancient music (the oldest then known in China).Thereupon he gave himself up to the study of it for three months, to the entire neglect of his ordinary food.He was then heard to say, "I should never have thought that music could be brought to such perfection."

14. A disciple who was with Confucius on his travels while in a certain State, — speaking of the reigning prince of that State who , while his father was driven to exile, succeeded, on his grandfather's death, to the throne, and was then opposing the attempt of his father to return to the country, — said to another disciple: "Is the master in favour of the son, the present ruler?"

"Oh," replied the other disciple, "I will ask him."

The other disciple accordingly went in where Confucius was, and said to him: "What kind of men were Po-yi and Shuh-ts'i?" "They are ancient worthies," answered Confucius."But," asked the disciple, "did they complain of the world?" "No," replied

11. 子曰："富而可求也,虽执鞭之士,吾亦为之。如不可求,从吾所好。"

　　有一次,孔子说:"如果有必然的途径可以致富,即使不得不去做一个马夫喂马,我也愿意成为那样的一个人。但因为的确没有必然的途径可以致富,我宁愿去从事合意于我的嗜好。"

12. 子之所慎:齐、战、疾。

　　孔子认为,一个人在一生中,在三种情况之下必须做最慎重的考虑:在礼拜、战争以及疾病的情况下。

13. 子在齐闻《韶》,三月不知肉味,曰:"不图为乐之至于斯也!"

　　孔子在旅途中来到某个国家,他第一次听到一首古乐(那时所知中国最古老的)的演奏。于是,他沉浸于对它的研究之中达三个月,并完全忽视了日常饮食。那时,有人听到他说:"我从来没想到过,音乐竟然能被演奏到如此完美的境界。"

14. 冉有曰:"夫子为卫君乎?"子贡曰:"诺。吾将问之。"入,曰:"伯夷、叔齐何人也?"曰:"古之贤人也。"曰:"怨乎?"曰:"求仁而得仁,又何怨。"出,曰:"夫子不为也。"

　　一位跟随孔子游历到某个国家的学生——谈论起那个国家执政的国君,当这位国君的父亲被流放在外时,他因他祖父的死而继承了王位,而后却反对他父亲回国——对另一个学生说:"老师是站在这个儿子,现在的掌权者这一边吗?""噢,"另外那个学生回答说,"我去问问他。"

　　这位学生于是走进孔子在的地方,对他说:"伯夷和叔齐是什么样的人?""他们是古代的俊杰啊。"孔子回答说。"那么,"这位学生问,"他们对这个世界有抱怨吗?""没有,"孔子回答说,"他们在生活中追

Confucius, "What they sought for in life was to live a high moral life, and they succeeded in living a high moral life. What had they then to complain of the world?"The disciple then went out and said to the other disciple, "No, the master is not in favour of the present ruler."

15. Confucius remarked, "Living upon the poorest fare with cold water for drink, and with my bended arms for a pillow, — I could yet find pleasure in such a life, whereas riches and honours acquired through the sacrifice of what is right, would be to me as unreal as a mirage."

16. Confucius once remarked, after he had begun the study of the I-king, "If I could hope to live some years more, long enough to complete my study of the I-king, I should then hope to be without any great shortcomings in my life."

17. The subjects upon which Confucius loved to talk were: Poetry, history, and the rules of courtesy and good manners. He frequently talked on these subjects.

18. The reigning prince of a small principality asked a disciple of Confucius, the intrepid Chung Yu, to give his opinion of Confucius. The disciple did not say anything in reply. When Confucius afterwards heards of the enquiry, he said to his disciple: "Why did you not say to him thus:'He is a man who, in the efforts he makes to overcome the difficulty in acquiring knowledge, neglects his food, and in the joy of its attainment, forgets his sorrows of life; and, who thus absorbed, becomes oblivious that old age is stealing on him?' "

求的是过一种高尚的道德生活,并且,他们成功地过上了一种高尚的道德生活。他们还对这个世界抱怨什么呢?"这位学生然后走出去对那个学生说:"不,老师不是站在目前的掌权者这边。"

15. 子曰:"饭疏食饮水,曲肱而枕之,乐亦在其中矣。不义而富且贵,于我如浮云。"

　　孔子说:"以最简陋的饭菜为食,喝冷水,用弯曲的手臂作枕头——在这样的生活中,我也能找到快乐,然而,如果财富和荣誉是通过牺牲道义来获取的话,对我来说就像海市蜃楼那样不真实。"

16. 子曰:"加我数年,五十以学《易》,可以无大过矣。"

　　有一次,孔子在开始研究《易经》之后说:"如果我能够多活几年,足够让我完成对《易经》的研究,那么,我就可能在生活中没有大的缺点。"

17. 子所雅言,《诗》、《书》、执礼,皆雅言也。

　　孔子喜爱谈及的话题是:诗歌、历史,以及谦恭与良好礼仪的规则。他经常谈及这些话题。

18. 叶公问孔子于子路,子路不对。子曰:"女奚不曰,其为人也,发愤忘食,乐以忘忧,不知老之将至云尔。"

　　一个小型公国的执政国君问孔子的一个学生,那位刚勇的仲由,他对孔子的看法。这位学生什么也没回答。当后来孔子听说这个询问之后,他对他的学生说:"你为何不对他这样说:'他是一个这样的人,在为获取学问而克服困难的努力中,他忽略了食物;在获得知识的快乐中,他忘记了生活里的忧伤;而且,他如此专注,竟未曾察觉老年正在悄悄接近他。'"

19. Confucius remarked, "I am not one born with understanding. I am only one who has given himself to the study of Antiquity and is diligent in seeking for understanding in such studies."

20. Confucius always refused to talk of supernatural phenomena; of extraordinary feats of strength; of crime of unnatural depravity of men; or of supernatural beings.

21. Confucius remarked, "When three men meet together, one of them who is anxious to learn can always learn something of the other two. He can profit by the good example of the one and avoid the bad example of the other."

22. Confucius, on one occasion of great personal danger to his person from an enemy, was heard to say, "God has given me this moral and intellectual power in me: what can that man do to me?"

23. But on another occasion Confucius remarked to his disciple, "Do you think, my friends, that I have some mysterious power within me? I have really nothing mysterious in me, — to you, of all others. For if there is anyone who shows to you everything which he does, I am, you know, my friends, that person."

24. Confucius through his life and teaching taught only four things: a knowledge of literature and the arts, conduct, conscientiousness and truthfulness.

19. 子曰："我非生而知之者,好古,敏以求之者也。"

    孔子说："我并不是一个生来就有智慧的人。我只是一个已沉湎于古代研究,并勤勉地在这样的研究中寻求智慧的人而已。"

20. 子不语怪,力,乱,神。

    孔子总是拒绝谈论超自然的现象、非凡的力量技能、人们违背人性的堕落的罪恶,以及超自然的存在。

21. 子曰："三人行,必有我师焉。择其善者而从之,其不善者而改之。"

    孔子说："当三个人遇到一起时,如果其中一个人渴望学习,总会从其他两个人那里学到东西。他可以从其中一个人的好的事例中获益,并避免另一个人的不好的事例。"

22. 子曰："天生德于予,桓魋其如予何?"

    有一次,孔子面临着来自一个敌人的巨大的人身危险,有人听到他说："上天已经给了我道德与理智的力量在我内心:那个人又能对我怎么样呢?"

23. 子曰："二三子以我为隐乎? 吾无隐乎尔。吾无行而不与二三子者,是丘也。"

    但另有一次,孔子对他的学生们说:"我的朋友们,你们认为我具有某种神秘的力量吗? 我确实没有什么神秘的东西——对你们,以及其他所有的人来说。如果有一个人对你们展现了他所做的每件事情,你们知道,我的朋友们,那个人就是我。"

24. 子以四教:文,行,忠,信。

    孔子通过他的生活与学说,只传授四件事情:关于文学与艺术的学问、行为举止、良心与真诚。

25. Confucius once, speaking of the men and state of the society of his time, remarked, "Holy, sainted men I do not expect to see; if I could only meet with wise and good men I would be satisfied."

"Perfectly honest men I do not expect to see; if I could only meet with scrupulous men I would be satisfied. But in a state of society in which men must pretend to possess what they really do not possess; pretend to have plenty, when they have really nothing; and pretend to be in affluence when they are in actual want: — in such a state of society, it is difficult to be even a scrupulous man."

26. Confucius sometimes went out fishing, but always with the rod and angle; he would never use a net; He sometimes went out shooting, but he would never shoot at a bird except on the wing.

27. Confucius once remarked, "There are, perhaps, men who propound theories which they themselves do not understand. That is a thing I never do. I read and learn everything and, choosing what is excellent, I adopt it; I see everything and take note of what I see; that is, perhaps, next to having a great understanding."

28. A certain place was noted for the bad character of the people in it. When Confucius allowed a young man of that place to be presented to him, his disciples were astonished. But Confucius said, "Why should one be too severe? When a man reforms and comes to me for advice, I accept his present reformation without

25. 子曰："圣人,吾不得而见之矣;得见君子者,斯可矣。"子曰:"善
人,吾不得而见之矣;得见有恒者,斯可矣。亡而为有,虚而为
盈,约而为泰,难乎有恒矣。"

　　　　有一次,孔子谈及他那时的人与社会的状况,说:"圣洁德高的人我
是不指望能见到了;只要能见到明智而良善的人,我就满足了。"

　　　　"完全诚实的人我是不指望能见到了,只要能见到审慎耿直的人,
我就满足了。但是在一个社会状态下人们必须假装拥有那些他们确实
没有的东西;当他们确实没有什么时,又必须假装大量地拥有;当他们
实际上匮乏时,又必须假装丰富充足——在这样的一个社会状况下,即
使做一个审慎耿直的人也是困难的啊。"

26. 子钓而不纲,弋不射宿。

　　　　有时,孔子也外出打渔,但总是用鱼竿和鱼钩,他从来不用渔网。
他有时也外出射猎,但除了飞翔中的鸟,他从不射杀。

27. 子曰:"盖有不知而作之者,我无是也。多闻择其善者而从之,多
见而识之,知之次也。"

　　　　孔子曾说:"或许有提出连他们自己都搞不明白的学说的人。这
是我绝不会做的事情。我研究与学习每件事情,并选出优秀的来采用。
我观察每件事情,并对看到的东西作好记录;也许,这仅次于拥有一个
杰出的智力吧。"

28. 互乡难与言,童子见,门人惑。子曰:"与其进也,不与其退也,唯
何甚! 人洁己以进,与其洁也,不保其往也。"

　　　　某个地方因其人民的不良品行而见称。当孔子允许那个地方的一
个年轻人被引见给他时,他的学生们都感到非常惊讶。但孔子说:"一
个人为什么要过于苛刻呢? 当一个人改过自新并前来向我请教时,我

inquiring what his past life has been.I am satisfied if I find that, for the present, he has really reformed, without being able to guarantee that he will not relapse again.But why should one to too severe?"

29. Confucius then went on to remark, "Is moral life something remote or difficult? If a man will only wish to live a moral life — there and then his life becomes moral."

30. A minister of justice in a certain State enquired of Confucius, while he was in that State on his travels, if the reigning prince in Confucius' native State was a man of propriety in his life."Yes," answered Confucius, "he is."

After a while, when Confucius had left, the minister beckoned to a disciple of Confucius to approach, and said to him: "I have always been taught to believe that a good and wise man is impartial in his judgment. But now I find it is not so. The reigning prince of your State married a princess from the reigning house of a State whose family surname is the same as that of your prince; and, to conceal the impropriety, your prince changed her surname in the title given to her a Court.Now if , after this, your prince can be considered a man of propriety in life, who may not be considered so?"

Afterwards when the disciple told Confucius of what the minister said, Confucius remarked, "I am glad that whenever I make a mistake, people always know it."

接受他目前的改善，而不会质问他过去的生活是怎样的。如果我发现目前他确实已经改善了，我就很满意了，却无法保证他将来不会故态复萌。但一个人为什么要过于苛刻呢？"

29. 子曰："仁远乎哉？我欲仁，斯仁至矣。"

　　然后孔子接着说："道德生活是件遥远或艰难的事吗？一个人一旦想过道德的生活——立刻，他的生活就变得道德了。"

30. 陈司败问昭公知礼乎？孔子曰："知礼。"孔子退，揖巫马期而进之，曰："吾闻君子不党，君子亦党乎？君取于吴为同姓，谓之吴孟子。君而知礼，孰不知礼？"巫马期以告。子曰："丘也幸，苟有过，人必知之。"

　　孔子在游历途中到了某个国家，那个国家的一位法务大臣询问孔子，孔子故国的执政国君是否是一个生活中合乎礼仪的人。"是的，"孔子回答说，"他是这样的。"

　　过了一会儿，孔子离开之后，这位大臣招手示意孔子的一个学生靠近，并对他说："我总是听说，一个良善而明智的人在他的评判中是公正的。但现在我发现不是这样。你们国家那位执政的国君，从一个国家的王室那里娶了一位和他同姓的王妃，而且，为了去遮掩这种无礼的行为，你们国君还在她的称号中改变了她的姓来取悦她。那么，如果就此之后你们的国君可以被视为一个在生活中合乎礼仪的人，谁还不能被视为这样呢？"

　　后来，当这位学生把那位大臣说的话告诉孔子之后，孔子说："每当我犯错误的时候，人们总会知道，我很高兴。"

31. When Confucius asked a man to sing, if he sang well, Confucius would make him sing again the same song, accompanying him with his own voice.

32. Confucius remarked, "In the knowledge of letters and the arts, I may perhaps compare myself with other men.But as for the character of a good and wise man who carrises out in his personal conduct what he professes, — that is something to which I have not yet attained."

33. Confucius then went on to say, "And as for the character of a holy, sainted man or even a moral character, — how should I dare even to pretend to that.That I spare no pains in striving after it and am indefatigable in teaching others to strive for it, — that, perhaps, may be said of me."

    A disciple, who heard what was said, thereupon remarked, "That is where we, your disciples, cannot follow you."

34. On one occasion when Confucius was sick, a disciple asked that he would allow prayers to be offered for his recovery."Is it the custom?"asked Confucius."Yes," replied the disciple, "in the Book of Rituals for the Dead it is written, 'Pray to the Powers above and pray to the Powers below.' "

    "Ah," said Confucius then, "my prayer has been a long — lifelong — one."

31. 子与人歌而善,必使反之,而后和之。

　　孔子请一个人唱歌时,如果那人唱得很好,孔子就会请他把同一首歌再唱一遍,而且用自己的歌声去陪他一起唱。

32. 子曰:"文,莫吾犹人也。躬行君子,则吾未之有得。"

　　孔子说:"在关于文学与艺术的学问方面,我或许可以拿我自己去和其他人比较。但至于一位良善而明智的人把他所信奉的贯彻于个人行为这样的品格——这是我还没有达到的东西。"

33. 子曰:"若圣与仁,则吾岂敢? 抑为之不厌,诲人不倦,则可谓云尔已矣。"公西华曰:"正唯弟子不能学也。"

　　然后,孔子接着说:"而至于圣洁德高的人,或即使有道德的人——我怎敢这样自诩呢。我不遗余力地争取这样,并不知疲倦地教导别人去为之奋斗——这,也许可以用来说我吧。"

　　一位学生听到了这些话,于是说:"这就是我们,您的学生们,难以效仿您的地方啊。"

34. 子疾病,子路请祷。子曰:"有诸?"子路对曰:"有之。《诔》曰:'祷尔于上下神祇。'"子曰:"丘之祷久矣。"

　　有一次,孔子病了,一位学生请求能够允许为他的康复祈祷。"这是习俗吗?"孔子问。"是的,"那位学生回答说,"《逝者的礼法之书》上说:'向在上的神灵祷告,并向在下的神灵祷告。'"

　　"啊,"孔子于是说,"我的祈祷已是一个长久的——终生之久的——祈祷了。"

35. Confucius remarked, "Extravagance leads to excess; thrift to meanness: but it is better to be mean than to be guilty of excess."

36. Confucius remarked, "A wise and good man is composed and happy; a fool is always worried and full of distress."

37. Confucius, in his look, was gracious but serious; he was awe-inspiring but not austere; he was earnest but unaffected.

35. 子曰:"奢则不孙,俭则固。与其不孙也,宁固。"

　　孔子说:"奢侈导致浪费过度,而节俭会带来吝啬:但是吝啬总比有浪费过度的罪过好。"

36. 子曰:"君子坦荡荡,小人长戚戚。"

　　孔子说:"一个明智而良善的人是从容而快乐的;一个愚蠢的人则总是焦虑并充满忧苦的。"

37. 子温而厉,威而不猛,恭而安。

　　孔子,在他的神情上是和蔼可亲而又严肃庄重的;他令人敬畏,却不严峻苛刻;他热心诚挚而又安详淡然。

【评述】

1. 文中，"述"，辜鸿铭译为"transmit the old truth"，"传承古老的真理"；"作"，译为"originate any new theory"，"发明新的理论"；"信而好古"，译为"well acquainted and love the study of Antiquity"，"精通并且热爱对古代的研究"。辜鸿铭认为，孔子热爱研究古代，致力于继承古代探索出的真理，而非发明自己的理论。最后，他保留了"老彭"的名字，并注释说：

> 那时一位著名的古文物研究者。

2. 文中，"默"，辜鸿铭译为"in silence"，"静默"；"识"译为"meditate"，"沉思，冥想"。"默而识之"指自己能够经常严肃地、深入地沉思，思考一些较深入的问题。"学"，译为"acquire knowledge"，"获得学问"。这里的翻译与他一贯将"学"视为品德修养不同，此处指对知识、学问的学习。"诲人不倦"，译为"teach it to others"，"把它教给别人"，"它"即指上面所说的"默而识之，学而不厌"。这里的意思是，孔子不仅自己按照这样的方式来自我修习，而且把这种方式传授给别人。

3. 文中，"德"，辜鸿铭译为"godliness"，"神圣、虔敬"。他认为，此处的"德"并不是泛指道德，而是重点指"虔诚"这一种德性。"学之不讲"，译为"study without understanding"，"研究而不理解"；"义"，译为"right"，"正确的"或"正义的"。"闻义不能徙"，意思就是不能真正地按照自己的是非标准去行事，无法自由地做正确的事情。而辜鸿铭认为，真正的自由，恰恰在于自由地做正确的事。他在《文明与无政府状态或远东问题的道德难题》一文中说："在新的文明下，受教育者的自由并不意味着他们可以随心所欲，而是可以自由地做正确的事情。……他行为端正是因为他喜欢为善；他不做错事，也不是出于卑鄙的动机或胆怯，而是因为他讨厌为恶。在生活品行的所有细则上，他循规蹈矩不是由于外在的权威，而是听从于内在的理性与良心的使唤。"（夏丹等选编，《辜鸿铭作品精选·中国人的精神》，第149页）

4. 文中，"燕居"，辜鸿铭译为"in his disengaged hours"，"在空闲时间里"。这一节说的是孔子闲暇时的样子。"申申如"，译为"serene"，"宁静的、祥和的"；"夭夭如"，译为"cheerful"，"活泼的、愉快的"。这里的意思指孔子在生活中是放松、舒缓、活泼、愉悦的心灵状态。

5. 文中，"吾衰"，历来学者多解释为"老衰"，辜鸿铭译为"mental powers have decayed"，指的是精神、脑力方面的衰退。句子开头，辜鸿铭的译文中说"只有一次在年老

152

的时候孔子才被听到这样说",意思是,孔子一生追求真理与良好社会,只在自己的身体衰败之后,才流露出这样的感叹。对于周公,辜鸿铭注释认为,相当于《旧约》中的先知摩西或古希腊立法家梭伦,他说:

> 中国历史上的摩西或梭伦,也是孔子的故国鲁国(古代中国的英格兰)的建立者。一位同时拥有圣·奥古斯丁的虔敬与英格兰国王阿尔弗雷德的政治才能的人。

6. 文中,"志于道",辜鸿铭译为"seek for wisdom","寻求智慧"。此处对"道"的翻译与第一章第2节"本立而道生"中的"道"翻译相同,都泛指智慧。"据于德",译为"hold fast to godliness","坚持虔敬之心","据"为坚持之意。此处,辜鸿铭对"德"的翻译与本章第3节"德之不修"相同,都译为"godliness","虔敬,虔诚"。"依于仁",译为"live a moral life","过道德的生活"。"游于艺",译为"enjoy the pleasures derived from the pursuit of the polite arts","享受来自追求高雅艺术的快乐"。"艺",传统学者多指"六艺",即"礼、乐、射、御、书、数",辜鸿铭译为"polite arts","高雅的艺术"。这里的意思是,在高雅艺术的氛围中享受乐趣。

7. 在翻译本句时,辜鸿铭添加了一句"in teaching men, I make no difference between the rich and the poor","在教授别人的时候,富者和贫者在我眼中没有区别"。这句话点明了主旨,表达了孔子对贫富一视同仁的思想。"束脩",译为"the barest presentation gift","最起码的晋见之礼"。孔子这句话是说,只要求学者已经尽了自己的心意,无论礼品本身贵贱,都是值得教授的。

8. 孔子这段话阐明了他的教学方式与特点。其中,"举一隅不以三隅反"一句中,"隅"译为"the bearing of a subject in one direction",即"从某个角度来看主题的意义";"反"译为"see its bearings into other directions",即"见到它在其他角度的意义"。

9. 这一节表现了孔子平时面对丧事的态度。

10. 这节是说,孔子主张人要懂得运用理性。

11. 本节是讲,世上并不存在必然的生财之路,所以,遵循嗜好,做自己感兴趣的事才是有意义的。

12. 文中"慎"字,辜鸿铭译为"exercise the most mature deliberation","做最慎重

的考虑"。所考虑者，即以下所说的三件事，是孔子一生中最谨慎的："齐"（通斋），译为
"worship"，"做礼拜、敬神"；"战"、"疾"，辜鸿铭分别译为"war"、"sickness"，指战争与
疾病。

13. 对于本节提到的《韶》乐，辜鸿铭注释说：

> 见第三章第25节。

在该节，辜鸿铭称《韶》乐为"一首非常著名的乐曲（那时所知中国最古老的）"。

14. 在本节中，冉有问孔子是支持卫世子蒯聩，还是他的儿子卫出公辄。子贡通过询问
孔子对伯夷、叔齐的看法，而猜测孔子的想法。辜鸿铭对伯夷、叔齐的说明，见第五章第23
节。在该节中，辜鸿铭称伯夷和叔齐是"因生活与人格的纯粹与圣洁而闻名的古代名士。"

15. 文中，"不义而富且贵"，辜鸿铭译为"riches and honours acquired through the
sacrifice of what is right"，即以牺牲道义的代价来获取财富与荣誉。他一贯将"富贵"译为
"财富与荣誉"。"浮云"，译为"a mirage"，"海市蜃楼"。这里的意思是，牺牲道义的代价
而换来的财富与荣誉，虽然看上去像真的一样华丽，然而，实质是虚假的，就像海市蜃楼的
景象。

16. 孔子在本节中谈了对《易》的看法。辜鸿铭首先对《易》进行了大段注释，他说：

> 对于外国人来说，这本书被作为"变化之书"而广泛知晓，是中国圣经中的所谓五
> 经之一。对我们来说，这本书是在数理上与精确科学上陈述心理现象和道德问题的一
> 种尝试。它或许可以被称作"流变的理论"（The Theory of Fluxions），最初，该原理用于
> 自然中的物质力的作用，但是现在，就像它被认为的——用于这个世界的道德力与智
> 力。阿查利爵士发表过关于这本书的仅有的一篇明了易懂的论文，任何对这个课题感
> 兴趣的人，都应该查阅一下。

接着，"五十以学易"一句，辜鸿铭在翻译中没有体现出"五十"这一数字，而是译
为"long enough to complete my study of the I-king"，即有足够长的时间完成对《易经》的
研究。"无大过"一句，译为"I should then hope to be without any great shortcomings in my
life"，"我就可能在生活中不犯任何大过"。这里意思是研究《易》对于人生有重要意义。
值得注意的是，辜鸿铭本人就对《易》非常推崇，他自号"汉滨读易者"、"读易老人"等，

他的一部中文著作也取名《读易草堂文集》。

17. 文中，"雅言"，辜鸿铭译为"the subjects upon which Confucius loved to talk"，"喜爱谈及的话题"。另外，辜鸿铭将"《诗》《书》"译为"poetry"和"history"，而传统学者多理解为《诗经》《尚书》。"poetry"，"诗歌"，泛指诗歌这种文学形式。"history"，"历史"，是对《尚书》的延伸翻译，因为《尚书》本是一部史书，所以，代指历史。

18. 文中，"发愤忘食，乐以忘忧"是孔子对自己心态的总结。

19. 文中，"生而知之"，辜鸿铭译为"born with understanding"，"生而聪明"，即"我非生而知之者"。这一节是说，孔子说自己并不是一个天生就很聪明的人，而后面的"好古"与"敏以求之"则是其自我完善的途径。

20. 文中，"不语"，辜鸿铭译为"refuse to talk of"，"拒绝谈论"。"怪，力，乱，神"，辜鸿铭的翻译是："怪"，译为"supernatural phenomena"，"超自然现象"，即不正常的、不合自然规律的怪异的现象；"力"译为"extraordinary feats of strength"，"非凡的力量技能"，也是指不正常的、超出常人的力量与技能；"乱"，译为"crime of unnatural depravity of men"，"违背人性的堕落的罪恶"；"神"译为"supernatural beings"，"超自然的存在"。以上话题是孔子拒绝谈论的。

21. 文中，辜鸿铭翻译中第一句中的"anxious to learn"，"渴望学习"，指一个人首先要具有求学之心，然后才会从其他人那里取长补短。

22. 文中，"天"，辜鸿铭译为"God"，"上帝或上天"。前面我们讲过，在他眼中，中国哲学中的"天"在意义上相当于西方宗教哲学中的"上帝"，都是宇宙中最高秩序或规律的代名词。"生"译为"give"，"赋予，给予"；"德"译为"moral and intellectual power"，"道德与理智的力量"。此处有几分自嘲的意味，但也表达了一种使命的心态。

23. 文中，"隐"，学者多理解为隐瞒之意，辜鸿铭译为"some mysterious power"，"某种神秘的力量"，指的是学生们怀疑孔子作为圣人，或者说能够成为圣人，一定有某种常人所不具备的神秘力量。而孔子的回答，则告诉大家，他也是平凡的人，并无特殊能力，"吾无行而不与二三子"，即向别人展示他所做的任何事情，坦诚、无所隐瞒之意。

24. 文中，"子以四教"，按辜鸿铭的翻译，指孔子学说的四项主要内容。

25. 本节一开始，辜鸿铭在翻译中添加了一句"Confucius once, speaking of the men and state of the society of his time"，"有一次，孔子谈及他那时的人与社会的状况"，这点明了这段话的主旨。从"圣人"句到"善人"句，表现了孔子退而求其次的无奈心情。

下文中，在对"亡而为有，虚而为盈，约而为泰，难乎有恒矣"这句话的翻译中，辜鸿铭表达出了孔子对当时社会状态的不满之情。

26. 文中，"钓"，辜鸿铭译为"always with the rod and angle"，"总是使用鱼竿与鱼钩"，指钓鱼；"纲"，译为"use a net"，"使用渔网"，指用网捕鱼，这里的意思是指孔子打渔从不使用渔网；"弋"，译为"shooting"，"射猎"，泛指用箭射鸟；"宿"，译为"except on the wing"，"除了飞翔时"，这里的意思是指但凡没有在飞翔的鸟，都是宿鸟，这种鸟是不射杀的。

27. 文中"不知而作之"一句中，"作"，辜鸿铭译为"propound theories"，"提出或创下某些理论、学说"；"不知"，译为"they themselves do not understand"，"他们自己都搞不明白"。这种事情，孔子是不会去做的。最后一句"知之次也"的"知"，译为"a great understanding"，"杰出的智力"，意思是，在生活中留心好学而努力获得知识与智慧，也仅次于具有杰出的智力。

28. 文中，"互乡难与言"一句，辜鸿铭略去了"互乡"的地名，"难与言"，译为"was noted for the bad character of the people in it"，"因其人民的不良品格而见称"，指当地人民的品德不好。"进"，译为"reformation"，"改善"，取该字所包含的进步、前进的意思；"退"，译为"what his past life has been"，"他过去的生活"，指的是他过去的"品德不好"的生活。前后两个"与"字，辜鸿铭进行了不同的翻译：针对"改善"，辜鸿铭译"与"为"accept"，"赞成，接受"。针对"他过去的生活"，译"与"为"inquire"，"询问，质问"。"与其进也，不与其退也"，意思是，对待那些不善的人，也应怀着一颗宽容、帮助的心，他们之前的"不善"不会阻止他们在今天及将来"向善"，希望能看到他们的进步。最后一句中，"洁"，译为"has really reformed"，"确实已改善"。按辜鸿铭的翻译，与前面的"进"字同义。"往"，译为"relapes again"，"故态复萌"，意为无法保证他以后的德行。但即使无法保证以后，只要眼前有改善的希望，且其已经有所改善，那么也是好的。

29. 文中的"仁"，辜鸿铭译为"moral life"，"道德的生活"，这是他最常见的翻译。"远"，译为"remote or difficult"，"遥远或艰难的"，指人过不过道德的生活，完全取决于自己，并不是很困难的事。

30. 文中，"知礼"，辜鸿铭译为"of propriety in his life"，"在生活中合乎礼仪"；"君子

不党",辜鸿铭将"不党"译为"impartial in his judgment","在评判中是公正的"。这一节是说,君子的评判应是公正的,无偏袒的。

"君取于吴为同姓,谓之吴孟子"一句,辜鸿铭在翻译中添加了两个细节:一是指出昭公的这一行为是"the impropriety",即"无礼的行为",而且昭公刻意通过给王妃改名而掩饰这种行为;而给王妃改名则又是为了"given to her a Court","取悦她"。通过这两个细节,可以更明显地看出昭公为了自己享乐而不惜掩饰错误的无礼行为。

最后,辜鸿铭通过注释而阐明了在古代中国的一项婚姻习俗:

> 在过去及现在的中国,一个男人去娶嫡亲的堂表妹,或者即使是娶和他同姓的女人,都是非常无礼的,若是同姓,这可能证明那个女人或许是一个远房的嫡亲堂表妹。

31. 文中,"和之",辜鸿铭译为"accompanying him with his own voice","用自己的歌声去陪他一起唱",指与人唱歌时的情景。朱熹注释说:"反,复也。必使复歌者,欲得其详而取其善也。而后和之者,喜得其详而与其善也。此见圣人气象从容,诚意恳至,而其谦逊审密,不掩人善又如此。"(《四书章句集注》,第101页)

32. "文,莫吾犹人也"一句,辜鸿铭的翻译是:"文",按照一贯的方式译为"letters and arts","文学与艺术";"莫",译为"perhaps","或许",体现了孔子不肯定的语气;"犹",译为"compare with","比较"。这里的意思是,在文学与艺术的修养方面,"我"或许可以拿出来跟别人比一下,与别人差不多。

下文"躬行君子",译为"the character of a good and wise man who carrises out in his personal conduct what he professes",即"一位良善而明智的人把他所信奉的贯彻于个人行为这样的品格",简略地说,指"知行合一"这样的品格。"吾未之有得",译为"I have not yet attained","我还没有达到",即没有达到这样的品格。

33. 文中,孔子首先举例说"若圣与仁,则吾岂敢"。"圣",辜鸿铭译为"character of a holy, sainted man","圣洁、德高的人";"仁",译为"a moral character","有道德的人";"岂敢",译为"how should I dare to pretend to that","怎敢这样自诩"。孔子不敢以这样的人自诩。"为之不厌,诲人不倦"是孔子自评。"之",代指前文所说的"圣与仁",那么,"为之"即"in striving after it","争取它";"不厌",译为"spare no pains","不遗余力地",表现其努力程度;"诲人",译为"teach others to strive for it","教导别人去为之奋斗";"不倦",译为"indefatigable","不知疲倦地,不屈不挠地"。"不厌"指努力程度;"不倦"指精神面貌。这里的意思是,尽管自己还未达到"圣与仁"的程度,但自己所做的,以及教给别人的,都是去寻求它,以之为人生的目标。

34. 文中,"祷",辜鸿铭译为 "prayers to be offered for his recovery",指子路为孔子的康复而祈祷。"有诸",译为 "Is it the custom?","这是习俗吗?" 子路的回答中,《诔》,辜鸿铭译为 "Book of Rituals for the Dead","逝者的礼法之书",指一部典籍的名称。子路是拿出相关的典籍,来证明自己的想法是有凭据的。"久",译为 "my prayer has been a long — lifelong — one",即祷告长达终生之久,指孔子正是按照这样的方式来终生寻求真理与天道的,因此,如果说这就是祈祷,那么孔子的一生都是在祈祷。

35. 文中,"奢",辜鸿铭译为 "extravagance","奢侈, 挥霍"之意;"不孙",译为 "excess",指"过度,过分,无节制"。这里的意思是,如果人惯于过奢侈的生活,那么,就会养成过度无节制的性格。"俭",译为 "thrift","节俭";"固"译为 "meanness","吝啬"。这里的意思是,如果惯于过节俭的生活,即会养成吝啬的性格。在辜鸿铭看来,孔子认为,相比起来,"吝啬"要好于"奢侈"。最后,辜鸿铭在注释中引用了另一种译法:

> 阿查利爵士译为:"奢侈导致罪恶,节俭让人吝啬:但是吝啬总比罪恶好。"
> (Extravagance leads to sin; thrift makes men mean: but it is better to be mean than to sin.)

36. 文中,"坦荡荡",辜鸿铭译为 "composed and happy","从容而快乐的",指一种乐观从容的心态;"戚戚",译为 "worried and full of distress","焦虑并充满忧苦的",意指消极悲观的心态;"小人",译为 "a fool","蠢人",这也是辜鸿铭比较常见的译法,带有嘲讽的意味。

37. 辜鸿铭在翻译中添入 "in his look" 一句,即本节内容说的是孔子的外在气度、神情。"温而厉"一词,辜鸿铭译为 "gracious but serious","和蔼可亲而又严肃庄重"。指孔子看上去是亲切的,然而又不失严肃。既有亲和力,又有威严。对此,他还在注释中引用了席勒的诗句加以形容,这里引用钱春绮先生的汉译(见《席勒诗选·异国的姑娘》,人民文学出版社,1984,第71—72页):

> 她一来到,就使人欣慰,
>   大家都感到衷心欢喜,
>   可是有一种崇尚和高贵,
>   使人们无从跟她亲昵。

CHAPTER VIII
泰伯第八

1. Confucius speaking of a remote Founder of the Imperial House of Chou, the then ruling dynasty, remarked: "He was a man, it may be said, of the highest moral greatness.He three times refused the government of the Empire; although the world, not knowing this, does not speak much of him."

2. Confucius remarked, "Earnestness without judgment becomes pedantry; caution without judgment becomes timidity; courage without judgment leads to crime; uprightness without judgment makes men tyrannical.

"When the gentlemen of a country are attached to the members of their own family, the people will improve in their moral character; when the gentlemen do not discard their old connections, the people will not become grasping in their character."

3. When a disciple of Confucius was on his death bed, he called to him his own disciples and said to them: "Uncover my feet; uncover my hands.The Psalm says: —

Walk with fear and with trembling

As on the brink of a gulf;

For the ground you are treading

Is with thin ice covered above.

But now, my young friends, I shall from henceforth be free from all these things."

1. 子曰："泰伯,其可谓至德也已矣! 三以天下让,民无得而称焉。"

   孔子谈论一位当时的统治王朝周朝的久远的创立者,说："可以说,他是一个具有最高道德的伟大的人。他三次都拒绝了帝国的统治权,尽管世人不知道这个而没有常常提及他。"

2. 子曰："恭而无礼则劳,慎而无礼则葸,勇而无礼则乱,直而无礼则绞。君子笃于亲,则民兴于仁;故旧不遗,则民不偷。"

   孔子说："认真而没有判断力,则变得迂腐;谨慎而没有判断力,则变得怯懦;勇敢而没有判断力,则会导致罪过;正直而没有判断力,则让人专横。

   "如果一个国家的正人君子们都深爱他们自己的家人,人民在他们的道德品质方面就会改善,如果正人君子们不抛弃他们的旧亲故友,人民在他们的品质方面就不会变得贪婪。"

3. 曾子有疾,召门弟子曰："启予足! 启予手!《诗》云:'战战兢兢,如临深渊,如履薄冰。'而今而后,吾知免夫! 小子!"

   孔子的一个学生临终时,把他自己的学生们叫过来,对他们说:"掀开我的脚,掀开我的手。《诗篇》上说:

   敬畏而发抖地走着,

   　　就像在深渊的边缘;

   　　因你所踩踏的地上,

   　　　覆盖着薄薄的冰面。

   但是现在,我年轻的朋友们,从今以后我就要摆脱这所有的事情而得自由了。"

4. On the same occasion as mentioned above, when a young noble of the Court came to see him, the disciple said to him, "When the bird is dying, its song is sad; when a man is dying, his words are true.

"Now a gentleman in his education should consider three things as essential.In his manners, he aspires to be free from excitement and familiarity.In the expression of his countenance, he seeks to inspire confidence.In the choice of his language, he aims at freedom from vulgarity and unreasonableness.As to the knowledge of the technical details of the arts and sciences, he leaves that to professional men."

5. A disciple of Confucius remarked, "Gifted himself, yet seeking to learn from the ungifted; possessing much information himself, yet seeking it from others possessing less; rich himself in the treasures of his mind, yet appearing as though he were poor; profound himself, yet appearing as though he were superficial: — I once had a friend who thus spent his life."

6. A disciple of Confucius remarked, "A man who could be depended upon when the life of an orphan prince, his master's child, is entrusted to his care, or the safety of a kingdom is confided to his charge, — who will not, in any great emergency of life and death, betray his trust, — such a man I would call a gentleman; such a man I would call a perfect gentleman."

4. 曾子有疾，孟敬子问之。曾子言曰："鸟之将死，其鸣也哀；人之将死，其言也善。君子所贵乎道者三：动容貌，斯远暴慢矣；正颜色，斯近信矣；出辞气，斯远鄙倍矣。笾豆之事，则有司存。"

　　也是上面提到的那一次，一位年轻的宫廷贵族来看望他，这位学生对他说："鸟要死的时候，它的啼叫是悲伤的；人死的时候，他的话是真实的。

　　"那么，一位正人君子在他的教育中，应该把三件事视为必不可缺的。在他的举止上，他追求摆脱激动轻浮与亲狎无礼。在他的脸色表达上，他力求激发信任感。在他的语言表述的选择上，他以避免粗俗与不合理为目标。至于艺术与科学上的技术细节的知识，他留给那些专业人士。"

5. 曾子曰："以能问于不能，以多问于寡；有若无，实若虚，犯而不校，①昔者吾友尝从事于斯矣。"

　　孔子的一位学生说："他自己有天赋，却试图向那些没有天赋的人学习；他自己拥有大量的学问，却向那些拥有较少学问的人那里寻求它；他自己具有丰富的思想财富，却表现得好像他是贫乏的；他自己见解深刻，却表现得好像他是肤浅的——我曾经有一位朋友这样度过了他的一生。"

6. 曾子曰："可以托六尺之孤，可以寄百里之命，临大节而不可夺也。君子人与？君子人也。"

　　孔子的一位学生说："一个人，当一位孤儿王子——他主人的孩子——的性命可以委托给他照顾，或者一个王国的安全可以交给他掌控的时候，值得信赖——并且他在任何生死攸关的重大危机时刻都不会背叛他的职责——这样一个人，我将称他为一位正人君子；这样一个人，我将称他为一位完全的正人君子。"

―――――――――――
① "犯而不校"一句，辜鸿铭未译。

7. A disciple of Confucius remarked, "An educated gentleman may not be without strength and resoluteness of character.His responsibility in life is a heavy one, and the way is long.He is responsible to himself for living a moral life; is that not a heavy responsibility? He must continue in it until he dies; is the way then not a long one?"

8. Confucius remarked, "In education sentiment is called out by the study of poetry; judgment is formed by the study of the arts; and education of the character is completed by the study of music."

9. Confucius remarked, "The common people should be educated in what they ought to do; not to ask why they should do it."

10. Confucius remarked, "A man of courage who hates to be poor will be sure to commit a crime.A man without moral character, if too much hated, will also be sure to commit a crime."

11. Confucius remarked, "A man may have abilities as admirable as our Lord of Chou, but if he is proud and mean, you need not consider the other qualities of his mind."

12. Confucius remarked, "A man who educates himself for three years without improvement is seldom to be found."

7. 曾子曰:"士不可以不弘毅,任重而道远。仁以为己任,不亦重乎? 死而后已,不亦远乎?"

　　孔子的一位学生说:"一位受过教育的正人君子不可以缺少力量与果敢的品质。他在生命中的责任是沉重的,而路途是久远的。他有责任让自己过一种有道德的生活,这难道不是个重大的责任吗? 他必须持续这样直到死去,这条道路难道不是长久的吗?"

8. 子曰:"兴于《诗》,立于礼。成于乐。"

　　孔子说:"在教育中,情感是通过诗歌的研究而唤起的;鉴别力是通过艺术的研究而形成的;而品格的培养是通过音乐的研究而完备的。"

9. 子曰:"民可使由之,不可使知之。"

　　孔子说:"一般的民众,应该教育他们该做些什么,而不是教育他们问为什么要这样做。"

10. 子曰:"好勇疾贫,乱也。人而不仁,疾之已甚,乱也。"

　　孔子说:"一个有勇气的人而憎恨贫穷,必会犯罪。一个没有道德品质的人,如果被过多地憎恨,也必会犯罪。"

11. 子曰:"如有周公之才之美,使骄且吝,其余不足观也已。"

　　孔子说:"一个人可能拥有像我们的周公那样出色的才能,但如果他妄自尊大而且品行卑劣,那么你就无需考虑他才智中的其他特性了。"

12. 子曰:"三年学,不至于谷,不易得也。"

　　孔子说:"很少会发现一个人自我修习三年而没有进步的。"

13. Confucius remarked, "A man who is scrupulously truthful, cultured and steadfast to the death in the path of honesty, such a man should not serve in a country where the government is in a state of revolution nor live in a country where the government is in an actual state of anarchy.When there is justice and order in the government of the world, he should be known, but when there is no justice and order in the government of the world he should be obscure.When there is justice and order in the government of his own country, he should be ashamed to be poor and without honour; but when there is no justice in the government of his own country he should be ashamed to be rich and honoured."

14. Confucius remarked, "A man who is not in office in the government of a country, should never give advice as to its policy."

15. Confucius speaking of the performance of a great musician of the time remarked, "The volume of sound at the commencement and the clash and commingling of harmony at the end of that ancient ballad he played were magnificent.How it seemed to fill the ears!"

16. Confucius remarked, "Appearance of high spirit without integrity; Of dullness without humility; of simplicity without honesty; — of such men I really do not know what to say."

17. Confucius remarked, "In education study always as if you have not yet reached your goal and as though apprehensive of losing it."

13. 子曰："笃信好学,守死善道。危邦不入,乱邦不居。天下有道则见,无道则隐。邦有道,贫且贱焉,耻也;邦无道,富且贵焉,耻也。"

　　孔子说:"一个审慎诚实、有教养,而又到死也要毫不动摇地走正直之路的人,这样一个人,不应该在政治处于革命状态的国家任职服务,也不应该在一个政治实际上正处于无政府状态的国家生活。当世界的统治中有正义与秩序时,他应该为人所知,但当世界的统治中没有正义与秩序时,他应该默默无闻。当他自己的国家在统治中有正义与秩序时,他应该为自己的贫穷以及缺少荣誉而感到羞耻;但当他自己的国家在统治中没有正义与秩序时,他又应该为自己的富有与荣誉而感到羞耻。"

14. 子曰："不在其位,不谋其政。"

　　孔子说:"一个不在国家政府中任职的人,绝不应就它的政策提出建议。"

15. 子曰："师挚之始,《关雎》之乱,洋洋乎! 盈耳哉。"

　　孔子谈论那时一位伟大音乐家的表演,说:"他演奏这首古代民谣,开始时的音量与最后和音的撞击与混合是宏伟壮丽的。它是多么满满地充盈了耳朵啊!"

16. 子曰："狂而不直,侗而不愿,悾悾而不信,吾不知之矣。"

　　孔子说:"看上去精神崇高却不正直;看上去反应迟钝却不谦逊;看上去简单朴素却不坦诚——对于这样的人,我真不知道该怎样形容。"

17. 子曰："学如不及,犹恐失之。"

　　孔子说:"在接受教育的求学过程中,你经常仿佛并没有达到你的目标,而又总是好像担心失去它。"

18. Confucius remarked, "How toweringly high and surpassingly great in moral grandeur was the way by which the ancient Emperors Shun and Yü came to the government of the Empire, and yet they themselves were unconscious of it."

19. Confucius remarked, "Oh! How great, as a ruler of men, was Yao The Emperor! Ah! how toweringly high and surpassingly great: Yao's moral greatness is comparable only to the greatness of God.How vast and infinite: the people had no name for such moral greatness. How surpassingly great he was in the works he accomplished!How glorious he was in the arts he established."

20. The great Emperor Shun had five great Public Servants and the Empire had peace.King Wu said, "I had ten great Public Servants who assisted me in restoring order in the Empire."

　　Confucius, remarking on the above, observed: "It was said of old that men of great ability are difficult to find.The saying is very true. The great men who lived during the period between the reigns of T'ang and Yü (the title of Shun) have never been equalled. Among the ten great Public Servants mentioned above, there was one woman: so that there were really only nine great men.

　　"The House of Chou then had two-thirds of the Empire under them, while still acknowledging the sovereignty of the House of Yin.The moral greatness of the early Emperors of the House of Chou may be considered perfect."

18. 子曰:"巍巍乎! 舜禹之有天下也,而不与焉。"

　　孔子说:"古代帝王舜与禹通向帝国统治的道路,在道德威严上是多么杰出地高尚与卓越地伟大啊,然而他们自己却没有意识到。"

19. 子曰:"大哉尧之为君也! 巍巍乎! 唯天为大,唯尧则之。荡荡乎! 民无能名焉。巍巍乎! 其有成功也;焕乎,其有文章!"

　　孔子说:"噢! 作为一位统治者,尧是多么伟大的帝王! 啊! 多么杰出地崇高与卓越地伟大:尧的道德的伟大只能拿上帝的伟大来比照了。多么广博而无限:人民无法为这样的道德的伟大而取名描述。在他完成的事业中他是多么卓越地伟大! 在他创建的艺术中他是多么地荣耀!"

20. 舜有臣五人而天下治。武王曰:"予有乱臣十人。"孔子曰:"才难,不其然乎? 唐虞之际,于斯为盛。有妇人焉,九人而已。三分天下有其二,以服事殷。周之德,其可谓至德也已矣。"

　　那位伟大的帝王舜有五位杰出的公务人员而帝国就拥有了和平。武王说:"我有十位杰出的公务人员辅助我重建帝国的秩序。"

　　孔子就此评论说:"过去常说有杰出才能的人很难找到。这种说法千真万确啊。生活在唐(帝王尧的称号)和虞(舜的称号)的统治时期之间的杰出人士,从来没人能比得上。上面提到的十位杰出的公务人员之中,有一位是女人:所以,真正只有九位杰出的人士。

　　"后来,周王室拥有帝国的三分之二,还依然承认殷王朝的统治君权。周王室早期帝王们的道德的伟大可以说是完美的。"

21. Confucius remarked, "I have not been able to find a flaw in the character of the ancient Emperor, the Great Yü.He was extremely simple in his own good and drink, but lavish in what he offered in sacrifice.His ordinary clothing was coarse and poor, but when he went to worship he appeared in rich and appropriate robes.The palace where he lived was humble and mean, but he spared no expense in useful public works for the good of the people.In all this I cannot find a flaw in the character of the Great Yü!"

21. 子曰："禹，吾无间然矣。菲饮食，而致孝乎鬼神；恶衣服，而致美乎黻冕；卑宫室，而尽力乎沟洫。禹，吾无间然矣。"

　　孔子说："我无法在那位古代帝王，那位伟大的禹的品行中找到一点瑕疵。他在自己的饮食方面极端简朴，但在祭祀时却慷慨大方。他日常的衣服粗糙而陈旧，但他去做礼拜时却穿上合适的华美的礼服。他居住的宫殿简陋而破旧，但他在对人民有益的公共建设方面却不惜代价。在这一切里，我无法在伟大的禹的品行中找到一点瑕疵。"

【评述】

1. 辜鸿铭在翻译中略去了"泰伯"的名字,泰伯为周太王古公亶父的儿子、周文王的叔父,辜鸿铭介绍他是"a remote Founder of the Imperial House of Chou","周帝国的一位久远的创立者"。根据《史记》记载,周太王想立文王之父"季历"与文王"昌"为储,泰伯于是为了成全父亲的想法,"奔荆蛮,文身断发,示不可用",后来成为吴国之祖。不过,这一段历史的真实性历来颇有争议。孔子称他"至德",辜鸿铭译为"the highest moral greatness","最高道德的伟大",指道德修养的最高程度;"无得",译为"not know this","不知道这个",指世人不知道泰伯主动让出储位继承的事情;"称",译为"speak much of him","过多地谈论他"。这里的意思是,由于泰伯之"让"很隐蔽,世人不得而知,不大提及他。

2. 文中,辜鸿铭将"礼"译为"判断力"(judgment),是指人在品格修养过程中如果不注意培养自己的判断力,就会形成看似相同实则有本质不同的微妙差别。接下来,孔子谈了亲情的意义。"君子笃于亲,则民兴于仁"一句,学者多理解为是"国君"(君子)与"人民"(民)的上行下效的关系,但辜鸿铭译"君子"为"the gentlemen","绅士,正人君子",强调这是民间的普遍行为,即民风;"笃",译为"are attached to","依恋,深爱";"亲",译为"the members of their own family","自己的家人";"兴",译为"improve","改善";"仁",译为"moral character","道德品质"。这里的意思是,如果这个国家的正人君子们能够深爱他们的家人,那么,这个国家的人民就会普遍地提高他们的道德品质,从而形成好的民俗民风。所以,他对此注释说:

> 这就是为什么说痛恨那些无亲戚的蠢人的苏格兰人,是一个特别道德的民族。

3. 文中,"疾",辜鸿铭译为"on his death bed","临终"。这一节表达的是曾子临终时的感慨与举动。"启",译为"uncover",指掀开被子,露出手足来;《诗》,译为"The Psalm",字面意思是《旧约》中的《诗篇》,这里指《诗经》。辜鸿铭对《诗经》的翻译与解释,见第二章第2节。在该节,辜鸿铭称《诗经》是"那本关于民谣、诗歌与赞美诗的文学典籍"。"吾知免夫"的"免"译为"be free from all these things","摆脱这所有的事情"。这一节的意思是,人活着战战兢兢,生活中充满种种考验与责任,死后终于可以摆脱这些凡俗之累了。

4. 文中,"鸟之将死,其鸣也哀。人之将死,其言也善"一句,辜鸿铭将"善"译为"true","真实的"。这里的意思是,人临死的时候,会说出真实的话。

下文中,"君子所贵乎道者三"一句,辜鸿铭译为"a gentleman in his education should

consider three things as essential", "一位正人君子在他的教育中,应该把三件事视为必不可缺的"。第一,"动容貌,斯远暴慢矣"。"容貌",译为"manner","举止,态度";"远"译为"be free from","摆脱,避免";"暴慢"译为"excitement and familiarity","激动轻浮与亲狎无礼"。意思是,自己要在举止上避免轻浮、无礼。

第二,"正颜色,斯近信矣"。"颜色",译为"the expression of his countenance","脸色的表达";"近信",译为"seeks to inspire confidence","力求激发信任感"。意思是,在意见表达或人际交往中,要通过你的脸色表达,让别人信任自己。

第三,"出辞气,斯远鄙倍矣"。"辞气",译为"language",指"语言表述";"远",译为"aims at freedom from","以避免……为目标";"鄙倍",译为"vulgarity and unreasonableness","粗俗与不合理"。意思是,说话的修养,应避免粗俗,文雅合理。

后面说"笾豆之事,则有司存","笾豆"指一种礼器,"有司"指主管祭祀或礼仪等事的官员。辜鸿铭没有按原意翻译,而是做了引申。"笾豆",译为"the knowledge of the technical details of the arts and sciences",比喻"艺术与科学上的技术细节的知识";"有司",译为"professional men",比喻"专业人士"。

这一节是说,君子应从"举止"、"表情的表达"、"语言"三个方面进行德行的修养,并以之为人生必不可少的,至于那些人类文化中技术性的知识与技能,则交给专业人士去研究、传承。

5. 文中,"能"与"不能",辜鸿铭译为有无"天赋"(gifted/ungifted);"多"与"寡",则译为获得学问之多少(possessing much information/less);"有"与"无",指思想财富的丰富与贫乏(rich in the treasures of mind/poor);"实"与"虚",指见解的深刻与肤浅(profound/superficial)。

6. 文中,辜鸿铭将后面一个"君子"译为"a perfect gentleman",即"完全的正人君子",加强了语气。

7. 文中,"士",辜鸿铭译为"an educated gentleman","受过教育的正人君子";"弘毅",历来学者多解释为心胸宽大、坚强果断之意,辜鸿铭译为"with strength and resoluteness of character","具有力量与果敢的品质"。"士不可以不弘毅"指受过教育的正人君子应该具有力量以及果敢的品质。所谓"道远",即指整个人生之路。"仁以为己任"的"仁",译为"live a moral life",即"过一种道德的生活",意思是,人生的责任即过道德的生活;"死而后已",译为"continue in it until he dies","持续这样直到死去"。

8. "兴于诗"一句中,"诗",辜鸿铭译为"poetry","诗歌",指诗歌这种文学形式;

"兴"，译为 "sentiment is called out"，"唤起情感"。这一节的意思是，在教育中，通过研究诗歌，能够唤起学生的情感。对于诗歌的意义，他在此作如下注释：

> 华兹华斯认为，诗歌应该是这样的："在她的成长中滋养想象，/并给她领悟能力的思想；/凭此，她可以迅速去认识，/道德的本质与万物的范畴。"

"立于礼"一句中，"立"，辜鸿铭译为 "judgement"，"判断力"，这是他对"立"最常见的翻译；"礼"，译为 "arts"，"艺术"。这里的意思是，研究与学习艺术，可以建立一个人的判断力。

"成于乐"一句中，"成"，译为 "complete the education of the character"，"完成品格的培养"；"乐"，译为 "music"，"音乐"。这里指研究学习音乐，能最终完成品格的培养。

9. 辜鸿铭认为，"民可使由之，不可使知之"指教育普通大众，应该教给他们什么是生活的义务，而不是教给他们追问其背后的原因。

辜鸿铭始终认为"普通大众"无法理解某些高深的东西，但他又认为，人民的意志是可畏的。他在此专门注释说：

> 宋代注释家程子，此处注释说："孔子这样说，并不是因为他不希望人民去理解，而是因为让他们去理解是不可能的。但如果你说孔子并不希望人民去理解，那将意味着，他将通过耶稣会教义的把戏（jugglery of Jesuitism）统治人民，就像后代的人们有时做的那样———一个荒谬的假设。"
>
> 歌德在他晚年的时候更倾向于认为，马丁·路德使欧洲文明倒退了，因为他呼吁大众去评判那些他们本身并不能理解的事情。另一方面，其实现代民主真正的原则被包含在孔子的这句话里："极大地畏惧人民的愿望（那些难以言喻的，而不仅仅是清楚地表达出来的愿望）。"

注释最后所引用的孔子的这句话，就是出自《大学》的"大畏民志"。辜鸿铭在这句话后边留下了"大畏民志"这四个汉字做标识。

10. "人而不仁，疾之已甚"，辜鸿铭译"不仁"为 "without moral character"，"没有道德品质"。

11. 此处，辜鸿铭再次将周公称作"中国历史上的摩西或梭伦"，见第七章第5节评述所引辜鸿铭的注释（本书第152—153页）。这句话是说，不管一个人的才能多么出色，如

174

果他品行恶劣,那么也是不足观的。

12. 文中,"学",辜鸿铭译为"educates himself","自我学习、修炼";"谷",译为"improvement","进步、改善";"得",译为"find","找到"。这一节的意思是,如果一个人真心想要学习,只要坚持三年,没有不进步的。

13. "笃信好学,守死善道"一句中,辜鸿铭译"善道"为"the path of honesty","正直之路"。这句话意思是,为人审慎诚实,到死也要坚持正直。辜鸿铭认为,下面所说的,是如上描述的这样一个人所应遵守的。其中,"天下有道则见,无道则隐"一句中,"道",译为"there is justice and order in the government","统治中有正义与秩序"。这是他对于政治意义上的"道"的一贯译法。这句话是说,如果政治有序、公平正义,那么,他可以为人所知,并努力履行自己的职责;而如果政治混乱,没有公平正义存在,那么,他最好选择默默无闻。

14. 学者多认为这一节指官员各司其职之意。辜鸿铭将这句话所描述的对象设定为一个不在政府任职的普通人,实则代指普通大众。他认为,普通大众不应对国家政策提出建议。他在《上德宗景皇帝条陈时事书》中批判西方政治制度时,就对现代报纸提出批判:"如商人议院,则政归富人;民立报馆,则处士横议;官设警察,则以匪待;民讼请律师,则吏弄刀笔。"(汪堂家编译,《乱世奇文·读易草堂文集》,第432页)在《上湖广总督张书》一文中,他同样批判了中国近代以来"好论时事"的现象:"……《春秋》尊王之旨,要在明义利之分,而本乎忠恕之教。义利之分明,故中国之士知君臣之相属以义也,非以利也;忠恕之教行,故中国士人知责己而不责人。责人犹不可,况家国有艰难而敢以责其君父乎?自是中国尊王之义存。故自春秋至今日两千余年,虽有治乱,然政体未闻有立民主之国,而士习亦未闻有开报馆之事。此殆中国之民所赖以存至于今日也。乃近日中国士人不知西洋乱政所由来,好论时事,开报馆,倡立议院,汤生窃谓此实非盛事。至于《时务报》载有君权太重之论,尤骇人听闻。……然窃恐中国士人开报馆、论时势之风渐盛,其势必至无知好事之辈创立异说,以惑乱民心,甚至奸民藉此非谤朝廷,要胁官长。种种辨言乱政,流弊将不可以收拾。"(同上,第438页)

15. 文中,"始",辜鸿铭译为"at the commencement","开始";"乱"译为"at the end","结束"。这一节讲的是孔子观赏师挚演奏《关雎》时的描述与感受。

16. 文中,辜鸿铭在开头用了"appearance"一词,他认为,这一节是批判那些伪善的人。

17. 学者多认为，"不及"与"失之"的对象，是"学"或学到的知识。而辜鸿铭则把"不及"与"失之"分别译为"you have not yet reached your goal"与"losing it"，分别指"没有达到"与"失去""你的目标"。同时，"学"译为"in education study"，"在接受教育的求学过程中"；"犹"译为"always as if"，即"好像，仿佛"。这一节是说，人在接受教育的学习过程中，他会有自己的目标，而且会经常担心自己并没有达到目标，以及担心会失去它。这是种保持谨慎、自我反思的心态。

18. 文中，"不与"，辜鸿铭译为"they themselves were unconscious of it"，指舜禹"他们自己都没意识到"。没意识到什么呢？即前面的"之有天下"，译为"the way by which the ancient Emperors Shun and Yü came to the government of the Empire"，"舜禹通向帝国统治的道路"。这条道路怎么样？"巍巍"即其形容，译为"how toweringly high and surpassingly great in moral grandeur"，"道德的崇高性与伟大性非常地杰出卓越"。简单说就是，舜禹成为帝王的道路走得非常高尚，但他们自己都没意识到。对于"舜禹"，辜鸿铭在此处添加注释，将他们比作《旧约》中犹太人的祖先"以撒"与"雅各"：

中国历史上的以撒与雅各：两个人在中国的早期氏族时代起于田间而登上帝位。（公元前2255—前2205年与公元前2205—前2197年）

19. 对于尧，辜鸿铭首先在注释中将他比作《旧约》中犹太人的祖先亚伯拉罕：

中国历史上的亚伯拉罕。（公元前2356—前2258年）

"唯天为大，唯尧则之"一句，辜鸿铭将"大"译为"toweringly high and surpassingly great"，"杰出地崇高与卓越地伟大"；"天"译为"God"，"上帝"；"则之"译为"comparable only to"，"与之相比"。这里的意思是，尧的道德的伟大能够与上帝相比。
另外，下文中的"文章"，辜鸿铭译为"the arts he established"，指"尧所创建的艺术"。他一贯将"礼"理解为"艺术"，所以，此处的翻译也应包含传统学者所认为的"礼仪法度"的意思。

20. 对于武王，辜鸿铭在注释中将他比作《旧约》中富有智慧的所罗门王：

那位武士国王或征服者：中国历史上的所罗门王。（公元前1122—前1115年）

"五人"，历来多认为指"禹、稷、契、皋陶、伯益"。辜鸿铭译为"five great Public

Servants"，"五位杰出的公务人员"，"人"即"臣"的意思。"乱臣十人"，历来多认为指"文母、周公旦、召公奭、太公望、毕公、荣公、太颠、闳夭、散宜生、南宫适"。"乱"字多解释为"治"，与上一句之"治"同义，包含在"assisted me in restoring order in the Empire"一句中，即帮助武王重建帝国秩序。

21. 文中，"吾无间然矣"一句中，"间"，辜鸿铭译为"flaw in the character"，"性格上的瑕疵，缺陷"。"菲饮食，而致孝乎鬼神"一句，辜鸿铭的翻译是："菲"，译为"extremely simple"，"极端简朴"；"致孝乎鬼神"译为"lavish in what he offered in sacrifice"，"在祭祀时慷慨大方"。"恶衣服"，译为"ordinary clothing was coarse and poor"，"日常的衣服粗糙而陈旧"；"致美乎黻冕"，译为"when he went to worship he appeared in rich and appropriate robes"，"去做礼拜时穿上合适的华美的礼服"。"卑宫室，而尽力乎沟洫"一句，"卑宫室"，译为"the palace where he lived was humble and mean"，即居住的宫殿简陋破旧；"尽力乎沟洫"，译为"spared no expense in useful public works for the good of the people"，"在对人民有益的公共建设方面不惜代价"，即禹不惜一切代价，把全部工作重点都放在民生建设上。

CHAPTER IX
子罕第九

1. Confucius in his conversation seldom spoke of interests, of religion or of morality.

2. A man of a certain place remarked, "Confucius is certainly a great man.He is a man of very extensive acquirements, but he has not distinguished himself in anything so as to make himself a name."

   When Confucius heard of the remark, he said to his disciples, "Now what shall I take up to distinguish myself? Shall I take up driving or shall I take up archery? I think I will take up archery."

3. Confucius remarked, "Linen hats were considered good taste, but now people generally wear silk ones.The latter are less expensive; therefore I follow the general practice.It was considered correct form at one time to make your bow, as you enter, from the lower part of the room; but now the practice is to make your bow from the upper end of the room.The latter practice presumes too much; therefore I continue to make my bow from the lower part of the room."

4. There were four things from which Confucius was entirely free:He was free from self-interest, from prepossessions, from bigotry and from egoism.

5. On one occasion, when Confucius was in fear for his personal safety from the violence of men of a certain place, he said to those about him, "Be not afraid. Since the death of King Wan (who founded this civilisation) is not the cause of this civilisation with us here now? If God is going to destroy all civilisation in the world, it would not

1. 子罕言利与命与仁。

　　孔子在他的谈话中很少谈及利益、宗教及道德。

2. 达巷党人曰："大哉孔子！博学而无所成名。"子闻之，谓门弟子曰："吾何执？执御乎？执射乎？吾执御矣。"

　　某地的一个人说："孔子的确是个伟大的人。他是一个学识非常广博，然而却没有在任何领域让自己扬名以便为自己赢得声誉的人。"

　　当孔子听到了这句话，对他的学生们说："那么，我应该拿什么来替自己扬名呢？我应该用御术，还是应该用射术？我想我会用射术。"①

3. 子曰："麻冕，礼也；今也纯，俭。吾从众。拜下，礼也；今拜乎上，泰也。虽违众，吾从下。"

　　孔子说："亚麻的帽子，被认为是一种高品位，但现在人们通常戴丝质的帽子。后者花费更少，因此，我遵从这种做法。从房屋较低的一边进入时弯腰作揖，一度被认为是正确的方式，但现在的做法是从较高的一边进入时弯腰作揖。后者的做法太放肆了，因此我继续坚持从较低的一边进入房间时弯腰作揖。"

4. 子绝四：毋意，毋必，毋固，毋我。

　　有四件事情，孔子完全杜绝：他杜绝利己主义，杜绝先入为主的偏见，杜绝顽固狭隘，杜绝自我中心主义。

5. 子畏于匡。曰："文王既没，文不在兹乎？天之将丧斯文也，后死者不得与于斯文也；天之未丧斯文也，匡人其如予何？"

---

① 原文中孔子说"吾执御矣"，辜鸿铭译为"I will take up archery"，"我会用射术"，这大概是他的失误。

have been given to a mortal of this late generation to understand this civilisation.But if God is not going to destroy all civilisation in the world — what can the people of this place do to me?"

6. A minister of a certain State asked a disciple of Confucius, saying, "Your teacher — he is a holy man, is he not? What a variety of acquirements he seems to possess." The disciple replied, "God has certainly been bountiful to him to make him a holy man.Besides he has himself acquired knowledge in many things."

When Confucius afterwards heard of the conversation, he remarked, "Does the minister know me? When I was young, I was in a low position in life: therefore I had to acquire knowledge in many things; but they were merely ordinary matters of routine. You think a wise and good man requires much knowledge to make him so; no, he does not require much."

A disciple also once remarked, "I have heard the Master say: 'I have not been called to act in public life; therefore I have had time to acquaint myself with many arts.' "

7. Confucius once remarked to someone, "Do you think I have a great understanding? I have no great understanding at all.When an ordinary person asks my opinion on a subject, I myself have no opinion whatever of the subject; but by asking questions on the pros and cons, I get to the bottom of it."

有一次，孔子在某地众人的暴力威胁下而为自己的人身安全感到不安，他对那些人谈论自己说："不要担心。难道文王的死不正是我们现在这个文明的起始吗？如果上帝要毁灭世上的全部文明，就不会让晚辈中的一个凡夫俗子来通晓这个文明了。如果上天不打算毁灭世上的全部文明——这个地方的人又能对我怎么样呢？"

6. 大宰问于子贡曰："夫子圣者与？何其多能也？"子贡曰："固天纵之将圣，又多能也。"子闻之，曰："大宰知我乎！吾少也贱，故多能鄙事。君子多乎哉？不多也。"牢曰："子云：'吾不试，故艺。'"

某国的一位大臣问孔子的一位学生，说："你的老师——他是一个神圣的人，不是吗？他看上去拥有多么广博的学识啊。"那位学生回答说："上帝确实慷慨地让他成为了一个神圣的人。另外，他自己也从很多事务中学到了知识。"

后来孔子听到了这段对话，他说："那位大臣了解我吗？当我年轻的时候，我在生活中地位低下：因此，我不得不从很多事务中学习知识；但它们都仅仅是些日常生活中的琐事。你认为一个明智而良善的人是通过获取大量知识而变得如此；不，他并没有学到多少。"

一位学生也曾说："我听到老师说：'我并没有受命去公共生活中尽职责；因此，我有时间去通过一些艺术来认知自己。'"

7. 子曰："吾有知乎哉？无知也。有鄙夫问于我，空空如也。我叩其两端而竭焉。"

孔子曾对某人说："你认为我有出色的智力吗？我并没有出色的智力。当一位普通人问我关于某个问题的意见时，我自己对这个问题竟没有任何想法；但通过从正反两方面来提出问题，我找到了它的本质。"

8. Confucius was once heard to exclaim, "Ah, woe's me.I do not see any signs either in heaven or on earth that we are near the end of the present period of disorder and anarchy and that we are about to inaugurate a new order of things in the world."

9. When Confucius met a person dressed in deep mourning, an officer in full uniform or a blind person, on their approach, although such persons were younger than himself, he would always stand up, and, when walking past them, he would respectfully quicken his steps.

10. A disciple, the favourite Yen Hui, speaking in admiration of Confucius' teaching, remarked: "The more I have looked up to it the higher it appears.The more I have tried to penetrate into it the more impenetrable it seems to be.When I have thought I have laid hold of it here, lo! it is there.But the Master knows admirably how to lead people on step by step.He has enlarged my mind with an extensive knowledge of the arts, while guiding and correcting my judgment and taste.Thus I could not stop in my progress, even if I would.But when I have exhausted my efforts and thought I have reached it, the goal would still stand clear and distinct away from me, and I have no means of reaching it, make what efforts I will."

11. On one occasion, when Confucius was seriously sick, his disciple, the intrepid Chung Yu, made arrangements, in case of the decease of the sick man, that each of the disciples should assume the function of an officer in the household of a great noble.When Confucius came

8. 子曰："凤鸟不至,河不出图,吾已矣夫!"

　　孔子曾被听到这样感叹:"啊,我真是不幸。无论是在天上还是在地上,我都没见到任何结束目前这种混乱与无政府时代,进而开创一个万物新秩序的世界的迹象。"

9. 子见齐衰者、冕衣裳者与瞽者,见之,虽少必作;过之,必趋。

　　当孔子遇到穿着深色丧服的人、穿着整套制服的官员或一位盲人的时候,尽管这样的人比他自己更年轻,但接近他们时,他总是站起身来,而走过他们时,他会恭敬地加快自己的步子。

10. 颜渊喟然叹曰:"仰之弥高,钻之弥坚;瞻之在前,忽焉在后。夫子循循然善诱人,博我以文,约我以礼。欲罢不能,既竭吾才,如有所立卓尔。虽欲从之,末由也已。"

　　一位学生,那位最受喜爱的颜回,赞美孔子的教学,说:"我越是仰望它,它就越显得高深。我越试着去洞察它,它就好像越不可捉摸。当我认为我已经在这儿抓住它时,瞧! 它在那儿。但是老师很清楚如何一步一步去引导人们发展。他用艺术方面的广博的知识拓展了我的思维,同时指导与矫正了我的判断力与审美力。这样,我无法停止我的进步,即使我想。但当我耗尽精力与思想后触及到了它,而目标仍然清晰地站在一边离我很远,我没有办法达到它,无论付出什么努力。"

11. 子疾病,子路使门人为臣。病间,曰:"久矣哉! 由之行诈也,无臣而为有臣。吾谁欺? 欺天乎? 且予与其死于臣之手也,无宁死于二三子之手乎? 且予纵不得大葬,予死于道路乎?"

　　有一次,孔子病得很厉害,他的学生,那位刚勇的仲由,为了防备

to know of what the disciple did, he , in a remission of his sickness, remarked: "I have for this long while observed that Yu (Chung Yu) practises self-deception in his actions.To pretend to have public officers when I have none; whom do I want to impose upon by that? Do I want to impose upon God? Besides, is it not better that I should die in the arms of you, my friends, than in the arms of mere unsympathetic officers? Again, even if I should never be buried with the honours of a public funeral, am I likely to be left unburied on the public road?"

12. A disciple once said to Confucius, "There is a beautiful gem here. Shall I put it in a case and lay it by; or shall I seek for a good price and sell it?"

    "Sell it by all means," answered Confucius, "Sell it by all means; but , if I were you, I should wait until the price were offered."

13. On one occasion Confucius said he would go and live among the barbarous tribes in the East: "You will there," remarked somebody, "feel the want of refinement."

    "Where a wise and good man lives," replied Confucius, "there will be no want of refinement."

14. Confucius remarked, "When I finally returned from my travels, to my native State, I completed my work of reforming the State Music and arranging the Songs and Psalms in the Book of Ballads, Songs and Psalms, assigning each piece to its proper place in the book."

病人死去,就安排每位学生承担起家务官员的职责,就像在大贵族家中。孔子知道了学生们做的事,在病情缓和的时候说:"我观察很久了,由(仲由)在行为中经常自欺欺人。我明明没有公务官员,却假装有;我要去欺骗谁呢?欺骗上天吗?另外,死在你们的怀抱中,我的朋友,不比死在冷漠无情的官员的怀抱中更好吗?再说,即使我永远不会在公共葬礼的荣誉下被埋葬,难道我会被扔在大路上而不被埋掉吗?"

12. 子贡曰:"有美玉于斯,韫椟而藏诸?求善贾而沽诸?"子曰:"沽之哉!沽之哉!我待贾者也。"

　　一位学生曾对孔子说:"这里有一块美丽的宝玉。我应该把它放在盒子里保存起来,还是寻求一个好的价格卖掉它呢?"

　　"务必卖掉它,"孔子回答说,"务必卖掉它;但如果我是你,我就会等到有人主动给出价格。"

13. 子欲居九夷。或曰:"陋,如之何!"子曰:"君子居之,何陋之有?"

　　有一次,孔子说他将去东方的野蛮部落中去生活。"你到那里去,"有人说,"将会感到教养的缺乏。"

　　"明智而良善的人生活的地方,"孔子回答说,"那里将不会缺乏教养。"

14. 子曰:"吾自卫反鲁,然后乐正,《雅》《颂》各得其所。"

　　孔子说:"当我最后从旅途回到我的故国的时候,我完成了改革国家音乐,以及改编那部关于诸多民谣、诗歌和赞美诗的文学典籍中的诗歌与赞美诗,将它们每一篇编入书中恰当位置的工作。"

15. Confucius remarked, "In public life to do one's duty to the nobles and princes whom one serves under; in private life to do one's duty to the members of one's family; in performing the last offices to the dead, to spare no pains lest anything should be neglected; and in using wine, to be able to resist the temptation of taking it to excess: — which one of these things can I say that I have been able to do?"

16. Confucius once standing by a stream, remarked, "How all things in nature are passing away even like this, — ceasing neither day nor night!"

17. Confucius once remarked, "I do not now see a man who can love moral worth in man as he loves beauty in woman."

18. Confucius remarked, "Suppose a man wants to raise a mound and, just as it wants only one basket more of earth to complete the work, suppose he were suddenly to stop: the stopping depends entirely upon himself. Suppose again a man wants to level a road, although he has just thrown over it only one basket of earth; to proceed with the work also depends entirely upon himself."

19. Confucius remarked of his disciple, the favourite Yen Hui: "He was the only man who was never tired and inattentive while I talked with him."

15. 子曰："出则事公卿，入则事父兄，丧事不敢不勉，不为酒困，何有于我哉？"

　　孔子说："在公务生活中，为自己所服侍的贵族与君主尽责；在私人生活中，为家庭的成员尽责；为死者举办丧礼不遗余力，以防止任何事情被遗漏；饮酒时，能够抵制住过量饮用的诱惑——这些事情中的哪一项，我能说我已经做到了呢？"

16. 子在川上，曰："逝者如斯夫！不舍昼夜。"

　　孔子曾站在一条河边上，说："大自然中的万物正如此般消逝啊——日夜不止。"

17. 子曰："吾未见好德如好色者也。"

　　孔子曾说："我现在见不到一个人能够像热爱女人的美那样，去热爱人的道德品格。"

18. 子曰："譬如为山，未成一篑，止，吾止也；譬如平地，虽覆一篑，进，吾往也。"

　　孔子说："假设一个人想堆一个土丘，而当它仅仅只差一筐土就完成时，假设他突然停止了：那么，停止完全取决于他自己。再假设一个人想整平一条路，尽管他才只扔上去了一筐土；继续工作也完全取决于他自己。"

19. 子曰："语之而不惰者，其回也与！"

　　孔子评价他的学生，那位他最喜爱的颜回："他是唯一一个在我和他谈话时从不厌倦与懈怠的人。"

20. Confucius remarked of the same disciple: "Alas! He is dead. I have observed his constant advance; I never saw him stop in his progress."

21. Confucius once, speaking of the career of his many disciples, remarked: "Some only sprout up, but do not flower; some only flower, but do not ripen into fruit."

22. Confucius remarked, "Youths should be respected. How do we know that their future will not be as good as we are now? Only when a man is forty or fifty without having done anything to distinguish himself, does he then cease to command respect."

23. Confucius remarked, "If you speak to a man in the strict words of the law, he will probably agree with you; but the important point is that he should so profit by what you say to him as to change his conduct.If you speak to a man in parables, he will probably be pleased with your story; but the important point is that he should apply the moral to himself.Now when I find a man who agrees with me in what I say, without being able so to profit by it as to change his conduct, or one who is pleased with my parable without being able to apply the moral to himself, — I can do nothing for such a man."

24. Confucius remarked, "Make conscientiousness and sincerity your first principles. Have no friends who are not as yourself.When you have bad habits do not hesitate to change them."

20. 子谓颜渊,曰:"惜乎！吾见其进也,未见其止也。"

    孔子评论同一个学生:"哎！他死了。我注意到了他持续的成长；我从没看到过他停止进步。"

21. 子曰:"苗而不秀者有矣夫！秀而不实者有矣夫！"

    孔子曾谈论他一些学生的事业,说:"有些只发芽了,但没有开花；有些只开花了,但没有成熟结果。"

22. 子曰:"后生可畏,焉知来者之不如今也？四十、五十而无闻焉,斯亦不足畏也已。"

    孔子说:"年轻人应被尊重。我们怎么知道他们的将来不如我们现在好呢？只有当一个人四十岁或五十岁还仍没有做出任何事情而让自己扬名,那时,他就不再值得尊重了。"

23. 子曰:"法语之言,能无从乎？改之为贵。巽与之言,能无说乎？绎之为贵。说而不绎,从而不改,吾末如之何也已矣。"

    孔子说:"如果你对一个人用严厉的法律用语讲话,他将可能同意你；但重点是他应该从你说的话中受益,进而改变他的行为。如果你对一个人讲寓言故事,他将可能会因你的故事而高兴；但重点是他应该把寓意运用在他自己身上。现在,我发现一个人同意我所说的话,却不能够从中受益去改变他的行为,或者一个人因我讲的寓言故事而高兴,却不能够把寓意运用于他自身——我对这样的一个人束手无策。"

24. 子曰:"主忠信,毋友不如己者,过则勿惮改。"

    孔子说:"使良心与真诚成为你的第一原则。没有与你自己不同的朋友。当你有坏习惯时,要毫不犹豫地改掉它们。"

25. Confucius remarked, "The general of an army may be carried off, but a man of the common people cannot be robbed of his free will."

26. Confucius remarked of his disciple, the intrepid Chung Yu, "Dressed in an old shabby suit of russet cloth and standing among a crowd dressed in costly furs without being ashamed, — that is Yu! (the disciple's familiar name): —

Without envy, without greed,

What he does is good indeed."

Afterwards, when the intrepid Chung Yu kept repeating those two lines of poetry, Confucius remarked, "That alone is not good indeed."

27. Confucius remarked, "When the cold of winter comes, it is then you know that the pine tree and the cypress are the last to lose their green."

28. Confucius remarked, "Men of intelligence are free from doubts, moral men from anxiety, and men of courage from fear."

29. Confucius remarked, "Some men there are with whom you can share your knowledge of *facts*, but who cannot follow you in arriving at *principles*. Some can follow you to *particular* principles, but they cannot arrive with you at *general* principles.Some can arrive with you at general principles but they cannot apply the general principles under exceptional circumstances."

25. 子曰:"三军可夺帅也,匹夫不可夺志也。"

孔子说:"一支军队的将军可以被夺去生命,但一个普通人的自由意志不能被剥夺。"

26. 子曰:"衣敝缊袍,与衣狐貉者立,而不耻者,其由也与?'不忮不求,何用不臧?'"子路终身诵之。子曰:"是道也,何足以臧?"

孔子评论他的学生,那位刚勇的仲由:"穿着一套由土气简朴的布料制成的陈旧破烂的衣服,站在一群穿着昂贵的皮毛衣服的人中间而并不感到那是种耻辱——那就是由!(那位学生的令人熟悉的名字)——'从不嫉妒,从不贪婪,/他所做的,真正良善。'"

后来,刚勇的仲由坚持不断地重复那两句诗,孔子说:"仅仅那样并不是真正的好啊。"

27. 子曰:"岁寒,然后知松柏之后彫也。"

孔子说:"当冬天的寒冷到来之时,你才会知道松树和柏树是最后才失去它们的绿色的。"

28. 子曰:"知者不惑,仁者不忧,勇者不惧。"

孔子说:"智慧之人免于困惑,有德之人免于忧虑,而勇敢之人免于恐惧。"

29. 子曰:"可与共学,未可与适道;可与适道,未可与立;可与立,未可与权。"

孔子说:"有些人,你可以与他们分享你关于事实的知识,但他们不能跟随你达到掌握原理的程度。有些人可以跟随你达到掌握特定原理的程度,但他们却不能与你一起掌握普遍的原理。有些人能够与你一起获得普遍的原理,但他们却不能够在特殊情况下运用这种普遍的原理。"

30.　　How they are waving, waving,

The blossoming myrtles gay;

Do I not think of you, love?

Your home is far away.

　　Confucius, repeating those lines, remarked, "That is because men do not think. Why is it far away?"

30. "唐棣之华，偏其反而。岂不尔思？室是远而。"子曰："未之思也，夫何远之有？"

> 孔子诵读了这几句话：

> > 它们如此飘舞着，飘舞着，

> > 开满繁花的桃金娘如此绚烂；

> > 是我不想念你吗，亲爱的？

> > 你的家是那样遥远。

> 他说："这是因为人们并没有想啊，怎么就遥远呢？"

【评述】

1. 文中，"罕"，辜鸿铭译为"seldom"，"很少"；"言"，译为"spoke of"，"谈论"；"利"，译为"interests"，"利益"；"命"，译为"religion"，"宗教信仰"；"仁"，译为"morality"，"道德、道义"。这句话是说，孔子很少谈论利益、宗教信仰与道德。辜鸿铭的意思大概是，"利益"是孔子所不主张的，所以很少谈；至于"宗教信仰"与"道德"，孔子是很少把它们当作哲学话题来谈，那样会远离现实的生活。

2. 文中"博学而无所成名"一句，"博学"，辜鸿铭译为"of very extensive acquirements"，指学问非常广博；"无所成名"，译为"has not distinguished himself in anything so as to make himself a name"，"没有在任何领域让自己扬名以便为自己赢得声誉"。这里叹惜孔子虽然学问广博，但没有在任何领域赢得名声。

下文中，"执"，辜鸿铭译为"take up to distinguish myself"，"从事……为自己扬名"。值得注意的是，"take up"一词，有"拿起"之意，也有"从事"之意。这一翻译与经文一样，具有双关意义。"御"与"射"分别译为"driving"与"archery"，即驾驶与射术。

3. 文中，"麻"，辜鸿铭译为"linen"，"亚麻"。"冕"，西汉孔安国解释为"缁布冠也"，即黑色帽子。朱熹认为"麻冕"才是"缁布冠"。辜鸿铭译冕为"hat"，"帽子"。"麻冕"，即"亚麻的帽子"。"礼"，这里译为"be considered good taste"，"被视为好的品味或审美"。"纯"，历来解释颇复杂，有学者认为指"丝"，也有人认为"缁"字之误，指的是"黑布"或"黑帛"。辜鸿铭译为"silk"，取的是"丝"的意思。"俭"，朱熹解释为用料节省。辜鸿铭译为"less expensive"，"花费更少"。"从众"，译为"follow the general practice"，"遵从这种做法"。"麻冕，礼也。今也纯，俭，吾从众"意思是，虽然向来亚麻的帽子被认为更有品位，但眼下都戴丝质的帽子已经成了新的现象，我决定顺应这种现象，原因是它更节省。

对于"拜下"、"拜上"，辜鸿铭的翻译是："拜下"，译为"make your bow, as you enter, from the lower part of the room"，"从房屋较低的一边进入时弯腰作揖"；"礼"，译为"correct form"，"正确的方式"；"拜上"译为"make your bow from the upper end of the room"，"从房屋较高的一边进入时弯腰作揖"；"泰"译为"presumes too much"，指这种放肆、冒昧的做法太多。"拜下，礼也。今拜乎上，泰也。虽违众，吾从下"意思是，虽然从"拜下"到"拜上"也是一种习惯的转变（就像上面所说的帽子的转变），但由于"拜上"的这种做法本身太无礼，所以，这是一种不好的转变，不予遵从，还是坚持原来的做法。

4. "绝四"，辜鸿铭译为"there were four things from which Confucius was entirely free"，即孔子完全地杜绝四件事情，指的后面说的"意、必、固、我"。下面逐个看辜鸿铭是如何翻译这四个问题的。

"毋意"，译为"free from self-interest"，"杜绝利己主义"，指的是个人要有公平的价值观；"毋必"，译为"（free）from prepossessions"，"杜绝先入为主的偏见"，指个人要有真正的判断力；"毋固"，译为"（free）from bigotry"，"杜绝顽固狭隘"，指应该具有广阔的视野与心胸，而不是拘泥于一种见识或思维习惯；"毋我"，译为"（free）from egoism"，"杜绝自我中心主义"，指做任何事情，都不能只以自我为中心，而不顾及其他。

5. 文中，"畏"，辜鸿铭译为"in fear for his personal safety from the violence of men"，"在暴力威胁下为人身安全感到不安"。翻译略去了具体典故，突出的是孔子危险的处境和不安的心态。"文王"，指周文王，辜鸿铭保留了他的名字，并在括号中注为"who founded this civilisation"，"他创建了这个文明"，指周文明。"文不在兹乎"中的"文"，辜鸿铭译为"this civilisation"，指周文明；"兹"，译为"us here now"，"我们现在这里"，意指目前这个时代。辜鸿铭是强调，文王是这个文明的创立者，他死后，周文明延续至今。"天"，辜鸿铭译为"God"，"上帝，上天"；"丧"，译为"destroy"，"毁灭"。下文中"未丧"，译为"is not going to destroy"，"不打算毁灭"。"后死者"，辜鸿铭译为"a mortal of this late generation"，"晚辈中的一个凡夫俗子"，孔子自指。不过，辜鸿铭用"late generation"一词，隐含着文明从周文王延续至今的意思。"与"，译为"give ... to understand"，"让……通晓"，指如果上天要毁灭这个文明的话，就不会让孔子通晓、了解这个文明了。

6. 文中，"多能"，辜鸿铭译为"what a variety of acquirements he seems to possess"，"他拥有广博的学识"。"天纵之将圣"一句中，"纵"，译为"bountiful to him"，"对他慷慨大方"，指上天对孔子的眷顾；"将"，译为"make him a holy man"，即上天要孔子成为一个神圣的人；"又多能也"，辜鸿铭单独译成一句，翻译为"he has himself acquired knowledge in many things"，"从很多事务中学到知识"。这里的意思是，除了上天给孔子的眷顾之外，孔子自身也做了大量的努力。这是子贡的看法。"吾少也贱，故多能鄙事"一句中，"贱"，译为"in a low position in life"，"在生活中地位低下"；"鄙事"，译为"ordinary matters of routine"，"日常生活中的琐事"，这里的意思是，孔子幼时社会地位低下，所以生活琐事都需要亲自动手去做。"君子多乎哉？不多也"一句中，"多乎哉"，译为"requires much knowledge to make him so"，"获取很多知识让他变得这样"；"不多"，译为"he does not require much"，"他没有获得很多知识"。这句话，孔子提醒了一般人对获取知识的误解，认为一个君子往往并不是单单通过书本学习来获取知识的，而是通过生活的磨炼。"吾不试，故艺"一句中，"试"，辜鸿铭译为"called to act in public life"，"去公共生活中尽职责"，"不试"则指不出仕；"艺"，译为"acquaint myself with many arts"，指通过对一些艺术的研究来认知自己。

7. 文中，"知"，辜鸿铭译为"great understanding"，"出色的智力"。这句话意思是，别人以为孔子具有出色的智力，但孔子说自己根本没有。

下文"我叩其两端而竭焉"指孔子的应对方式。辜鸿铭的翻译是："扣其两端"，译为"asking questions on the pros and cons"，"从正反两方面来提出问题"，指从正、反两个角度来反问询问者或向自己提出；"竭"，译为"get to the bottom of it"，"bottom"，"底部、尽头"，意指"找到了它的本质"。

8. 辜鸿铭将后面"吾已矣夫"放到了开头，译为"woe's me"，意为"我真是不幸"，英文中用于夸大哀叹自己的遭遇，增强了语气。在翻译中，辜鸿铭全部略去了原文中"凤鸟"、"河图"这些典故素材，它们本是古代的"祥瑞"，朱熹注释说："凤，灵鸟，舜时来仪，文王时鸣于岐山。河图，河中龙马负图，伏羲时出。皆圣王之瑞也。"（《四书章句集注》，第111页）辜鸿铭将这些祥瑞译为"sign"，"迹象"，即"near the end of the present period of disorder and anarchy"与"we are about to inaugurate a new order of things in the world"的迹象，"混乱与无政府时代的终结"与"万物新秩序世界的开创"。也就是说，孔子感到的只是世界无限的混乱状态，所以他才作此悲叹。

9. 这一节说的是孔子对待服丧者、执行公务的官员及盲人的三种态度。即使他们比自己年少，孔子对他们也会非常尊重。文中有两个"见"，辜鸿铭把第一个"见"译为"met"，"遇到"，而把第二个"见"译为"on their approach"，"接近他们时"。后面的"过之"译为"when walking past them"，"走过他们时"。指的是在路上偶然碰到的情景。碰到他们，孔子就会这么做。

10. "仰之弥高，钻之弥坚"一句，辜鸿铭的翻译是："仰"，译为"looked up to"，"仰望"；"弥高"，译为"higher it appears"，"显得更高深"；"钻"，译为"penetrate into"，"洞察"；"坚"，译为"impenetrable"，"不可测知，难以理解"。这里的意思是，越仰望，它越显得崇高、高深；越洞察，它就越不可捉摸，指孔子之道高深难测，难以把握。"瞻之在前，忽焉在后"，辜鸿铭译为"When I have thought I have laid hold of it here, lo! it is there""当我认为我已经在这儿抓住它时，瞧！它在那儿。"其中，"瞻"译为"lay hold of it"，"捉住、占有"；"前""后"分别译为"here"和"there"。这里意指无法掌握它。这是一种难以琢磨、变幻莫测的感觉。"循循然善诱人"一句中，"循循"，辜鸿铭译为"step by step"，"一步一步"，也即有次序的意思；"诱"，译为"lead people on"，"引导人们发展"，也是这个意思。这句话是说，指尽管孔子之道如此高深难以琢磨，但孔子却非常善于教导别人一步一步向前发展。"博我以文，约我以礼"一句中，"博"，辜鸿铭译为"enlarged my mind"，"拓展我的思维"；"文"，译为"an extensive knowledge of the arts"，"艺术方面的广博的知识"。"博我以文"，意思就是用艺术方面的广博的知识来拓宽"我"的思维。"约我以礼"，译为

"guiding and correcting my judgment and taste"，"指导与矫正我的判断力与审美力"。这句话的意思是，指在思维的广度与深度，以及判断力上不断提升整体的文化修养。这就是孔子教导别人一步一步向前发展的方式。"欲罢不能"，辜鸿铭译为"I could not stop in my progress, even if I would"，指在孔子循循教导下，自己无法停止进步。"既竭吾才，如有所立卓尔"一句中，"竭吾才"，译为"I have exhausted my efforts and thought"，"我耗尽精力与思想"，指的是颜渊自己竭尽全力去做；"如有"，译为"I have reached it"，"我触及到了它"，指通过努力而触及到孔子之道；"所立卓尔"，译为"stand clear and distinct away from me"，指它清晰地站在一边离我很远，感觉达到了，而且也已经看到了，但实际上仍有一段距离，并未真正达到。下面"虽欲从之，末由也已"一句即对这种状态的感叹，辜鸿铭译为"I have no means of reaching it, make what efforts I will"，即无论付出什么努力，都无法达到它。

11. 文中，"疾病"，辜鸿铭译为"seriously sick"，"病得很严重"。病得很严重，所以子路怀疑孔子要死。"子路使门人为臣"一句中，"臣"，辜鸿铭译为"an officer in the household of a great noble"，"大贵族家族中的官员"，学者所理解的"家臣"之意。子路想在孔子死后，令孔子的学生像贵族的家臣一样置办丧礼，虽然孔子并不是贵族。"病间"，辜鸿铭译为"in a remission of his sickness"，指"病情缓和"。"由之行诈也"一句，译为"Yu practises self-deception in his actions"，"由在行为中经常自欺欺人"。这里的意思是，孔子自己本非贵族、无家臣，完全可以按照目前的礼仪来办丧事，但子路却要假装有家臣，就像贵族家中那样。"且予与其死于臣之手也，无宁死于二三子之手乎"一句中，"死于臣之手"，译为"die in the arms of mere unsympathetic officers"，"死在冷漠无情的官员的怀抱中"；"死于二三子之手"，译为"die in the arms of you, my friends"，"死在你们的怀抱中，我的朋友"。孔子想告诉子路，与其要虚假的礼仪，不如要真挚的情感。

12. 文中，"沽之哉"一句，孔子重复了两遍。辜鸿铭译为"sell it by all means"，"务必卖掉它"。用"务必"一词加强了语气。"待贾者"的"贾"，历来学者多认为指"贾人"即商人。朱熹注释说："子贡以孔子有道不仕，故设此二端以问也。孔子言固当卖之，但当待贾，而不当求之耳。"（《四书章句集注》，第113页）辜鸿铭译"贾"为"wait until the price were offered"，指等待别人主动来给出价格。"贾"指价格。

13. 文中，"九夷"，辜鸿铭译为"the barbarous tribes in the East"，"东方的野蛮部落"。"陋"，译为"the want of refinement"，"教养的缺乏"。指野蛮未开化。"何陋之有"，译为"will be no want of refinement"，"不再缺少教养"。指君子到那里居住，就会把教养带过去。

14. 辜鸿铭认为，孔子这一节讲了"正乐"与"《雅》《颂》各得其所"两件事。其中，"正乐"即"reform the State Music"，"改革国家的音乐"；《雅》《颂》各得其所"，即"arranging the Songs and Psalms in the Book of Ballads, Songs and Psalms, assigning each piece to its proper place in the book"，指恰当编排《诗经》中的《雅》(诗歌)与《颂》(赞美诗)诗篇的次序。

15. 这一节孔子强调的是人的"义务"与"自我节制"。"出则事公卿，入则事父兄"一句中，"出"与"入"，辜鸿铭分别译为"in public life"和"in private life"，"在公务生活中"与"在私人生活中"。这是社会人的两大生活领域。

16. 文中，"逝者"，辜鸿铭译为"all things in nature are passing away"，"自然万物在不断消逝"；"如斯"译为"even like this"，"正如这样"，指像川水一样消逝；"不舍昼夜"，译为"ceasing neither day nor night"，"日夜不止"。这里的意思是，自然界的万事万物，像眼前的川水一样，日夜不停地在不断消逝。这是孔子对大自然的感叹。

17. "德"，辜鸿铭译为"moral worth in man"，"人的道德品格"；"色"，译为"beauty in woman"，"女人的美"。这里的意思是，像热爱女人的美那样热爱道德品格，指的是对道德的热爱发自内心的，完全真诚的。孔子说，他没见过这样的人。

18. 辜鸿铭首先给本节添加了一条注释：

我们面前的生活，就像一位建筑师面前的巨大的采石场。除非他能够把最节省、最合适与最可塑的材料从这些偶然的材料中结合起来，有些构成了来自于他自己精神的模型，否则他就不会被称作建筑师。……请相信我，大部分在这个世界上被称作罪恶的不幸与灾祸，源于人们过于疏忽去恰当地认识他们的目标，而当他们确实认识到它时，又疏忽于通过坚持不懈的工作去达成它们。他们对我来说，就像一群人突然产生了一个必须要建立一座高楼的念头，但他们所依赖的却是连建成一座小栅屋都不够的石料与工人。(歌德，《威廉·麦斯特》)

下文中，"止，吾止也"与"进，吾往也"两句即反映的这一道理。前者，辜鸿铭译为"the stopping depends entirely upon himself"，"停止完全取决于他自己"；后者译为"to proceed with the work also depends entirely upon himself"，"继续工作也完全取决于他自己"。这里意在说明人在设定并达成一个目标时"个人"是决定性的。很多时候，目标没有达成，只是因为自己选择了放弃而已。

19. "语之而不惰者，其回也与"，辜鸿铭译为"He was the only man who was never

tired and inattentive while I talked with him", 指颜回是唯一一个对孔子所说的话从不感到厌倦与懈怠的人。

20. "惜乎", 辜鸿铭译为 "Alas! He is dead", "哎！他死了", 一种无奈、痛惜的感叹。"吾见其进也，未见其止也"一句中，"进"译为"constant advance", "持续的成长"；"止"译为"stop in his progress", "停止进步"。这里是指，颜渊每日都在不断进步，完善自我。

21. 这一节是指学生们的事业发展程度不同，但都还未真正取得成功。辜鸿铭将"子曰"译为"speaking of the career of his many disciples", "谈论他一些学生的事业", 也就是说，孔子的话中"苗"、"秀"、"实"等字即比喻学生们事业的不同状态。"苗而不秀", 译为"only sprout up, but do not flower", "只发芽了，但没有开花", 指事业只是初露端倪，但尚未取得很大进展；"秀而不实", 译为"only flower, but do not ripen into fruit", "只开花了，但没有成熟结果", 指事业取得很大发展，看似昌盛，然而却没有取得真正的成果。

22. 文中，"后生可畏", 辜鸿铭译为"youths should be respected", "年轻人应被尊重"；"闻", 译为"having done anything to distinguish himself", "做出什么事情让自己扬名"；"不足畏", 译为"does he then cease to command respect", "他不再值得尊重"。这里的意思是，如果到四十或五十岁，还没有值得称道的成就，那么，就不再值得尊重了。

23. 文中，"法语之言", 传统学者多理解为"正言"或"正道", 辜鸿铭译为"the strict words of the law", "严厉的法律用语"。"法", 理解为"法律"；"从", 译为"agree with", "同意"；"改", 译为"he should so profit by what you say to him as to change his conduct", "受益于你说的话从而改变他的行为"。"法语之言，能无从乎？改之为贵"的意思是，纵然严厉的法律用语会强迫一个人同意你，但关键是他自己要真正想改。"巽与之言，能无说乎"一句中，"巽", 译为"parable", "寓言故事"；"说", 译为"be pleased with your story", "因你的故事而高兴", 即被你所讲的故事所娱乐；"绎", 译为"apply the moral to himself", "把寓意运用于自身", 即从故事的寓意中获得启发。这句话是说，寓言故事可以给人以娱乐，然而，最重要的是能够从故事的寓意中受到教益。

下文，辜鸿铭在翻译中调换了"说而不绎，从而不改"两句的位置，以与上文的论述顺序相合。

24. 辜鸿铭注释：

第一章第8节的重复。

25. 文中，"三军可夺帅"，辜鸿铭译为"The general of an army may be carried off"，"一支军队的将军可以被夺去生命"。"夺"，指夺去生命之意。"匹夫不可夺志也"一句中，"志"，译为"free will"，"自由意志"；"夺"译为"be robbed of"，"被剥夺"；"匹夫"译为"the common people"，"普通人"。这句的意思是，即使是普通人，他们的自由意志也是不可被剥夺的。

26. 文中，"衣敝缊袍"一句中，辜鸿铭将"敝"译为"old shabby"，"陈旧破烂的"；"缊袍"，译为"suit of russet cloth"，"布料土气简朴的衣服"。这句话是说，穿着陈旧破烂的、布料土气简朴的衣服，形容衣着极为寒酸。"与衣狐貉者立，而不耻"一句中，"狐貉"译为"costly furs"，"昂贵的皮毛"；"不耻"译为"without being ashamed"，"不感到那是种耻辱"。这里的意思是，自己衣着寒酸，然而与衣着华丽的人在一起，也并不感到那是种耻辱。"不忮不求，何用不臧"，辜鸿铭的翻译是："忮"译为"envy"，"嫉妒"；"求"，译为"greed"，"贪婪"；"臧"译为"good indeed"，"真正的好"。这一句的意思是，如果人没有嫉妒与贪婪之心，才是真正的好。"终身诵之"，辜鸿铭译为"keep repeating those two lines of poetry"，"坚持不断地重复那两句诗"。"是道"，译为"that alone"，"仅仅那样"，指仅仅按那诗句所说的做；"何足以臧"，译为"be not good indeed"，"不是真正的好"，即只那样做是不够的。

27. 文中，"彫"，传统学者也有写作"凋"的，多理解为"伤"，应之"伤残"之意。三国时何晏《论语集解》："大寒之岁，众木皆死，然后知松柏之凋伤。"辜鸿铭的翻译是："岁寒"，译为"when the cold of winter comes"，即冬天的寒冷到来之时；"后彫"，译为"the last to lose their green"，"最后失去它们的绿色"，即凋落。这里的意思是，在寒冷的冬天，万物凋敝，是松柏在冷寂环境中，最晚才渐渐褪去绿色。这句话代表了一种困境中的坚强意志。辜鸿铭最后还引用罗马诗人奥维德《爱的艺术》中的诗句加以注释：

> 正如黄金唯有在烈火中才得检验，
> 信仰也只有在艰难时刻方能验证。

28. 文中，"知者不惑"，辜鸿铭把"知者"译为"men of intelligence"，"有智慧的人"；"惑"译为"doubt"，"困惑，疑惑"，指有智慧的人不会有任何困惑。"仁者不忧"，辜鸿铭把"仁者"译为"moral men"，"有道德的人"；"忧"译为"anxiety"，"焦虑，忧虑，不安"。这里的意思是，有道德的人不会感到焦虑不安的。"勇者不惧"，"勇者"，辜鸿铭译为"men of courage"，"勇敢的人"；"惧"译为"fear"，"恐惧"。这里的意思是，真正勇敢的人，心中不会有恐惧。

29. 文中，"可与共学，未可与适道"一句，"共学"，辜鸿铭译为"share your knowledge

of facts"，"分享你关于事实的知识"；"适道"译为"follow you in arriving at principles"，"跟随你达到掌握原理的程度"。翻译中，辜鸿铭分别把前面的"facts"（事实）与后面的"principles"（原理）加了斜体。意在对比：关于事实的知识容易掌握，而更深一层的原理，则是较难理解的。"可与适道，未可与立"一句，"道"译为"particular principles"，"特定的原理"；"立"，译为"arrive with you at"，"与你一起掌握"之意。这句话指，即使有些人能够懂得你的某一方面、某个领域或某种程度上的原理，但他们却不懂得有普遍的原理，即超越于所有特定状态之上的普遍原理。"可与立，未可与权"一句，"权"，译为"apply the general principles under exceptional circumstances"，"在特殊情况下运用这种普遍的原理"，重点在于"运用"，也即知行合一。这句话指，有些人可能也在理论上懂得了普遍原理，然而，他们却无法付诸实践。

30. 本节的诗句，学者多认为是孔子引述的当时的"逸诗"，后来没有被保存下来。辜鸿铭将"唐棣"译为"myrtles"，"桃金娘"，一种常绿灌木。他调换了"唐棣之华，偏其反而"两句的前后位置。"偏其反而"译为"How they are waving, waving"，"它们如此飘舞着，飘舞着"；"唐棣之华"译为"The blossoming myrtles gay"，"开满繁花的桃金娘如此绚烂"。这两句诗描述的是桃金娘开满繁花的美景。本诗重点在于"尔"字，这个字是本诗的"主人公"，能最终体现诗句的含义。朱熹认为这个"尔""不知其何所指"，辜鸿铭译为"you, love"，指"爱人"。"岂不尔思"译为"Do I not think of you, love?"，"是我不想念你吗，亲爱的？"辜鸿铭认为，这句诗讲的是对爱人的思念。

下文中"未之思也，夫何远之有"，译为"That is because men do not think. Why is it far away?""这是因为人们并没有想啊，怎么就遥远呢？"强调的是"想念之心"，"心"怎么会有距离呢？

另外，辜鸿铭在最后还引用了歌德长篇小说《威廉·迈斯特的漫游时代》的《迷娘曲》给本节进行注释：

和风从蓝天之际徐徐吹来，
桃金娘亭亭玉立而玉桂树高插云霄。
你知道那是哪儿吗？快去吧！快去吧！
啊，我的爱人，我愿与你一同前行。

并且还补充说：

但是理想——我们的美国，就像《威廉·麦斯特》中的年轻人所说的——就在眼前，真实，也并不遥远。

CHAPTER X
乡党第十

1. Confucius in his life at home was shy and diffident, as if he were not a good speaker.In public life, however, in courts and councils, he spoke readily, but with deliberation.

2. At court, in conversation with junior officers, he spoke with frankness; With the senior officers, he spoke with self-possession.

   In the presence of his prince, he looked diffident, awe-inspired, but composed.

3. When his prince called to him to see a visitor out, he would start up with attention, make obeisance to receive the command; then, bowing right and left to officers in attendance and adjusting the folds of his robes, he would quicken his step, and walk out, not stiffly, but with dignity and ease. When the visitor had left, he would return to his place, announcing simply, "The guest has retired."

4. In entering the rooms of the palace, he would bend low his body at the door as if it were not high enough to admit him.In the room he would never stand right before the door, nor, in entering it, step on the door sill.

   In passing into the Presence Chamber; he would start up with attention and speak only in whispers.Then, holding up the folds of his robes, he would ascend the steps leading to the throne, bending low his body and holding in his breath as if he were afraid to breathe.

1. 孔子于乡党，恂恂如也，似不能言者。其在宗庙朝廷，便便言，唯
    谨尔。①

    在家庭生活中，孔子腼腆而羞怯，仿佛他是一个不善言辞的人。然
    而，在公共生活中，在朝廷与会议上，他却乐意讲话，但非常慎重。

2. 朝，与下大夫言，侃侃如也；与上大夫言，訚訚如也。君在，踧踖如
    也，与与如也。

    在朝廷上，与下级官员交谈时，他说话坦诚；与上级官员交谈时，他
    说话沉着。

    在国君面前，他看上去胆怯，敬畏，但是镇静。

3. 君召使摈，色勃如也，足躩如也。揖所与立，左右手。衣前后，襜
    如也。趋进，翼如也。宾退，必复命曰："宾不顾矣。"

    当他的国君要求他送宾客出去时，他就会态度殷勤起来，向国君致
    礼并接受命令；然后，向右边与左边列席的官员们鞠躬行礼，并整理他
    礼服的褶层，他会加快他的步子走出去，高贵、从容而不生硬。宾客离开
    后，他会返回他的位置，简要地宣告："客人已经离开了。"

4. 入公门，鞠躬如也，如不容。立不中门，行不履阈。过位，色勃如
    也，足躩如也，言其似不足者。摄齐升堂，鞠躬如也，屏气似不息
    者。出，降一等，逞颜色，怡怡如也。没阶趋，翼如也。复其位，踧
    踖如也。

    进入宫殿的时候，他会在门口弯下他的身体就像是门不够高而通不
    过他。在宫殿里，他从不正对着门站立，也不会进门时踩到门槛。

---

① "其在宗庙朝廷"一句，在原文中为《乡党》第2节。辜鸿铭在英译文中将第1节和第2节合
二为一。

After the audience, when he had descended one step away from the throne, he would relax his countenance and assume his ordinary look.After clearing the last steps, he would quicken his pace and walk with ease the dignity to resume his place among the courtiers, looking diffident, with awe and attention.

5. When he had to carry the sceptre of the prince, he would bend low his body as if the weight were too heavy for him; holding it not higher than his forehead nor lower than his chest, and, with his look all awe and attention, walk with slow, measured steps.

   At a public reception in the foreign courts to which he was sent, he behaved with great dignity.At a private audience in such courts, he was genial and engaging in his manners.

6. Confucius considered the following details necessary for a gentleman to observe in matters of dress: —

   A gentleman should never permit anything crimson or scarlet in colour to be seen in any part of his dress; even in his underclothing he should avoid anything red or of a reddish colour.

   In summer, when dressed in a single suit of gauze or grass-cloth, he should always wear something underneath, worn next to the skin. In winter he should line a black suit with lambskin; a light suit with fawn skin; a yellow suit with fox skin.His fur underclothing should be made long, with the right sleeve a little short.

   He should always have a change of night-dress, which should be as long again as the trunk of his body.

   When at home in winter, he should be dressed in a suit of fox or

进入接见大厅时,他的态度会殷勤起来,只会低声说话。然后,提起礼服的褶层,攀登通向王座的台阶,他弯下身体,屏住呼吸,就像是不敢呼吸一样。

觐见之后,一旦走下王座的第一个台阶,他就会放松表情,呈现出平常的样子。走下最后几级台阶后,他会从容而高贵地加快步子,重返位于朝臣中的他的位置,敬畏而殷勤,看上去胆怯的样子。

5. 执圭,鞠躬如也,如不胜。上如揖,下如授。勃如战色,足缩缩,如有循。享礼,有容色。私觌,愉愉如也。

当他不得不手拿国君的权杖时,他会弯下身体,就像是对他来说太重一样;他不会把它举得高于额头,也不会低于胸口,他的表情全是敬畏与殷勤,走路时,步子缓慢而有节奏。

在他被派往国外宫廷的公开接见会上,他表现得非常高贵庄严。而在这个宫廷的私人会见上,他的举止则是亲切而吸引人的。

6. 君子不以绀緅饰。红紫不以为亵服。当暑,袗绤绤,必表而出之。缁衣羔裘,素衣麑裘,黄衣狐裘。亵裘长。短右袂。必有寝衣,长一身有半。狐貉之厚以居。去丧,无所不佩。非帷裳,必杀之。羔裘玄冠不以吊。吉月,必朝服而朝。

孔子认为,下面的细节,对于一位绅士来说有必要在衣着方面予以留意:

一位绅士应该永远不会允许被人看到在他的衣服的任何部位有深红或鲜红的颜色;即使是在他的内衣上,他也应避免任何部分是红色的或发红的颜色。

夏天,当穿一件薄纱或夏布的单衣时,他应该在底下再穿点什么,贴着皮肤。冬天,他应该用羔羊皮给黑色衣服、幼鹿皮给浅色衣服、狐狸皮给黄色衣服作衬里。他的皮毛制的内衣应该做得长些,而右面的袖子应做得短一些。

badger skin. When not in mourning, he may have any ornaments or appendages on the girdle of his dress.His under-garment, except when it is worn as an apron (like the Free Masons now) on State occasions, he should always have cut pointed on the upper part.

On a visit of condolence he should never wear a suit of lamb's fur or a dark blue hat.On the first day of the month he should always put on his full uniform when he goes to Court.

7. On days when he fasts and gives himself up to prayer, he should always put on a bright clean suit of plain cloth.On such days he should always change the ordinary articles of his food, and move out of his usual sitting-room.

8. The following are the details which Confucius observed in matters of food and eating: —

In his food, he liked to have the rice finely cleaned and the meat, when stewed, cut in small pieces. Rice injured by damp and heat, or turned sour, he would not take; nor fish or flesh which was gone. He would not take anything that had an unwholesome colour or unwholesome flavour; nor any articles of food which had been spoilt in cooking; nor anything out of its season. Meat not properly cut he would not take; nor any dish served without its proper sauce.

Although there might be plenty of meat on the table, he would never allow the quantity of meat he took to exceed a due proportion to the rice he took. It was only in wine that he did not set himself a limit; but he never took it to excess.

He would not take wine or meat bought where it had been exposed for

他应该经常更换睡衣，而睡衣应该比他的身躯长一半。

冬天在家，他应该穿一件狐狸皮或獾皮的衣服。只要没有在办丧事，他可以在衣服腰带上佩戴任何装饰或附属物。除非在国家重大场合把衬衣当一件围裙穿（就像现在的共济会员），否则他总会把衣服上面的部分明显地剪掉。

吊唁时，他从不穿羔羊皮的衣服、戴深蓝色的帽子。每月的第一天，去朝廷时，他总会穿上全套礼服。

7. 齐，必有明衣，布。齐，必变食，居必迁坐。

在斋戒与专心祈祷的日子里，他应该穿一套由简朴的布料制成的鲜亮干净的衣服。这样的日子里，他应该改变通常的饮食，并且从平日居住的起居室里搬出去。

8. 食不厌精，脍不厌细。食馑而餲，鱼馁而肉败，不食。色恶，不食。臭恶，不食。失饪，不食。不时，不食。割不正，不食。不得其酱，不食。肉虽多，不使胜食气。惟酒无量，不及乱。沽酒市脯不食。不撤姜食，不多食。祭于公，不宿肉。祭肉不出三日。出三日，不食之矣。食不语，寝不言。虽疏食菜羹，瓜祭，必齐如也。

下面是孔子在饮食方面注意的一些细节：

在他的食物方面，他习惯把米好好清洗，炖肉时，把肉切成细小的块。如果米因为湿热而损坏，或者变得酸腐，他就不会去吃，鱼或者肉如果变质，同样如此；任何食物有腐败的颜色或腐败的味道，他都不会去吃，任何事物在烹饪时损坏、任何不符合时令的食物，同样如此；如果肉没有恰当地切割，他不会去吃，任何肉用盘子准备好，却没有合适的酱，同样如此。

尽管可能餐桌上有大量的肉，但他从不允许他所吃的肉量超过与他所吃的米饭量的合适比例。只有在饮酒上，他不会为自己设限，但从不

sale. He would always have ginger served on the table. He never ate much.

After a public sacrifice, he would never keep the portion of meat he received over night.The meat he used in sacrifice at home he would never keep over three days; if kept over three days, he would not allow it to be eaten.

At table, while eating he would not speak.When in bed he would not talk.

Although he might have the plainest fare on the table, he would always say grace before he ate.

9. In ordinary life, unless the mat used as a cushion was properly and squarely laid, he would not sit on it.

10. When at a public dinner in his native place, he would always leave the table as soon as the old people left.

In his native place on the occasion of the Purification Festival, when the procession of villagers passed his house, he would always appear in full uniform on the steps of his house, standing on the left-hand side of the house.

11. When he had occasion to entrust a message of enquiry after the health of a friend in another country to any person, he would always, on the person entrusted with the message leaving him, make obeisance twice and see him to the door.

On one occasion when a noble, who was the minister in power in his native State, sent him a present of some medicines, he received it respectfully, but said to the messenger: "Tell your Master I do not know the nature of the drugs: therefore I shall be afraid to use it."

会过量。

　　从暴露在外而出售的地方买的酒肉,他不会去吃。他总是会在餐桌上准备生姜。但他从不会多吃。

　　公共祭祀之后,他从不会把自己收到的那份肉保留过夜。在家祭祀用的肉,他从不保留超过三天,如果保留超过三天,他就不许再吃了。

　　在餐桌旁,吃东西时他不讲话。躺在床上,他不交谈。

　　尽管他的餐桌上可能是最简朴的食物,但他总会在吃饭之前祈祷。

9. 席不正,不坐。

　　在日常生活中,除非用作坐垫的席子被正确地、成直角地放置,否则他不会坐上去。

10. 乡人饮酒,杖者出,斯出矣。乡人傩,朝服而立于阼阶。

　　在他的家乡举行的公共宴会上,一旦年长的人离开,他就总会离开餐桌。

　　在他的家乡举行的净扫节日的活动上,当村民的队列经过他的家时,他总会穿整套礼服站在他家的台阶上,在房子的左手边。

11. 问人于他邦,再拜而送之。康子馈药,拜而受之。曰:“丘未达,不敢尝。”

　　当有机会委托别人问候其他国家的一位朋友时,他总会在那位捎信的人离开时两次行礼致敬,并送他出门。

　　有一次,一位在他故国当权的贵族送给他一些药品作为礼物,他恭敬地接受它,但对那位使者说:“告诉你的主人,我不了解这些药物的性能,因此我不敢使用它。”

12. On one occasion when, as he was returning from an audience at the palace, he heard that the State stable was on fire, his first question was, "Has any man been injured?"He did not ask about the horses.

13. When his prince sent him a present of dish of cooked meat, he would always have it properly served on the table, and he himself would taste it before he allowed others to taste it.When his prince sent him uncooked meat as a present, he would have it cooked and then offer it first in sacrifice before his ancestors.When his prince sent him a live animal, he would keep it alive.

   When he had the honour to sit with his prince at table, after the prince had said grace he would first taste the dishes.

   When he was sick, on his prince coming to see him, he would lie with his head to the east and have his court uniform laid over him with the girdle drawn across.

   When he received a summons form his prince he would immediately go on foot, without waiting for his carriage.

14. When he attended the service at the Great Cathedral (ancestral temple of the reigning prince) he always enquired what he should do at every stage of the service.

15. When any friend died who had no one to perform the last offices, he would always say: "Leave it to me: I will bury him."

   When friends sent him presents, although these might consist of carriages and horses, he would not on receiving them make obeisance. The only present which he received with an obeisance was meat which had been used in sacrifice.

12. 厩焚。子退朝,曰:"伤人乎?" 不问马。

　　有一次,当孔子从官殿觐见回来后,听说政府的马厩曾失火,他的第一个问题是:"有人受伤了吗?"他没有询问马的情况。

13. 君赐食,必正席先尝之;君赐腥,必熟而荐之;君赐生,必畜之。侍食于君,君祭,先饭。疾,君视之,东首,加朝服,拖绅。君命召,不俟驾行矣。

　　当国君送给他一盘做熟的肉作为礼物时,他总会得体地端到餐桌上,然后在给其他人品尝之前,自己先尝。当国君送给他生肉作为礼物时,他会做熟它,然后首先把它作为祭品献到祖先面前。当国君送给他一只活的动物,他会饲养起来。

　　当他荣幸地与国君坐在一起吃饭时,国君祈祷完毕后,他会首先尝一下食物。

　　当他生病国君前来探望时,他会把头朝向东方躺着,用朝服盖住自己,并拖过束带横在身体上。

　　当他接到国君的传唤时,他会立刻步行前去,而不会等他的马车。

14. 入太庙,每事问。

　　当他参加在大祠堂(在位国君的祖先祠堂)的祭拜仪式时,他总是询问仪式的每个环节他应该怎么做。

15. 朋友死,无所归,曰:"于我殡。"朋友之馈,虽车马,非祭肉,不拜。

　　当他的任何一个朋友死掉而没人为他举行葬礼时,他总会说:"让我来吧:我会埋葬他的。"

　　当朋友们送给他礼物时,尽管这些礼物有可能是马车与马,他也不会在接受它们时行礼致敬。唯一让他在接受时行礼致敬的礼物,是祭祀用过的肉。

16. In bed, he was never seen to lie straight on his back like a corpse.In ordinary life at home, he would never use formality.

When he met anyone dressed in deep mourning, although the person might be a familiar acquaintance, he would always look grave and serious.When he met with an officer in full uniform or a blind person, although he himself might be in undress, he would always behave with ceremony and punctiliousness.

When driving in his carriage, on meeting with a funeral cortege, he would always bend his head forward out of the carriage, to bow. He would behave in the same way when he met the procession carrying the mortality returns of the population.

At a dinner, whenever a dish *en grand tenue* was bought to the table, he would look serious and rise up to thank the host.

On sudden clap of thunder or during a violent storm, he would look grave and serious.

17. When about to mount his carriage he would stand in a proper position, holding the cord in his hand.When in the carriage he would look straight before him without turning his head.He would not talk fast or point with his fingers.

18. As they turned to look at it, it instantly rose and, hovering about, it settled again. Somebody said, "Ah! pheasant on the hill! Ah! pheasant on the hill! You know the times! You know the times!"Confucius' disciple, the intrepid Chung Yu, conned it over three times; then, suddenly understanding the meaning of the remark, made an exclamation, rose, and went away.

16. 寝不尸，居不容。见齐衰者，虽狎，必变。见冕者与瞽者，虽亵，必以貌。凶服者式之。式负版者。有盛馔，必变色而作。迅雷风烈，必变。

在床上，他从未被看到过像具尸体一样直直地仰面躺着。在家里的日常生活中，他从不会拘泥于礼节。

遇到任何穿着深色丧服的人时，尽管这个人可能是个熟悉认识的人，他也总会显得严肃而庄重。遇到一位身穿全套礼服的官员，或者一位盲人，尽管他自己可能身穿便服，他也总会表现得礼貌而谨慎。

驾驶马车而遇到一队葬礼的行列时，他总会向前把头伸到马车外面，弯腰行礼。当遇到运送人口死亡数据的队列时，他会表现出同样的举止。

在宴会上，当饭菜以盛大的礼仪端上餐桌时，他会表情庄重，并且站起来向主人致谢。

突然响起雷电的霹雳声，或发生猛烈的暴风时，他会显得庄重而严肃。

17. 升车，必正立执绥。车中，不内顾，不疾言，不亲指。①

将要登上马车时，他会站在合适的位置，把绳子抓在手里。在马车里，他会正视前方，而不会回头。他也不会快速讲话或用手指到处指。

18. 色斯举矣，翔而后集。曰："山梁雌雉，时哉！时哉！"子路共之，三嗅而作。

当他们回头看它时，它立刻飞了起来，盘旋不定，然后又栖息了下来。有人说："啊！山上的野鸡！啊！山上的野鸡！你懂得时机啊！你懂得时机啊！"孔子的学生，那位刚勇的仲由，默念了它超过三遍；然后，他突然明白了这句话的意思，感叹了一声，站起来，离开了。

---

① 在原文中，此节文字与第16节为一段，辜鸿铭英译文将其拆分为独立一节。

【评述】

1. 这一节是对孔子在家庭与工作两种场合下言行的对比。

"乡党"，辜鸿铭译为"his life at home"，"家中的生活"。他强调的是孔子在家中的生活表现；"恂恂"译为"shy and diffident"，"腼腆而羞怯"；"不能言"译为"he were not a good speaker"，"不善言辞"。这一句说明了孔子在家中是腼腆羞怯的，不善言辞的。

"宗庙朝廷"，译为"courts and councils"，"朝廷与会议"，传统学者多将"宗庙"理解为祖庙，"朝廷"理解为国君处理政事的地方。辜鸿铭的翻译没有包含"宗庙"这层意思，他把"宗庙朝廷"理解为对处理政事地方的泛指，与前面的"home"是相对的；"便便"，译为"readily"，"乐意地"，"便便言"，即乐意说话，与前面"不善言辞"相对；"谨"译为"with deliberation"，"慎重，审慎"。"在宗庙朝廷，便便言，唯谨尔"是说，如果在朝廷或者在会议上，在这样的正式场合，孔子就会乐于讲话，但说的话都是经过深思熟虑的。

2. 文中，"下大夫"、"上大夫"辜鸿铭分别"junior officers"与"senior officers"，即"下级官员"与"上级官员"。这句话指的是孔子对上下级的不同说话方式。"侃侃"，译为"frankness"，"坦诚"，意思是，对下级官员凡事坦诚相告；"訚訚"，译为"self-possession"，"沉着，冷静"，意思是，对上级官员冷静沉着。"与下大夫言，侃侃如也；与上大夫言，訚訚如也"表现了孔子在工作中的为人风格。"踧踖"，传统学者多理解为"恭敬"，辜鸿铭译为"diffident, awe-inspired"，"胆怯，敬畏"，指表现出对君主的敬畏；"与与"，译为"composed"，"镇静"，指尽管要对君主表示敬畏，但同样要以镇静的心情面对他。"君在，踧踖如也，与与如也"表现了孔子对待君主的方式。

3. 文中，"傧"，传统学者多理解为"迎接宾客"，辜鸿铭的翻译正好相反，译为"see a visitor out"，"送宾客出去"。这一节是说孔子送宾客时的行事风格。

4. 这一节说的是孔子上朝时的一系列举止表现。

5. 这一节讲的是孔子出使他国进行"外交"时的礼仪气度，张弛有度，富有个人魅力。

6. 在这一节中，辜鸿铭翻译的第一句话即点名主旨，即这里讲的是孔子认为的绅士的穿衣注意事项，接着，又说了夏天穿衣的事项和冬天穿衣的事项。他在翻译"缁衣羊裘"之前，加了"in winter"一词，指明是冬天。另外，"非帷裳，必杀之"，辜鸿铭译为"His under-garment, except when it is worn as an apron（like the Free Masons now）on State occasions, he should always have cut pointed on the upper part"，"他的内衬衣，除非在国家重大场合当一件围裙来穿（就像现在的共济会员），否则他总会把衣服上面的部分明显地剪掉",其中,"帷裳"译为"an apron(like the Free Masons now)","围裙(像现在共济会会员的围裙)",应指一种礼服,此处他拿共济会会员出席会议穿的围裙来作比喻;"必杀之",译为"he should always have cut pointed on the upper part","总是被明显地剪掉上面的部分"。这里的意思是,除非当作一种类似共济会围裙的礼服来穿,否则内衣的"上面部分"是应该裁掉。不得不说,辜鸿铭翻译的这句话从字面来看令人费解,有待方家作进一步解读。而传统上,学者多释"杀"为"杀缝"。朱熹注释说:"……若深衣,……则无襞积而有杀缝矣。"(《四书章句集注》,第119页)

7. 这一节讲的是孔子斋戒祈祷时的穿衣、饮食、起居方式。"齐",传统学者多认为通"斋","明衣"多认为指"浴衣","布"指浴衣的材料。

8. 这一节说的是孔子日常在饮食上注意的细节。文中,"虽疏食菜羹,瓜祭,必齐如也"一句,传统上,学者多释"瓜"为"必",而后面的"祭",辜鸿铭认为与西方的"感恩祈祷"相近,他在此注释说:

> 在中国一种古老的习俗,含义与欧洲的"感恩祈祷"(saying grace)相近然而却不完全一样。有人告诉我,今天在中国的一些乡下奉行这种习俗。祈祷时,留出极少的一点米饭或肉在餐桌上,献给神明,献祭者向其表达能够吃到这些食物的感激之情。

9. 文中,"席不正"的"正",辜鸿铭译为"properly and squarely laid","正确地、成直角地放置";"席"译为"the mat used as a cushion",指拿席子作坐垫。这句话指如果放置的方式不正确、不方正,宁可不坐。对于这一做法,辜鸿铭注释说:

> 在古代中国,就像现在的日本,人们并没有椅子;人们都"席地而坐",即使是天子与诸侯国君主。

10. 这一节表现的是当时的风俗民情。"乡人傩,朝服而立于阼阶"一句中,"傩",传统学者多认为指驱除疫鬼的仪式,辜鸿铭译为"the occasion of the Purification Festival","在净扫节日举行的活动"。辜鸿铭对此注释说:

> 在古代中国以及大多数东方国家,公共卫生形成了宗教的一部分,而不是被警察或国家武力(gens darmes)强制执行。

11. "问人于他邦,再拜而送之"一句中,"问",辜鸿铭译为"entrust a message of

enquiry after the health of ... to ...", "问候"之意,指孔子委托别人问候其他国家的朋友。"再拜而送之",译为"make obeisance twice and see him to the door""两次行礼致敬,并送他出门"。这句说的是孔子对朋友的牵挂之情,以及对使者的尊重。

"拜而受之",辜鸿铭译为"received it respectfully","恭敬地接受",表现的是孔子对这份礼物的重视及感激之情。"丘未达,不敢尝",辜鸿铭将"达"译为"know the nature of the drugs","了解药性";"尝"译为"use","使用",指孔子恭敬地接受礼物,但使用却很谨慎。

12. "厩",辜鸿铭译为"the State stable","政府的马厩",指的是国厩,即国家的马棚;"不问马",译为"he did not ask about the horses",他没有询问马的情况,表达的是孔子对人的关切。

13. 本节第一句反映的是孔子对国君所赐的不同礼物的不同处理方式。后面三句说的是孔子的待君之道。

14. 这一节与第三章第15节部分内容有所重复。辜鸿铭的翻译与第三章第15节有所不同。前面,他把"入大庙"译为"when Confucius first attended the service at the State Cathedral",指的是"孔子第一次在国家总庙参加祭拜仪式"。此处,他把"入太庙"译为"when he attended the service at the Great Cathedral",泛指孔子"参加在大祠堂的祭拜仪式"。所以,这一段与前面第三章第15节有所不同,因此辜鸿铭没有注明"重复"。根据辜鸿铭的翻译,唯一的不同之处在于:前面说的是孔子初次参加该祭拜仪式时的表现;这一节则泛指孔子每次去该处参加祭拜仪式时的表现。

15. 文中,"无所归",辜鸿铭译为"had no one to perform the last offices","没人为他举行葬礼";"于我殡",译为"leave it to me: I will bury him","让我来吧:我会埋葬他的"。这里指孔子对朋友始终如一的责任心。"朋友之馈,虽车马,非祭肉,不拜"一句中,"祭肉",译为"meat which had been used in sacrifice","祭祀用过的肉";"拜",译为"make obeisance","行礼致敬"。这句话指朋友馈赠多么贵重的财物,接时都不必对他行礼致敬。但关乎信仰祭祀,则必须行礼致敬。

16. 这一节说的是孔子在日常生活中的一些细节特征。其中,"负版者",传统上学者多释为"持邦国图籍者"。辜鸿铭译为"the procession carrying the mortality returns of the population","运送人口死亡数据的队列"。"式负版者"指孔子对国家人口生死问题的严肃态度。

17. 文中，"升车，必正立，执绥"一句，"升车"，辜鸿铭译为"mount his carriage"，"登上马车"；"正立"，译为"stand in a proper position"，"站在合适的位置"；"绥"译为"the cord"，"细绳"。这句话说的是孔子登车的动作。"车中不内顾，不疾言，不亲指"一句，"不内顾"，译为"look straight before him without turning his head"，"正视前方，不回头"；"疾言"译为"talk fast"，"快速说话"；"亲指"译为"point with his fingers"，"用手指到处指"。这句话讲的是孔子在马车上的行为习惯。

18. 对于这一节的含义，辜鸿铭表示不明白，他注释说：

> 中国的注释家们放弃了本节的这个段落，承认他们无法理解它的含义。然而，阿查理爵士发现了一个对本段非常好的解释，不幸的是，我们记不清了。我们这里的解释是凭记忆做了一个猜测。

文中，"色斯举矣，翔而后集"一句，辜鸿铭的翻译是："色"，译为"as they turned to look at it"，指人们回头看那只雌雉；"举"，译为"rose"，"飞起来"；"翔"，译为"hovering about"，"盘旋"；"集"，译为"settle"，"栖息，停下"。这句话指人们抬头看时，那只雌雉飞起、盘旋，又停下栖息，描述的是雌雉的一系列动作。

"山梁雌雉，时哉！时哉！"一句，辜鸿铭的翻译是："曰"，译为"somebody said"，指这句话是某个人说的，既不是孔子，也不是子路。实际上，按辜鸿铭的翻译，本段中并没有出现孔子；"山梁雌雉"译为"pheasant on the hill"，"山上的野鸡"，而且用了重复的感叹句式；"时哉！时哉！"，译为"You know the times!You know the times!"，"你懂得时机"。

"子路共之，三嗅而作"一句，按辜鸿铭的翻译，应将"共之"与"三"连读，即"共之三"译为"conned it over three times"，"默念了三次"；"嗅"，译为"made an exclamation"，"感叹"；"作"，译为"rose, and went away"，"起身离开"。这句话指子路默念了上面那人说的那句话三遍，然后突然有所醒悟，感叹了一声，就起身离开了。

CHAPTER XI
先进第十一

1. Confucius remarked, "Men of the last generation, in matters of the arts and refinement, are considered to have been rude; men of the present generation are, in those matters, considered polite.But in my practice I prefer men of the last generation."

2. Confucius in his old age remarked, "Of all those who followed me and shared hardships with me in my wanderings in former years, I do not now see one at my door.

   "Distinguished for godliness and conduct there were Yen Hui, Min Tzu Ch'ien, Jen Pin-niu and Chung Kung; distinguished as good speakers there were Tsai Ngo and Tzu Kung; for administrative abilities, Jen Yu and Chung Yu; and for literary pursuits, Tzu Yu and Tzu Hsia."

3. Confucius remarked of his disciple, the favourite Yen Hui: "There was Hui — (the disciple's familiar name), he never gave me any assistance at all.There was nothing in what I said to him with which he was not satisfied."

4. Confucius remarked of another disciple, saying: "He was indeed a good son.People found nothing in him different from what his parents said of him."

5. A disciple of Confucius was fond of repeating the verse: —
   > A fleck on the stone may be ground away;
   > A word misspoken will remain always.
   Confucius married his niece to him.

1. 子曰："先进于礼乐，野人也；后进于礼乐，君子也。如用之，则吾从先进。"

　　孔子说："前一辈的人，在艺术与教养这些事情方面被认为是原始的；现代的人在这些方面被认为是文雅的。但按我的习惯，我更倾向于上一辈的人。"

2. 子曰："从我于陈、蔡者，皆不及门也。"德行：颜渊，闵子骞，冉伯牛，仲弓。言语：宰我，子贡。政事：冉有，季路。文学：子游，子夏。

　　在晚年的时候，孔子说："对于那些在我往昔的流浪中跟随我，并与我共同面对艰难的人，到现在我也没看见有谁来到我的门口。

　　"在信仰与品行方面卓著的，有颜回、闵子骞、冉伯牛和仲弓；作为善于辞令的人而卓著的有宰我和子贡；在行政能力方面卓著的，是冉有和仲由；在文学研究方面卓著的是子游和子夏。"

3. 子曰："回也非助我者也，于吾言无所不说。"

　　孔子谈论他的学生，那位他最喜爱的颜回："回（那位学生令人熟悉的名字）——他从来没有给我任何帮助。在我对他说的话中，他从来不会对任何一点表示不满意。"

4. 子曰："孝哉闵子骞！人不间于其父母昆弟之言。"

　　孔子谈论另外一个学生，说："他的确是一个好儿子啊。人们在他身上没有发现一点与他父母所说的不一样的地方。"

5. 南容三复白圭，孔子以其兄之子妻之。

　　孔子的一位学生喜爱反复背诵这些诗句："石头的斑点可以研磨不见；/而讲错的话却将永远留传。"孔子把他的侄女嫁给了他。

6. A noble who was the minister in power in Confucius' native State, asked him which one of his disciples he considered a man of real culture.

   Confucius answered, "There was Yen Hui; he was a man of real culture. But unfortunately he died in the prime of his life. Now there is no one like him."

7. When the favourite Yen Hui died, his father begged that Confucius would sell his carriage to buy an outer case for the coffin in which to bury him.

   Confucius answered, "Talented or without talents, a man's son will always be to him as no other man's son. When my own son died, he was buried in a simple coffin without the outer case. Now I cannot go on foot to buy a coffin case for your son.As I have the honour to sit in the State Council of the country I am not permitted to go on foot when I go out."

8. When Confucius first heard the news of the death of his disciple, the favourite Yen Hui, he cried out in an outburst of grief, "Oh! Oh! God has forsaken me!God has forsaken me!"

9. When his disciple, the favourite Yen Hui, died, Confucius burst into a paroxysm of grief.Those around him said, "Sir, you are grieving too exceedingly."

   "Am I?" he replied, "But if I do not grieve exceedingly for him, for whom then should I grieve exceedingly?"

6. 季康子问:"弟子孰为好学?"孔子对曰:"有颜回者好学,不幸短命死矣,今也则亡。"

一位在孔子故国当权的贵族大臣问他,他的学生中哪一位他认为是一个真正有教养的人。

孔子回答说:"有一个颜回;他是一个真正有教养的人。但不幸的是,在他年富力强的时候死了。现在没有人像他一样了。"

7. 颜渊死,颜路请子之车以为之椁。子曰:"才不才,亦各言其子也。鲤也死,有棺而无椁。吾不徒行以为之椁。以吾从大夫之后,不可徒行也。"

当那位最受喜爱的颜回死后,他的父亲请求孔子能够卖掉自己的马车去为埋葬他的棺材买一个外壳。

孔子回答说:"不管是有才能的,还是无才能的,自己的儿子对他来说总是与别人的儿子不一样。我自己的儿子死的时候,他是在一个简陋的没有外壳的棺材里被埋葬的。现在,我不能够走路去为你的儿子买一个棺材外壳。因为我还有任职国会的头衔,我外出时是不许步行的。"

8. 颜渊死。子曰:"噫! 天丧予! 天丧予!"

当孔子最先听到他的学生,那位他最喜爱的颜回死的消息时,他因悲痛的爆发而呼喊:"噢! 噢! 上帝已抛弃我了! 上帝已抛弃我了!"

9. 颜渊死,子哭之恸。从者曰:"子恸矣。"曰:"有恸乎? 非夫人之为恸而谁为!"

当他的学生,那位他最喜爱的颜回死的时候,孔子发作了爆发性的悲痛。周围的人说:"先生,你过度地悲伤了。"

"是吗?"他回答说:"但是如果我不为他过度悲伤,那么,我应该为谁过度悲伤呢?"

10. When the favourite, Yen Hui, died, Confucius' other disciples proposed to give him a great funeral. But Confucius said, "Do not do so for my sake."

The disciples nevertheless gave him a great funeral.

Confucius then said to his disciples: "Hui (the favourite disciple's familiar name) behaved to me as to a father, but I have not been able to treat him as a son. It is not my fault. Ah! gentlemen, it is your fault."

11. A disciple (the intrepid Chung Yu) enquired how one should behave towards the spirits of dead men.

Confucius answered, "We cannot as yet do our duties to living men; why should we enquire about our duties to dead men?"

The disciple went on to enquire about death. Confucius answered, "We do not as yet know about life; why should we enquire about death?"

12. On one occasion several of his disciples were standing in attendance on Confucius. One was calm and self-possessed. The intrepid Chung Yu stood upright and soldier-like. Two others looked frank and engaging. Confucius, looking on them, was pleased. He remarked, however, "There is Yu (Chung Yu's name) there, — I am afraid he will not die a natural death."

13. A party in Confucius' native State proposed to build a new State-house. A disciple of Confucius remarked, "Why not keep the old building and modify it to suit the present circumstances? Why

10. 颜渊死,门人欲厚葬之,子曰:"不可。"门人厚葬之。子曰:"回也视予犹父也,予不得视犹子也。非我也,夫二三子也。"

　　当他最喜爱的学生颜回死的时候,孔子的其他学生打算为他办一个大型的葬礼。但孔子说:"为了我,不要这样做。"

　　学生们还是给他办了一个盛大的葬礼。

　　孔子于是对他的学生们说:"回(那位最受喜爱的学生的令人熟悉的名字)对我就像对待一位父亲,但我没能够像对儿子那样对他。这不是我的错。啊! 先生们,这是你们的错。"

11. 季路问事鬼神。子曰:"未能事人,焉能事鬼?"敢问死。曰:"未知生,焉知死?"

　　一位学生(那位刚勇的仲由)询问一个人应该如何对待死者的灵魂。

　　孔子回答:"我们尚且不能够为活着的人尽责;为何还要询问对死者的责任呢?"

　　那位学生接着询问死亡的问题。孔子回答:"我们尚且还不了解生命;为何还要询问死亡呢?"

12. 闵子侍侧,訚訚如也;子路,行行如也;冉有、子贡,侃侃如也。子乐。"若由也,不得其死然。"

　　有一次,他的一些学生站着侍奉孔子。其中一个镇静而沉着。刚勇的仲由笔直地站着,气势豪迈。其他两个看上去直率而亲切。孔子看着他们,十分高兴。然而,他说:"由(仲由的名字)啊——我担心他将不会正常地死去。"

13. 鲁人为长府。闵子骞曰:"仍旧贯,如之何? 何必改作?"子曰:"夫人不言,言必有中。"

　　孔子故国的一些人提议修建一座新的政府议事大厅。孔子的一位

construct a new building?"

"That man," said Confucius, referring to the disciple, "seldom speaks; but when he does speak, he always hits the mark."

14. Confucius on one occasion speaking in rebuke of his disciple, the intrepid Chung Yu, said: "That man with his trumpet-blowing should not be permitted to come to my house."

After that the other disciples began to look down upon Chung Yu. But Confucius said, "That man, in his education, has entered the gate, but not the house."

15. A disciple of Confucius, referring to two other disciple, enquired which of the two was the better man. Confucius answered, "One goes beyond the mark; the other does not come up to it." "Then," replied the disciple, "the first man is better than the last."

"No," answered Confucius, "to go beyond the mark is just as bad as not to come up to it."

16. The head of a powerful family of nobles in Confucius' native State had amassed immense wealth. A disciple of Confucius, who was in that nobleman's service, was very exacting in collecting imposts for him from the people on his estate, thus increasing his master's already great wealth."He is no disciple of mine," exclaimed Confucius, referring to the disciple mentioned above, and speaking to his other disciples, "Proclaim it aloud, my children, and assail him!"

学生说:"为什么不保留旧有的大厦并改造它去适应目前的状况呢? 为何还要修建一座新的大厦?"

"这个人,"孔子提及那位学生说,"很少说话;但每次开口总能切中要害。"

14. 子曰:"由之瑟奚为于丘之门?"门人不敬子路。子曰:"由也升堂矣,未入于室也。"

有一次,孔子指责他的学生,那位刚勇的仲由,说:"不允许吹奏喇叭的那个人来我的屋子。"

之后,其他学生开始轻视仲由。但孔子说:"那个人,在他的教育培养方面,已经进了门,但还没有进屋子。"

15. 子贡问:"师与商也孰贤?"子曰:"师也过,商也不及。"曰:"然则师愈与?"子曰:"过犹不及。"

孔子的一个学生,提及其他两个学生,询问那两个里面谁是更优秀的人。孔子回答说:"一个超过了要求;另一个未达到要求。""那么,"这位学生说,"头一个要比后一个更优秀。"

"不,"孔子回答说,"超过要求与未达到要求一样糟糕。"

16. 季氏富于周公,而求也为之聚敛而附益之。子曰:"非吾徒也。小子鸣鼓而攻之,可也。"

一位孔子故国里有权势的贵族家族的当家人,积聚起了巨大的财富。孔子的一个为那位贵族服务的学生,在征敛课税时,凭借他的社会地位而对人民非常严厉,由此来增加他主人已然很多的财富。"他绝不是我的学生,"孔子提到上面的那位学生时大声地说,又对他的其他学生说,"大声宣告出去,我的孩子们,去抨击他!"

17. Confucius, speaking of his four disciples, remarked, "One was simple; another was dull; another was specious; and the last was coarse."

18. Confucius, speaking of his disciple, the favourite Yen Hui, and of another disciple, remarked, "There is Hui, — (Yen Hui's name) — he is almost perfect as a man; yet he is often reduced to want. The other man does not even believe in religion; yet his possessions go on increasing. Nevertheless, the latter is often right in his judgment of things."

19. A disciple of Confucius enquired what constituted an honest man.

"An honest man," answered Confucius, "does not *cant* neither does he profess esoterism." *i. e.* the secret of any-ism.

20. Confucius then went on to say, "Men now are earnest in what they profess. Are they really good and wise men? or are they serious only in appearance? That is what I should like to know."

21. A disciple, the intrepid Chung Yu, asked if he might at once carry out into practice any truth which he had learnt.

"No," answered Confucius, "You have the wishes of your parents and of your old people at home to consult. How can you take upon yourself to carry at once into practice what you have learnt."

Another disciple on another occasion asked the same question.

"Yes," replied Confucius, "carry it out at once."

Afterwards another disciple ventured to enquire of Confucius

17. 柴也愚,参也鲁,师也辟,由也喭。

　　孔子谈到他的四个学生,说:"一个愚笨;另一个迟钝;再一个徒有其表;最后一个粗野低俗。"

18. 子曰:"回也其庶乎,屡空。赐不受命,而货殖焉,亿则屡中。"

　　孔子谈到他的学生,那位最受喜爱的颜回,和另外一个学生,说:"回(颜回的名字)啊,他作为一个人来说,几乎是完美的;然而,他经常陷于贫困。另一个人甚至没什么信仰;而他的财产不断地增加。不过,后者对事情的判断经常是正确的。"

19. 子张问善人之道。子曰:"不践迹,亦不入于室。"

　　孔子的一个学生询问如何才算是一个诚实正直的人。

　　"一个真诚的人,"孔子回答说,"不会伪善地说教,也不会信奉秘教。"即,关于任何信仰的隐秘。

20. 子曰:"论笃是与,君子者乎? 色庄者乎?"

　　孔子接着继续说:"现在人们对他们的信仰是真诚的。他们真的是良善而明智的人吗? 还是仅仅看上去认真严肃而已? 这是我想要知道的。"

21. 子路问:"闻斯行诸?"子曰:"有父兄在,如之何其闻斯行之?"冉有问:"闻斯行诸?"子曰:"闻斯行之。"公西华曰:"由也问闻斯行诸,子曰'有父兄在';求也问闻斯行诸,子曰'闻斯行之'。赤也惑,敢问。"子曰:"求也退,故进之;由也兼人,故退之。"

　　一个学生,那位刚勇的仲由,问他能否立刻把获知的原理付诸实践。

　　"不行,"孔子回答说,"你要和家中的父母与长辈去商议。你怎么能够擅自大胆地将获知的原理马上实践呢。"

　　另一次,又一个学生问同一个问题。

why he gave two totally different answers to the same question.

"That is because," answered Confucius, "the one man is too diffident; I therefore said that to encourage him; the other man, however, is too froward; therefore I said that to pull him back."

22. When on an occasion Confucius and his disciples on their travels were threatened with danger from the violent men of a certain place, his disciple, the favourite Yen Hui, was separated from the party. Afterwards, when the disciple rejoined him, Confucius said, "I was afraid you had been killed." "While you live," answered the disciple, "how should I dare to allow myself to be killed?"

23. A member of a family of nobles who were in power in Confucius' native State, referring to two disciples of his who were in the service of that powerful family, enquired whether those two disciples could be considered statesmen. "Oh!" replied Confucius, "I thought you had something extraordinary to ask my opinion about. You wish to have my opinion on these men: is that all you want? Men I call statesmen are those who will serve their master according to their sense of duty; who, however, when they find they cannot do that, consistently with their sense of duty, will resign. As to those two men you refer to, — they may be considered as states-functionaries, not statesmen."

"But," the noble went on to ask, "will these two men carry out anything they are called upon to do?" "An act of parricide or regicide they will not carry out."answered Confucius.

"可以，"孔子回答说，"要马上去实践它。"

后来，另外一个学生谨慎地询问孔子，为什么他对同一个问题给出了完全不同的两个答案。

"这是因为，"孔子回答说，"其中一个人太胆怯，因此我那样说去鼓励他；但是，另一个人太冒进，因此我那样说让他有所收敛。"

22. 子畏于匡，颜渊后。子曰："吾以女为死矣。"曰："子在，回何敢死？"

有一次，孔子和他的学生们在旅途中受到了某个地方的暴徒的威胁，他的学生，那位他最喜爱的颜回，与队伍走散了。后来，当那位学生重新与他相聚时，孔子说："我一直担心你已经被杀死了。""您还活着，"那位学生回答说，"我怎敢让自己被杀死呢？"

23. 季子然问："仲由、冉求可谓大臣与？"子曰："吾以子为异之问，曾由与求之问。所谓大臣者：以道事君，不可则止。今由与求也，可谓具臣矣。"曰："然则从之者与？"子曰："弑父与君，亦不从也。"

孔子故国的一个当权贵族家族的人，谈及孔子的两个在那个家族中服务的学生，询问那两个学生能否被视为政治家。"噢！"孔子回答说，"我想，你是有特别的东西想问吧。你希望我对这两个人说出看法：这就是你想要的全部吗？我称其为政治家的人，是那些将通过他们的责任感来服务主人的人；不过，当他们发现不能够一贯地按照责任感那样做时，他们就会辞职不做。至于你所提到的两个人——他们可以视为政治官员，并不是政治家。"

"但是，"那位贵族继续问，"他们两个人会执行要求他们要去做的任何事情吗？""如果是杀父母或者杀君主的任务，他们就不会去执行。"孔子回答说。

24. A disciple of Confucius, the intrepid Chung Yu, on one occasion got a very young man appointed Chief Magistrate of an important town."You are ruining a good man's son," said Confucius to him.

"Why," answered the disciple, "he has the large population to deal with; he has questions of the interests of the country to decide upon.Why must one read books in order to educate himself?"

"That," replied Confucius, "is the reason why I hate men who are always ready with an argument."

25. On one occasion five of his disciple were sitting in attendance on Confucius.

Confucius then said to them, "I am only a little older than you, gentlemen.Do not mind that.Now living a private life, you all say that you are not known and appreciated by men in authority; but suppose you were known, tell me now, each of you, what would you be able to do ?"

"I could," answered the intrepid Chung Yu at once, without hesitation, "if I had the conduct of affairs in a States of even the first power which was hemmed in between two States of great power and which was embroiled in the midst of a war, and hence harassed by famine and distress — I could, if I had the conduct of affairs in such a State for three years, make the people brave and, moreover, know their duty."

On hearing this, Confucius only smiled; and, turning to another disciple, said: "And you — what do you say?"

"I could," answered the disciple appealed to, "If I had the conduct of the government of a State, say, of the third or fourth

24. 子路使子羔为费宰。子曰:"贼夫人之子。"子路曰:"有民人焉,有社稷焉。何必读书,然后为学?"子曰:"是故恶夫佞者。"

　　孔子的一个学生,那位刚勇的仲由,有一次把一个非常年轻的人任命为一个重要城镇的主要行政官。"你正在毁一个好人的儿子。"孔子对他说。

　　"为什么,"那位学生回答,"他有众多的人口要去治理;他有关于国家利益的一些问题需要裁决。为什么一个人非要读书才能自我学习呢?"

　　"这,"孔子回答说,"就是我憎恶那些总是准备争论的人的原因。"

25. 子路、曾皙、冉有、公西华侍坐。子曰:"以吾一日长乎尔,毋吾以也。居则曰:'不吾知也!'如或知尔,则何以哉?"子路率尔而对曰:"千乘之国,摄乎大国之间,加之以师旅,因之以饥馑;由也为之,比及三年,可使有勇,且知方也。"夫子哂之。"求!尔何如?"对曰:"方六七十,如五六十,求也为之,比及三年,可使足民。如其礼乐,以俟君子。""赤!尔何如?"对曰:"非曰能之,愿学焉。宗庙之事,如会同,端章甫,愿为小相焉。""点!尔何如?"鼓瑟希,铿尔,舍瑟而作。对曰:"异乎三子者之撰。"子曰:"何伤乎?亦各言其志也。"曰:"莫春者,春服既成。冠者五六人,童子六七人,浴乎沂,风乎舞雩,咏而归。"夫子喟然叹曰:"吾与点也!"三子者出,曾皙后。曾皙曰:"夫三子者之言何如?"子曰:"亦各言其志也已矣。"曰:"夫子何哂由也?"曰:"为国以礼,其言不让,是故哂之。""唯求则非邦也与?""安见方六七十如五六十而非邦也者?""唯赤则非邦也与?""宗庙会同,非诸侯而何?赤也为之小,孰能为之大?"

　　有一次,孔子的五个学生坐着服侍他。①

---

① 这里辜鸿铭误译为"五个学生"。

power, I could in such a case, after three years, make the people live in plenty. As to education in higher things, I would leave that to the good and wise men who will come after me."

Confucius then turned to another disciple and said: "Now you — what do you say?"

"I do not say," replied the disciple, "that in what I am going to suppose I *could do* what I propose; only, I would *try* to do it. Suppose then there were functions to be performed in any Court such as public receptions and general assemblies, — dressed in an appropriate uniform, I think I could be the vice-presiding officer."

"And now you," said Confucius to the last of the four disciples, "What do you say?"

The disciple thus last appealed to, then laid aside the harpsichord which he was thrumming, stood up and answered: "What I have in my mind differs entirely from what those three gentlemen have proposed."

"What harm is there in that?" replied Confucius, — "we are all only speaking out each his own mind." "Then," answered the disciple, "we will suppose now that we are in the latter days of spring, when we have changed all our winter clothing for fresh, new, light garments for the warmer weather. I would then propose that we take along with us five or six grown-up young friends and six or seven still younger men. We will then bathe in that romantic river; after which we will go to the top of that ancient terrace to air and cool ourselves; and at last we will return, singing on our way as we loiter back to our homes."

"Ah!" said Confucius then , with a sigh, "I agree with him."

孔子对他们说:"先生们,我只比你们年长一点而已,不要介意。嗨,在你们的个人生活中,你们都说不被权威的人理解和赏识;但如果假设你们是被理解的,现在告诉我,你们每个人能做些什么?"

"我能够,"刚勇的仲由立刻回答,毫不犹豫,"如果我从事一个哪怕是一流实力的国家的事务管理,而这个国家被两个实力强大的国家包围,卷入了一场战争之中,并且因此而被饥荒与穷困所拖累——如果我从事这样一个国家的事务管理三年,我能够让人民勇敢,还可以让他们了解自己的责任。"

听到这些,孔子只是笑了笑。然后,他转向另一个学生,说:"你呢——你要说什么?"

"我能够,"被问到的学生回答说,"如果我从事一个国家的政治管理,比如说,一个三流或四流实力的国家,在这样的情况下,我能够在三年之后让人民过上富庶的生活。至于更高级的教育,我会留给继我之后的良善而明智的人。"

孔子于是转向另一个学生说:"你呢——你要说什么?"

"我不能够确定,"那位学生回答说,"我是否能胜任所要假设的事情。我只是试着去做。假设任何官廷要举办社交集会,就像公务接见以及通常的集会——穿上合适的礼服,我想我能够做副主持官。"

"那么,现在你呢,"孔子对四个学生中的最后一个说,"你要说什么?"

这个最后被问到的学生,把刚刚还在拨弄的古琴放在一边,站起来回答:"我所想的与这些先生们打算的完全不同。"

"这有什么妨碍呢?"孔子回答说,"我们大家只是说出自己的想法而已。""那么,"这位学生回答说,"我们假设现在正处于春天的最后几天,我们都把冬天的衣服换成了适合这个温暖天气的清爽、崭新而轻巧的衣服。然后我就计划我们带上五六位成年的年轻朋友,以及六七个更年轻一些的人和我们一起,在那条浪漫情调的河中沐浴,之后,我们

Afterwards, when three of the above four disciple had left, the one who spoke the last word and who remained behind, enquired of Confucius, saying: "What do you think of what those three gentlemen said?"

"They, of course," answered Confucius, "only spoke out, each his own mind."

"But," asked the disciple, "why did you smiled at the first speaker?"

"Oh," replied Confucius, "To rule a country requires judgment and modesty. But what the first speaker said was not modest, — therefore I smiled at him."

"But the second speaker," the disciple went on to ask, "Did he not speak of the affairs of a nation?" "Why," answered Confucius, "Did you ever hear of a State of even the third or fourth power that is not a nation?" "Well then," the disciple went on further to ask, — "the third speak, — did he not also mean the affairs of a great nation in what he said?"

"Where there are courts, public receptions, general assemblies," answered Confucius, — "Where do you find such things except in the Courts of the princes of the Empire. The third speaker modestly said he would be a vice-presiding officer at such functions. If such a man as he is fit only to be a vice-president who would be fit to be the president?"

还要登上那座古老的露台的顶端,去吹风乘凉;最后,我们要返回,散步着回家时在路上唱歌。"

"啊!"孔子感叹地说,"我赞同他。"

后来,当上面四位学生中的三个离开后,最后说话的这个学生留在了后面,他询问孔子说:"你觉得那三位先生说得怎么样?"

"他们,当然,"孔子回答说,"只是说出了每个人的想法而已。"

"但是,"那位学生问:"你为何冲第一个发言的人笑呢?"

"噢,"孔子回答说,"管理一个国家需要判断力与谦虚谨慎的态度。但是那第一个说话的人并不谦虚谨慎——因此我对他笑了笑。"

"那么第二个呢,"那位学生继续问,"他难道没有在谈论一个国家的事务吗?""为何,"孔子回答说,"你就知道哪怕是三流或四流实力的国家就不是一个国家呢?""那么,"这位学生继续问,"第三个说话的人,他所说的难道不也是指的一个大国的事务吗?"

"宫廷、公共接见、通常的集会,"孔子回答说,"除了在帝国的诸侯国国君们的宫廷里,你哪里能找到这样的事情呢。第三个说话的人谦虚地说他要在这样的集会中做副主持官。如果像他这样一个人仅仅适合做一名副主持官,那么谁能够适合做主持官呢?"

【评述】

1. 文中，"先进"，辜鸿铭译为"men of the last generation"，"前一辈的人"；"后进"译为"men of the present generation"，"现代的人"（指孔子当时的人）；"礼乐"译为"matters of the arts and refinement"，"艺术与教养方面的事情"；"野"译为"rude"，"原始的"；"君子"译为"considered polite"，"被认为是文雅的"；"用"译为"in my practice"，"在我的习惯中"；"从"译为"prefer"，"更倾向于"。这一节是说，之前的人，在艺术、教养方面是原始的，更加质朴的，现在的人，往往被认为很文雅，然而孔子更倾向于原始与质朴。

2. 文中，"从我于陈、蔡者，皆不及门也"，"陈、蔡"指"陈、蔡之厄"，辜鸿铭译为"hardships … in my wanderings in former years"，"往昔流浪中的艰难"；"门"译为"my door"，"我的门口"。这句话指，虽然那些弟子跟从孔子经历过共同的苦难，然而，在思想上、学问上，他们仍然没有真正开始理解孔子。"德行"、"言语"、"政事"、"文学"。辜鸿铭的翻译是："德行"，译为"godliness and conduct"，"信仰与品行"，侧重的是人内在的品性修养，其中"godliness"一词主要是"虔敬"、"虔诚"之意，指的是人自身的一种神圣本性，对真理、正义、神圣的一种天然的热爱；"言语"，译为"as good speakers"，"善于辞令"的意思；"政事"，译为"administrative abilities"，"行政能力"；"文学"，译为"literary pursuits"，"文学的研究或追求"。辜鸿铭认为，这四项是孔子概括的弟子们的所成。

3. 文中，"助"，辜鸿铭译为"gave me any assistance"，"给我帮助或益处"；"说"译为"satisfied"，"满意，信服"。孔子的意思，颜回对孔子说的话，没有不满意不信服的，所以，对于孔子自身来说并不能带来益处。

4. 文中，"孝"，辜鸿铭依然按常规的方式译为"a good son"，"好儿子"；"人不间于其父母昆弟之言"，译为"people found nothing in him different from what his parents said of him"，即人们发现真实的他与他父母口中的他，是一致的。

5. 文中，"三复白圭"，学者多指诵读《诗经·大雅·抑》中"白圭之玷，尚可磨也；斯言之玷，不可为也"一句。朱熹注释说："《诗·大雅·抑之篇》曰：'白圭之玷，尚可磨也；斯言之玷，不可为也。'南容一日三复此言，事见《家语》，盖深有意于谨言也。"（《四书章句集注》，第124页）《论语》该段中并没有诗句原文，而辜鸿铭则在文中补译了诗句。

6. 文中，"好学"，辜鸿铭译为"of real culture"，"真正有教养"。"有教养"，是辜鸿铭对"好学"或"学"的一贯翻译。颜回在孔子眼中，是个真正有教养的人。

7. 文中，"请子之车以为之椁"，辜鸿铭译为"his father begged that Confucius would sell his carriage to buy an outer case for the coffin in which to bury him"，即颜回之父请求孔子卖了自己的车为颜回买一个棺材的外壳（椁）。"才不才，亦各言其子也"，译为"talented or without talents, a man's son will always be to him as no other man's son"，"不管是有才能的，还是无才能的，自己的儿子对他来说总是与别人的儿子不一样"。即人各爱其子之意。"以吾从大夫之后，不可徒行也"一句，"从大夫之后"，译为"have the honour to sit in the State Council of the country"，即任职国会之意；"不可徒行"，译为"I am not permitted to go on foot when I go out"，即外出时不允许不行。因还有官职在身，外出不许步行，所以，无法卖车买椁。

8. 文中，"子曰"，辜鸿铭译为"he cried out in an outburst of grief"，"他因悲痛的爆发而呼喊"。"天丧予"一句，"天"，译为"God"，"上帝"；"丧"译为"forsake"，"抛弃，遗弃"。这句话是孔子的悲叹。

9. 文中，"恸"，辜鸿铭译为"grieve too exceedingly"，"过度地哀伤"。这句话是说，孔子哀伤有些过度了。"夫人"，译为"him"，"他"，指颜回。"非夫人之为恸而谁为"，意思是，不为颜回过度哀伤，还能为谁过度哀伤呢？

10. 本节的核心是"回也视予犹父也，予不得视犹子也"。根据辜鸿铭的翻译，这一节的意思是，孔子的儿子孔鲤死的时候，孔子没有厚葬。如今，颜回死了，孔子也想像对自己的儿子一样不予厚葬。所以，他说"do not do so for my sake"，"为了我不要那样做"，指希望门人们不要厚葬颜回。但门人们没听，所以，孔子说"it is your fault"，"这不是我的错"。

11. 文中，"鬼神"，辜鸿铭译为"the spirits of dead men"，"死者的灵魂"。"未能事人，焉能事鬼？"一句，"事"，辜鸿铭译为"do our duties to"，"尽责任"；"人"译为"living men"，"活着的人"；"死"译为"dead men"，"死去的人"。孔子这句话的意思就是：我们对活着的人尚未能尽好责任，又何谈对死去的人呢？这是儒家思想关注现实生活的一个观点。"未知生，焉知死？"一句，"生"，译为"life"，"生命"；"死"，译为"death"，"死亡"。含义与上一句是相同的，都指教人关注现实人生。

12. 文中，"不得其死然"，学者多理解为"不得以寿终"。辜鸿铭译为"will not die a natural death"，即不会正常死亡。这是孔子通过观察仲由的秉性而对他人身安危的担忧。辜鸿铭对此注释说：

243

这句预言最后变成了现实。后来,刚勇而具有武士精神的仲由,在一次暴乱中对抗暴民保卫一座城镇时被杀死了。临死前,他的头盔在战斗中被打歪到了一侧,他镇定地整理好它,说:"一个君子,必须衣装齐整地死去。"

13. 文中,"鲁人为长府"一句,"长府"辜鸿铭译为"State-house","政府议事大厅"。这句话指修建一座新的政府议事大厅。

14. 文中,"由之瑟奚为于丘之门"一句,学者多认为指仲由鼓瑟音调有杀伐之声或不合于《雅》《颂》。按辜鸿铭的翻译,孔子的第一句话在门人中对仲由造成不好的影响。于是,孔子加以弥补,在原来那句话的基础上,延伸出"登堂入室"的概念:"由也升堂矣,未入于室也",即"在教育方面,他已经进了门,但还没进屋子"。

15. 本节讲的是"过"与"不及"两个概念的关系。"过",辜鸿铭译为"go beyond the mark","超过了标准、要求";"不及"译为"do not come up to it","未达到标准、要求"。这种标准,应该指的是道德修养的程度。有的过于拘泥道德了,有的则未完全达到道德要求。孔子认为这两者(拘泥于道德与未达到道德)一样糟糕。

16. 文中,"富于周公",辜鸿铭译为"had amassed immense wealth","积聚起了巨大的财富"。"求也为之聚敛而附益之"一句中,"聚敛"译为"very exacting in collecting imposts for him from the people","征敛课税时对人民非常严厉";"附益之",译为"thus increasing his master's already great wealth","由此来激增他主人已然很多的财富"。这里的意思是,冉求损害人民来扩充富有者。"小子鸣鼓而攻之,可也",辜鸿铭译为"proclaim it aloud, my children, and assail him","大声宣告出去,我的孩子们,去抨击他"。"鸣鼓"即代指"宣告出去",即宣告前面的"非吾徒也",然后,让学生们都去抨击他。

17. 本节开头前面并没有"子曰"两字,但学者多认为是孔子谈论"柴"、"参"、"师"、"由"四个学生的话。辜鸿铭也认为如此。

18. 文中,"庶",辜鸿铭译为"he is almost perfect as a man",指他几乎是一个完美的人;"空",译为"reduced to want","陷于贫困";"屡空"即指颜回经常陷入贫困。"回也其庶乎,屡空"指颜回在品德、性格方面几乎是一个完美的人,然而却经常陷入贫困。

下文,孔子谈了子贡与颜回截然不同的精神与生活的状态。"不受命",译为"does not even believe in religion","甚至不信宗教",指没有精神信仰的意思;"货殖",译为"his possessions go on increasing","财富不断增长";"亿则屡中",译为"is often right in his judgment of things", 指在对事物的判断上总是正确的。

19. 文中, "善人之道", 辜鸿铭译为 "what constituted an honest man", "怎样才算一个诚实正直的人", 指询问 "善人" 的定义。"不践迹, 亦不入于室" 一句, "不践迹", 译为 "does not cant", "不伪善地说教"。在此, 辜鸿铭添加注释说:

> 字面意思是 "不按照别人踩出来的足迹走路", 或者卡莱尔所说的老套的程式 (formula)。

"不入于室", 译为 "neither does he profess esoterism", "不信奉密教"。后面, 辜鸿铭又加了一句 "the secret of any-ism" 来解释 "密教", 这句话的意思是, 不伪善, 不热衷于追求隐秘的或神秘的信仰, 就算一个诚实正直的人。

20. 文中, "论笃", 辜鸿铭译为 "earnest in what they profess", "在信仰上是真诚的"。后面的两个问句: "君子者乎" 译为 "are they really good and wise men", 即 "他们真的是良善而明智的人吗"; "色庄者乎" 译为 "or are they serious only in appearance", "还是仅仅看上去认真严肃而已"。根据辜鸿铭的翻译, 这句话的意思是, 孔子很怀疑当时的一些现象, 即有些人看上去非常虔诚, 然而, 却不知他们是否真的虔诚。

21. 文中, "闻斯行", 辜鸿铭译为 "at once carry out into practice any truth which he had learnt", 即学到某理论后马上付诸实践; "有父兄在", 译为 "you have the wishes of your parents and your old people at home to consult", "你有家中的父母与长辈去商议", 指做事不擅自做主, 与家中长辈商议。"求也退, 故进之。由也兼人, 故退之" 一句中。"退", 译为 "too diffident", "太过胆怯"; "进之", 译为 "encourage him" "鼓励他"; "兼人", 译为 "too froward", "太过冒进"; "退之", 译为 "pull him back", "把他拉回", 即让他有所收敛。

22. 文中的 "子畏于匡", 指孔子在匡地因自己长得像阳虎而被匡人误会并围困的典故, 辜鸿铭译为 "Confucius and his disciples on their travels were threatened with danger from the violent men of a certain place", "孔子及其学生在旅途中受到了某个地方的暴徒的威胁", "死", 译为 "be killed", 指 "被杀死"。

23. 文中, "大臣" 一词, 辜鸿铭译为 "statesmen", "政治家"。季子然是问仲由、冉求算不算政治家。那么, 这一段, 即孔子对 "政治家" 的理解。

24. 文中"子路使子羔为费宰"一事。学者多认为指孔子"堕三都"之后，"费"、"郈"两地已堕，子路令子羔在"费"地作宰（官名），或是在两地都作宰。辜鸿铭在翻译中略去了人名、地名、官名，"使子羔为费宰"译为"on one occasion got a very young man appointed Chief Magistrate of an important town"，"把一个非常年轻的人任命为一个重要城镇的主要行政官"。辜鸿铭在翻译"子羔"时用的是"a very young man"，"一个非常年轻的人"。

25. 文中，"子路、曾皙、冉有、公西华侍坐"。辜鸿铭译为"five of his disciple were sitting in attendance on Confucius"，"孔子的五个学生坐着服侍他"，照例略去了学生的名字。

CHAPTER XII
颜渊第十二

1. A disciple of Confucius, the favourite Yen Hui, enquired what constituted a moral life. Confucius answered, "Renounce yourself and conform to the ideal of decency and good sense."

"If one could only," Confucius went on to say, "live a moral life, renouncing himself and conforming to the ideal of decency and good sense for one single day, the world would become moral. To be moral, a man depends entirely upon himself and not upon others."

The disciple then asked for practical rules to be observed in living a moral life.

Confucius answered, "Whatsoever things are contrary to the ideal of decency and good sense, do not look upon them. Whatsoever things are contrary to the ideal of decency and good sense, do not listen to them. Whatsoever things are contrary to the ideal of decency and good sense, do not utter them with your mouth. Lastly, let nothing in whatsoever things you do, act or move, be contrary to the ideal of decency and good sense."

2. Another disciple of Confucius on another occasion asked what constituted a moral life.

Confucius answered, "When going out into the world, behave always as if you were at an audience before the Emperor; in dealing with the people, act as if you were at worship before God. Whatsoever things you do not wish that others should do unto you, do not do unto them.In your public life in the State as well as in your private life in your family, give no one a just cause of complain against you."

The disciple then said: "Unworthy and remiss though I am, I shall try to make what you have just said the rule of my life."

1. 颜渊问仁。子曰："克己复礼为仁。一日克己复礼，天下归仁焉。为仁由己，而由人乎哉？"颜渊曰："请问其目。"子曰："非礼勿视，非礼勿听，非礼勿言，非礼勿动。"颜渊曰："回虽不敏，请事斯语矣。"①

    孔子的一位学生，那位最受喜爱的颜回，询问怎样才算是一种道德的生活。孔子回答说："舍弃自我并遵从高尚文雅与良好感知的理想。"

    "如果一个人哪怕仅仅能够，"孔子继续说，"只过一天道德的生活，即舍弃自我并遵从高尚文雅与良好感知的理想，世界就会变得道德。要变得道德，一个人完全取决于他自己而不是别人。"

    那位学生又问要过一种道德生活需要遵循的实践规则。

    孔子回答说："无论什么违背高尚文雅与良好感知的理想的事情，都不要去看。无论什么违背高尚文雅与良好感知的理想的事情，都不要去听。无论什么违背高尚文雅与良好感知的理想的事情，都不要用你的嘴去讲。最后，无论你做什么事情，都不要违背高尚文雅与良好感知的理想。"

2. 仲弓问仁。子曰："出门如见大宾，使民如承大祭。己所不欲，勿施于人。在邦无怨，在家无怨。"仲弓曰："雍虽不敏，请事斯语矣。"

    孔子的另一个学生在另一个场合问怎样才算是道德的生活。

    孔子回答："外出进入社会后，要常表现得像在觐见帝王；在治理人民时，就像在崇拜上帝。任何事情你不希望别人对你做的，也不要对他们做。在国家的公务生活以及在家庭的私人生活中，不要给人哪怕仅仅是对你不满的理由。"

    然后那位学生说："尽管我是拙劣而粗心的，我也会试着把您刚才说的话作为我生活的准则。"

---

① 最后一句，辜鸿铭漏译了。

3. Another disciple asked what constituted a moral character.

Confucius answered, "A man of moral character is one who is sparing of his words."

"To be sparing of words: does that alone," asked the disciple, "constitute a moral character?"

"Why," replied Confucius, "When a man feels the difficulty of living a moral life, would he be otherwise than sparing of his words?"

4. The same disciple asked what constituted a good and wise man.

Confucius answered, "A good and wise man is without anxiety and without fear." "To be without anxiety and without fear: does that alone," asked the disciple, "constitute a good and wise man?"

"Why," replied Confucius, "When a man finds within himself no cause for self-reproach, what has he to be anxious about; what has he to fear?"

5. A disciple of Confucius was unhappy, exclaiming often: "All men have their brothers: I alone have none."Upon which another disciple said to him, "I have heard it said that Life and Death are pre-ordained, and riches and honours come from God. A good and wise man is serious and without blame. In his conduct towards others he behaves with earnestness, and with judgment and good sense. In that way he will find all men within the corners of the Earth his brothers. What reason, then, has a good and wise man to complain that he has no brothers in his home? "

3. 司马牛问仁。子曰:"仁者其言也讱。"曰:"其言也讱,斯谓之仁已乎?"子曰:"为之难,言之得无讱乎?"

　　另外一个学生问什么是道德品质。

　　孔子回答说:"一个有道德品质的人是个爱惜言辞的人。"

　　"爱惜言辞:仅仅这样做,"那位学生问,"就是一种道德品质吗?"

　　"为什么这么问,"孔子回答说,"当一个人感到过一种道德生活的困难,他怎么会不爱惜言辞呢?"

4. 司马牛问君子。子曰:"君子不忧不惧。"曰:"不忧不惧,斯谓之君子已乎?"子曰:"内省不疚,夫何忧何惧?"

　　那同一个学生问怎样才算是一个良善而明智的人。

　　孔子回答说:"一个良善而明智的人没有忧虑与恐惧。""没有忧虑与恐惧:仅仅这样做,"那位学生问,"就算是一个良善而明智的人吗?"

　　"什么,"孔子回答说,"当一个人发现他自己内心中没有自我谴责的理由,他还忧虑什么呢;他还恐惧什么呢?"

5. 司马牛忧曰:"人皆有兄弟,我独亡。"子夏曰:"商闻之矣:死生有命,富贵在天。君子敬而无失,与人恭而有礼。四海之内,皆兄弟也。君子何患乎无兄弟也?"

　　孔子的一个学生不快乐,经常感叹:"所有的人都有兄弟:只我没有。"关于这个,另一个学生对他说:"我曾听说,生与死是先定的,而富有与荣耀来自上天。一个良善而明智的人是严肃庄重而不受指责的。在他对待别人的言行中,他表现得诚挚、有判断力而且合乎情理。那样,他会发现,世界的每个角落里的所有人都是他的兄弟。那么,一个良善而明智的人还有什么理由去抱怨在家中没有兄弟呢?"

6. A disciple of Confucius enquired what constituted perspicuity.

Confucius answered, "A man who can resist long-continued attempts of others to insinuate prejudice into him, or one who cannot be influenced by a sudden appeal to his own personal safety: — such a man may be considered a man of perspicuity. Indeed, a man who can resist such an influence, or such an appeal, must be a really superior man."

7. A disciple on one occasion enquired what was essential in the government of a country.

Confucius answered, "There must be sufficient food for the people; and efficient army; and confidence of the people in their rulers."

"But," asked the disciple then, "If one were compelled to dispense with one of those three things, which one of them should go first?"

"Dispense with the army," replied Confucius.

"But still," the disciple went on to ask, "If one were compelled to dispense with one of those two things remaining, which one of them should go first?"

"Dispense with the food," replied Confucius, "For from of old men have died, but without the confidence of the people in their rulers, there can be no government."

8. An officer of a certain State on one occasion remarked to a disciple of Confucius, saying: "A wise and good man wants only the substance; why should he trouble about the style?"

"I am sorry to hear you make such a statement," replied Confucius' disciple, "What you would say is true; but, stated in that

6. 子张问明。子曰:"浸润之谮,肤受之愬,不行焉。可谓明也已矣。浸润之谮肤受之愬不行焉,可谓远也已矣。"

孔子的一个学生问什么才算是明达。

孔子回答说:"一个能够抵抗住别人长期使他形成偏见的企图的人,或者一个不会被突如其来的危及其自身安全的事情所左右的人——这样一个人可以被视为明达之人。实际上,能够抵抗住这样的影响,或者这样的吸引的人,一定是一个真正优秀的人。"

7. 子贡问政。子曰:"足食。足兵。民信之矣。"子贡曰:"必不得已而去,于斯三者何先?"曰:"去兵。"子贡曰:"必不得已而去,于斯二者何先?"曰:"去食。自古皆有死,民无信不立。"

有一次,一位学生问对于一个国家的治理来说,什么是必需的。

孔子回答说:"必须要有充足的食物给人民;一支有力的军队;以及人民对他们的统治者的信任。"

"但是,"那位学生接着问,"如果要被迫摈弃这三件事中的一件,其中哪一件可以首先去除?"

"摈弃军队。"孔子回答说。

"但是仍然,"那位学生继续问,"如果要被迫摈弃剩下的两件事中的一件,其中哪一件可以先去除?"

"摈弃食物,"孔子回答说,"因为,自古以来人都要死,但没有人民对他们的统治者的信任,就不可能有治理。"

8. 棘子成曰:"君子质而已矣,何以文为?"子贡曰:"惜乎! 夫子之说,君子也。驷不及舌。文犹质也,质犹文也。虎豹之鞟犹犬羊之鞟。"

有一次,某国的一位官员对孔子的一位学生说:"一个明智而良善的人只是想要本质,为什么他应该为形式而费心呢?"

way, it is impossible for men not to misunderstand your meaning. To be sure, the style comes out of the substance, but the substance also comes out of the style. For the substance in the skin of a tiger or a leopard is the same as the substance in the skin of a dog or a sheep."

9. The reigning prince of Confucius' native State on one occasion asked one of Confucius' disciple, saying: "The year now is one of scarcity: we cannot make the revenue meet the public expenditure. What should be done?"

The disciple answered, "Why not tithe (take one-tenth) the people?" "Why," replied the prince, "with two-thirds, even, we cannot make ends meet: how should we be able to do so with one-tenth?" To which the disciple answered, "When the people have plenty, the prince will not want. But if the people want, the prince will not have plenty."

10. A disciple of Confucius enquired how to raise the moral sentiment and to dispel delusions in life.

Confucius answered, "Make conscientiousness and sincerity your first principles. Act up to what is right. In that way you will raise the moral sentiment in you.

"You wish to live and hate to die. But while clinging to life, you yet hanker after those things which can only shorten life: that is a great delusion in life.

Truly your wealth and pelf avail you nought.

To have what others want, is all you sought."

"很抱歉听到你这样说，"孔子的学生说，"你这拿不准的看法是对的；但是，用这种方式来说，不可能不被人误解你的意思。无疑，形式产生于本质，但本质也产生于形式。因为老虎或豹子的皮毛所包含的本质与狗或羊的皮毛所包含的本质就是一样的。"

9. 哀公问于有若曰："年饥，用不足，如之何？"有若对曰："盍彻乎？"曰："二，吾犹不足，如之何其彻也？"对曰："百姓足，君孰与不足？百姓不足，君孰与足？"

有一次，孔子故国的执政国君问孔子的一位学生，说："今年是个萧条的年份：我们无法让财政收入满足公共支出。应该怎么做呢？"

那位学生回答："为什么不让人民缴纳什一税（收十分之一）呢？""为什么这么说，"那位国君说，"即使是收取三分之二，我们也无法让结果满足：我们怎能这样收十分之一呢？"那位学生对此说："当人民充足的时候，国君就不会匮乏。但如果人民匮乏，那么国君也将不会充足。"

10. 子张问崇德、辨惑。子曰："主忠信，徙义，崇德也。爱之欲其生，恶之欲其死。既欲其生，又欲其死，是惑也。'诚不以富，亦只以异。'"

孔子的一位学生问如何在生活中激发道德情感并消除困惑。

孔子回答说："把遵循良心做事与真诚作为你的第一原则。根据正义原则行事。这样，你就会激发你的道德情感。

"你愿活着而不愿死去。但当你留恋生命时，却又渴望那些只会缩短生命的东西：这在生活中是个巨大的困惑。'财富与金钱真的对你徒然无益，/拥有别人所匮乏的，正是你的全部动机。'"

11. The reigning prince of a certain State asked Confucius what was essential in the government of a country.

Confucius answered, "Let the prince *be* a prince, and the public servant *be* a public servant. Let the father *be* a father, and let the son *be* a son."

"It is very true," replied the prince, "Indeed, if the prince *is* not a prince, and the public servant *is* not a public servant, and if the father *is* not a father and the son *is* not a son, — in such a state of things, even though I had my revenue, how should I enjoy it?"

12. Confucius, speaking of his disciple, the intrepid Chung Yu, remarked:

"One who can settle a dispute with half a sentence — that is Yu."(Chung Yu's name)

It was also remarked of the same disciple that he never slept a night over a promise.

13. Confucius on one occasion after he had been appointed Chief Justice in his native State, remarked: "While sitting in court, in deciding upon the suits that come before me, I am no better than other men. But what I always try to do is to make even the suits unnecessary."

14. A disciple of Confucius enquired what was the essential thing in the conduct of the government of a country.

Confucius answered, "Be patient in maturing your plans and then carry them out with conscientiousness."

11. 齐景公问政于孔子。孔子对曰："君君，臣臣，父父，子子。"公
曰："善哉！信如君不君，臣不臣，父不父，子不子，虽有粟，吾得
而食诸？"

    某国的执政国君问孔子，在一国治理中什么是必需的。

    孔子回答说："让国君像个国君，公务人员像个公务人员。让父亲
像个父亲，让儿子像个儿子。"

    "非常对啊，"那位国君回答，"的确，如果国君不像个国君，而公务
人员不像个公务人员，父亲不像个父亲，儿子不像个儿子——在这样的
状态下，尽管我拥有财政收入，我还能够享用它吗？"

12. 子曰："片言可以折狱者，其由也与？"子路无宿诺。

    谈到他的学生，那位刚勇的仲由，孔子说："一个人能够用半句话就
解决一场争执——那就是由（仲由的名字）。"

    这句话也是对这位学生从来不留着诺言过夜的评论。

13. 子曰："听讼，吾犹人也，必也使无讼乎！"

    有一次，在被任命为其故国的首席法官之后，孔子说："当我坐在法
庭上，对提交给我的诉讼做出裁决时，我并不比别人做得更好。但我一
直试着去做的，就是让诉讼变得多余。"

14. 子张问政。子曰："居之无倦，行之以忠。"

    孔子的一位学生问在一个国家的政治治理中，什么是必需的事情。

    孔子回答说："要耐心地慎重思考你的计划，然后按照良心实施
它们。"

15. Confucius remarked: "A man who studies extensively the arts and literature, and directs his studies with judgment and taste, is not likely to get into a wrong track."

16. Confucius remarked, "A good and wise man encourages men to develop the good qualities in their nature, and not their bad qualities; whereas, a bad man and a fool does the very opposite."

17. A noble who was the minister in power in Confucius' native State asked him to define government.

    "Government means order, " answered Confucius, " If you yourself, sir, are in order, who will dare to be disorderly?"

18. The noble mentioned above was distressed at the frequency of robberies in the country, He asked Confucius what should be done.

    "If you yourself," answered Confucius, "show them that you do not wish for wealth, although you should reward them for stealing, the people would not steal."

19. The same noble again asked about government , saying, "What do you say to putting to death the wicked in the interests of the good? "

    "In your government," answered Confucius, "why should you think it necessary to depend upon capital punishments? Wish for honesty, and the people will be honest. The moral power of the rulers is as the wind, and that of the people is as the grass. Whithersoever the wind blows, the grass is sure to bend. "

15. 子曰:"博学于文,约之以礼,亦可以弗畔矣夫!"

　　孔子说:"一个广博地研究艺术与文学,并用判断力和审美力来指导他的研究的聪明人,不太可能走上错误的方向。"

16. 子曰:"君子成人之美,不成人之恶。小人反是。"

　　孔子说:"良善而明智的人鼓励人们去发展他们本性中好的品质,而不是坏的品质;然而,恶劣的人和愚蠢的人却完全相反。"

17. 季康子问政于孔子。孔子对曰:"政者,正也。子帅以正,孰敢不正?"

　　一个在孔子的故国做当权大臣的贵族,让孔子界定政治。

　　"政治意味着秩序,"孔子回答,"如果你自身,先生,处于秩序中,那么,谁敢混乱无序呢?"

18. 季康子患盗,问于孔子。孔子对曰:"苟子之不欲,虽赏之不窃。"

　　上面提到的那位贵族因国内盗窃事件的频繁发生而烦恼,他问孔子应该怎么办。

　　"如果你自身,"孔子回答说,"展示给他们你并不渴望财富,即使你奖赏他们去偷窃,人民也不会去偷的。"

19. 季康子问政于孔子曰:"如杀无道,以就有道,何如?"孔子对曰:"子为政,焉用杀? 子欲善,而民善矣。君之子德风,小人之德草。草上之风,必偃。"

　　同一位贵族再次询问政治,说:"为了好人的利益而把恶人处死,你认为怎么样?"

　　"在你的治理中,"孔子回答说,"为什么要认为必须依靠死刑呢?你向往正直,人民就会变得正直。统治者的道德力量就像是风,而人民的道德就像是草,无论风吹到何处,草必然会弯下。"

20. A disciple of Confucius enquired, "What must an educated gentleman do in order to be distinguished?"

"What do you mean by being distinguished? "asked Confucius.

"I mean," replied the disciple, "that whether in public life or in private life he will be heard of by the world. "

"That," answered Confucius, "is to be notorious, not distinguished.

"Now a man who is really a man of distinction is one who stands upon his own integrity and loves what is right: who forms a correct judgment of men by observing how they look as well as by regarding what they say. Reflection makes him humble in his estimate of himself as compared with other men. Such a man, whether he be in public life or in private life, will be a distinguished man.

"As to the notorious man: he is one who wants to be moral in his look and outward appearance, but really is not so in his life. He prides himself on such an appearance without misgiving. Such a man in public life or in private life, will also certainly be heard of and known."

21. A disciple of Confucius on one occasion was in Confucius' company when he went out for a walk on a terrace built for a religious purpose. The disciple then took the occasion to ask him what one should do in order to elevate the moral sentiment; to discover the secret vices and failings in one's inmost mind; and, lastly, to dispel the delusions of life.

"That is a very good question indeed," answered Confucius.

"Make it a rule," he then said, "to *work* for it before you accept anything as your own: that is, perhaps, the best way to elevate the

20. 子张问："士何如斯可谓之达矣?"子曰："何哉,尔所谓达者?"子张对曰："在邦必闻,在家必闻。"子曰："是闻也,非达也。夫达也者,质直而好义,察言而观色,虑以下人。在邦必达,在家必达。夫闻也者,色取仁而行违,居之不疑。在邦必闻,在家必闻。"

孔子的一位学生问:"为了变得杰出,一位有教养的君子必须怎么做?"

"你说的杰出指的是什么?"孔子问。

"我是指,"那位学生回答说,"无论是在公共生活中,还是在私人生活中,他将被世界知晓。"

"这个,"孔子回答说,"是出名,不是杰出。

"一个真正杰出的人,是个坚持他自己的正直,并且热爱正义的事情;通过观察人们如何表现并倾听他们说什么,来形成对人们的正确评价的人。深思让他在评价自己时比评价别人更谦逊。这样一个人,无论是在公共生活还是在私人生活中,将是一个杰出的人。

"至于出名的人:他是个只想看上去有道德,但实际在生活中并不如此的人。他得意于这样的表现而没有疑虑。这样的人,在公共生活或私人生活中,当然也会被知晓并且闻名。"

21. 樊迟从游于舞雩之下,曰:"敢问崇德、修慝、辨惑。"子曰:"善哉问! 先事后得,非崇德与? 攻其恶,无攻人之恶,非修慝与? 一朝之忿,忘其身,以及其亲,非惑与?"

有一次,孔子在一座为宗教而修建的露台上散步时,他的一位学生陪着他。那位学生抓住机会问他,一个人要提升道德情感,要发现思想最深处的隐秘的弱点与缺陷,以及消除生活中的困惑,应该怎么做。

"这的确是个很好的问题,"孔子回答说。

"要制定这样的常规,"他接着说,"任何事情在你并未有任何收获之前,就要尽力去做:或许,这就是提升道德情感的最好方式。

moral sentiment.

"Make it a habit to assail your own vices and failings before you assail the vices and failings of others: that is , perhaps, the best way to discover the secret vices of your inmost mind.

"If a man allows himself to lose his temper and forget himself of a morning, in such a way as to become careless for the safety of his own person and for the safety of his parents and friends — is that not a case of a great delusion in life?"

22. The same disciple mentioned above asked, "What does a moral life consist in?"

"The moral life of a man," answered Confucius, "consists in loving men."

The disciple then asked, "What does understanding consist in? "

"Understanding," answered Confucius, "consists in understanding men."

The disciple, however, did not seem to comprehend the meaning of what was said. Thereupon Confucius went on to say, "Uphold the cause of the just, and put down every cause that is unjust in such a way that the unjust will be made just."

When the disciple left, he met on the way another disciple, and said to him: "Just a little while ago I saw the Master, and enquired of him what understanding consisted in, and he answered, 'Uphold the cause of the just, and put down every cause that is unjust in such a way that the unjust will be made just.' What did he mean by that? "

"It is a saying," replied the other disciple, "very wide indeed in its application. When the ancient Emperor Shun came to the

"要养成这样的习惯,在批评其他人的弱点与缺陷之前,先批评自己的弱点与缺陷:或许,这就是发现你思想最深处的隐秘的弱点与缺陷的最好方式。

"如果一个人在早上发脾气、忘掉自己,并用这样的方式去变得对自身的安全以及他父母和朋友的安全漠不关心——这难道不是生活中巨大困惑的一个例子吗?"

22. 樊迟问仁。子曰:"爱人。"问知。子曰:"知人。"樊迟未达。子曰:"举直错诸枉,能使枉者直。"樊迟退,见子夏。曰:"乡也吾见于夫子而问知。子曰:'举直错诸枉,能使枉者直',何谓也?"子夏曰:"富哉言乎!舜有天下,选于众,举皋陶,不仁者远矣。汤有天下,选于众,举伊尹,不仁者远矣。"

上面提到的同一位学生问:"道德生活指的是什么?"

"一个人的道德生活,"孔子回答,"在于爱人。"

那位学生接着问:"聪明指的是什么?"

"聪明,"孔子回答,"在于理解人。"

然而,那位学生好像没有明白这句话的意思。于是,孔子继续说:"坚持正义的主张,而抑制每种不义的主张,这样,不义的将变成正义的。"

当这位学生离开时,在路上遇到另一个学生,对他说:"就在刚才,我看望老师并询问他理解力指的是什么,他回答说:'坚持正义的主张,而抑制每种不义的主张,这样,不义的将变成正义的',他这样说是什么意思?"

"这是一句,"那另外的学生回答说,"寓意确实非常广博的话啊。当古代帝王舜开始统治帝国时,他从人民中选拔,并晋升皋陶为法务大

government of the Empire and, selecting from among the people, advanced Kao Yao to be Minister of Justice: from that moment all immoral people disappeared. When the ancient Emperor the great T'ang came to the government of the Empire and, choosing from among the people, advanced I-yin to be Prime Minister: from that moment, all immoral men disappeared."

23. A disciple of Confucius enquired how one should behave to a friend.

Confucius answered, "Be conscientious in what you say to him! Lead him on gently to what you would have him be; if you find you cannot do that, stop. Do not quarrel with him only to get insulted."

24. A disciple of Confucius remarked, "A wise man makes friends by his taste for art and literature. He uses his friends to help him to live a moral life."

臣：从那时起,所有不道德的人都消失不见了。当古代帝王,那位伟大的汤,开始统治帝国时,从人民中选拔,并晋升伊尹为首要大臣：从那时起,所有不道德的人都消失不见了。"

23. 子贡问友。子曰："忠告而善道之,不可则止,无自辱焉。"

孔子的一位学生问一个人应该如何一位对待朋友。

孔子回答说："对他说话要凭良心！和善地引导他成为你希望他所是的样子。如果你发现你做不到这个,就停下来。不要和他争吵,那样只会让自己受到侮辱。"

24. 曾子曰："君子以文会友,以友辅仁。"

孔子的一位学生说："一个明智的人,会根据他对艺术与文学的品位来结交朋友。他会让他的朋友来帮助他过一种道德的生活。"

【评述】

1. 文中,"克己复礼为仁",辜鸿铭译为 "renounce yourself and conform to the ideal of decency and good sense","舍弃自我并遵从高尚文雅与良好感知的理想"。其中,"克"指舍弃;"己"指"自我";"复"指"遵从";"礼"指"高尚文雅与良好感知的理想"。意思是,应该舍弃自我的固有局限,追求一种美好的道德理想:高尚文雅、良好感知。对此,辜鸿铭注释说:

> 达朗伯认为,如果古代的斯多各派狄奥根尼仅仅拥有"高尚文雅的礼节",他将是欧洲古代最伟大的人。
>
> 第一点是歌德所说的"自我牺牲"(Entsagen):"什么时候你还不解/这'死与变'的道理,/你就只是个忧郁的过客,/在这黑暗的尘世。"([回译者注]汉译诗句采自《外国文学经典:歌德抒情诗选萃》,杨武能译,四川人民出版社,2009)
>
> 第二点是礼的必需的原则——就其自身来说,就像歌德所说的,是希腊人与意大利人的宗教。

2. 文中,"出门如见大宾",辜鸿铭译为 "when going out into the world, behave always as if you were at an audience before the Emperor","外出进入社会后,要常表现得像在觐见帝王",存有觐见帝王一样的敬意与谨慎。"使民如承大祭",译为 "in dealing with the people, act as if you were at worship before God","在治理人民时,就像在崇拜上帝",即把人民当作上帝那样敬畏、崇拜、热爱。"己所不欲,勿施于人",译为 "whatsoever things you do not wish that others should do unto you, do not do unto them","任何事情你不希望别人对你做的,也不要对他们做"。"在邦无怨,在家无怨"一句,"在邦",译为 "in your public life in the State","在国家的公务生活中";"在家",译为 "in your private life in your family","在家庭的私人生活中",这句即指生活、工作两个方面;"无怨",译为 "give no one a just cause of complain against you","不要给人哪怕仅仅是对你不满的理由",即无论在工作上,还是在私人生活上,都不要引起别人对你的不满。

3. 文中,"仁者其言也切"一句,辜鸿铭译为 "a man of moral character is one who is sparing of his words","一个有道德品质的人是个爱惜言辞的人"。"切"解释为"爱惜言辞",即不多说话,更不作妄语。"为之难,言之得无切乎",辜鸿铭译为 "when a man feels the difficulty of living a moral life, would he be otherwise than sparing of his words","当一个人感到过一种道德生活的困难,他怎么会不爱惜言辞呢",指有过道德生活的追求,就会让自己变得谨慎,因而就会爱惜言辞。

4. 文中,"不忧不惧",辜鸿铭译为"is without anxiety and without fear","没有忧虑与恐惧",指心中没有忧愁、过多的思虑和恐惧等负面情绪;"内省不疚",译为"a man finds within himself no cause for self-reproach","发现自己内心中没有自我谴责的理由",即问心无愧之意。孔子认为,这两点是君子(a good and wise man)的内心特质。

5. 文中"死生有命,富贵在天"一句,"死生有命"辜鸿铭译为"Life and Death are pre-ordained","生与死是先定的";"富贵在天"译为"riches and honours come from God","富有与荣耀来自上帝"。"天"辜鸿铭一贯译为"上帝",他对"天"即"上帝"的具体解释见第二章第4节评述(本书第39页)

。"富贵"的"贵",辜鸿铭一贯译为"荣耀",见第四章第5节。"君子敬而无失,与人恭而有礼"一句中,"敬而无失",译为"is serious and without blame","严肃庄重而不受指责"。"敬",即保持自己内心的严肃与庄重;"失"指受到指责。这句话是说,君子要尽量保持自身行为的完美无缺,不被人指责。"与人恭而有礼"译为"in his conduct towards others he behaves with earnestness, and with judgment and good sense","在他对待别人的言行中,他表现得诚挚、有判断力而且合乎情理"。"恭"即真诚、诚挚之意;"有礼"即有判断力、合乎情理。这句话指君子在对待别人时是真诚的,而且是有理性的,有判断力的。"四海之内,皆兄弟也。君子何患乎无兄弟也?"一句,传统学者多指这是孔子"大道之行,不独亲其亲,不独子其子"的思想,也即宋代张横渠所说的"民吾同胞",指"天下一家"的理想状态。辜鸿铭的翻译是:"四海之内"译为"within the corners of the Earth","世界的每个角落之中",指整个世界上的人。这句话说,司马牛叹息的是自己家中没有亲兄弟,而子夏强调的则是整个世界的人都可以成为兄弟。

6. 文中,"明",辜鸿铭译为"perspicuity","明白颖悟,明达,通达"。"浸润之谮,肤受之愬,不行焉。可谓明也已矣"一句中,"浸润之谮",译为"long-continued attempts of others to insinuate prejudice into him","别人长期使他形成偏见的企图",指试图使他形成偏见;"肤受之愬"译为"a sudden appeal to his own personal safety","危及其自身安全的突发事情";"不行"分别译为"can resist"与"cannot be influenced",前者指在别人影响自己时,能够不形成偏见;后者指的是在面临突如其来的危险时,自己的冷静和判断力能够不受到影响。"可谓远也已矣",辜鸿铭译为"Indeed, a man who can resist such an influence, or such an appeal, must be a really superior man",意思是,如果他真能做到这样,他不止是个明达之人,也必定是个真正优秀的人。

7. 文中,"问政",辜鸿铭译为"enquired what was essential in the government of a country",即子贡问的是国家治理必须具备的条件。下面的文字是孔子的阐述。

8. 辜鸿铭认为，本节讨论的是形式与本质的关系。"君子质而已矣，何以文为？"译为 "A wise and good man wants only the substance; why should he trouble about the style？" "一个明智而良善的人只是想要本质，为什么他应该为形式而费心呢？"其中，"质"是"本质"，"文"是"形式"。"驷不及舌"，传统学者多认为这句话说的是棘子成的失言，辜鸿铭译为"what you would say is true; but, stated in that way, it is impossible for men not to misunderstand your meaning"，"你这拿不准的看法是对的；但是，用这种方式来说，不可能不被人误解你的意思"。即很容易被人误解成根本不需要外在形式。"文犹质也，质犹文也"一句，辜鸿铭译为 "the style comes out of the substance, but the substance comes out of the style"，"形式产生于本质，而本质也产生于形式"，指事物的"形式"与"本质"，是可以相互影响，相互生发的。"虎豹之鞟犹犬羊之鞟"，译为 "the substance in the skin of a tiger or a leopard is the same as the substance in the skin of a dog or a sheep"，"老虎或豹子的皮毛所包含的本质与狗或羊的皮毛所包含的本质是一样的"，指如果忽略了形式，那么本质相同的"虎豹之鞟"与"犬羊之鞟"，该如何区别呢？最后，辜鸿铭在注释中引用了爱默生的话，表达形式的重要性：

> 谈到文学上的风格，华兹华斯说："无疑，这是形式，但是，你知道，内容往往产生于形式。"（爱默生，《英国人的特性》）

9. 文中，哀公问"年饥，用不足"，辜鸿铭译为 "the year now is one of scarcity: we cannot make the revenue meet the public expenditure"，"今年是个萧条的年份：我们无法让财政收入满足公共支出"。"彻"，译为"tithe（take one-tenth）the people"，"让人民缴纳什一税（收十分之一）"。"二"，译为"with two-thirds"，"交三分之二的税"，指人民拿出三分之二的收入来交税。收十分之一税，是有若给出的建议。"百姓足，君孰与不足？百姓不足，君孰与足？"一句，辜鸿铭译为 "when the people have plenty, the prince will not want. But if the people want, the prince will not have plenty"，"当人民充足的时候，国君就不会匮乏。但如果人民匮乏，那么国君也将不会充足"。

10. 文中，"主忠信"，辜鸿铭译为 "make conscientiousness and sincerity your first principles"，"把遵循良心做事与真诚作为你的第一原则"。把"忠"译为良心，以及"信"译为真诚，是辜鸿铭通常采用的译法。最后一句"诚不以富，亦只以异"出自《诗经·小雅·我行其野》，辜鸿铭最后注释说：

> 一位中国的注释家认为，这些诗句应该被用到第十六章第12节。

11. 文中，"政"，辜鸿铭译为"what was essential in the government of a country"，"一国治理中必需的东西"，即为政的必要条件。"君君，臣臣，父父，子子"，辜鸿铭译为："let the prince be a prince, and the public servant be a public servant.Let the father be a father, and let the son be a son"，"让国君像个国君，公务人员像个公务人员。让父亲像个父亲，让儿子像个儿子"，即每个人都按照自己的身份行事，承担相应的义务。孔子认为，这是治理国家所必需的。

12. 文中，"片言可以折狱"，辜鸿铭译为"settle a dispute with half a sentence"，"能够用半句话就解决一场争执"；"无宿诺"，辜鸿铭译为"he never slept a night over a promise"，"从来不留着诺言过夜"，"宿"，即"过夜"之意，指孔子赞扬子路的"信誉"。

13. 文中"听讼，吾犹人也"一句，"听讼"，辜鸿铭译为"sitting in court, in deciding upon the suits that come before me"，"坐在法庭上，对提交给我的诉讼做出裁决"；"犹人"，译为"no better than other men"，"不比别人做得更好"。"必也使无讼乎"一句，"必也"译为"what I always try to do"，"我一直试着去做的"，指孔子真正努力去做的事；"使无讼"译为"make even the suits unnecessary"，"让诉讼变得多余"，即不再有诉讼。在《文明与无政府状态或远东问题的道德困境》中，辜鸿铭表达了对理想文明状态的畅想，或许可以视作孔子"必也使无讼乎"的理想状态："在新的文明中，受过教育的人的自由并不意味着随心所欲，而是自由地干公正的事情。……处于新的文明中的自由人是这样一种人，对他来说，皮鞭、警察或炼狱再也没有必要。他之所以公正行事，是因为他喜欢这么做；他之所以不去作恶，并不是由于自感卑下或胆怯，而是由于他讨厌作恶。在人格修养方面，他并不是服从外在的权威，而是服从内在的理性与良心。"（汪堂家编译，《乱世奇文·尊王篇》，第134页）

14. 文中，"政"，辜鸿铭译为"the essential thing in the conduct of the government of a country"，"一个国家的政治管理中必需的事情"。"居之无倦，行之以忠"，译为"be patient in maturing your plans and then carry them out with conscientiousness"，"耐心地慎重思考你的计划，然后按照良心实施它们"。其中，"居"，辜鸿铭理解为"思考计划"；"行"理解为"实施计划"；"无倦"理解为"耐心、慎重"；"以忠"理解为"按照良心"。

15. 辜鸿铭注释说：

第六章第5节的重复。

这里有误，应为第六章第25节。

16. 文中，"成人之美，不成人之恶"一句，辜鸿铭译为"encourages men to develop the good qualities in their nature, and not their bad qualities"，"鼓励人们去发展他们本性中好的品质，而不是坏的品质"。"成"即"鼓励发展"的意思；"美"即本性中好的品质；"恶"即不好的品质。此处，辜鸿铭把"小人"译为"a bad man and a fool"，"恶劣的人和愚蠢的人"。

17. 文中，"问政"，辜鸿铭译为"asked him to define government"，即问孔子"政治"的定义；"正"是孔子对"政"的解释，"政者，正也"译为"government means order"，"政治意味着秩序"，"正"即"秩序"之意。

18. 文中，"患盗"，辜鸿铭译为"was distressed at the frequency of robberies in the country"，"因国内盗窃事件的频繁发生而烦恼"。"苟子之不欲，虽赏之不窃"一句，辜鸿铭的翻译是："子之不欲"译为"you yourself show them that you do not wish for wealth"，"你展示给他们你自己并不渴望财富"，"欲"指的是对财富的贪欲，指你自己本身并不贪婪；"虽赏之不窃"译为"although you should reward them for stealing, the people would not steal"，"即使你奖赏他们去偷窃，人民也不会去偷的"，指作为管理者，治下的问题往往出自自身。

19. 文中，"杀无道，以就有道"一句，辜鸿铭译为"put to death the wicked in the interests of the good"，"为了好人的利益而把恶人处死"，"无道"指的是恶人；"有道"指的是"好人"；"就"指的是维护某人的利益。"子为政，焉用杀？"译为"in your government why should you think it necessary to depend upon capital punishments?"，"在你的治理中，为什么要认为必须依靠死刑呢？"孔子对季康子的统治思维提出质疑。"子欲善而民善矣"，译为"wish for honesty, and the people will be honest"，"你向往正直，人民就会变得正直"，指统治者要以身作则。"君之子德风，小人之德草，草上之风，必偃"，译为"the moral power of the rulers is as the wind, and that of the people is as the grass.Whithersoever the wind blows, the grass is sure to bend"，"统治者的道德力量就像是风，而人民的就像是草，无论风吹到何处，草必然会弯下"，指统治者的道德力量对人民的道德状况具有决定性的影响作用。

20. 文中，"达"，辜鸿铭译为"distinguished"，"卓著的，卓越的，杰出的"。子张问的是怎样才能做到真正的杰出。"在邦必闻，在家必闻"是子张对"达"即"杰出"的理解。辜鸿铭译为"whether in public life or in private life he will be heard of by the world"，"无论是在公共生活中，还是在私人生活中，他将被世界知晓"。"是闻也，非达也"，辜鸿铭译为"that is to be notorious, not distinguished"，"这是出名，不是杰出"。孔子认为，子张混淆了"出名"和"杰出"的区别。下面，就是孔子的具体论述。

21. "崇德、修慝、辨惑"一句，"崇德"辜鸿铭译为"to elevate the moral sentiment"，"提升道德情感"。提升或激发道德情感，是辜鸿铭对"崇德"的比较常见的翻译，如对第十二章第10节"崇德"的翻译。"修慝"，译为"to discover the secret vices and failings in one's inmost mind"，"发现思想最深处的隐秘的弱点与缺陷"，指人应对本性深处的一些弱点与缺陷有所察觉。"辨惑"译为"to dispel the delusions of life"，"消除生活中的困惑"。樊迟问的即一个人如何才能做到以上三种行为。下面的文字是孔子的具体阐述。

22. 文中，"爱人"，辜鸿铭译为"loving men"，"热爱人们"；"仁"即指博爱。辜鸿铭进一步注释说：

中国字"仁"，我们一直翻译为"道德生活或道德品质"，字面意思是"博爱"。

"知"，译为"understanding"，"理解力、领悟力、聪明"；"知人"，译为"understand men"，"理解别人"。"举直错诸枉，能使枉者直"，辜鸿铭译为"uphold the cause of the just, and put down every cause that is unjust in such a way that the unjust will be made just"，"坚持正义的主张，而抑制每种不义的主张，这样，不义的将变成正义的"。"富哉言乎"，辜鸿铭译为"It is a saying very wide indeed in its application"，"这是一句寓意确实非常广博的话"，指子夏称赞孔子的话。下面的文字是子夏对孔子的话的理解与阐发。

23. 文中，"友"，辜鸿铭译为"how one should behave to a friend"，指"一个人应该如何一位对待朋友"。这一节，孔子讲的是朋友的相处之道。

24. 文中，"以文会友"，辜鸿铭译为"makes friends by his taste for art and literature"，"根据他对艺术与文学的品位来结交朋友"，即只结交在文化修养、艺术品位上与自己契合的人做朋友；"以友辅仁"，译为"he uses his friends to help him to live a moral life"，"让他的朋友来帮助他过一种道德的生活"。这一节指交友要能提高自身的品行修养。

271

CHAPTER XIII
子路第十三

1. A disciple of Confucius enquired how to conduct the government of a country.

Confucius answered, "Go before the people with your example; show them your exertion." The disciple asked for something more. "Be indefatigable in that," replied Confucius.

2. Another disciple, who was in the service of a powerful noble in Confucius' native State, enquired how to conduct the government of the country.

Confucius answered, "Leave the initiative in the details of government to the responsible heads of the departments.Overlook small short-comings; and advance men of ability and worth."

"But," answered the disciple, "how am I to know who are men of ability and worth?"

"Advance those," replied Confucius, "whom you already know: there is then no fear that those whom you do not know will be neglected."

3. A disciple, the intrepid Chung Yu, said to Confucius on one occasion when the reigning prince of a certain State was negotiating for Confucius to enter his service: "The prince is waiting, sir, to entrust the government of the country to you. Now what do you consider the first thing to be done?"

"If I must begin," answered Confucius, "I would begin by defining the names of things."

"Oh! Really," replied the disciple, — "but you are too impractical. What has definition of names to do here?"

"Sir," replied Confucius, "you have really no manners. A gentleman,

1. 子路问政。子曰："先之，劳之。"请益。曰："无倦。"

    孔子的一个学生问如何治理国家。

    孔子回答说："做好你的榜样领先人民；向他们展示你的努力。"那位学生问还应做什么。"其间要坚持不懈，"孔子回答。

2. 仲弓为季氏宰，问政。子曰："先有司，赦小过，举贤才。"曰："焉知贤才而举之？"曰："举尔所知。尔所不知，人其舍诸？"

    另一个学生为孔子故国的一个有权势的贵族服务，询问如何去治理一个国家的政治。

    孔子回答："把政治上细节问题的决断权留给相应部门的负责人。原谅小的缺点，并提拔有能力与美德的人。"

    "但是，"那位学生回答，"我怎么知道谁是有能力与美德的人呢？"

    "提拔那些，"孔子回答，"你已经知道的。不要担心那些你不知道的会被忽视掉。"

3. 子路曰："卫君待子而为政，子将奚先？"子曰："必也正名乎！"子路曰："有是哉，子之迂也！奚其正？"子曰："野哉由也！君子于其所不知，盖阙如也。名不正，则言不顺；言不顺，则事不成；事不成，则礼乐不兴；礼乐不兴，则刑罚不中；刑罚不中，则民无所措手足。故君子名之必可言也，言之必可行也。君子于其言，无所苟而已矣。"

    一位学生，那位刚勇的仲由，当有一次某国的执政国君要协商让孔子进入他的政府任职时，对孔子说："先生，那位国君正在等着把这个国家的政治交托给您。那么，您认为最先需要做的事情是什么？"

    "如果我必须要开始去做，"孔子回答，"我就要从确定事物的名称

when he hears anything he does not understand, will always wait for an explanation.

"Now, if names of things are not properly defined, *words* will not correspond to *facts*. When words do not correspond to facts, it is impossible to perfect anything. Where it is impossible to perfect anything, the arts and institutions of civilisation cannot flourish. When the arts and institutions of civilisation cannot flourish, law and justice cannot attain their ends; and when law and justice do not attain their ends, the people will be at a loss to know what to do.

"Therefore a wise and good man can always specify whatever he names; whatever he can specify, he can carry out. A wise and good man makes it a point always to be exact in the words he uses."

4. A disciple of Confucius requested to be taught farming. Confucius answered, "For that I am not as good as an old farmer."

The disciple then asked to be taught gardening. "For that," replied Confucius, "I am not as good as an old gardener."

After the disciple had left, Confucius remarked, "What a petty-minded man he is!"

"When the rulers of a country," he then went on to say, "encourage education and good manners the people will never fail in respect! When the rulers encourage the love of justice, the people will never fail in obedience; when the rulers encourage good faith, the people will never fail in honesty. In such case, people from all quarters will flock to that country: — what need then has a ruler to know about husbandry?"

开始。"

"噢！真的，"那位学生回答"但是您太不切实际了。要确定名称干什么呢？"

"先生，"孔子回答说，"你真的没有礼貌啊。一个绅士当他听到任何不明白的事情时，都会等着解释。

"如果事物的名称没有被恰当地确定，那么言语就会与事实不符。当言语与事实不符时，要完善任何事情是不可能的。当完善任何事情都不可能，那么艺术与文明的制度就无法繁荣。当艺术与文明的制度无法繁荣，法律与司法就无法达到它们的目的；而法律与司法无法达到它们的目的，人民就会茫然而不知道应做些什么。

"因此，一个明智而良善的人，总是能够详细地说明任何他命名的事情；任何他能详细说明的事情，他就能够实行。一个明智而良善的人总是会特别注意准确用语。"

4. 樊迟请学稼，子曰："吾不如老农。"请学为圃。曰："吾不如老圃。"樊迟出。子曰："小人哉，樊须也！上好礼，则民莫敢不敬；上好义，则民莫敢不服；上好信，则民莫敢不用情。夫如是，则四方之民襁负其子而至矣，焉用稼？"

孔子的一个学生请求教给他耕作。孔子回答说："就此而言，我比不上老练的农夫。"

那位学生然后要求教给他园艺。"就此而言，"孔子回答说，"我比不上老练的园丁。"

那位学生离开之后，孔子回答说："他是一个多么器量狭小的人啊！"

"当一个国家的统治者，"他继续说，"鼓励教育与良好的礼仪，人民就不会不尊敬！当统治者鼓励对正义的热爱，人民就不会不服从；当统治者鼓励好的信义，人民就不会不诚实。这种情况下，来自四面八方的人民就会拥入这个国家——那么，一个统治者有什么必要了解农事呢？"

5. Confucius remarked, "A man who can recite three hundred pieces of poetry by heart, but who, when the conduct of the affairs of a nation is entrusted to him, can do nothing, and who, when sent on a public mission to a foreign country, has nothing to say for himself, — although such a man has much learning, of what use is it? "

6. Confucius remarked, "If a man is in order in his personal conduct, he will get served even without taking the trouble to give orders. But if a man is not in order in his personal conduct, he may give orders, but his orders will not be obeyed. "

7. Confucius remarked of the state of government of his own State and that of another State in his time: "The one is about the same as the other."

8. Confucius remarked of a public character of the time that he was admirable in the way in which he ordered the economy of his home. Confucius said: "When he had saved something from his income, he would remark, 'I have just made ends meet.' Later on, when he had increased his saving, he would remark, 'I have just managed to pay for all I require.' Finally, when he had saved a large surplus, he would remark, 'Now I can just manage to get along pretty well.' "

9. When Confucius on his travels was on one occasion entering a certain State in company with a disciple who was driving the carriage for him, he remarked, "What a large population is here!"

    "With such a large population," asked the disciple, "what should

5. 子曰:"诵《诗》三百,授之以政,不达;使于四方,不能专对;虽多,亦奚以为?"

　　孔子说:"一个人能够背诵三百首诗,但当国家事务交托给他处理时,不能做任何事情;当身负公务使命派往外国时,无法为自己辩护——尽管这样一个人拥有大量的学问,可这有什么用呢?"

6. 子曰:"其身正,不令而行;其身不正,虽令不从。"

　　孔子说:"如果一个人的自身言行是合乎秩序的,即使不用费力地下达命令,也会达到效果。但如果一个人的自身言行并不合乎秩序,他可以下达命令,但他的命令将不会被服从。"

7. 子曰:"鲁卫之政,兄弟也。"

　　孔子谈到他的国家与同时代另一个国家的政治状态说:"一个与另一个大致相同。"

8. 子谓卫公子荆,"善居室。始有,曰:'苟合矣。'少有,曰:'苟完矣。'富有,曰:'苟美矣。'"

　　孔子谈到那个时代的一位公众人物,他居家理财非常出色。孔子说:"当他从收入中有所积蓄时,他就会说:'我只是能够收支相抵了。'后来,他增长了他的积蓄,会说:'我只是能够支付我全部的需求了。'最后,他已经积蓄了大量的盈余,他会说:'现在我只是能够非常好地继续生活了。'"

9. 子适卫,冉有仆。子曰:"庶矣哉!"冉有曰:"既庶矣。又何加焉?"曰:"富之。"曰:"既富矣,又何加焉?"曰:"教之。"

　　有一次,孔子在他的旅途中进入了某个国家,与他一起的一位学生为他驾驶着马车。他说:"这里的人口这么多啊!"

be done? " "Enrich them," answered Confucius. "And after that?" asked the disciple. "Educate them." replied Confucius.

10. Confucius on one occasion remarked, "If I were given the conduct of the government of a country now, in one year I should have accomplished something; after three years, I should have put everything in order."

11. Confucius went on to remark, "It is a common saying that if good honest men had the rule of a country for a hundred years, they could make deeds of violence impossible and could thus dispense with capital punishment. It is a very true saying! "

12. Confucius finally remarked, "If a really God-sent great man were to become Emperor now, it would still take a generation before the people could be moral."

13. Confucius remarked, "If a man has really put his personal conduct in order, what is there in the government of a country that he should find any difficulty in it? But if a man has not put his personal conduct in order, how can he put in order the people of a country? "

14. On one occasion when a disciple who was in official employment returned from the palace, Confucius said to him, "Why are you so late?" "Oh!" answered the disciple, "We have just had State affairs." "You mean 'business'! For if there had been State affairs, although I am not now in office, I should still have been consulted."

"这么多的人口，"那位学生问，"应该如何去对待呢？""使他们富裕。"孔子回答说。"那之后呢？"那位学生问。"教育他们。"孔子回答。

10. 子曰："苟有用我者，期月而已可也，三年有成。"

有一次，孔子说："现在如果让我治理一个国家，一年之内，我能够让事情有所完善；三年后，我能够让每件事情都处于秩序之中。"

11. 子曰："善人为邦百年，亦可以胜残去杀矣。诚哉是言也！"

孔子继续说："俗话说，如果良善而正直的人统治一个国家一百年，他们会让暴力行为变得不可能，并因此而免除死刑。这确实是一句非常正确的话。"

12. 子曰："如有王者，必世而后仁。"

最后，孔子说："即使是一个真正的天赐伟人，现在就要成为帝王，那么，仍然需要花费一代人的时间让人民变得有道德。"

13. 子曰："苟正其身矣，于从政乎何有？不能正其身，如正人何？"

孔子说："如果一个人已经真正地把自身言行纳入秩序之中，那么，他在一个国家的统治中还能发现什么困难呢？但如果一个人并没有把自身言行纳入秩序之中，他又如何能够把一国的人民纳入秩序之中呢？"

14. 冉子退朝。子曰："何晏也？"对曰："有政。"子曰："其事也。如有政，虽不吾以，吾其与闻之。"

有一次，在官方任职的一个学生从官殿回来，孔子对他说："为什么这么晚？""噢！"那位学生回答说，"我们刚才有国家政事。""你是指'公事'！如果有国家政事的话，尽管我现在不在职了，我仍然会被征询意见的。"

15. The reigning prince of Confucius' native State enquired if the principle to make a country prosperous could be expressed in one single sentence. Confucius answered, "One cannot expect so much meaning from a single sentence. There is, however, a saying which the people have, 'To be a ruler of men is difficult and to be a public servant is not easy.' Now if one only knew that it is difficult to be a ruler of men, would not that alone almost make a country prosperous? "

The prince then asked if the principle to ruin a country could be expressed in one single sentence.

Confucius answered, "So much meaning is not to be expected from one single sentence. There is, however, a saying among the people:'I find no pleasure in being a ruler of men, except in that whatsoever I order no man shall oppose.' Now if what is ordered is right, it is well and good that no one oppose it; but if what is ordered is not right and no one opposes it, — is not that alone enough to ruin a country? "

16. The prince of a small principality asked what was essential in the government of a country.

Confucius answered, "When there is good government in a country the people at home are happy, and the people in other countries will come."

17. A disciple of Confucius who was appointed chief magistrate of an important town enquired what was essential in government.

Confucius answered, "Do not be in a hurry to get things done. Do not consider petty advantages. If you are in a hurry to get things

15. 定公问:"一言而可以兴邦,有诸?"孔子对曰:"言不可以若是其几也。人之言曰:'为君难,为臣不易。'如知为君之难也,不几乎一言而兴邦乎?"曰:"一言而丧邦,有诸?"孔子对曰:"言不可以若是其几也。人之言曰:'予无乐乎为君,唯其言而莫予违也。'如其善而莫之违也,不亦善乎?如不善而莫之违也,不几乎一言而丧邦乎?"

　　孔子故国的执政国君问,是否能够把让一个国家繁荣昌盛的原则用一句话表达出来。孔子回答说:"不能指望用一句话包含这么多含义。然而,人民有一句谚语:'做一个人民的统治者是困难的而做一名公务人员也不容易。'那么,如果一个人知道做人民的统治者是困难的,那不就几乎能让一个国家繁荣昌盛了吗?"

　　那位国君又问,灭亡一个国家的原则能否用一句话表达出来。

　　孔子回答说:"不要指望用一句话来包含如此多的含义。然而,人民有一句谚语:'我发现做一个人民的统治者一点都不快乐,除非我下达任何命令都没人反对。'那么,如果命令的是正确的,没人反对它就是良好有益的;但如果命令的是不正确的而没人反对它——那不就足够灭亡一个国家了吗?"

16. 叶公问政。子曰:"近者说,远者来。"

　　一个小型公国的国君问在一国的政治中什么是必需的。

　　孔子回答说:"当一个国家中有良好的政治时,国内的人民就会快乐,而其他国家的人民就会前来归附。"

17. 子夏为莒父宰,问政。子曰:"无欲速,无见小利。欲速,则不达,见小利,则大事不成。"

　　孔子的一位被任命为一个重要城镇的主要行政官的学生,问在政治治理中什么是必需的。

done, things will not be done thoroughly and well. If you consider petty advantages, you will never accomplish great things."

18. The reigning prince of a small principality said to Confucius, "Among my people there are men to be found who are so upright that when a father steals a sheep the son is ready to bear witness against him."

"In our country," replied Confucius, "The upright men are different from that. They consider it consistent with true uprightness for a father to be silent regarding the misdeed of his son and for a son to be silent concerning the misdeed of his father."

19. A disciple of Confucius enquired what was essential in a moral life. Confucius answered, "In dealing with yourself, be serious; in business, be earnest; in intercourse with other men, be conscientious. Although you may be living among barbarians and savages, these principles cannot be neglected. "

20. A disciple of Confucius enquired, "What must one be in order to be considered a gentleman?" Confucius answered, "He must be a man of strict personal honour; when sent on a public mission to any country, he will not disgrace his mission. Such a man may be considered a gentleman."

The disciple then asked for a type of gentleman next in degree to the one mentioned above. Confucius answered, "One whom the members of his family hold up as a good son and his fellow citizens hold up as a good citizen."

孔子回答说："不要匆忙地把事情做完。不要关注琐碎的利益。如果你匆忙地把事情做完，事情就不会被充分彻底地完成。如果你关注琐碎的利益，你就无法完成重大的事情。"

18. 叶公语孔子曰："吾党有直躬者，其父攘羊，而子证之。"孔子曰："吾党之直者异于是。父为子隐，子为父隐，直在其中矣。"

     一个小型公国的执政国君对孔子说："在我的人民中，有些人被发现是如此正直，甚至当父亲偷了一只羊时，儿子就会准备作证。"

     "在我们国家，"孔子回答说，"正直的人与此不同。他们认为，父亲对儿子的罪行选择缄默以及儿子对父亲的罪行选择缄默，与真正的正直是一致的。"

19. 樊迟问仁。子曰："居处恭，执事敬，与人忠。虽之夷狄，不可弃也。"

     孔子的一个学生问在道德的生活中，什么是必需的。孔子回答说："对待自己，要认真严肃；做事要热心诚恳；与别人交往，要有良心。即使你可能生活于未开化的野蛮人之中，这些原则也不要忽视。"

20. 子贡问曰："何如斯可谓之士矣？"子曰："行己有耻，使于四方，不辱君命，可谓士矣。"曰："敢问其次。"曰："宗族称孝焉，乡党称弟焉。"曰："敢问其次。"曰："言必信，行必果，硁硁然小人哉！抑亦可以为次矣。"曰："今之从政者何如？"子曰："噫！斗筲之人，何足算也。"

     孔子的一个学生问："怎样才会被视为一个绅士？"孔子回答说："他必须是一个具有严格的个人荣誉感的人。当因公共使命被派到任何一个国家时，他都会不辱使命。这样一个人可以被视为一位绅士。"

     那位学生又问在程度上仅次于上面所提到一种绅士。孔子回答

The disciple went on to ask for a type of gentleman still next in degree.

Confucius answered, "One who makes it a point to carry out what he says and to persist in what he undertakes, a dogged, stubborn little gentleman though he is; such a man may also be considered a type of gentleman next in degree."

The disciple finally asked, saying, "But now what is your opinion of the gentlemen now in the public service? " "They are," replied Confucius, "only red-taped bureaucrats not worth taking into account."

21. Confucius remarked, "If I cannot find equitable and reasonable men to have to do with, upon necessity I would choose men of enthusiastic or even fanatical character. Enthusiastic men are zealous and there are always limits which fanatical men would not pass."

22. Confucius remarked, "The southern people have a saying, 'A man without perseverance cannot be a doctor or a magician.' How true!

"Again, it is said in the *I-king*, 'The reputation for a virtue once acquired unless persevered in will lead to disgrace.' "

Commenting on this, Confucius remarked, "It is much better not to assume the reputation for the virtue at all."

23. Confucius remarked, "A wise man is sociable, but not familiar. A fool is familiar but not sociable."

说:"一个被他的家庭成员提出是一个好儿子,以及他的同胞提出是一个好公民的人。"

那位学生继续问再次一个程度的绅士。

孔子回答说:"一个特别注意把所说的话付诸实践,并且坚持做已经开始的事情的人,尽管他可能是一个顽固倔强的微不足道的绅士,但也会被视为这一程度的绅士。"

那位学生最后问:"那么现在,您对公职中的绅士们有怎样的看法呢?""他们,"孔子回答说,"只是些繁文缛节的官僚主义者罢了,不值得重视。"

21. 子曰:"不得中行而与之,必也狂狷乎! 狂者进取,狷者有所不为也。"

孔子说:"如果我无法找到公正而明理的人相伴,有必要的话,我会选择满腔热情甚至狂热入迷的人。满腔热情的人是热忱的,而狂热入迷的人总有些限度他们不会超过。"

22. 子曰:"南人有言曰:'人而无恒,不可以作巫医。' 善夫!""不恒其德,或承之羞。"子曰:"不占而已矣。"

孔子说:"南方的人民有一句谚语:'一个没有毅力的人不能够成为一名医生或巫师。'多么正确啊!

"还有,《易经》上说:'一旦获得美德的声誉,除非坚持下去,否则将导致名誉扫地。'"

孔子对此评论说:"还是不要僭取有美德的声誉比较好。"

23. 子曰:"君子和而不同,小人同而不和。"

孔子说:"一个明智的人是友善随和的,而不是过分亲热的。一个愚蠢的人则是过分亲热的,而不是友善随和的。"

24. A disciple of Confucius enquired of him, saying, "What do you say of a man who is popular with all his fellow townsmen in a place? "

"He is not necessarily a good man," answered Confucius.

"What do you say then," asked the disciple, "of a man who is unpopular with all his fellow townsmen? "

"He is neither," replied Confucius, " necessarily a good nor a bad man. A really good man is he who is popular with the good men of a place and unpopular with the bad men."

25. Confucius remarked, "A wise and good man is easy to serve, but difficult to please. If you go beyond your duty to please him, he will not be pleased. But in his employment of men, he always takes into consideration their capacity. A fool, on the other hand, is easy to please, but difficult to serve. If you go beyond your duty to please him, he will be pleased. But in his employment of men, he expects them to be able to do everything."

26. Confucius remarked, "A wise man is dignified, but not proud. A fool is proud, but not dignified."

27. Confucius remarked, "A man of strong, resolute, simple character approaches nearly to the true moral character."

24. 子贡问曰:"乡人皆好之,何如?"子曰:"未可也。""乡人皆恶之,何如?"子曰:"未可也。不如乡人之善者好之,其不善者恶之。"

　　孔子的一位学生问他:"一个人在一个地方受到他所有同乡人的喜爱,您认为怎么样?"

　　"他未必是一个好人。"孔子回答说。

　　"那你认为,"那位学生问,"如果一个人他的所有同乡人都不喜欢他,是怎样的?"

　　"他必然既不是,"孔子回答说,"一个好人,也不是一个坏人。一个真正的好人,是一个受该地的好人喜爱而不受坏人喜爱的人。"

25. 子曰:"君子易事而难说也:说之不以道,不说也;及其使人也,器之。小人难事而易说也:说之虽不以道,说也;及其使人也,求备焉。"

　　孔子说:"一个明智而良善的人,你很容易去为他服务,但很难取悦他。如果你超出你的职责范围去取悦他,他不会高兴。但他在差使人的时候,总会顾及他们的能力。另一方面,一个愚蠢的人,你很容易去取悦他,却很难去为他服务。如果你超出你的职责范围去取悦他,他会很高兴。但他在差使人的时候,会希望他们能够做全部的事情。"

26. 子曰:"君子泰而不骄,小人骄而不泰。"

　　孔子说:"一个明智的人是高贵的,而不是高傲的。一个愚蠢的人是高傲的,而不是高贵的。"

27. 子曰:"刚毅、木讷,近仁。"

　　孔子说:"一个刚强、坚毅、朴素的人,几乎接近有真正的道德品质了。"

28. A disciple of Confucius enquired, "What must a man be in order to be considered a gentleman?" Confucius answered, "He must be sympathetic, obliging and affectionate: sympathetic and obliging to his friends and affectionate to the members of his family. "

29. Confucius remarked, "A good honest man, after educating the people for seven years, will be able to lead them to war."

30. Confucius remarked, "To allow a people to go to battle without first instructing them, is to betray them. "

28. 子路问曰："何如斯可谓之士矣?" 子曰："切切、偲偲、怡怡如也，可谓士矣。朋友切切、偲偲，兄弟怡怡。"

　　孔子的一个学生问："要必须怎样做，才能被视为绅士?" 孔子回答说："他必须有同情心，乐于助人，并充满关爱：有同情心与乐于助人是对他的朋友而言的，充满关爱是对他的家人而言的。"

29. 子曰："善人教民七年，亦可以即戎矣。"

　　孔子说："一个良善正直的人，教育人民七年之后，就能够带领他们参加战争。"

30. 子曰："以不教民战，是谓弃之。"

　　孔子说："允许人民去作战，而没有事先指导他们，就等于陷害他们。"

【评述】

1. 文中，"政"，辜鸿铭译为"how to conduct the government of a country"，"如何治理国家的政治"，指为政之道；"先之，劳之"，译为"go before the people with your example; show them your exertion"，"做好你的榜样领先人民；向他们展示你的努力"，指的是统治者自身的"努力"，即勤劳，这样的一种精神状态；"无倦"，译为"be indefatigable in that"，"其间要坚持不懈"，指做上述事情时，要坚持不懈，使之成为一种统治的方式。

2. 文中，"先有司，赦小过，举贤才"一句，"先有司"，辜鸿铭译为"leave the initiative in the details of government to the responsible heads of the departments"，"把政治上细节问题的决断权留给相应部门的负责人"，指具体问题让各职责部门负责；"赦小过"，译为"overlook small short-comings"，"原谅小的缺点"；"举贤才"，译为"advance men of ability and worth"，"提拔有能力与美德的人"。这一节讲的是统治者应当遵循的统治原则。

3. 文中，"名不正，则言不顺"，辜鸿铭译为"if names of things are not properly defined, words will not correspond to facts"，"如果事物的名称没有被恰当地确定，那么言语就会与事实不符"。翻译中，辜鸿铭把"words"与"facts"两词设为斜体，意在进行对比强调。"事不成，则礼乐不兴"，辜鸿铭译为"where it is impossible to perfect anything, the arts and institutions of civilisation cannot flourish"，"当完善任何事情都不可能，那么艺术与文明制度就无法繁荣"。此句中，辜鸿铭把"礼"译为"art"，艺术，这是他较为常见的翻译；"乐"译为"institutions of civilisation"，"文明制度"，大概用"乐"字来代指文明制度；"兴"译为"flourish"，"繁荣"，这句话的意思指如果任何事情都无法完善的话，那么整个文明制度就无法真正取得繁荣。"君子名之必可言也，言之必可行也"，辜鸿铭译为"a wise and good man can always specify whatever he names; whatever he can specify, he can carry out"，"一个明智而良善的人，总是能够详细地说明任何他命名的事情；任何他能详细说明的事情，他就能够实行"。所以，孔子指出，"君子于其言，无所苟而已矣"，辜鸿铭译为"a wise and good man makes it a point always to be exact in the words he uses"，"一个明智而良善的人总是会特别注意准确用语"。其中，"无所苟"指"特别注意准确用语"之意。对此，辜鸿铭注释说：

> 字面意思是"不粗心大意"，孔子在这里是把这个问题作为他那个时代的特征而指出的。不久前，史密斯牧师在他的《中国人的特性》中很聪明地指出今天的中国人的特性，即'缺乏精确性'，说无论什么地方、无论任何时候，它都存在着，并使得艺术与文明不可能繁荣。但我们认为，在言辞的使用上，"缺乏精确性"现在并不完全局限于中国。见第六章第23节的注释。

4. 文中，"请学稼"，辜鸿铭译为 "requested to be taught farming"，"请求教给他耕作"，"稼" 泛指农业劳作；"请学为圃"，译为 "asked to be taught gardening"，"要求教给他园艺"。总之，樊迟是要求孔子教给他具体的农活。孔子称樊迟 "小人"，辜鸿铭译为 "a petty-minded man"，"器量狭小的人"。最后一段，孔子谈的是治理国家的原则要点："好礼"、"好义"、"好信"。"好" 译为 "encourage"，"鼓励"，指政府的政策指导。

5. 文中，"授之以政，不达"，辜鸿铭译为 "when the conduct of the affairs of a nation is entrusted to him, can do nothing"，"当国家事务交托给他处理时，不能做任何事情"。"达" 指毫无做事能力。意思是，虽然能背诵《诗经》，但无法做好实际事务。

6. 本节所表达的含义包含于第十二章第19、22节中，说的是统治者自身对一般民众的德行具有决定性的影响作用。所以，统治者必须先做好表率。文中，辜鸿铭把 "正" 译为 "in order"，"合乎秩序"。

7. 文中，"政"，辜鸿铭译为 "the state of government"，"政治的状态"；"兄弟" 译为 "the one is about the same as the other"，"一个与另一个大致相同"，指鲁、卫两国政治状态大致相同。

8. "善居室"，辜鸿铭译为 "he was admirable in the way in which he ordered the economy of his home"，"他居家理财非常出色"。辜鸿铭后面的翻译遵循了传统上对这一节的理解，呈现了公子荆正确的财富观。

9. 文中，"庶"，辜鸿铭译为 "a large population"，人口众多之意；"富之"，译为 "enrich them"，"使他们富裕"；"教之" 译为 "educate them"，"教育他们"。这一节反映了孔子的实际治国思路。

10. 文中，"苟有用我者"，辜鸿铭译为 "if I were given the conduct of the government of a country"，"如果让我治理一个国家的政治"；"期月而已可也"，译为 "in one year I should have accomplished something"，"一年之内，我能够让事情有所完善"，这里的意思是指初步取得治理成果。"三年有成"，译为 "after three years, I should have put everything in order"，"三年后，我能够让每件事情都处于秩序之中"，指用三年时间，能够建立良好稳定的社会秩序。

11. 这一节表达的是孔子对 "善人为邦百年，亦可以胜残去杀矣" 这一说法的认可。"善人"，辜鸿铭译为 "good honest men"，"良善而正直的人"；"为邦百年" 译为 "had the

rule of a country for a hundred years",统治一个国家一百年";"胜残去杀"译为"make deeds of violence impossible and could thus dispense with capital punishment","让暴力行为变得不可能,并因此而免除死刑"。

12. 文中,"王者",辜鸿铭译为"a really God-sent great man were to become Emperor","一个真正的天赐伟人要成为帝王";"世而后仁"一句,译为"it would still take a generation before the people could be moral","仍然需要花费一代人的时间让人民变得道德","世"解释为"代";"仁"解释为"道德"。

13. 文中,"正身"、"正人",辜鸿铭对"正"的翻译与本章第6节相同,都指国家、社会的秩序而言。"正身"译为"put his personal conduct in order","把自身言行纳入秩序之中";"正人"译为"put in order the people of a country","把一国的人民纳入秩序之中"。

14. 孔子问冉子"何晏也",辜鸿铭译为"Why are you so late","为什么这么晚"。指的是冉有此次退朝晚于平时很久。下文中,孔子对"政"与"事"进行了区分。"政",译为"State affairs","国家政事";"事",译为"business","公事"或"公事",指一般性事务。"虽不吾以,吾其与闻之",译为"如果有国家政事的话,尽管我现在不在职了,我仍然会被征询意见的"。辜鸿铭注释说:

> 那时,孔子是国会的成员。

15. 文中,"一言而可以兴邦",辜鸿铭译为"the principle to make a country prosperous could be expressed in one single sentence","把让一个国家繁荣昌盛的原则用一句话表达出来"。"为君难,为臣不易",译为"to be a ruler of men is difficult and to be a public servant is not easy","做一个人民的统治者是困难的而做一名公务人员也不容易"。"臣",辜鸿铭一贯译为"公务人员"。

16. 文中,"政",辜鸿铭译为"what was essential in the government of a country","政治中什么是必需的";即政治的必要因素;"近者说,远者来",辜鸿铭译为"when there is good government in a country the people at home are happy, and the people in other countries will come","当一个国家中有良好的政治时,国内的人民就会快乐,而其他国家的人民就会前来"。这一节的意思是,良好的政治能使本国人快乐,并且能吸引其他国家的人前来。

17. 文中,"欲速则不达,见小利则大事不成"一句,辜鸿铭的翻译是:"欲速则不达",

译为"if you are in a hurry to get things done, things will not be done thoroughly and well"，"如果你匆忙地把事情做完，事情就不会被充分彻底地完成"。"速"指"匆忙地把事情做完"；"达"指"充分彻底地完成"。"见小利则大事不成"，译为"if you consider petty advantages, you will never accomplish great things"，"如果你关注琐碎的利益，你就无法完成重大的事情"；"小利"指"琐碎的利益"；"不成"指"无法完成"。

18. 文中，"吾党有直躬者"一句，辜鸿铭译为"among my people there are men to be found who are so upright"，意思是，在该国人民中，有些人被发现非常正直。"其父攘羊，而子证之"，译为"when a father steals a sheep the son is ready to bear witness against him"，"当父亲偷了一只羊时，儿子就会准备作证"。其中"攘"意思是"偷盗"；"证"意思是"准备为之作证"。叶公认为，这是正直的表现。"父为子隐，子为父隐，直在其中矣"，辜鸿铭译为"they consider it consistent with true uprightness for a father to be silent regarding the misdeed of his son and for a son to be silent concerning the misdeed of his father"，"父亲对儿子的罪行选择缄默以及儿子对父亲的罪行选择缄默，才是真正的正直"。"隐"，指对罪行保持沉默。

19. 本节孔子谈了道德生活的几项行为原则。文中，"与人忠"，译为"in intercourse with other men, be conscientious"，"与别人交往，要有良心"。"忠"指有良心，遵循良知。

20. 子贡问"士"，辜鸿铭译为"gentleman"，"绅士"。指优秀、高贵的人。

"行己有耻"，译为"he must be a man of strict personal honour"，指具有严格的个人荣誉感。也可以理解为拥有强烈的自尊心。"使于四方，不辱君命"，译为"when sent on a public mission to any country he will not disgrace his mission"，"当因公共使命被派到任何一个国家时，他都会不辱使命"。指能够承担重大的外交任务。这是最高程度的绅士。

"宗族称孝焉，乡党称弟焉"，译为"one whom the members of his family hold up as a good son and his fellow citizens hold up as a good citizen"，"一个被他的家庭成员提出是一个好儿子，以及他的同胞提出是一个好公民的人"，指同时在家庭及社会角色上都十分优秀，获得认可。辜鸿铭一贯把"弟"与"悌"解释为"好的公民"。在家中讲"孝"，在社会上讲"弟"，这是中国人现实生活的两个构成维度。这是次一等的绅士。

"言必信，行必果，硁硁然小人哉"，辜鸿铭译为"one who makes it a point to carry out what he says and to persist in what he undertakes, a dogged, stubborn little gentleman though he is"，指"一个特别注意把所说的话付诸实践，并且坚持做已经开始的事情的顽固倔强的微不足道的绅士"。在本句中，辜鸿铭把"小人"译为"little gentleman"，"微不足道的绅士"，指的是地位低微，身份渺小的人，如果能够"言必信，行必果"，即使有顽固倔强等性格缺点，也可以称为一个绅士。这是较低层次的绅士。

子贡问"今之从政者",孔子称其为"斗筲之人"。辜鸿铭译为"only red-taped bureaucrats not worth taking into account","只是些繁文缛节的官僚主义者罢了"。这里，"斗筲"译为"red-taped"，指"繁文缛节"。对此，辜鸿铭还添加注释做了进一步说明：

> 中文对"繁文缛节"的表达是"配克与筐子"（pecks and hampers）（［回译者注］这里都是计量单位），源自这样的事实，古代那些仅仅负责日常事务的官员职责是，去称量从人民那里征收来的谷物与其他产物。

这是孔子对彼时从政者的评价。

21. 文中，"不得中行而与之，必也狂狷乎"一句，辜鸿铭译"中行"为"equitable and reasonable,"指公正而明理的人；"狂"译为"enthusiastic"，指满腔热情的人；"狷"译为"fanatical"，指狂热入迷的人。对于"狷"字，辜鸿铭注释说：

> 字面意思是指顽固的——中文的意思是一种凶猛的、顽固的像一只哈巴狗的动物。其实是指观念僵化的人。

"狂者进取，狷者有所不为"，辜鸿铭译"进取"为"zealous"，指热忱，即积极主动的心态。另外，"有所不为"指的不是消极无为，而是对自己的行为有理性的克制。

22. 文中，"人而无恒，不可以作巫医"一句，辜鸿铭译为"a man without perseverance cannot be a doctor or a magician"，"一个没有毅力的人不能够成为一名医生或巫师"。其中，"恒"译为"perseverance"，"毅力"；"巫医"译为"a doctor or a magician"，"医生或巫师"。

"不恒其德，或承之羞"是《易经·恒卦》的爻辞，学者多认为指如果道德不能恒久，就会蒙受羞辱。辜鸿铭译此句为"the reputation for a virtue once acquired unless persevered in will lead to disgrace"，"一旦获得美德的声誉，除非坚持下去，否则将导致名誉扫地"。

"不占而已矣"，传统学者多认为指不为"无恒"之人占卜。辜鸿铭译为"it is much better not to assume the reputation for the virtue at all"，"还是不要僭取有美德的声誉比较好"。其中，把"占"译为"assume"，假装、僭取之意。指实际不具有美德，却僭取了美德的声誉。辜鸿铭对自己的翻译作了注释：

> 中国伟大的注释家朱夫子放弃了最后一段，说不理解它。（［回译者注］朱熹在《四书章句集注》中说此段"其义未详"，见第147页）在此，我们通过这样的翻译来冒险地给出这一段的解释。

23. 文中，"和"，辜鸿铭译为"sociable"，"友善随和的"；"同"，译为"familiar"，"过分亲热的"。"和而不同"就是"友善随和而非过分亲热的"；"同而不和"就是"过分亲热非友善随和的"。按照辜鸿铭的翻译，这句话是说"君子"与"小人"在与人相处时的不同表现。

24. 文中，"不如乡人之善者好之，其不善者恶之"一句，辜鸿铭认为，这是孔子对真正的"好人"的看法，译为"a really good man is he who is popular with the good men of a place and unpopular with the bad men"，"一个真正的好人，是一个被当地的好人喜爱而不被坏人喜爱的人"。

25. 文中，"说之不以道，不说也"一句，辜鸿铭译为"if you go beyond your duty to please him, he will not be pleased"，"如果你超出你的职责范围去取悦他，他不会高兴"。"道"指你的职责，"不以道"即超出你的职责范围，指你做出不应做的事情去取悦他，则君子不会因此而被取悦。

26. 文中，"泰"，辜鸿铭译为"dignified"，"高贵的，有尊严的"；"骄"，译为"proud"，"高傲的，傲慢的"。"泰而不骄"意思就是"高贵而不高傲"；"骄而不泰"意思是"高傲而不高贵"。

27. 文中，"刚"，辜鸿铭译为"strong"，"刚强，坚强"；"毅"，译为"resolute"，"坚毅，果敢"；"木讷"，译为"simple"，"朴素，简朴"；"近仁"，译为"approaches nearly to the true moral character"，"几乎接近真正的道德品质"。

28. 文中，"切切、偲偲、怡怡如也"一句中，"切切偲偲"译为"sympathetic and obliging"，"有同情心及乐于助人"；"怡怡"译为"affectionate"，"充满关爱的，温柔亲切的"。同时，辜鸿铭将"兄弟"译为"the members of his family"，"家人"。这一节是说，作为一个绅士，应该对朋友富有同情心，并乐于提供帮助；对家人，应该是关爱的、亲切的。

29. 文中，"善人"，辜鸿铭译为"a good honest man"，"一个良善正直的人"；"即戎"译为"lead them to war"，"带领他们参加战争"。这一节指人民在"善人"的教育之下，七年即可被带领去作战。

30. 文中，"不教"，辜鸿铭译为"without first instructing them"，"没有事先指导他们"，指没有对人民事先进行军事训练与指导；"弃"译为"betray"，"出卖，陷害，背叛"。这一节指不对人民进行指导训练就使他们作战，就等于陷害他们。

CHAPTER XIV
宪问第十四

1. A disciple of Confucius enquired what constituted dishonour. Confucius answered, "When there is justice and order in the government of the country, to think only of pay is dishonourable. When there is no justice and order in the government of the country, to think only of pay is also dishonourable."

2. The same disciple went on to ask, saying: "A man with whom ambition, vanity, envy and selfishness have ceased to act as motives, — may he be considered a moral character? " "What you suggest," answered Confucius, "may be considered as something difficult to achieve; but I cannot say that it constitutes a moral character."

3. Confucius remarked, "A gentleman who only thinks of the comforts of life, cannot be a true gentleman."

4. Confucius remarked, "When there is justice and order in the government of the country a man may be bold and lofty in the expression of his opinions as well as in his actions. When, however, there is no justice and order in the government of the country, a man may be bold and lofty in his action, but he should be reserved in the expression of his opinion."

5. Confucius remarked, "A man who possesses moral worth will always have something to say worth listening to; but a man who has something to say is not necessarily a man of moral worth. A moral character always has courage; but a man of courage is not necessarily a moral character."

1. 宪问耻。子曰:"邦有道,谷;邦无道,谷,耻也。"

　　孔子的一个学生问什么是耻辱。孔子回答说:"当国家的政治中有正义与秩序时,仅仅关心薪水,是耻辱的。当国家的政治中没有正义与秩序时,仅仅关心薪水,也是耻辱的。"

2. "克、伐、怨、欲不行焉,可以为仁矣?"子曰:"可以为难矣,仁则吾不知也。"

　　那同一个学生继续问:"如果一个人停止了把野心、虚荣、妒忌和自私作为他的做事基调——他可以被视为一个有道德的人吗?""你所建议的,"孔子回答说,"可以被视为难以实现的事情。但我无法确定这样就能成为一个有道德的人。"

3. 子曰:"士而怀居,不足以为士矣。"

　　孔子说:"一个绅士只考虑生活的安逸,就不会成为真正的绅士。"

4. 子曰:"邦有道,危言危行;邦无道,危行言孙。"

　　孔子说:"当国家的政治中有正义与秩序时,一个人可以在他意见的表达与行为上勇敢而且高尚。然而,当国家的政治中没有正义与秩序时,一个人在他的行为上可以勇敢而且高尚,但在他的意见表达上应该含蓄。"

5. 子曰:"有德者必有言,有言者不必有德;仁者必有勇,勇者不必有仁。"

　　孔子说:"一个有道德的人,总是会有一些值得聆听的话去说,但一个有话去说的人,未必是一个有道德的人。一个有道德的人总有勇气的,但一个有勇气的人未必是一个有道德的人。"

6. A disciple of Confucius on one occasion remarked in his presence: "There was a famous man in ancient time who was an excellent marksman in archery, and there was another man famous for his feats of strength: both of these men eventually came to an unnatural end. On the other hand, there were also in ancient time two men who worked in the fields and toiled as husbandmen: both these latter finally came to the government of the Empire."

Confucius at the time did not say anything in reply. But when the disciple had left, Confucius said: "What a really wise and good man he is! How much he honours moral worth in what he has said!"

7. Confucius remarked, "There are wise men who are not moral characters; but a fool is never a moral character."

8. Confucius remarked, "Where there is affection, exertion is made easy; where there is disinterestedness, instruction will not be neglected."

9. Confucius, speaking of the great merits of the State documents of a certain State of the time, remarked: "In the preparation of these State documents, one minister would first sketch out the draft; another would then discuss the several points; another minister after that would make the necessary corrections; and finally, another minister would polish the style and give it a last finishing touch. "

6. 南宫适问于孔子曰："羿善射,奡荡舟,俱不得其死然;禹稷躬稼,而有天下。"夫子不答,南宫适出,子曰："君子哉若人! 尚德哉若人!"

　　有一次,孔子的一位学生到场时说:"古代有一个著名的人,他是一位神射手,还有一个人则是以力量的技艺而知名:他们两个人最后都没有善终。另一方面,古代也有两个作为农夫而在田地里长期劳作的人:他们两个人最后都成了帝国的统治者。"

　　当时,孔子并没有作任何回答。但当那位学生离开后,孔子说:"他是一位真正明智而良善的人啊! 他在言辞间是多么尊崇道德啊!"

7. 子曰："君子而不仁者有矣夫,未有小人而仁者也。"

　　孔子说:"有些聪明人并不是有道德的人;但一个蠢人却永远不会成为一个有道德的人。"

8. 子曰："爱之,能勿劳乎? 忠焉,能勿诲乎?"

　　孔子说:"哪里有爱慕之心,努力就会变得容易。哪里公正无私,教诲就不会被忽视。"

9. 子曰："为命:裨谌草创之,世叔讨论之,行人子羽修饰之,东里子产润色之。"

　　孔子谈到那时某国的一份国家文件的巨大价值,说:"在这些国家文件的预备阶段,一位大臣会首先草拟出初稿。然后,另一位会论述许多要点。这之后,再一位会作必要的修改。最后,另一位大臣会文饰语言风格,并完成最后一笔。"

10. Someone on one occasion asked Confucius' opinion of the character of a famous statesman (the Colbert of the time). Confucius answered, "He was a generous man."

The enquirer asked of the character of another notorious statesman. "Why, that man! That man! Why speak of him at all? "

The enquirer finally asked of the character of Kuan Chung (the Bismarck of the time). Confucius answered, "As a man he was able to take possession of an estate, confiscated from the head of an old noble family in the country, in such a way that the former owner, although he was thus obliged to live in great poverty to the end of his days, yet had nothing to say in complaint against Kuan Chung."

11. Confucius remarked, "To be poor without complaining is not easy; but it is easy to be rich without being proud."

12. Confucius remarked of a public character of the time: "As an officer in the retinue of a great noble, he would be excellent, but he is not fit to be councillor of State even in a small principality."

13. A disciple of Confucius enquired what constituted a perfect character. Confucius, referring to the different famous known men of the time, said: "A perfect character should have the intellect of such another man; the disinterestedness of such another man; the gallantry of such another; the accomplishments of such another man. In addition to those qualities, if he would culture himself by the study

10. 或问子产。子曰:"惠人也。"问子西。曰:"彼哉! 彼哉!"问管
    仲。曰:"人也。夺伯氏骈邑三百,饭疏食,没齿无怨言。"

    有一次,有人问孔子对一位著名的政治家(那个时代的柯尔伯特)
的品质的看法。孔子回答说:"他是一个慷慨宽厚的人。"

    那位提问者问另一个臭名昭著的政治家的品质。"哎呀! 那个
人! 那个人! 为什么要谈论他呢?"

    最后,那位提问者问管仲(那个时代的俾斯麦)的品质。孔子回答
说:"作为一个人,他能够从该国一个古老的贵族家族的当家人手中没
收地产,尽管那位之前的拥有者不得不因此而在最后的日子里过上了
非常贫穷的生活,然而对管仲却没有任何抱怨。"

11. 子曰:"贫而无怨难,富而无骄易。"

    孔子说:"贫穷而不抱怨,是不容易的。但富有而不高傲则是容
易的。"

12. 子曰:"孟公绰为赵魏老则优,不可以为滕薛大夫。"

    孔子谈到那时的一位公众人物:"作为一位显赫贵族的随从官员,
他可以说是优秀的,但不适合成为一位政务委员,即使是在一个小型
公国。"

13. 子路问成人。子曰:"若臧武仲之知,公绰之不欲,卞庄子之
    勇,冉求之艺,文之以礼乐,亦可以为成人矣。"曰:"今之成人
    者何必然? 见利思义,见危授命,久要不忘平生之言,亦可以
    为成人矣。"

    孔子的一个学生问怎样才算是一个完美的人。孔子提到那时一
些闻名的人,说:"一个完美的人应该拥有像另一个人同样的智力,另一

of the arts and institutions of the civilised world, he would then be considered a perfect character."

"But," Confucius went on to say, "now-a-days it is not even necessary to be all that in order to be a perfect character. One who, when he sees a personal advantage, can think of what is right and, in presence of personal danger, is ready to give up his life; and who, under long-continued trying circumstances, does not belie the professions of his life: — such a man may also be considered a perfect character."

14. Confucius on one occasion enquired about a teacher from one of his disciples, saying: "Is it true that your teacher seldom speaks and seldom laughs; and that he never accepts anything from anybody?" "They are mistaken who say that," replied the teacher's disciple, "My teacher speaks when it is time to speak:therefore people never lose patience when he does speak. He laughs when he is really delighted; therefore people never lose patience when he does laugh. He accepts when it is consistent with right to accept: therefore people never lose patience when he accepts anything." Confucius then said, "So! is it really so with him?"

15. Confucius, speaking of a powerful noble of his native State, remarked, "He took possession of an important military town when sending a message to the prince to beg him to appoint a successor to his own family estate. Although it is said that on that occasion he did not use intimidation with the prince, his master, I do not believe it."

个人同样的超然无欲的心态，另一个人同样的勇敢，另一个人同样的才艺。除了这些品质外，如果他会通过研究这个文明社会的艺术及制度来培养自己，那么，他就会被视为一个完美的人。"

"但是"，孔子继续说，"现今要成为一个完美的人甚至不必全部如此。一个人，当他看到个人利益时能够考虑到正义，面对人身危险能够准备好放弃生命，以及处于长期令人难以忍受的环境下而不会违背他的人生誓言——这样一个人也可以被视为是一个完美的人。"

14. 子问公叔文子于公明贾曰："信乎夫子不言、不笑、不取乎？"公明贾对曰："以告者过也。夫子时然后言，人不厌其言；乐然后笑，人不厌其笑；义然后取，人不厌其取。"子曰："其然，岂其然乎？"

有一次，孔子从一个老师的学生那里询问他的老师："你的老师很少说话，很少笑，并且他从来不从任何人那里接受任何东西，是真的吗？""这样说的人理解错了，"那位老师的学生回答，"我的老师是在该说话的时候才说话，因此人们在他说话时从来不会变得不耐烦。他是在当真高兴的时候才笑，因此人们从来不在他笑的时候变得不耐烦。他是在符合道义时才接受，因此人们从来不会在他接受任何东西的时候变得不耐烦。"孔子然后说："这样啊！他真的是这样吗？"

15. 子曰："臧武仲以防求为后于鲁，虽曰不要君，吾不信也。"

孔子谈及他故国的一位有权势的贵族，说："当他向国君传递消息，请求委任一个继承者来继承他的家产之际，他正占据着一座军事重镇。尽管有人说在那种情况下他没有胁迫国君——他的主人，但我不信。"

16. Confucius, speaking of the characters of the two most famous princes of his time, remarked: "One (the Frederic the Great of the time) was crafty and without honour.The other (Wilhelm I of Germany) was a man of honour and without any craftiness in his character."

17. A disciple, speaking of the famous statesman Kuan Chung (the Bismarck of the time), remarked, "Kuan Chung and another officer were given charge, as tutors, of the elder of two princes. When the younger of the two princes, in order to succeed to the throne, slew his elder brother, the other officer preferred to die with his pupil and charge, but Kuan Chung did not die. Did not Kuan Chung in this show that he was not a moral character?"

Confucius answered, "It was due to the great services of Kuan Chung that the prince, his master, was able to call together the princes of the Empire to a Congress which prevented a general war during the time. What has one to say against the moral character — what has one to say against the moral character of man like that?"

18. Another disciple then remarked, "But Kuan Chung not only did not die with the elder prince, his pupil and charge; he even served the younger prince, the very man who murdered his pupil and charge. Did he not in this show that he was not a moral character? "

Confucius answered, "Kuan Chung as Prime Minister enabled the prince, his master, to exercise Imperialism over the prince of the time, to unite the Empire and give it peace. Down to the present day the people are enjoying the benefits due to his great services. But for Kuan Chung we should now be living like savages. He was

16. 子曰:"晋文公谲而不正,齐桓公正而不谲。"

   孔子谈及他那个时代两位最著名的国君的品质,说:"其中一个(那个时代的弗里德里克大帝)狡诈而没有正义感。另一个(德国的威廉一世)是个品质中充满正义感却没有丝毫狡诈的人。"

17. 子路曰:"桓公杀公子纠,召忽死之,管仲不死。"曰:"未仁乎?"子曰:"桓公九合诸侯,不以兵车,管仲之力也。如其仁!如其仁!"

   一位学生谈起那位著名的政治家管仲(那时的俾斯麦),说:"管仲与另一位官员被任命为两位王子中那位大王子的私人教师。当小王子为了继承王位而杀害他兄长的时候,那位官员宁愿伴随他的学生也就是他所照顾的人一起死,但管仲没有死。管仲不是有道德的人吧?

   孔子回答说:"正因为管仲的伟大工作,国君——他的主人,才能够把帝国的诸侯国君们召集到国会,在这期间防止了一场全面的战争。为什么还要声讨这位有道德的人——为什么还要声讨像这样一位有道德的人呢?"

18. 子贡曰:"管仲非仁者与? 桓公杀公子纠,不能死,又相之。"子曰:"管仲相桓公,霸诸侯,一匡天下,民到于今受其赐。微管仲,吾其被发左衽矣。岂若匹夫匹妇之为谅也,自经于沟渎而莫之知也?"

   另一个学生又说:"但是管仲不仅没有陪伴他的大王子——他的学生、他所照顾的人死去,他甚至又辅佐小王子,正是这位小王子谋杀了他的学生、他所照顾的人。管仲不是有道德的人吧?"

   孔子回答说:"作为首要大臣,管仲能够使国君,他的主人,完成霸业,并赋予和平。直到今天,人民还在享受着应归功于他伟大工作的好

certainly not like your faithful lover and his sweetheart among the common people, who, in order to prove their constancy, go and drown themselves in a ditch, nobody taking any notice of them. "

19. A noble of a certain State (who after his death was given the title of Beauclerc), when he was called to office in the government, chose for his colleague an officer who had been serving in his retinue. Confucius, remarking on this, said: "Such a man certainly deserves the title of 'Beauclerc'."

20. Confucius on one occasion was commenting on the scandalous life of the prince of a certain State, when somebody remarked, "If he was such a man — how did he not lose his throne? " "That was because," replied Confucius, "he had great and able men to carry on the different departments of his administration."

21. Confucius remarked, "From a man who is not bashful in his talk, it is difficult to expect much in the way of action."

22. On one occasion, having heard that the Prime Minister of a neighbouring State had murdered the prince, his master, Confucius, after purifying himself as when going to worship, presented himself before the prince of his own State, and said: "The minister of the neighbouring State has murdered the Prince, his master. I beg that steps to bring him to a summary punishment may be at once undertaken. "But the prince only answered: "Go and tell our

处。要不是管仲，我们现在应该像野蛮人那样生活了吧。他当然不会像你所说的普通人中，忠实的爱人与他的恋人那样，为了证明他们的贞节，去溺死在一条沟渠中，没人会注意到他们。"

19. 公叔文子之臣大夫僎，与文子同升诸公。子闻之，曰："可以为文矣。"

    　　某国的一位贵族（他死后被赋予了杰出文士的称号）当他被征召去政府任职时，他把他的一位随从官员选为同僚。孔子对此评论说："这样一个人的确应授予'杰出文士'的称号啊。"

20. 子言卫灵公之无道也，康子曰："夫如是，奚而不丧？"孔子曰："仲叔圉治宾客，祝鮀治宗庙，王孙贾治军旅。夫如是，奚其丧？"

    　　有一次，孔子正在评论某国一位国君的可耻生活，有人说："如果他是这样一个人——他怎么没有丢掉他的王位呢？""这是因为，"孔子回答说，"他有杰出而有才干的人去从事他的行政机关中的不同职责。"

21. 子曰："其言之不怍，则为之也难。"

    　　孔子说："从一个谈话时不觉羞怯的人那里，很难在行为方式上期待很多。"

22. 陈成子弑简公。孔子沐浴而朝，告于哀公曰："陈恒弑其君，请讨之。"公曰："告夫三子！"孔子曰："以吾从大夫之后，不敢不告也。君曰'告夫三子'者。"之三子告，不可。孔子曰："以吾从大夫之后，不敢不告也。"

    　　有一次，听到一个邻国的首要大臣谋杀了国君——他的主人，孔子就像祭祀时那样沐浴斋戒之后，见到了他自己国家的国君，说："邻国的大臣谋杀了国君——他的主人。我请求立刻采取措施惩罚他。"但国

ministers in the government."

Confucius then went out, saying as he went: "As I have the honour to sit in the State council of the country, I have thought it my duty to bring this to the notice of my prince; but he, my prince, now tells me to go and inform the ministers."Confucius accordingly went to see the ministers then in power, and told them what he had said to the prince; but the ministers also would not do anything in the matter. Confucius then said: "As I have the honour to be a member of the State council of the country, I have done my duty in bringing this to your notice."

23. A disciple of Confucius enquired how one should behave towards the prince, his master. Confucius answered, "Do not impose upon him and, if necessary, withstand him to his face. "

24. Confucius remarked, "A wise and good man looks upwards in his aspirations; a fool looks downwards. "

25. Confucius remarked, "Men in old times educated themselves for their own sakes, Men now educate themselves to impress others."

26. An officer of a certain State, who was an old friend of Confucius, sent a messenger with a message of enquiry to him. Confucius, after making the messenger sit down with him, said to him: "What has your master been doing?" "My master," replied the messenger, "has been trying to reduce the number of his shortcoming without,

君仅仅回答说："去告诉我们政府中的大臣们吧。"

孔子于是就出来了，出来的时候说："因为我有任职这个国家国会的头衔，我把让我的国君对这件事引起注意视为我的职责，但是他，我的国君，现在却告诉我去通知大臣们。"孔子于是去见当权的大臣们，并告诉他们他对国君所说过的话。但大臣们在这件事上同样什么也不做。孔子于是说："因为我有任职这个国家的国会成员的头衔，我已尽了职责让你们对这件事引起注意。"

23. 子路问事君。子曰："勿欺也，而犯之。"

孔子的一位学生问一个人应该以怎样的言行举止对待国君——他的主人，孔子回答说："不要欺骗他，如果必要的话，要当着他的面反对他。"

24. 子曰："君子上达，小人下达。"

孔子说："明智而良善的人在他的志向方面是向上看的，蠢人是向下看的。"

25. 子曰："古之学者为己，今之学者为人。"

孔子说："古时候的人，自我学习是因为他们自己的原因；今天的人，自我学习是为了让别人铭记他。"

26. 蘧伯玉使人于孔子。孔子与之坐而问焉，曰："夫子何为？"对曰："夫子欲寡其过而未能也。"使者出。子曰："使乎！使乎！"

某国的一位官员，是孔子的老朋友，派一位使者问候孔子。孔子让使者与他坐在一起之后，对他说："你的主人在忙什么？""我的主人，"

however, being able to do so."

When the messenger had left, Confucius exclaimed, "What a messenger! What a messenger!"

27. Confucius remarked, "A man who is not in office in the government of a country should not give advice as to its policy."

28. A disciple of Confucius remarked, "A wise man should never occupy his thoughts with anything outside of his position."

29. Confucius remarked, "A wise man is ashamed to say much; he prefers to do more. "

30. Confucius once remarked, "A wise and good man may be known in three ways which I am not able to show in my own person. As a moral man he is free from anxiety; as a man of understanding he is free from doubt; and as a man of courage he is free from fear."

A disciple, who heard what Confucius said, then remarked, "That is only what you *say* of yourself, sir."

31. A disciple of Confucius was fond of criticising men and making comparisons. Confucius said to him, "You must be a very superior man to be able to do that. For myself, I have no time for it."

那位使者回答说,"正在试着减少他的缺点,然而却做不到。"

当那位使者离开后,孔子感叹:"好一位使者! 好一位使者!"

27. 子曰:"不在其位,不谋其政。"

孔子说:"一个不在一国政府中任职的人,绝不应就它的政策提出建议。"

28. 曾子曰:"君子思不出其位。"

孔子的一个学生说:"一个明智的人,绝不应把他的思虑用于超出他职务之外的事情。"

29. 子曰:"君子耻其言而过其行。"

孔子说:"一个明智的人耻于说过多的话,他宁愿去做更多的事情。"

30. 子曰:"君子道者三,我无能焉:仁者不忧,知者不惑,勇者不惧。"子贡曰:"夫子自道也。"

孔子有一次说:"一个明智而良善的人,会通过三种方式被人知晓,而我自身无法表现出来。作为一个道德的人,他免于忧虑;作为一个智慧通达的人,他免于困惑;以及作为一个有勇气的人,他免于恐惧。"

一位学生听到了孔子说的话,然后说:"这说的正是您自己啊,先生。"

31. 子贡方人。子曰:"赐也贤乎哉? 夫我则不暇。"

孔子的一个学生喜欢评论人并加以比较。孔子对他说:"你能够做这个,一定是个非常优秀的人。像我自己,我就没工夫干这个。"

32. Confucius remarked, "Be not concerned that men do not know you; be concerned that you have no ability. "

33. Confucius remarked, "A man who does not anticipate deceit nor imagine untrustworthiness, but who can readily detect their presence, must be a very superior man."

34. A practical character of the time said once to Confucius, "What do you mean by rambling about with your talk? I am afraid you are also but a self-seeking good talker. " "I do not wish," replied Confucius, "to be a good talker; but I hate narrow-minded bigotry in men. "

35. Confucius remarked, "A good horse is considered so, not because of its mere brute strength, but because of its moral qualities. "

36. Someone on one occasion enquired of Confucius, saying: "What do you say of requiting injury with kindness?" Confucius replied, "How will you then requite kindness? Requite injury with justice and kindness with kindness."

37. Confucius on one occasion remarked, "Ah! There is no one who understands me." Thereupon a disciple asked, "What do you mean, sir, in saying that no one understands you?" Confucius then answered, "I do not repine against God, nor do I complain of men. My studies are among lowly things; but my thoughts penetrate the sublime. Ah! There is perhaps only God who understands me. "

32. 子曰:"不患人之不己知,患其不能也。"

　　孔子说:"不要担心人们并不知道你;而要担心你自己没有才能。"

33. 子曰:"不逆诈,不亿不信,抑亦先觉者,是贤乎!"

　　孔子说:"一个人并不预先忧虑别人欺诈,也不去臆测别人不可信赖,却能够轻而易举地发现它们的存在,就一定是个非常优秀的人。"

34. 微生亩谓孔子曰:"丘何为是栖栖者与? 无乃为佞乎?"孔子曰:"非敢为佞也,疾固也。"

　　那个时代的一位实干家有一次对孔子说:"你四处演讲闲逛,用意何在? 我担心你也只是个追逐私利的娴熟说客罢了。""我并不希望,"孔子回答说,"成为一个娴熟的说客,但我厌恶人们思想狭隘的顽固偏见。"

35. 子曰:"骥不称其力,称其德也。"

　　孔子说:"一匹好马之所以为好马,并不是因为它的蛮力,而是因为它的道德品质。"

36. 或曰:"以德报怨,何如?"子曰:"何以报德? 以直报怨,以德报德。"

　　有一次,有人问孔子说:"你认为用善意来回报伤害怎么样?"孔子回答说:"那么你又将如何来回报善意呢? 用公正回报伤害,用善意回报善意。"

37. 子曰:"莫我知也夫!"子贡曰:"何为其莫知子也?"子曰:"不怨天,不尤人。下学而上达。知我者其天乎!"

　　孔子有一次说:"啊! 没有人理解我。"一位学生于是问:"先生,您说没有人理解您,是什么意思?"孔子回答:"我不对上天不满,也不对人们抱怨。我的学问存在于卑微的事物之中,但我的思想却洞悉崇高的东西。啊! 也许只有上天理解我。"

38. A man having on one occasion slandered Confucius and his disciple, the intrepid Chung Yu, to a noble of the Court, somebody informed Chung Yu of it. Chung Yu afterwards, in speaking of it to Confucius, said, "My Lord — is being led astray by that man; but I am strong enough to exterminate that man and expose his carcase on the market-place." Upon which Confucius said, "Whether or not I shall succeed in carrying out my teaching among men, depends upon the will of God. What can that man do against the will of God."

39. Confucius remarked on one occasion: "Men of real moral worth now retire from the world altogether. Some of less degree of worth avoid or retire from certain countries. Some of still less degree of worth retire as soon as they are looked upon with disfavour. Some of the least degree of worth retire when they are told to do so."

40. Confucius went on to say, "I know of seven men who have written books."

41. A disciple of Confucius, the intrepid Chung Yu, had on one occasion to pass a night before the gate of a city. The keeper of the gate, on seeing him , asked, "Where are you from, sir?" "I am from Confucius," replied Chung Yu. "Oh," said the other, "isn't it he who knows the impracticalness of the times, and is yet trying to do something? "

38. 公伯寮愬子路于季孙。子服景伯以告,曰:"夫子固有惑志于公伯寮,吾力犹能肆诸市朝。"子曰:"道之将行也与? 命也。道之将废也与? 命也。公伯寮其如命何!"

   有一次,一个人向一位朝廷的贵族造谣,诋毁孔子和他的学生——那位刚勇的仲由,有人把这件事通知给了仲由。然后,在向孔子谈到这件事情时,仲由说:"那位大人——正在被那个人导向歧途;但是我足以能消灭那个人并把他的尸体暴露在集市上。"说到这个,孔子说:"我是否能成功地在人们中间实现我的学说,取决于上天的意志。那个人能够把上天的意志怎么样呢?"

39. 子曰:"贤者辟世,其次辟地,其次辟色,其次辟言。"

   有一次,孔子说:"现在真正有道德的人都遁世了。有些在程度上次一等的人会逃避或从某些国家退隐。有些在程度上再次一等的人只有在他们备受冷落的时候才会退隐。有些在程度上最次的人会在他们被告诉去这样做的时候退隐。"

40. 子曰:"作者七人矣。"

   孔子继续说:"我知道有七个已写有著作的人。"

41. 子路宿于石门。晨门曰:"奚自?"子路曰:"自孔氏。"曰:"是知其不可而为之者与?"

   孔子的一位学生,那位刚勇的仲由,有一次不得不在一座城市的大门前度过了一夜。大门的看守者看到他后问:"你从哪里来,先生?""从孔夫子那里。"仲由回答说。"噢!"那人说,"他不是那个明明知道这个时代不可实行,却仍在试着去做些事情的人吗?"

42. Confucius was on one occasion playing upon a musical instrument when a man carrying a basket passed the door of the house. "Ah!" said the man on hearing the sound of the music, "He has his heart full, the musician who is playing there!" After a while, he said, "How contemptible to go on thrumming like that when nobody takes any notice of you: you should stop!

You must swim over when the water is high.

But in low water you may 'paidle' and keep dry."

On hearing what the man said, Confucius remarked: "That certainly shows determination; But it is not difficult."

43. A disciple of Confucius enquired of him, saying, "What is meant when the Book of Records says that an ancient Emperor while observing the period of Imperial mourning, keep silence for three years? "

Confucius answered, "That was the rule not only in the case of that particular Emperor: it was a general rule with all princes of antiquity. When the sovereign died, for three years all public functionaries received their orders from the Chief Minister."

44. Confucius remarked, "When the rulers encourage education and good manners, the people are easily amenable to government."

45. A disciple of Confucius enquired what constituted a wise and good man.

Confucius answered, "A wise and good man is one who sets himself seriously to order his conversation aright?" "Is that all?"

42. 子击磬于卫。有荷蒉而过孔氏之门者,曰:"有心哉! 击磬乎!"
既而曰:"鄙哉! 硁硁乎! 莫己知也,斯己而已矣。深则厉,浅则
揭。"子曰:"果哉! 末之难矣。"

　　有一次,孔子在演奏一个乐器,这时一个人扛着一只筐从家门口经
过。"啊!"听到音乐声的那个人说,"那位正在演奏的乐师,他非常用
心!"过了一会儿,他说:"像这样继续乱弹而没人给予一丁点的注意是
多么可鄙啊:你应该停下来! '水深时你必须得游过去,/浅水中你却
可以"趟过"并保持不湿。'"

　　听到那个人说的话,孔子说:"这样的确表现出了坚定果断,但它并
不困难。"

43. 子张曰:"《书》云:'高宗谅阴,三年不言。'何谓也?"子曰:"何
必高宗,古之人皆然。君薨,百官总己以听于冢宰三年。"

　　孔子的一位学生问他:"《尚书》上说一位古代的帝王在举办帝国
的丧事期间,保持沉默了三年,是什么意思?"

　　孔子回答说:"这不仅是该事例中那位帝王的规则:它是古代所有
国君的普遍规则。君主去世后,三年之内,所有的公务官员都会听从来
自首要大臣的命令。"

44. 子曰:"上好礼,则民易使也。"

　　孔子说:"当统治者鼓励教育与良好的礼仪时,人民就会很容易甘
愿接受统治。"

45. 子路问君子。子曰:"修己以敬。"曰:"如斯而已乎?"曰:"修己
以安人。"曰:"如斯而已乎?"曰:"修己以安百姓。修己以安百
姓,尧舜其犹病诸!"

　　孔子的一位学生问怎样才算是一个明智而良善的人。

asked the disciple. "Yes," replied Confucius, "He wants to order his conversation aright for the happiness of others." "Is that all?" asked the disciple again. "Yes," replied Confucius, "He wants to order his conversation aright for the happiness of the world; and, judged by that, even the great ancient Emperors felt their shortcomings."

46. A worthless man, well known to Confucius, was on one occasion squatting on his heels, and did not rise up when Confucius passed by him. Confucius then said to him: "A wilful man and a bad citizen in your youth, in manhood you have done nothing to distinguish yourself, and now you are dishonouring your old age: such a man is called a rascal!" With that, Confucius lifted his staff and hit him on the shanks.

47. A youth of a certain place was employed by Confucius in his house to answer the door and introduce visitors. Someone remarked to Confucius, "I suppose he has improved in his education." "No," replied Confucius, "I have observed him sitting where a youth of his age should not sit, and walking side by side with people who are his seniors. He is not one who seeks to improve his education; he is only one who is in a great hurry to become a grown-up man."

孔子回答说:"一个明智而良善的人就是让自己严肃认真地去使他的谈吐正确恰当的人。""只是这样吗?"那位学生问。"是的,"孔子回答说,"他是为了别人的快乐才使他的谈吐恰当的。""只是这样吗?"那位学生又问。"是的,"孔子回答说,"他是为了世人的幸福使他的谈吐恰当的;如果用这个来判断的话,即使是伟大的古代帝王们也会感到他们的不足。"

46. 原壤夷俟。子曰:"幼而不孙弟,长而无述焉,老而不死,是为贼!"以杖叩其胫。

　　孔子所熟知的一个卑劣无用的人,有一次孔子经过时,他蹲着没有起身。孔子对他说:"你在年轻的时候是个任性固执的人和不良公民,成年以后你没有做出任何让自己杰出的事情,现在,你又让你的晚年蒙羞:这样一个人就是恶棍无赖!"说着,孔子举起拐杖敲他的小腿。

47. 阙党童子将命。或问之曰:"益者与?"子曰:"吾见其居于位也,见其与先生并行也。非求益者也,欲速成者也。"

　　某地的一个年轻人被孔子雇来在家看门并引导来访者。有人对孔子说:"我想他在学识上有所提高了。""不,"孔子回答说,"我发现他常坐在像他这个年龄的年轻人不该坐的地方,而且与比他年长的人并肩走路。他不是一个寻求提高自己学识的人,他只是个急于要变成熟的人。"

【评述】

1. 文中，"邦有道"，辜鸿铭译为 "there is justice and order in the government of the country"，"国家的政治中有正义与秩序"。这是他对政治含义的"道"的常见译法。"邦无道"即其否定句式。两个"谷"字，辜鸿铭译为"to think only of pay"，"仅仅关心薪水"。"耻"译为"dishonour"，"耻辱的，丢脸的"，指无论国家是否有"道"，如果一个人只关心自己的收入，是可耻的。

2. 文中，"克、伐、怨、欲"，辜鸿铭的翻译是："克"译为"ambition"，"野心"；"伐"译为"vanity"，"虚荣"；"怨"译为"envy"，"妒忌"；"欲"译为"selfishness"，"自私自利"，即"野心、虚荣、妒忌、自私"。另外，这里的"仁"，辜鸿铭译为"a moral character"，"有道德的人"。所问的是，如果一个人能够抑制住上面所说的这四种心理或性格的话，算不算是个有道德的人？

3. 文中，"怀居"，辜鸿铭译为"only thinks of the comforts of life"，"只考虑生活的安逸"；"不足以为士"，译为"cannot be a true gentleman"，"不会成为真正的绅士"。

4. 文中，"危言危行"，辜鸿铭译为"bold and lofty in the expression of his opinions as well as in his actions"，"在意见的表达与行为上勇敢而且高尚"。"危"即"勇敢、高尚"之意。"危行言孙"中，"孙"译为"reserved"，"含蓄的，矜持的，有保留的"，指行为可以坚持勇敢高尚，但要注意意见的表达方式，要含蓄谨慎。

5. 文中，"有德者必有言，有言者不必有德"一句，"有德者"，辜鸿铭译为"a man who possesses moral worth"，"一个拥有道德的人"；"有言"，译为"have something to say"，"有话去说"。"仁者必有勇，勇者不必有仁"一句中，"仁者"，译为"a moral character"，"一个有道德的人"；"有勇"译为"has courage"，"有勇气"，指有德之人必然会有话说、有勇气，反之则未必。

6. 文中，"羿善射，奡荡舟，俱不得其死然"一句。"羿善射"，辜鸿铭译为"a famous man in ancient time who was an excellent marksman in archery"，"古代有一个著名的人，他是一位在箭术方面的神射手"；"奡荡舟"译为"there was another man famous for his feats of strength"，"因体力的技艺而著名的人"。"不得其死"，译为"came to an unnatural end"，"没有正常死亡"，即没有善终。"禹稷躬稼，而有天下"。"禹稷躬稼"译为"two men who worked in the fields and toiled as husbandmen"，"两人作为农夫而在田地里长期劳作"；"有天下"译为"finally came to the government of the Empire"，"最后都成了帝国的统治者"。

以上两句话将禹和稷与前面的羿和奡的不同特征及结果进行了对比。

"君子哉若人！尚德哉若人！"这是孔子在听到南宫适讲了上面一段话之后，对他的评价。"君子"，辜鸿铭译为"a really wise and good man"，"一个真正明智而良善的人"；"尚德"译为"he honours moral worth"，"尊崇道德"。孔子肯定南宫适通过历史典故的表述而对个人价值作出的判断。

7. 文中，辜鸿铭将"君子"译为"wise men"，"聪明人"；"小人"译为"a fool"，"蠢人"，指有些"君子"（聪明人）未必是道德的，而"小人"（蠢人）则总是不道德的。

8. 文中，"爱之，能勿劳乎"，辜鸿铭译为"where there is affection, exertion is made easy"，"哪里有爱慕之心，努力就会变得容易"。其中，"爱"译为"affection"，"有爱慕、热爱的情感"；"劳"译为"exertion"，"努力，尽力"，意思是，"爱"的情感能赋予人动力，使人努力。"忠焉，能勿诲乎"，译为"where there is disinterestedness, instruction will not be neglected"，"哪里公正无私，教诲就不会被忽视"。其中，"忠"译为"disinterestedness"，"公正无私"；"诲"译为"instruction"，"教训，教诲"，意思是，公正无私的环境能使人注重道德的教诲。

9. 这一节说的是在制作一份国家文献时，不同大臣之间的分工合作。"为命"的"命"，辜鸿铭译为"the State documents of a certain State of the time"，"某国的一份国家文件"。"为命"，即这一文件的制定。学者多认为指国与国之间的"聘会之书"，一种外交文书。

10. 文中，辜鸿铭略去了"子产"的名字并将之比作柯尔贝尔（见第五章第15节）。同时，再次将管仲比作德国政治家俾斯麦（见第三章第22节）

11. 文中，"贫而无怨"，辜鸿铭译为"To be poor without complaining"，"贫穷而不抱怨"；"富而无骄"译为"to be rich without being proud"，"富有而不高傲"。孔子认为，前者不易做到，后者则不难做到。

12. 文中，"为赵魏老"，辜鸿铭译为"as an officer in the retinue of a great noble"，"作一位显赫贵族的随从官员"。"优"译为"be excellent"，"优秀的"，指做一个显赫贵族的随从他是优秀的；"不可以"译为"he is not fit to"，"不适合去……"，"为滕薛大夫"译为"be councillor of State even in a small principality"，"成为一位政务议员，即使是在一个小型公国"。这是孔子对孟公绰的评价。

13. 文中，"成人"，辜鸿铭译为"a perfect character"，"完美无缺的人"。辜鸿铭认为，本节是孔子讨论如何算是一个完美无缺的人。辜鸿铭略去了"臧武仲""公绰""卞庄子"、"冉求"的人名，而"知"、"不欲"、"勇"、"艺"是这四人的特质。辜鸿铭的翻译是："知"译为"intellect"，"智力"；"不欲"译为"disinterestedness"，"超然无欲"；"勇"译为"gallantry"，"勇敢"；"艺"译为"accomplishments"，"才艺"。也就是说，作为一个"完人"应同时具备这四方面的特质。但仅如此仍不是"成人"，还须"文之以礼乐"，辜鸿铭译为"culture himself by the study of the arts and institutions of the civilised world"，"通过研究这个文明社会的艺术及制度来培养自己"。其中，"文"指"培养、教化"之意；"礼乐"指"这个文明社会的艺术及制度"。

14. 文中，"子问公叔文子于公明贾"一句，辜鸿铭译为"enquired about a teacher from one of his disciples"，"从一个老师的学生那里询问他的老师"，即"公叔文子"是"公明贾"的老师，略去了两人名字，但指出了他们的师生关系。"夫子不言、不笑、不取"一句，"不言"译为"seldom speaks"，"很少说话"。"不笑"译为"seldom laughs"，"很少笑"。"不取"译为"never accepts anything from anybody"，"从来不从任何人那里接受任何东西"。前两个"不"是很少的意思；后一个"不"是绝不的意思。孔子问公明贾他的老师公叔文子是否如此。

15. 文中，"以防求为后于鲁"一句，"防"，辜鸿铭译为"an important military town"，"一个军事重镇"；"求为后于鲁"，译为"sending a message to the prince to beg him to appoint a successor to his own family estate"，"向国君传递消息，请求委任一个继承者来继承他的家产"。"后"指的是自己的继承者。"虽曰不要君，吾不信也"一句中，"要君"，译为"use intimidation with the prince"，"胁迫国君"，即要挟之意。这句话指，尽管有人说臧武仲没有要挟国君，但孔子不信。

16. 本节，辜鸿铭略去了"晋文公"、"齐桓公"的称呼，但开头指出这句话是孔子对当时两位国君的评价。另外，辜鸿铭在翻译中把"晋文公"这位春秋霸主比作17世纪普鲁士弗里德里希大帝（1712—1786），后者统治普鲁士46年，使普鲁士确立了欧洲大国的地位，并为普鲁士统一德意志奠定了基础；把"齐桓公"比作19世纪普鲁士国王威廉一世（1797—1888），德意志帝国第一任皇帝，俾斯麦称他是一位谦恭有礼的绅士。

17. 辜鸿铭在翻译子路的话时首先介绍了这段谈话的背景，即"管仲"与"召忽"都被任命为"公子纠"的老师。这一节讨论的是，当公子纠的弟弟齐桓公杀死他之后，管仲与召忽作为其老师的截然不同的表现——召忽选择陪他学生一起死去，管仲则没有。

文中，"未仁乎？"辜鸿铭译为"Did not Kuan Chung in this show that he was not a moral character?"，"管仲不是有道德的人吧？"指子路质疑管仲"不仁"。下文是孔子针对这一质疑而对管仲进行的评价。

"桓公九合诸侯，不以兵车，管仲之力也"。辜鸿铭译："九合诸侯"为"call together the princes of the Empire to a Congress"，"把帝国的诸侯国君们召集到一起举行会议"，意思是，管仲使诸侯和平谈判，从而避免了全面的战争。辜鸿铭对齐桓公"九合诸侯"注释说：

那时的柏林会议。

指1878年俾斯麦代表德国邀请欧洲各国与奥匈帝国在柏林召开会议，商讨解决英国、奥匈帝国与俄国之间在巴尔干半岛等地的矛盾。"如其仁，如其仁"，辜鸿铭译为"what has one to say against the moral character — what has one to say against the moral character of man like that?"，"为什么还要声讨这位有道德的人，为什么还要声讨像这样一位有道德的人呢？"强调人们只看到了管仲貌似"不仁"的地方，却没有看到管仲实际为和平所做出的贡献。

18. 辜鸿铭认为，这是子贡接着上一节子路的疑问，继续发问的。"桓公杀公子纠，不能死，又相之"一句，"相之"，译为"he even served the younger prince, the very man who murdered his pupil and charge"，"他甚至又辅佐小王子——就是谋杀了他的学生、他所照顾的人的那个人"，指管仲不仅没有像召忽那样，为他的学生公子纠去死，而是"背叛"了公子纠，给杀他的凶手齐桓公为相。这是子贡的进一步发问。孔子对此又做出阐述，接着提出反问："岂若匹夫匹妇之为谅也，自经于沟渎而莫之知也？"其中，"匹夫匹妇"，辜鸿铭译为"your faithful lover and his sweetheart among the common people"，"普通人中忠实的爱人与他的恋人"。这一句意指普通人可以为了固守某个信用而自由地选择为之默默死去。而管仲则不同，身负更多的使命和责任。

19. 对于"公叔文子"，辜鸿铭翻译时补充了他的身份："who after his death was given the title of Beauclerc"，"他死后被赋予了杰出文士的称号"。其中，"Beauclerc"也是对下文中"文"的翻译，即"杰出文士"。总的来看，这段话指公叔文子具有心胸坦荡、为人正直、不为自己的私利而埋没人才的品格。

20. 文中，"子言卫灵公之无道也"一句，"无道"，辜鸿铭译为"the scandalous life"，"可耻的生活"，指孔子谈得卫灵公的生活状况。辜鸿铭在注释中把他比作17世纪英国国王查理二世，据说此人奉行享乐主义。辜鸿铭注释说：

那时的查理二世,"一个愉快的帝王,可耻而拙劣。"他的妻子是第六章第26节提到的那个声名狼藉的王妃。

这句话指,卫灵公虽然私生活糜烂,但他有优秀的人才在打理国政,故不失国。

21. 文中,"言之不怍",辜鸿铭译为"is not bashful in his talk","谈话时不觉羞怯",即大言不惭之意。其中,"怍"是"bashful",羞怯,腼腆之意。"为之也难",译为"it is difficult to expect much in the way of action","很难在行为方式上期待很多",指惯于大言不惭的人,往往会只说不做,华而不实。

22. "陈成子弑简公"一句,指齐国大夫陈恒杀了齐国国君齐简公。辜鸿铭译为"the Prime Minister of a neighbouring State had murdered the prince","一个邻国的首要大臣谋杀了国君"。略去了齐国国名及陈成子(陈恒)的名字。而"告夫三子"一句,"三子",即当时在鲁国专权的"三桓",或称"三家",指孟孙(仲孙)、叔孙、季孙,辜鸿铭译为"go and tell our ministers in the government","去告诉我们政府中的大臣们吧",翻译中也没有特指"三桓"。最后一句"以吾从大夫之后,不敢不告也",辜鸿铭译为"as I have the honour to sit in the State council of the country, I have thought it my duty to bring this to the notice of my prince","因为我有任职这个国家国会的头衔,我把让我的国君对这件事引起注意视为我的职责","不敢不告",即自己履行这样的职责去告知此事。这显示了孔子尽责然而无奈的情绪。

23. 文中,"事君",辜鸿铭译为"how one should behave towards the prince","应该以怎样的言行举止对待国君",即问与国君应如何相处。

24. 文中,"上达",辜鸿铭译为"look upwards in his aspirations","在他的志向方面向上看";"下达"译为"look downwards","向下看",指人的追求不同,君子追求进步、提高,小人则惯于追求低级的东西。

25. 文中,"为己",辜鸿铭译为"for their own sakes","为了他们自己起见",即加强自身的修养;"为人",译为"to impress others","让别人铭记他,钦佩他,敬仰他",即获得外在的好处,功利性的。

26. 文中,"蘧伯玉",辜鸿铭译为"an old friend of Confucius","孔子的一位老朋友";"使人于孔子",译为"sent a messenger with a message of enquiry to him","派一位

使者问候孔子"。"夫子何为",译为"what has your master been doing","你的主人在忙什么"。这是孔子问蘧伯玉的使者。下文中使者的回答出乎孔子的意料。

"欲寡其过而未能也",辜鸿铭译为"trying to reduce the number of his shortcoming without, however, being able to do so","正在试着减少他的缺点,然而却做不到"。使者回答的是蘧伯玉道德修养的事情。这使孔子很感意外,于是他大为感叹。

27. 辜鸿铭注释说:

> 第七章第14节的重复。

这里辜鸿铭有误,应为第八章第14节。

28. 本节,学者多认为是曾子引用《周易·艮》"君子以思不出其位"的句子,来佐证上段孔子的话,指人应专注于自己的本职工作或分内之事,辜鸿铭译为"never occupy his thoughts with anything outside of his position","绝不应把他的思虑用于超出他职务之外的事情"。

29. 文中,"耻其言",辜鸿铭译为"is ashamed to say much","耻于说过多地话"。"过其行",译为"prefers to do more","宁愿去做更多的事情"。这同样表达了孔子重行而轻言的思想。

30. 文中,"君子道者三,我无能焉"一句,"君子道者三"译为"a wise and good man may be known in three ways","一个明智而良善的人,会通过三种方式被人知晓"。这三种方式即"仁者不忧,知者不惑,勇者不惧"。其中,"仁者不忧"译为"as a moral man he is free from anxiety","作为一个道德的人,他免于忧虑";"知者不惑"译为"as a man of understanding he is free from doubt","作为一个智慧通达的人,他免于困惑";"勇者不惧"译为"as a man of courage he is free from fear","作为一个有勇气的人,他免于恐惧"。孔子认为,这是君子应具有的三个典型特质。

31. 文中,"方人",辜鸿铭译为"criticising men and making comparisons","对人评论并作比较",指喜欢议论他人是非。这是子贡喜欢做的事。"赐也贤乎哉",辜鸿铭译为"you must be a very superior man to be able to do that","你能够做这个,一定是个非常优秀的人",指孔子说反话,讽刺子贡。"夫我则不暇",译为"for myself, I have no time for it","像我自己,我就没工夫干这个"。这是孔子对"方人"这一行为的不齿。

32. 文中，"能"，辜鸿铭译为"ability"，"才能"。本节与第四章第14节"不患无位，患所以立。不患莫己知，求为可知也"表达了同样的思想。

33. 文中，"不逆诈"，辜鸿铭译为"does not anticipate deceit"，"不预先忧虑别人欺诈"。其中，"逆"为"anticipate"，"预先假设、忧虑、考虑"之意；"诈"译为"deceit"，"欺骗、欺诈"。"不亿不信"，译为"nor imagine untrustworthiness"，"不去臆测别人不可信赖"。其中"亿"译为"imagine"，"臆测、猜想"；"不信"译为"untrustworthiness"，"不可信赖，不忠实"。"先觉"，译为"can readily detect their presence"，"能够轻而易举地发现它们的存在"，指能够轻易察觉前面所说的"欺诈"与"不可信赖"。"贤"，译为"a very superior man"，"非常优秀的人"。按辜鸿铭的说法：前两句（"不逆诈，不亿不信"）说的是与人相处时不要心存偏见，刻意忖度别人心存不良，然而，后一句（"先觉"）则指出，在与别人的相处过程中，却能够很清醒地察觉别人的不良心态。能做到如此，就是非常优秀的人。

34. 文中，辜鸿铭略去了"微生亩"的名字，译之为"a practical character"，"一位实干家"。说明此人过于务实，过于注重世俗利害。

35. 文中，"骥"，辜鸿铭译为"a good horse"，"好马"，泛指好马。"不称其力，称其德也"。"德"，学者多认为指驯服且有威仪。辜鸿铭译为"not because of its mere brute strength, but because of its moral qualities"，"不是因为它的蛮力，而是因为它的道德特性"。其中，"称"是指"马称为好马的原因"；"力"译为"brute strength"，"蛮力"；"德"译为"moral qualities"，"道德品质"。在《中国人的精神（在北京东方学会上所宣讲的论文）》一文中，辜鸿铭说："一匹纯种的阿拉伯骏马之所以能够明白其英国主人的意图，既不是因为它学过英语语法，也不是因为它对英语有本能的反应，而是因为它热爱并依恋它的主人。"（夏丹等选编，《辜鸿铭作品精选·中国人的精神》，第26页）这也可以视为他对马的"德性"的一种解释。

36. 文中，"以德报怨"辜鸿铭译为"requiting injury with kindness"，"用善意来回报伤害"。其中，"德"译为"kindness"，"善意，仁慈"；"怨"译为"injury"，"伤害，损害"；"报"译为"requite"，"回报，报答"。"以直报怨，以德报德"，辜鸿铭译为"requite injury with justice and kindness with kindness"，"用公正回报伤害，用善意回报善意"。其中，"直"译为"justice"，"公正"。

37. 文中，"莫我知也夫"，辜鸿铭译为"there is no one who understands me"，"没有人理解我"。这是孔子自叹，下面的文字是孔子自述。其中，"怨天"译为"repine against

God","对上帝不满",按照惯常的译法,把"天"译为"上帝"。

38. 文中,"公伯寮愬子路于季孙",辜鸿铭译为"A man having on one occasion slandered Confucius and his disciple, the intrepid Chung Yu, to a noble of the Court","有一次,一个人向一位朝廷的贵族造谣,诋毁孔子和他的学生——那位刚勇的仲由"。即公伯寮诋毁孔子和子路。"子服景伯以告"译为"somebody informed Chung Yu of it",即"有人把这件事通知给了仲由"。后面"曰"字,辜鸿铭译为"Chung Yu afterwards, in speaking of it to Confucius","然后,在向孔子谈到这件事情时,仲由说"。"吾力犹能肆诸市朝",译为"I am strong enough to exterminate that man and expose his carcase on the market-place","我足以能消灭那个人并把他的尸体暴露在集市上"。这是子路对公伯寮的诋毁行为的强烈反应,嫉恶如仇的性格,使他想杀人。下面的文字描述了孔子的反应。

39. 文中,"贤者辟世",辜鸿铭译为"men of real moral worth now retire from the world altogether","现在真正有道德品格的人都遁世了"。其中,"贤者"译为"men of real moral worth","真正有道德品格的人。""辟"译为"retire from","隐遁"之意。"其次辟地,其次辟色,其次辟言"是三种隐遁的方式。其中,"辟地",译为"avoid or retire from certain countries","逃避或从某些国家退隐";"辟色",译为"retire as soon as they are looked upon with disfavour","在他们备受冷落的时候退隐",指的是在国家或社会上不受充分尊敬与重用、价值因此无法实现;"辟言",译为"retire when they are told to do so","在他们被告诉去这样做的时候退隐",即别人告诉他们退隐,或劝说他们退隐的时候,他们才有可能退隐。

40. 辜鸿铭将"子曰"译为"Confucius went on to say","孔子继续说",即孔子承接上一节,继续谈话;"作者七人矣",译为"I know of seven men who have written books","我知道有七个已写有著作的人","作"即著书之意,但辜鸿铭又在此注释说对这种解释并不确定:

> 我们在此冒险地把"作"这个词翻译为"写有著作并提出学说"。那位伟大的中国注释家放弃了这一段,说他不理解所提到的内容。

> 朱熹注释说:"李氏曰:'作,起也。言起而隐去者,今七人矣。不可知其谁何。必求其人以实之,则凿矣。"(《四书章句集注》,第158页)

41. 文中,"宿于石门",辜鸿铭译为"pass a night before the gate of a city","在一座城市的大门前度过了一夜"。其中,"石门"指"城门",子路在城门外露宿了一夜;"晨门"译为"the keeper of the gate","大门的看守"。大门看守说孔子"知其不可而为之者",辜鸿铭译为"he who knows the impracticalness of the times, and is yet trying to do something","明明知道这个时代不可实行,却仍在试着去做些事情"。辜鸿铭在此注释认为,那时有品格的人都隐退了,包括此处大门的看守也是一位隐士:

> 在孔子时代,真正有品格的人都从世界隐退了:为了过一种正直的生活而从事于低微的工作,比如此处的那位大门看守者。在欧洲,那位世界著名的哲学家斯宾诺莎从事的是玻璃镜片的研磨!

42. 文中,"有心哉,击磬乎!"是荷蒉者感叹孔子击磬,辜鸿铭译为"he has his heart full, the musician who is playing there!","那位正在演奏的乐师,他非常用心!""有心",即用心、认真之意。下面荷蒉者继续说,"鄙哉硁硁乎! 莫己知也,斯己而已矣",辜鸿铭译为"how contemptible to go on thrumming like that when nobody takes any notice of you: you should stop!","像这样继续乱弹而没人给予一丁点的注意是多么可鄙啊: 你应该停下来!"其中,"鄙"译为"contemptible","可鄙的,卑劣的"。是形容孔子一味坚持自我。"硁硁乎"译为"go on thrumming like that","像这样乱弹"。指的就是孔子不管有没有听众,只一味自己弹奏。"莫己知也,斯己而已矣",译为"nobody takes any notice of you:you should stop","没人给予一丁点的注意: 你应该停下来"。明确表示,孔子应该停止做这种毫无意义的盲目坚持。

"深则厉,浅则揭"表达了荷蒉者的处事态度,意思是过河的方式根据水的深浅而定,不一定非要用一种过河方式,要知道权变处世。对于"揭"字,辜鸿铭还引用18世纪著名苏格兰诗人彭斯的《往昔的时光》中的一句话注释说:

> "Paidle","趟过"的苏格兰说法。"我们曾赤脚趟过河流。"([回译者注]汉译诗句引自《彭斯诗选》,王佐良译,人民文学出版社,第27页)

"果哉,末之难矣",辜鸿铭译为"That certainly shows determination; But it is not difficult","这样的确表现出了坚定果断,但它并不困难"。辜鸿铭最后注释说:

> 即在轻蔑与厌恶中远离世界。

指这样做并不困难。

43.文中,《书》(《尚书》),辜鸿铭译为"the Book of Record",记录之书。这是他对《尚书》较固定的翻译,与第二章第21节同。"高宗谅阴,三年不言",这是《尚书·周书·无逸》里的话,原文是:"其在高宗,时旧劳于外,爰暨小人。作其即位,乃或亮阴,三年不言。""高宗",指商王武丁。"谅阴",一般认为指高宗守孝。这句话辜鸿铭译为"an ancient Emperor while observing the period of Imperial mourning, keep silence for three years","一位古代的帝王在举办帝国的丧事期间,保持沉默了三年"。其中,"谅阴"辜鸿铭译为"while observing the period of Imperial mourning","办帝国丧事期间",也指守孝,略去了"高宗"的名字。

44. 文中,"礼",辜鸿铭译为"education and good manners","教育与良好的礼仪"。这也是辜鸿铭对"礼"比较常见的译法。"易使",译为"easily amenable to government","很容易甘愿接受统治",指的是民众在好的教育之下,更有遵守秩序、追求秩序之心。

45. "君子",辜鸿铭译为"a wise and good man","明智而良善的人"。指道德修养上的"君子"而言。最后一句的"病"字,传统学者多理解为"难",指尧舜也会感到这很困难。辜鸿铭译为"felt their shortcomings","感到他们的不足",即尧舜实际上也并未做到这样的纯粹与高尚。

46. 文中,"原壤夷俟"一句,"原壤"为人名,辜鸿铭略去人名,译为"A worthless man, well known to Confucius","孔子所熟知的一个卑劣无用的人";"夷俟",译为"squatting on his heels, and did not rise up when Confucius passed by him","孔子经过时,他蹲着没有起身"。孔子骂他"幼而不孙弟,长而无述焉,老而不死,是为贼"。"幼而不孙弟",辜鸿铭译为"a wilful man and a bad citizen in your youth","你在年轻的时候是个任性固执的人和不良公民","孙弟"即指做好人和好公民,这是辜鸿铭的通常译法;"长而无述"译为"in manhood you have done nothing to distinguish yourself","成年以后你没有做出任何让自己杰出的事情","述"即指做出杰出的事情,让社会来认可自己。

47. 文中,"阙党童子将命"一句,"阙党",地名;"将命",辜鸿铭译为"was employed by Confucius in his house to answer the door and introduce visitors","被孔子雇来在家看门并引导来访者"。"益者与",译为"I suppose he has improved in his education","我想他在学识上有所提高了"。"见其居于位也,见其与先生并行",译为"sitting where a youth of his age should not sit, and walking side by side with people who are his seniors","常坐在像他这个年龄的年轻人不该坐的地方,而且与比他年长的人并肩走路"。其中,"居于位"指坐到不该坐的地方;"与先生并行"指与年长的人并肩走路。这是孔子观察出的童子不守礼的细节。孔子认为他只是"欲速成",译为"in a great hurry to become a grown-up man","急于要变成熟的人"。

CHAPTER XV
卫灵公第十五

1. The reigning prince of a certain State where Confucius was on a visit on his travels, asked about military tactics. "I know a little about the arts of peace, but I have never studied the art of war." The next day he left the country.

   Then, going on in his travels, he arrived at another State. Their provisions having failed them, his party had to go without food, and were so reduced that they could not proceed. A disciple, the intrepid Chung Yu, with discontent in his look, then said to Confucius, "A wise and good man — can he, too, be reduced to such distress?" "Yes," replied Confucius, "a wise and good man sometimes also meets with distress; but a fool when in distress, becomes reckless."

2. Confucius once remarked to a disciple, "You think, I suppose, that I am one who has learned many things and remembers them all? " "Yes," replied the disciple, "but is it not so?"

   "No," answered Confucius, "I unite all my knowledge by one connecting principle."

3. Confucius on one occasion remarked to a disciple, "It is seldom that men understand real moral worth."

4. Confucius remarked, "The ancient Emperor Shun was perhaps the one man who successfully carried out the principle of no-government. For what need is there really for what is called government? A ruler needs only to be earnest in his personal conduct, and to behave in a manner worthy of his position."

1. 卫灵公问陈于孔子。孔子对曰："俎豆之事，则尝闻之矣；军旅之事，未之学也。"明日遂行。在陈绝粮，从者病，莫能兴。子路愠见曰："君子亦有穷乎？"子曰："君子固穷，小人穷斯滥矣。"

　　孔子在途中访问的某国的执政国君，询问军事策略。"我懂得一点有关和平的策略方法，"孔子回答说，"但我从没学过有关战争的策略方法。"第二天，他就离开了那个国家。

　　然后，在旅途中继续前进，他们到达了另一个国家。他们的粮食供给匮乏，他的队伍不得不在缺乏食物的情况下坚持着，但如此落魄以至于他们无法前进。一个学生，那位刚勇的仲由，脸上带着不满的表情，对孔子说："一个明智而良善的人——他也会落魄到如此的窘境吗？""是的，"孔子回答说，"一个明智而良善的人有时也会遇到窘境，但一个蠢人在窘境下会变得轻率鲁莽。"

2. 子曰："赐也，女以予为多学而识之者与？"对曰："然，非与？"曰："非也，予一以贯之。"

　　有一次，孔子对他的一个学生说："我想，你认为我是一个学了很多东西并已把它们全部记住的一个人吧？""是啊，"那位学生回答，"不是这样吗？"

　　"不是，"孔子回答说，"我是用一个连接性的原则统一了我全部的学问。"

3. 子曰："由！知德者鲜矣。"

　　有一次，孔子对一个学生说："懂得真正道德的人是很少见的。"

4. 子曰："无为而治者，其舜也与？夫何为哉，恭己正南面而已矣。"

　　孔子说："古代的帝王舜也许是唯一成功地实现了去政府原则的人。就他而言，哪里还需要所谓的政府呢？一个统治者只需在个人行为上真诚严肃，并表现出与其身份相匹配的礼仪举止即可。"

5. A disciple of Confucius enquired what one should do in order to get along well with men. Confucius answered, "Be conscientious and sincere in what you say; be earnest and serious in what you do; in that way, although you might be in barbarous countries, you will get along well with men. But if, in what you say, you are not conscientious and sincere, and in what you do, you are not earnest and serious, even in your own country and in your home, how can you get along well with men? Keep these principles constantly before you, as when, driving a carriage, you keep your eyes on the head of your horse. In that way you will always get along well with men."

The disciple had these words engraved on his belt.

6. Confucius, speaking of a famous historiographer of the time, remarked, "What a straightforward man he was! When there were justice and order in the government of his country, he was straight as an arrow; when there were no justice and order, he was still straight as an arrow."

Speaking of another public character of the time, Confucius remarked, "What a really wise and good man he was! When there were justice and order in the government of his country, he entered the public service; but when there were no justice and order, he rolled himself up and led a strictly private life."

7. Confucius remarked, "When you meet the proper person to speak to and do not speak out, you lose your opportunity; but when you meet one who is not a proper person to speak to and you speak to him, you waste your words. A man of intelligence never loses his opportunity, neither does he waste his words."

5. 子张问行。子曰:"言忠信,行笃敬,虽蛮貊之邦行矣;言不忠信,行不笃敬,虽州里行乎哉? 立,则见其参于前也;在舆,则见其倚于衡也。夫然后行。"子张书诸绅。

　　孔子的一个学生问应该怎么做才能与人们相处得好。孔子回答说:"说话要讲良心、真诚,做事情要认真、严肃:这样做,即使你可能身处野蛮的国家,你也会与人们相处得很好。但是,如果你说话不讲良心、不真诚,做事情不认真严肃,即使是在你自己的国家,在家乡,又怎能与人们相处得好呢? 你要经常把这个原则保持在你的面前,就像当你驾驶一驾马车的时候,你会保持你的双眼凝视马的正前方。这样做,你就总是会与人们相处得好。"

　　那位学生把这些话刻在了他的腰带上。

6. 子曰:"直哉史鱼! 邦有道,如矢;邦无道,如矢。""君子哉蘧伯玉! 邦有道,则仕;邦无道,则可卷而怀之。"

　　孔子谈到那时的一位著名的历史学家,说:"他是一个多么坦率正直的人啊! 当他国的政治中还有正义与秩序时,他正直得像箭;当没有正义与秩序时,他仍然正直得像箭。"

　　谈到那个时代另一个公众人物,孔子说:"他是一位多么明智而良善的人啊! 当他国的政治中有正义与秩序时,他参与公共事务,但当没有正义与秩序时,他就把自己卷藏起来,过一种完全的私人生活。"

7. 子曰:"可与言而不与之言,失人;不可与言而与之言,失言。知者不失人,亦不失言。"

　　孔子说:"当你遇到了适合对他说话的人,却没开口去说,就是错失良机;当你遇到了一个并不适合对他说话的人,却开口对他说话,就是浪费唇舌。一个有智慧的人从不错失良机,也不会浪费唇舌。"

8. Confucius remarked, "A gentleman of spirit or a man of moral character will never try to save his life at the expense of his moral character: he prefers to sacrifice his life in order to save his moral character."

9. A disciple of Confucius enquired how to live a moral life. Confucius answered, "A workman who wants to perfect his work first sharpens his tools. When you are living in a country, you should serve those nobles and ministers in that country who are men of moral worth, and you should cultivate the friendship of the gentlemen of that country who are men of moral worth."

10. A disciple of Confucius enquired what institutions he would adopt for the government of an Empire. Confucius answered, "I would use the calendar of the Hsia dynasty; introduce the form of carriage used in the Yin dynasty; and adopt the uniform of the present dynasty. For State music I would use the most ancient music. I would prohibit all the popular airs in the music of the present day, and I would banish all popular orators. The modern popular music provokes sensuality in the people, and popular orators are dangerous to the State."

11. Confucius remarked, "If a man takes no thought for the morrow, he will be sorry before to-day is out."

12. Confucius on one occasion was heard to say, "Alas! I do not now see a man who loves moral worth as he loves beauty in women."

8. 子曰："志士仁人，无求生以害仁，有杀身以成仁。"

    孔子说："一个有志气的绅士或一个有道德品质的人，绝不会试着以牺牲道德品质为代价来挽救生命：他宁愿为了挽救道德品质而牺牲生命。"

9. 子贡问为仁。子曰："工欲善其事，必先利其器。居是邦也，事其大夫之贤者，友其士之仁者。"

    孔子的一个学生问如何去过一种有道德的生活。孔子回答说："一个想要完成工作的工人，首先要使他的工具锋利。你生活在一个国家，就应该为那些该国中具有道德品质的贵族与大臣服务，应该建立起与该国那些有道德品质的绅士们之间的友谊。"

10. 颜渊问为邦。子曰："行夏之时，乘殷之辂，服周之冕，乐则《韶》、舞。放郑声，远佞人。郑声淫，佞人殆。"

    孔子的一个学生问他会为一个帝国的政治采取什么样的制度。孔子回答说："我会采用夏朝的历法，引进殷朝使用的马车样式，采取当今这个朝代的制服。在国家音乐方面，我会采用最古老的音乐。我会禁止所有当今音乐中的流行曲调，并放逐所有流行的说客。当代流行音乐会煽起人心中对声色的沉迷，而流行说客对国家则是危险的。"

11. 子曰："人无远虑，必有近忧。"

    孔子说："如果一个人不为明天操心忧虑，在今天结束之前，他会感到遗憾。"

12. 子曰："已矣乎！吾未见好德如好色者也。"

    有一次，孔子被听到说："啊！我现在见不到一个人能够像热爱女人的美貌那样，去热爱道德。"

13. Confucius, speaking of a public character of the time, remarked, "He was like one who had stolen his position. Although he knew the talents and virtues of a friend he had, yet when he came to office in the government he did nothing to bring his friend forward, and was afraid lest his friend should become his colleague. "

14. Confucius remarked, "A man who expects much from himself and demands little from others will never have any enemies."

15. Confucius remarked, "A man who does not constantly say to himself 'What is the right thing to do?' I can do nothing for such a man."

16. Confucius remarked, "When a body of men sit together for a whole day without turning their conversation to some principle or truth, but only amuse themselves with small wit and smart sayings, it is a bad case."

17. Confucius remarked, "A wise and good man makes Right the substance of his being; he carries it out with judgment and good sense; he speaks it with modesty; and he attains it with sincerity: — such a man is a really good and wise man!"

18. Confucius remarked, "A wise and good man should be distressed that he has no ability; he should never be distressed that men do not take notice of him."

13. 子曰："臧文仲其窃位者与？知柳下惠之贤，而不与立也。"

　　孔子谈到那时的一个公众人物，说："他就像是一个偷得自己职位的人。尽管他知道一个朋友的才能与美德，然而，当他到政府上任的时候，他没有推荐他的朋友，并唯恐他的朋友成为他的同事。"

14. 子曰："躬自厚而薄责于人，则远怨矣。"

　　孔子说："一个对自己要求多而对别人要求少的人，将不会有仇敌。"

15. 子曰："不曰'如之何如之何'者，吾末如之何也已矣。"

　　孔子说："一个不经常地对自己说'什么是应该做的正确的事情？'的人，我对这种人也做不了什么。"

16. 子曰："群居终日，言不及义，好行小慧，难矣哉！"

　　孔子说："一群人一整天凑到一起，而没有把话题转移到一些原则或真理上，只是用小聪明与俏皮话来娱乐自己，这真是一件糟糕的事。"

17. 子曰："君子义以为质，礼以行之，孙以出之，信以成之。君子哉！"

　　孔子说："一个明智而良善的人，把正义作为他秉性的本质；用判断力与良好感知来实行它；用谦逊的态度来诉说它；用真诚来达成它——这样一个人，是一个真正良善而明智的人。"

18. 子曰："君子病无能焉，不病人之不己知也。"

　　孔子说："一个明智而良善的人应该因自己没有才能而苦恼；他绝不应该因人们没有注意到他而苦恼。"

19. Confucius remarked, "A wise and good man hates to die without having done anything to distinguish himself."

20. Confucius remarked, "A wise man seeks for what he wants in himself; a fool seeks for it from others."

21. Confucius remarked, "A wise man is proud but not vain; he is sociable, but belongs to no party."

22. Confucius remarked, "A wise man never upholds a man because of what he says, nor does he discard what a man says because of the speaker's character."

23. A disciple of Confucius enquired: "Is there one word which may guide one in practice throughout the whole life?" Confucius answered, "The word 'charity' is perhaps the word. What you do not wish others to do unto you, do not do unto them."

24. Confucius on one occasion remarked, "In my judgement of men, I do not easily award blame nor easily award praise. When I have happened to praise a man in a way which might appear beyond his deserts, you may yet be sure that I have carefully weighed my judgment. The people of to-day — there is really nothing in them

19. 子曰:"君子疾没世而名不称焉。"

　　孔子说:"一个明智而良善的人,憎恨还没有做出什么事情让自己闻名就死去。"

20. 子曰:"君子求诸己,小人求诸人。"

　　孔子说:"一个明智的人会在自己身上寻求他想要的东西;而一个蠢人则会向别人去寻求。"

21. 子曰:"君子矜而不争,群而不党。"

　　孔子说:"一个明智的人骄傲而不自负;善于交际而不会隶属于任何党派。"

22. 子曰:"君子不以言举人,不以人废言。"

　　孔子说:"一个明智的人从来不会因为一个人所说的话而支持他,也不会因为说话者的人品而忽视他所说的话。"

23. 子贡问曰:"有一言而可以终身行之者乎?"子曰:"其恕乎! 己所不欲,勿施于人。"

　　孔子的一个学生问:"是否有一个词能够贯穿整个一生来指导人的实践?"孔子回答说:"'博爱'也许就是这个词。你不希望别人对你做的事情,也不要对他们做。"

24. 子曰:"吾之于人也,谁毁谁誉? 如有所誉者,其有所试矣。斯民也,三代之所以直道而行也。"

　　有一次,孔子说:"在我对人的判断中,我不会轻易地指责也不会轻易地赞扬。当我偶然赞扬一个人,可能表现得超过了他本来的优点时,你可以确信,我已经小心地权衡了我的判断。今天的人们——的确没

to prevent one from dealing honestly with them as the men of the good old times dealt with the people of their day."

25. Confucius in his old age remarked, "In my young days, I could still obtain books which supplied information on points which the standard historical books omitted; and a man who had a horse would willingly lend it to a friend to ride. But now such times and such manners have all disappeared."

26. Confucius remarked, "It is plausible speech which confuses men's ideas of what is moral worth. It is petty impatience which ruins great undertakings."

27. Confucius remarked, "When a man is unpopular, it is necessary to find out why people hate him. When a man is popular, it is still necessary to find out why people like him."

28. Confucius remarked, "It is the *man* that can make his religion or the principles he professes great; and not his religion or the principles which he professes, which can make the man great."

29. Confucius remarked, "To be wrong and not to reform is indeed to be wrong."

30. Confucius on one occasion remarked, "I have spent a whole day without taking food and a whole night without sleep, occupied with thinking. It was of no use. I have found it better to acquire knowledge from books."

有什么去阻止一个人,像过去的美好时代的人对待那个时代的人那样,公正地对待他们。"

25. 子曰:"吾犹及史之阙文也,有马者借人乘之。今亡已夫!"

孔子在晚年说:"在我年轻的时候,我还能够得到一些针对权威历史著作所遗漏的要点而提供信息的书籍;一个拥有一匹马的人,也会很乐意把它借给朋友去骑。但如今,这样的时代和习俗,都已经消失不见了。"

26. 子曰:"巧言乱德,小不忍则乱大谋。"

孔子说:"是貌似合理的言语混淆了人们关于道德品质的观念。是轻微的不耐烦毁坏了伟大的事业。"

27. 子曰:"众恶之,必察焉;众好之,必察焉。"

孔子说:"如果一个人是不受欢迎的,就有必要找出为什么人们厌恶他。如果一个人受到欢迎,仍然有必要找出为什么人们喜欢他。"

28. 子曰:"人能弘道,非道弘人。"

孔子说:"是人能够使他所信仰的宗教或原则变得伟大,而不是他所信仰的宗教或原则使他变得伟大。"

29. 子曰:"过而不改,是谓过矣。"

孔子说:"错了而不去改进,那就是真的错了。"

30. 子曰:"吾尝终日不食,终夜不寝,以思,无益,不如学也。"

有一次,孔子说:"我曾一整天不吃饭、一整夜不睡觉而忙于思考,没有用。我发现还是从书上获取学问更好一些。"

31. Confucius remarked, "A wise and good man is occupied in the search for truth; not in seeking for a mere living. Farming sometimes leads to starvation, and education sometimes leads to the rewards of official life. A wise man should be solicitous about truth, not anxious about poverty."

32. Confucius remarked, "There are men who attain knowledge by their understanding; but, if they have not moral character sufficient to hold fast to it, such men will lose it again. There are men again who have attained it with their understanding and have moral character sufficient to hold fast to it; but if they do not set themselves seriously to order their knowledge aright they will not inspire respect in the people. There are lastly men who have attained it with their understanding; who have moral character sufficient to hold fast to it; and who can set themselves seriously to put it in order; but if they do not exercise and make use of it in accordance with the ideals of decency and good sense, they are not yet perfect."

33. Confucius remarked, "A wise and good man may not show his quality in small affairs, but he can be entrusted with great concerns. A fool may gain distinction in small things, but he cannot be entrusted with great concerns."

34. Confucius remarked, "Men need morality more than the necessaries of life, such as fire and water. I have seen men die by falling into fire or water; but I have never seen men die from falling into morality."

31. 子曰："君子谋道不谋食。耕也,馁在其中矣;学也,禄在其中矣。君子忧道不忧贫。"

　　孔子说:"一个明智而良善的人是忙于探索真理的,而不是仅仅寻求生计。耕作有时会带来饥饿,而教育有时会带来公职生活的报酬。一个明智的人应该渴望真理,而不是担心贫穷。"

32. 子曰："知及之,仁不能守之;虽得之,必失之。知及之,仁能守之。不庄以莅之,则民不敬。知及之,仁能守之,庄以莅之。动之不以礼,未善也。"

　　孔子说:"有人通过他们的智力获得了学问,但如果他们因没有道德品质而无法坚持它,将会再次失去它。再比如,有人用他们的智力获得了它,并且有道德品质足以坚持它,但如果不认真地致力于恰当地把学问梳理得井井有条,他们将不会在人民心中赢得尊敬。最后,有人用智力获得了它,有道德品质足以坚持它,并且能够致力于将它梳理得井井有条,但如果他们不根据高雅礼仪和良好感知的理想来践行与使用它,也是不完美的。"

33. 子曰："君子不可小知,而可大受也;小人不可大受,而可小知也。"

　　孔子说:"一个明智而良善的人可能在小的事务中不会表现出他的特质,但可以委托给他重大的事情。一个蠢人可能在一些琐事上出名,但不可以委托给他以重大的事情。"

34. 子曰："民之于仁也,甚于水火。水火,吾见蹈而死者矣,未见蹈仁而死者也。"

　　孔子说:"与火和水这样的生活必需物相比,人们更需要道德。我见到过人因掉进火中或水中而死,但我没见过人因掉进道德中而死。"

35. Confucius remarked, "When the question is one of morality, a man need not defer to his teacher."

36. Confucius remarked, "A good, wise man is faithful, — not merely constant."

37. Confucius remarked, "In the service of his prince, a man should place his duty first; the matter of pay should be with him a secondary consideration."

38. Confucius remarked, "Among really educated men, there is no caste or race-distinction."

39. Confucius remarked, "Men of totally different principles can never act together."

40. Confucius remarked, "Language should be intelligible and nothing more."

41. A blind music-teacher having called on Confucius, When they came to the steps of the house Confucius said to him, "Here are the steps." When they came to the mat where they were to sit, Confucius again said to him, "Here is the mat." Finally, when they had sat down, Confucius said to him, "So-and-so is here, and So-and-so is here."

Afterwards, when the blind music-teacher had left, a disciple said to Confucius, "Is that the way to behave to a music-teacher?" "Yes," replied Confucius, "that is certainly the way to behave to blind people."

35. 子曰:"当仁不让于师。"

　　孔子说:"当问题是合乎道德的,一个人就不必顺从于他的老师。"

36. 子曰:"君子贞而不谅。"

　　孔子说:"一个良善明智的人是忠诚可靠的——而不是固执愚忠的。"

37. 子曰:"事君,敬其事而后其食。"

　　孔子说:"在为国君的服务中,一个人应把责任置于首位;薪酬的问题,对他来说应该是其次考虑的事情。"

38. 子曰:"有教无类。"

　　孔子说:"在真正有教养的人们之中,没有社会等级或种族区别。"

39. 子曰:"道不同,不相为谋。"

　　孔子说:"具有完全不同的原则的人,永远不可能共事。"

40. 子曰:"辞达而已矣。"

　　孔子说:"语言应该明白易懂,仅此而已。"

41. 师冕见,及阶,子曰:"阶也。"及席,子曰:"席也。"皆坐,子告之曰:"某在斯,某在斯。"师冕出。子张问曰:"与师言之道与?"子曰:"然,固相师之道也。"

　　一位盲人音乐教师拜访孔子,当他们来到屋子的台阶时,孔子对他说:"这里是台阶。"当他们来到他们要坐下的席子时,孔子又对他说:"这里是席子。"最后,当他们已经坐下时,孔子对他说:"某某人在这里,某某人在这里。"

　　后来,盲人音乐教师离开后,一个学生对孔子说:"这就是对待一位音乐教师的方式吗?""是啊,"孔子回答说,"这就是对待盲人的方式。"

【评述】

1. 文中，"陈"，多认为通"阵"，"兵阵"之意。辜鸿铭译为"military tactics"，"军事策略"。"俎豆之事，则尝闻之矣；军旅之事，未之学也"一句，其中，"俎豆"，历来学者或解释为礼器或解释为食器，在此为象征意义。这句话辜鸿铭译为"I know a little about the arts of peace, but I have never studied the art of war"，"我懂得一点有关和平的策略方法，但我从没学过有关战争的策略方法"。

2. 文中，"多学而识之"，辜鸿铭译为"has learned many things and remembers them all"，"学了很多东西并已把它们全部记住"。其中，"识"是"记住"的意思。"予一以贯之"，译为"I unite all my knowledge by one connecting principle"，"我是用一个连接性的原则统一了我全部的学问"。在此，"贯"辜鸿铭理解为"统一"之意；"一"理解为"连接性的原则"。第四章第15节中孔子表达过这样的思想。

3. 文中，"知德者鲜矣"，辜鸿铭译为"It is seldom that men understand real moral worth"，"懂得真正的道德品格的人是很少见的"。其中，"知"是懂得、理解的意思。这是孔子对当时社会道德状况的叹息。

4. 文中，"无为而治"，辜鸿铭译为"carry out the principle of no-government"，"实行去政府的原则"。在此，为避免与"anarchy"（无政府）一词混淆，我们把"no-government"一词译作"去政府"。辜鸿铭认为，"无为而治"指的是没有政府（或政府并不需发生作用），国家仍然可以正常运行的状态，也即民间自治。"恭己正南面而已矣"一句中，"恭己"，译为"to be earnest in his personal conduct"，"在个人行为上真诚严肃"；"正南面"，译为"to behave in a manner worthy of his position"，"表现出一种与他的身份相匹配的礼仪举止"。这是对统治者的德性要求。对于本节所表现出的"去政府"思想，辜鸿铭最后引用美国作家爱默生的文章进行注释。爱默生写道：

> 一个星期天，我的朋友们问是否存在一些具有美国思想的美国人？很有挑战性的问题，……我谈起无政府和不抵抗理论。……我说："我还的确没有在哪个国家看到一个人有足够的勇气而捍卫这条真理。我也明白，除了这个，没有任何勇气能赢得我的敬仰。我能轻易地看到滑膛枪崇拜的破产，尽管有些伟大的人们是滑膛枪崇拜者。它就像上帝存在一样无疑。一种枪不需要另一种枪来陪伴，唯有爱和正义的法则，才能带来一场干净的革命。"（《英国人的特性》）

5. 子张问"行"，辜鸿铭译为"what one should do in order to get along well with men"，

"应该怎么做才能与人们相处得好"。子张是问与人相处之道。

6. 文中，"直"，辜鸿铭译为"straightforward"，"坦率，正直"；"如矢"译为"straight as an arrow"，"正直得像箭"。"道"译为"justice and order in the government"，"政治中的正义与秩序"；这句话指，无论政府的政治合理与否，史鱼始终正直如一，这是种完全的正直。孔子感叹他的正直。"卷而怀之"，辜鸿铭译为"he rolled himself up and led a strictly private life"，"他就把自己卷藏起来，过一种完全的私人生活"，即归隐之意，指政治"有道"时，就入世从政，尽己之力；政治"无道"时，就归隐而去，避免迫害并洁身自守。这种人，孔子称之为"君子"。

7. 文中，"可与言而不与之言，失人"一句，辜鸿铭译为"When you meet the proper person to speak to and do not speak out, you lose your opportunity"，"当你遇到了适合对他说话的人，却没开口去说，就是错失良机"。其中，"可与言"指的是"适合对他说话的人"；"失人"指"错失良机"。后文的"失言"译为"waste your words"，"浪费唇舌"；"知者"译为"a man of intelligence"，"有智慧的人"。这再次表达了孔子爱惜言辞的思想。

8. 文中，"志士"，辜鸿铭译为"a gentleman of spirit"，"有气魄、气概、勇气、志气的绅士"；"仁人"译为"a man of moral character"，"有道德品质的人"。"求生以害仁"，译为"save his life at the expense of his moral character"，"以牺牲道德品质为代价来挽救生命"。"杀身以成仁"译为"sacrifice his life in order to save his moral character"，"为了挽救道德品质而牺牲生命"。这是"仁人志士"在"道德"与"生命"两者发生冲突时所应做出的选择。

9. 文中，"工欲善其事，必先利其器"一句，辜鸿铭译为"a workman who wants to perfect his work first sharpens his tools"，"一个想要完善自己工作的工人，首先要使他的工具锋利"。"事其大夫之贤者，友其士之仁者"一句。"事其大夫之贤者"译为"serve those nobles and ministers in that country who are men of moral worth"，"为该国中那些具有道德品格的贵族与大臣服务"。其中，"事"为服务之意。"友其士之仁者"，译为"cultivate the friendship of the gentlemen of that country who are men of moral worth"，"建立起与该国那些有道德品格的绅士们之间的友谊"。其中，"友"的意思是建立友谊。指与道德高尚的人同事、为友。

10. 文中，"颜渊问为邦"一句。"问为邦"，辜鸿铭译为"enquired what institutions he would adopt for the government of an Empire"，"问他会为一个帝国的政治采取什么样的制度"。"行夏之时，乘殷之辂，服周之冕"一句。辜鸿铭的解释是："行"、"乘"、"服"这些具体的动词,分别译为"use"、"introduce"与"adopt",均有"采用"之意。这表明,孔子是在谈制度,而不是谈具体事物。"夏之时"译为"the calendar of the Hsia dynasty","夏朝的历法"。"殷之辂"译为"the form of carriage used in the Yin dynasty","殷朝使用的马车样式"。"周之冕"译为"the uniform of the present dynasty","当今这个朝代的制服"。这是孔子想在历法与礼仪方面采取的三种制度。"乐则《韶》、舞",辜鸿铭译为"for State music I would use the most ancient music","在国家音乐方面,我会采用最古老的音乐"。这是孔子谈的对音乐制度的采用。"放郑声,远佞人"一句。"放郑声"译为"prohibit all the popular airs in the music of the present day","禁止所有当今音乐中的流行曲调"。"放"是禁止之意,"郑声"指流行曲调;"远佞人"译为"banish all popular orators","放逐所有流行的说客","远"是放逐之意;因为这是孔子在谈心中的理想制度。"郑声淫,佞人殆"一句中,"淫"译为"provokes sensuality in the people","煽起人心中对声色的沉迷";"殆"译为"dangerous to the State","对国家是危险的"。这两者,一者破坏社会道德,一者危害国家安全,所以,孔子要清除。

11. 文中,"无远虑"辜鸿铭译为"take thought for the morrow","不为明天操心、忧虑"。"忧"译为"be sorry","感到遗憾",指要有长远打算之意。

12. 本节内容与第九章第17节重复,请参看前文。

13. 文中,"窃位",辜鸿铭译为"had stolen his position","偷得他的职位";"贤"译为"the talents and virtues","才能与美德";"与立",按翻译是"bring his friend forward, become his colleague",即"推荐他的朋友并成为他的同事"之意。这句话指"臧文仲"虽然知道自己的朋友"柳下惠"具有优秀的才能与美德,但因为担心会与自己成为同事,因此不予举荐。这就像是他偷得了自己的职位一样。

14. 文中,"躬自厚"译为"expects much from himself","对自己要求多";"薄责于人"译为"demands little from others","对别人要求少";"远怨",译为"will never have any enemies","将不会有仇敌"。这一节意指"严于律己,宽以待人"。

15. 文中,"如之何如之何",辜鸿铭译为"What is the right thing to do","什么是应该做的正确的事情",指总是恪守道德,并在行为上追求更高的道德程度。"吾末如之何也已矣"译为"I can do nothing for such a man","我对这种人也做不了什么"。

16. 文中,"群居终日,言不及义,好行小慧"一句,辜鸿铭译为"a body of men sit

together for a whole day without turning their conversation to some principle or truth, but only amuse themselves with small wit and smart sayings", "一群人一整天凑到一起, 而没有把话题转移到一些原则或真理上, 只是用小聪明与俏皮话来娱乐自己"。其中, "义"指原则或真理, 也就是超越一般世俗生活之上的深刻性话题; "群居"泛指人群聚集到一处; "行小慧"指用小聪明与俏皮话来取乐; "难矣哉"译为 "it is a bad case", "这真是一件糟糕的事"。

17. 文中, "义以为质", 辜鸿铭译为 "makes Right the substance of his being", "把正义作为他秉性的本质", "质"指人的秉性本质。"礼以行之", 译为 "carries it out with judgment and good sense", "用判断力与良好感知来实行它", "礼"指判断力与良好感知。这是辜鸿铭对"礼"的比较常见的翻译。这句话指人以"正义"作为本质, 在此基础之上, 又需有怎样的"行为状态"。"孙以出之"译为 "speaks it with modesty", "用谦逊的态度来诉说它"。"孙"是谦逊; "出"是说出。这句话指人以"正义"为本质, 在此基础之上, 又需有怎样的"言语表达状态"。"信以成之"译为 "he attains it with sincerity", "用真诚来达成它"。"信"指真诚、诚挚的心态; "成"指达成、实现。这句话指人以"正义"为本质, 在此基础之上, 应有怎样的"总体心态"。

18. 文中, "病无能", 译为 "should be distressed that he has no ability", "应该因自己没有才能而苦恼", "能"指才华之意; "不己知", 译为 "men do not take notice of him", "没有注意到他"。这一节孔子还是强调人首先要完善自己, 不能只追求虚名。

19. 文中, "疾", 辜鸿铭译为 "hate", "憎恨, 厌恶"; "没世而名不称", 译为 "die without having done anything to distinguish himself", "还没有做出什么事情让自己闻名就死去", "没世"指死去。这一节意思是, 一生都没有做出可以称道的事情。辜鸿铭对本节注释说:

即白白度过了一生。

20. 文中, "求诸己", 译为 "seeks for what he wants in himself", "在自己身上寻求他想要的东西"; "求诸人", 译为 "seeks for it from others", "向别人去寻求"。指当一个人明确自己要追求什么或者需要什么时, 明智的做法是通过自己的努力去获取; 而非寄希望于别人。

21. 文中, "矜而不争", 辜鸿铭译为 "proud but not vain", "骄傲而不自负"。辜鸿铭对此注释说:

迪恩·史威夫特说:"一个真正骄傲的人正是因为过于骄傲而不会自负。"

22. 文中,"以言举人",辜鸿铭译为"upholds a man because of what he says","因为一个人所说的话而支持他"。其中"举"的意思是支持,即单凭别人说的话,就简单地决定自己对他支持或反对的态度。"以人废言",译为"discard what a man says because of the speaker's character","不会因为说话者的人品而忽视他所说的话"。其中"废"是忽视、忽略之意,即单单因为一个人的恶劣人品,就忽略或否定他所表达的意见的价值。这是孔子反对的两种做法。

23. 文中,"恕",辜鸿铭译为"charity","博爱,仁慈"。他理解的"恕",即为他人利益着想的博大的爱。他对此注释说:

> 当今时髦的说法是"利他主义"(altruism)。

"己所不欲,勿施于人",辜鸿铭译为"What you do not wish others to do unto you, do not do unto them","你不希望别人对你做的事情,也不要对他们做",可参看第十二章第2节辜鸿铭对这同一句话的翻译。

24. 文中,"斯民也,三代之所以直道而行也"一句中,"三代",学者多理解为夏商周,辜鸿铭未确指,他译为"The people of to-day — there is really nothing in them to prevent one from dealing honestly with them as the men of the good old times dealt with the people of their day","今天的人们——的确没有什么去阻止一个人,像过去的美好时代的人对待那个时代的人那样,公正地对待他们"。这一句的意思是,在今天,人们完全应该像"过去的美好时代的人"那样,得到公正的对待。

25. 文中,"吾犹及史之阙文也"一句,辜鸿铭译为"In my young days, I could still obtain books which supplied information on points which the standard historical books omitted","在我年轻的时候,我还能够得到一些针对权威历史著作所遗漏的要点而提供信息的书籍"。其中,"史"指权威的历史著作;"阙文"指包含权威历史著作所遗漏的要点的书籍。"有马者借人乘之",辜鸿铭译为"a man who had a horse would willingly lend it to a friend to ride","一个拥有一匹马的人,也会很乐意地把它借给朋友去骑"。"今亡已夫",辜鸿铭译为"But now such times and such manners have all disappeared","但如今,这样的时代和习俗,都已经消失不见了"。这是孔子对社会良好风气的逝去所作的叹息。

26. 文中，"巧言乱德"，辜鸿铭译为"It is plausible speech which confuses men's ideas of what is moral worth"，"是貌似合理的言语混淆了人们关于道德品格的观念"。其中，"巧言"意思是貌似合理的言语，与第一章第3节"巧言令色"中"巧言"的翻译是相同的。

27. 文中，"众恶之"，辜鸿铭译为"a man is unpopular"，"一个人不受欢迎"；"众好之"，译为"a man is popular"，"一个人受到欢迎"；两个"必察焉"分别译为"it is necessary to find out why people hate him"与"it is still necessary to find out why people like him"，即有必要搞清楚别人为什么讨厌他或喜欢他。

28. 文中，"道"，辜鸿铭译为"his religion or the principles he professes"，"他所信仰的宗教或原则"；"弘"译为"make ... great"，"使……变得伟大"。

29. 这一节辜鸿铭译为"To be wrong and not to reform is indeed to be wrong"，"错了而不去改进，那就是真的错了"。其中，前一个"过"译为"to be wrong"；后一个"过"译为"indeed to be wrong"，指错而不改这种行为本身是真的错了。

30. 文中，"终日不食，终夜不寝，以思"一句，辜鸿铭译为"spent a whole day without taking food and a whole night without sleep, occupied with thinking"，"一整天不吃饭、一整夜不睡觉而忙于思考"。"无益，不如学也"，译为"It was of no use. I have found it better to acquire knowledge from books"，"没有用。我发现还是从书上获取学问更好一些"。这里的"学"，辜鸿铭强调的是从书本上获得知识。

31. 文中，"君子谋道不谋食"一句，"谋道"译为"occupied in the search for truth"，"忙于探索真理"，"道"理解为真理；"谋食"译为"seek for a mere living"，"仅仅寻求生计"。这句话指君子是忙于前者而非后者。"耕也，馁在其中矣；学也，禄在其中矣"，辜鸿铭译为"farming sometimes leads to starvation, and education sometimes leads to the rewards of official life"，"耕作有时会带来饥饿，而教育有时会带来公职生活的报酬"。其中，"馁"译为"starvation"，"饥饿，挨饿"；"在其中"译为"sometimes leads to"，"有时会导致、带来"之意；"学"译为"education"，"教育"。"君子忧道不忧贫"，辜鸿铭译为"A wise man should be solicitous about truth, not anxious about poverty"，"一个明智的人应该渴望真理，而不是担心贫穷"。

32. 文中，"知及之"，辜鸿铭译为"attain knowledge by their understanding"，"通过他们的智力获得了学问"。这一节指人在获得学问之后如何能够守住，并有效运用。

33. 文中，"不可小知而可大受"，辜鸿铭译为 "may not show his quality in small affairs, but he can be entrusted with great concerns"，"可能在小的事务中不会表现出他的特质，但可以委托给他重大的事情"。其中，"小知" 即 "在小的事务中表现出特质"；"大受" 指 "can be entrusted with great concerns"，"可以委托给他重大的事情"。这句话说的是 "君子" 的特征。"不可大受而可小知"，译为 "gain distinction in small things, but he cannot be entrusted with great concerns"，"在一些琐事上出名，但不可以委托给他以重大的事情"。其中，"大受" 指 "可以委托给他重大的事情"；"小知" 指 "在琐事上出名"。这句话说的是 "小人" 的特征。

34. 文中，"民之于仁也，甚于水火"，辜鸿铭译为 "men need morality more than the necessaries of life, such as fire and water"，"与火和水这样的生活必需物相比，人们更需要道德"。其中，"水火"，辜鸿铭并未单单按照字面翻译，而是译为 "the necessaries of life, such as fire and water"，"火和水这样的生活必需物"。重点还是指出 "生活必需物"，即拿这种 "必需" 的东西与道德相比，还是道德更重要。

35. 文中，"当仁，不让于师"，辜鸿铭译为 "when the question is one of morality, a man need not defer to his teacher"，"当问题是合乎道德的，一个人就不必顺从于他的老师"。其中，"仁" 指 "合乎道德的问题"；"让" 指 "顺从、听从" 之意。

36. 文中，"贞"，辜鸿铭译为 "faithful"，"忠诚的"；"谅"，译为 "merely constant"，直译是 "仅仅一成不变地忠诚"，也即 "固执、愚忠" 之意。这一节指作为一个 "君子"，他会是忠诚的、可靠的，但绝不会愚忠于某人、某事。

37. 文中，"敬其事"，辜鸿铭译为 "should place his duty first"，"将责任置于首位"；"而后其食"，译为 "the matter of pay should be with him a secondary consideration"，即 "薪酬应该是其次考虑的事情"。

38. 文中，"有教无类"，译为 "among really educated men, there is no caste or race-distinction"，"在真正有教养的人们之中，没有社会等级或种族区别"。

39. 文中，"道不同，不相为谋"，辜鸿铭译为 "men of totally different principles can never act together"，"具有完全不同的原则的人，永远不可能一起共事"。其中，"道" 指行为原则、思想信念等价值观；"谋" 指一起做事、共事。

40. 文中,"辞达而已矣",辜鸿铭译为 "language should be intelligible and nothing more","语言应该明白易懂,仅此而已"。其中,"辞"泛指语言;"达"指明白易懂。这是孔子对语言功能的看法。

41. 文中,"师冕",多解释为盲人"乐人"或"乐师",其名为"冕"。辜鸿铭译为 "a blind music-teacher","一位盲人音乐教师"。"见",译为 "called on",即"拜访"。这一节说的是那位盲人音乐教师来拜访孔子时,孔子的举止与态度。"与师言之道与",译为 "is that the way to behave to a music-teacher?""这就是对待一位音乐教师的方式吗"。其中,"言",辜鸿铭引申为"对待";"相",译为 "behave to",即与上句的"言"相同,也是"对待"之意。辜鸿铭最后注释说:

古代中国所有伟大的音乐家都是盲人。

CHAPTER XVI
季氏第十六

1. The head of a powerful family of nobles in Confucius' native State was preparing to commence hostilities against a small principality within that State. Two of Confucius' disciples, who were in the noble's service, came to see Confucius and informed him of it. Confucius , turning to one of these disciples, said, "Sir, is not this due to your fault? The reigning family of this principality derived its titles from ancient Emperors: besides, its land is situate within our own territory; the ruler, therefore, is a prince of the Empire. What right, then, have you to declare war against a vassal of the Emperor?"

The disciple to whom the above was addressed, replied, "It is my lord, our Master, who wishes for this war; it is not we two, who are only his servants, that desire it."

Confucius then answered, "An ancient historian says:'Let those who can stand the fight fall into the ranks, and let those who cannot, retire.' What is the use of a guide to a blind man if, when he is in danger, the guide does not help him and, when he falls, the guide does not lift him up? Besides, you are wrong in what you have said to excuse yourself. When a tiger or a wild animal escapes from its cage, or when a tortoise-shell or a valuable gem gets broken in its casket: — who is responsible and to blame in such a case? "

"But now," argued one of the disciple, "this principality is very strongly fortified and is within easy reach of our most important town. If we do not reduce and take it now, it will in future be a source of anxiety and danger to the descendants of the family."

"Sir," answered Confucius, "A good man hates to make excuses when he ought to say simply 'I want it'.

"But for my part, I have been taught to believe that those who have

1. 季氏将伐颛臾。冉有、季路见于孔子曰："季氏将有事于颛臾。"孔子曰："求！无乃尔是过与？夫颛臾，昔者先王以为东蒙主，且在邦域之中矣，是社稷之臣也。何以伐为？"冉有曰："夫子欲之，吾二臣者皆不欲也。"孔子曰："求！周任有言曰：'陈力就列，不能者止。'危而不持，颠而不扶，则将焉用彼相矣？且尔言过矣。虎兕出于柙，龟玉毁于椟中，是谁之过与？"冉有曰："今夫颛臾，固而近于费。今不取，后世必为子孙忧。"孔子曰："求！君子疾夫舍曰欲之，而必为之辞。丘也闻有国有家者，不患寡而患不均，不患贫而患不安。盖均无贫，和无寡，安无倾。夫如是，故远人不服，则修文德以来之。既来之，则安之。今由与求也，相夫子，远人不服而不能来也；邦分崩离析而不能守也。而谋动干戈于邦内。吾恐季孙之忧，不在颛臾，而在萧墙之内也。"

孔子故国的一个有权势的贵族家族的当家人，正准备开始对国内的一个小型公国发动战争。孔子的两个为那位贵族服务的学生来看望他，并把这个消息告诉了他。孔子转向其中一个学生说："先生，这不是要归因于你们的过错吗？那个公国的当权家族，其爵位源自古代的帝王们；另外，它的国土位于我们自己的版图之内；因此，其统治者是帝国的一个诸侯国君。那么，你们有什么权利向帝王的一个诸侯宣战？"

上面被问到的那位学生回答说："是我的大人——我们的主人，希望这场战争；不是我们两个想要这样，我们只是他的佣仆。"

孔子于是回答说："一位古代的历史学家说：'让那些能够忍耐战斗的人排入队列，让那些不能的人，退出。'如果一个盲人处于危险之中，而他的向导不帮助他，当他跌倒时，他的向导也不把他扶起，那么这个向导对于这位盲人来说又有什么用呢？另外，你为自己辩解而说的话是错的。当一只老虎或一头野生动物从它的笼子里逃了出来，或者，当一片龟甲或一颗珍贵的宝石在匣子里坏掉——在这样的事情中，谁承担责任并应受谴责？"

kingdoms and possessions should not be concerned that they have not enough possessions, but should be concerned that possessions are not equally distributed; they should not be concerned that they are poor, but should be concerned that the people are not contented. For with equal distribution there will be no poverty; with mutual good will, there will be no want; and with contentment among the people, there can be no downfall and dissolution.

"This being so, when the people outside the country do not submit, a ruler should improve the moral education at home in order to attract them; when people from outside are attracted and come to his country, the ruler should make them happy and contented."

"Now you two gentlemen," continued Confucius, "while assisting your master in his government, have done nothing to attract people from outside when they have shown signs of insubmission. At present, when the country is actually internally torn by factions, dissensions, outbreaks and dissolutions, you are doing nothing to prevent them. Instead of this, you are now going to bring on the ravages and horrors of war within our own State. I am afraid the danger in future to the stability of the house of your noble lord will not come from that small principality against which you are now going to declare war, but will arise from within the walls of your master's own palace."

2. Confucius remarked, "In the normal state of the government of an empire, the initiative and final decision in matters of religion, education, and declaration of war from the supreme prerogative of the emperor. During abnormal conditions in the government of the empire, that prerogative passes into the hands of the princes

"但是现在，"其中一个学生争辩说，"那个公国在非常强有力地设防，很容易就会延伸到我们最重要的城镇。如果我们现在不加以限制并攻占它，将来对于这个家族的后代来说，它会是担忧与危险的根源。"

"先生，"孔子回答说，"一个良善的人，当他应该简单地说'我想这样'时，他会厌恶去找借口的。

"但对我来说，我的教育使我相信，那些拥有王国与财产的人，不应担心他们不具备足够的财产，而应该担心财产没有得到平均分配；他们不应担心他们匮乏，而应该担心人民不满意。因为平均分配，就会没有贫穷；相互友善，就会没有匮乏；人民满意，就不会衰落与消亡。

"这样，当国外的人民不顺服的时候，为了吸引他们，统治者应该改善国内的道德教育。当外面的人民被吸引来到他的国家时，统治者应该让他们快乐并感到满意。"

"现在，你们两位阁下，"孔子继续说，"在政治上辅佐你们的主人时，并没有做出任何事情，当外面的人民已经显现出不顺从的迹象时去吸引他们。目前，当国家实际上被各种派系、纠纷、暴动以及衰败而导致内部分裂时，你们没有做出任何事情去阻止它们。与此相反，你们正在我们国内引起战争的毁坏与恐惧。我担心，对于你们贵族主人的家族稳固来说，未来的危险将不会来自那个你们正打算对其宣战的小型公国，而会产生于你们主人自己宫殿的高墙内部。"

2. 孔子曰："天下有道，则礼乐征伐自天子出；天下无道，则礼乐征伐自诸侯出。自诸侯出，盖十世希不失矣；自大夫出，五世希不失矣；陪臣执国命，三世希不失矣。天下有道，则政不在大夫。天下有道，则庶人不议。"

孔子说："在一个帝国的政治的正常状态下，在宗教、教育，以及对外

of the empire: in which case it is seldom that ten generations pass before they lose it. Should that prerogative pass into the hands of the nobility of the empire, it has rarely happened that they have retained it for five generations. When subordinate officers have the power of government in their hands they generally lose their authority in the course of three generations.

"When there are order and justice in the government of a country, the supreme power of government will not be in the hands of the nobility or of a ruling class. When there are justice and order in the government of a country, the common people will not meddle with the government."

3. Confucius, speaking of the state of government in his native State, remarked, "It is now five generations since the appointments to offices in the State have been taken away from the scions of the reigning houses. It is now four generations since the powers of government have passed into the hands of the ruling class of nobility. Therefore the descendants of the most ancient houses have lost all power and are now living in obscurity."

4. Confucius remarked, "There are three kinds of friendship which are beneficial and three kinds which are injurious. Friendship with upright men, with faithful men, and with men of much information: such friendships are beneficial. Friendship with plausible men, with men of insinuating manners, and with glib-tongued men: such friendships are injurious."

宣战的问题上的主动权与最后决定权来自帝王的至高无上的权力。在帝国政治不正常的情况下,最高权力会落入帝国的诸侯国君手中:在这种情况下,他们在失去它之前,很少会度过十代。如果最高权力落入帝国的贵族阶层手中,他们能够维持上五代就很少见了。当从属官员手中拥有了政治权力,他们通常会在三代内就会丧失掉他们的权力。

"当一个国家的政治中有秩序与正义时,政治的至高权力就不会在贵族阶层或统治阶层手中。当一个国家的政治中有正义与秩序时,普通大众就不会干涉政治。"

3. 孔子曰:"禄之去公室,五世矣;政逮于大夫,四世矣,故夫三桓之子孙,微矣。"

孔子谈到其故国的政治状态,说:"在这个国家,自从对公职的委任权从执政家族的子孙手中被剥夺,至今已经五代了。自从各种政治权力落入贵族阶层手中已经四代了。因此,最古老家族的后代失去了所有权力并过着一种默默无闻的生活。"

4. 孔子曰:"益者三友,损者三友。友直,友谅,友多闻,益矣。友便辟,友善柔,友便佞,损矣。"

孔子说:"有三种友谊是有益处的,有三种是有害处的。与正直的人,与忠实的人,以及与有学问的人的友谊:这样的友谊是有益处的。与巧言善辩的人、与谄媚态度的人,以及与油嘴滑舌的人的友谊:这样的友谊是有害处的。"

5. Confucius remarked, "There are three kinds of pleasures which are beneficial and three kinds which are injurious. Pleasure derived from the study and criticism of the polite arts, pleasure in admiring and speaking of the excellent qualities of men, and pleasure in having many friends of virtue and talents: these pleasures are beneficial. Pleasure in dissipation; in extravagance; in mere conviviality: such pleasures are injurious."

6. Confucius remarked, "There are three kinds of errors to which men are liable when in the presence of their superiors. First, To speak out when one is not called upon to speak: that is called being froward. Secondly, To keep silence when called upon to speak: that is called being disingenuous. Thirdly, To speak out without taking into consideration the expression in the look of the person spoken to: that is called blindness."

7. Confucius remarked, "There are three things which a man should beware of in the three stages of his life. In youth, when the constitution of his body is not yet formed, he should beware of lust. In manhood, when his physical powers are in full vigour, he should beware of strife. In old age, when the physical powers are in decay, he should beware of greed."

8. Confucius remarked, "There are three things which a wise and good man holds in awe. He holds in awe the Laws of God, persons in authority, and the words of wisdom of holy men. A fool, on the other hand, does not know that there are Laws of God; he, therefore, has no reverence for them; he is disrespectful to persons in authority, and contemns the words of wisdom of holy men."

5. 孔子曰:"益者三乐,损者三乐。乐节礼乐,乐道人之善,乐多贤友,益矣。乐骄乐,乐佚游,乐宴乐,损矣。"

孔子说:"有三种快乐是有益处的,有三种是有害处的。来自对文雅艺术的研究与评论的快乐、在对人们优秀品质的称赞与谈论中的快乐、拥有很多有美德与才能的朋友的快乐:这样的快乐是有益处的。在浪费消遣中、挥霍奢侈中、欢宴作乐中的快乐:这样的快乐是有害处的。"

6. 孔子曰:"侍于君子有三愆:言未及之而言谓之躁,言及之而不言谓之隐,未见颜色而言谓之瞽。"

孔子说:"人们在他们的长者面前,容易犯三种错误。第一,没有要求说话时,却大声说话:这叫做刚愎自用。第二,要求说话时却保持沉默:这叫做不够坦诚。第三,大声说话而不顾及听者的面部表情:这叫做轻率鲁莽。"

7. 孔子曰:"君子有三戒:少之时,血气未定,戒之在色;及其壮也,血气方刚,戒之在斗;及其老也,血气既衰,戒之在得。"

孔子说:"一个人在他人生的三个阶段应该谨防三件事情。年少时,他身体的体格还未成形,他应该谨防色欲。成年时,他的体力处于全盛的状态,他应该谨防争斗。老年时,他的体力处于衰退中,他应该谨防贪婪。"

8. 孔子曰:"君子有三畏:畏天命,畏大人,畏圣人之言。小人不知天命而不畏也,狎大人,侮圣人之言。"

孔子说:"一个明智而良善的人对三件事情保持敬畏。他对上帝的律法、权威的人以及圣者的智慧话语保持敬畏。相反,一个蠢人并不知道存在上帝的律法,因此他对它们没有崇敬之心,他对权威的人无礼,并且侮辱圣者的智慧话语。"

9. Confucius remarked, "The highest class of men are those who are born with a natural understanding. The next class are those who acquire understanding by study and application. There are others again who are born naturally dull, but who yet by strenuous efforts, try to acquire understanding:such men may be considered the next class. Those who are born naturally dull and yet will not take the trouble to acquire understanding: such men are the lowest class of the people."

10. Confucius remarked, "There are nine objects which a wise man aims at. In the use of his eyes, his object is to see clearly. In the use of his ears, his object is to hear distinctly. In the expression of his look, his object is to be gracious. In his manners, his object is to be serious. In what he says, his object is to be sincere. In business, his object is to be earnest. In doubt, his object is to seek for information. In anger, his object is to think of consequences. In view of personal advantage, his object is to think of what is right. "

11. Confucius remarked, "Men who, when they see what is good and honest, try to act up to it, and when they see what is bad and dishonest try to avoid it as if avoiding scalding water: such men I have known and the expressions of such principles I have heard. But men who live in retirement in order to study their aims and who practise righteousness in order to carry out their principles: the expression of such principles I have heard, but I have not seen such men."

9. 孔子曰:"生而知之者,上也;学而知之者,次也;困而学之,又其次也;困而不学,民斯为下矣。"

   孔子说:"最高等的人是那些生来就有一种天赋智慧的人。次一等的是那些通过学习与应用而获取智慧的人。还有一些人,他们生来天性愚钝,但他们通过艰苦的努力试图获取智慧:这样的人可以视为再下一等的人。那些生来天性愚钝然而又不去费力获取智慧的人:这样的人是最下等的人。"

10. 孔子曰:"君子有九思:视思明,听思聪,色思温,貌思恭,言思忠,事思敬,疑思问,忿思难,见得思义。"

    孔子说:"一个明智的人力求达到九个目标。在眼睛的使用上,他的目标是能看得清晰。在耳朵的使用上,他的目标是能听得清楚。在脸色的表达上,他的目标是谦和。在他的态度上,他的目标是严肃庄重。在说话上,他的目标是真诚。在做事上,他的目标是认真。在困惑上,他的目标是寻求学问。在愤怒上,他的目标是考虑后果。看到个人利益时,他的目标是考虑到正义。"

11. 孔子曰:"见善如不及,见不善如探汤。吾见其人矣,吾闻其语矣。隐居以求其志,行义以达其道。吾闻其语矣,未见其人也。"

    孔子说:"看到优秀与正直时试着去遵守它,看到恶劣与不正直时试着去躲避它,就像躲避滚烫的开水:这样的人我看到过,这种行为准则的表述我也听到过。但是,为了研究他们的目标而隐居,以及为了实现他们的原则而依义行事的人:这种行为准则的表述我听到过,但我没见过这样的人。"

12. Confucius, speaking of a prince lately deceased, remarked, "In his lifetime, he had a thousand teams of horses: but on the day of his death, the people had not a good word to say of him. On the other hand, the ancient worthies Po Yi and Shuh Ts'i, who were starved to death at the foot of a lonely mountain, are held in honour by the people to this day. This is the meaning of the verse —

Truly your wealth and pelf avail you nought,
To have what others want, is all you sought."

13. A gentleman of the Court on one occasion enquired of Confucius' son, saying: "Have you had any special lesson from your father? " "No, I have not," replied Confucius' son, "Only once when he was standing alone, and I happened to pass through the hall, he said to me:'Have you studied poetry?' to which I replied, 'No, I have not.''Then,' said he, 'if you do not study poetry, you cannot make yourself agreeable in conversation.' After that I gave myself to the study of poetry. On another occasion when he was again standing alone, and I happened to pass through the hall, he said to me:'Have you studied the arts?' to which I replied, 'No, I have not.' 'Then,' said he, 'if you do not study the arts, you will lack judgment and taste.' After that, I gave myself to the study of the arts."

The gentleman of the Court, when he heard that, went away delighted, saying: "I have asked about one thing and now I have learnt about three things. In addition to what I have asked, I have learnt about the importance of the study of poetry and the arts, and also that a wise and good man does not treat even his own son with familiarity."

12. 齐景公有马千驷，死之日，民无德而称焉。伯夷叔齐饿于首阳之下，民到于今称之。其斯之谓与？

　　孔子谈到不久前死掉的一个国君，说："在他的一生中，他拥有一千队马；但他死的那一天，人民对他没有说一句好话。另一方面，古代的杰出人物伯夷和叔齐饿死在了在一座孤山脚下，受到人民的尊敬直到今天。这就是这些诗句的含义：'财富与金钱真的对你徒然无益，/拥有别人所匮乏的，正是你的全部动机。'"

13. 陈亢问于伯鱼曰："子亦有异闻乎？"对曰："未也。尝独立，鲤趋而过庭。曰：'学诗乎？'对曰：'未也。''不学诗，无以言。'鲤退而学诗。他日又独立，鲤趋而过庭。曰：'学礼乎？'对曰：'未也。''不学礼，无以立。'鲤退而学礼。闻斯二者。"陈亢退而喜曰："问一得三，闻诗，闻礼，又闻君子之远其子也。"

　　有一次，朝廷的一位绅士问孔子的儿子："你从你父亲那里学到特殊的课程了吗？""没有，我没有学到，"孔子的儿子回答说，"只有一次，当他独自站在那里时，我碰巧路过大厅，他对我说：'你研究过诗吗？'我对此回答说：'没有，没研究过。''那么，'他说，'如果你不研究诗，在谈话时就不会令人愉快。'之后，我专心于对诗的研究。又一次，他又独自站在那里，我碰巧路过大厅，他对我说：'你研究过艺术吗？'对此，我回答说：'没有，我没研究过。''那么，'他说，'如果你不研究艺术，你就会缺乏判断力与鉴赏力。'之后，我致力于艺术的研究。"

　　那位朝廷的绅士，当他听到这些话之后，高兴地离去了，说："我询问了一件事情，现在却学到了三件事情。除了我所问的事情之外，我还学到了研究诗与艺术的重要性，也学到一个明智而良善的人即使是对待自己的儿子也不会过分亲近。"

14. The wife of the reigning prince of a State is addressed by him as "Madame". She addresses him as "Sire". She is addressed by her people in her own State as "Madame, my lady", and her own people in speaking to people of another State, mention her as "Our good little princess." People of other States, speaking of her to her own people, all her "Madame, your princess".

14. 邦君之妻，君称之曰夫人，夫人自称曰小童；邦人称之曰君夫人，
    称诸异邦曰寡小君；异邦人称之亦曰君夫人。

    一个国家的执政国君的妻子，被他称为"夫人"。她称他为"陛下"。[①] 她被她国家的人民称为"夫人，我的女主人"，而她的人民对另一个国家的人民提到她时称"我们善良可爱的王妃"。其他国家的人民向她的人民谈到她时，称她"夫人，你们的王妃"。

---

① "小童"译为"Sire"，此处辜鸿铭有误，应为国君之妻自称，而不是称呼国君。

【评述】

1. "季氏将伐颛臾"一句中，"季氏"为鲁国"三桓"之一，为大夫，辜鸿铭译为"the head of a powerful family of nobles in Confucius' native State"，"孔子故国的一个有权势的贵族家族的当家人"。"颛臾"为鲁国的附庸国，辜鸿铭译为"a small principality within that State"，"国内的一个小型公国"。翻译中指出了两者的关系，即同在一国之内，一个是贵族官员，一个是诸侯公国。前者将讨伐后者。

"无乃尔是过与？"这是当孔子听到季氏要向颛臾发动战争的事情之后，强烈地谴责冉有。辜鸿铭译为"is not this due to your fault?"，"这不是要归因于你们的过错吗？"下文中孔子分析了谴责他们的原因。

"夫颛臾，昔者先王以为东蒙主，且在邦域之中矣，是社稷之臣也"。辜鸿铭的翻译是："昔者先王以为东蒙主"译为"The reigning family of this principality derived its titles from ancient Emperors"，"那个公国的当权家族，其爵位源自古代的帝王们"。其中，"东蒙主"应指"titles"，爵位之意；"在邦域之中"，译为"its land is situate within our own territory"，"它的国土位于我们自己的版图之内"；"社稷之臣"译为"the ruler is a prince of the Empire"，"其统治者是帝国的一个诸侯国君"，指颛臾国君是周朝的一个诸侯，就其身份而言的。下一句孔子反问："何以伐为？"辜鸿铭译为"What right, then, have you to declare war against a vassal of the Emperor?"意思是，季氏只是个"大夫"，而颛臾国国君则是个"诸侯"，季氏有何权利去征伐诸侯呢？

冉有辩驳说"夫子欲之，吾二臣者皆不欲也"。"夫子"，辜鸿铭译为"my lord, our Master"，"我的大人——我们的主人"，即指季氏，指自己并非战争主谋，真正的主谋是他们的主人季氏。下面又是孔子的回答。

"陈力就列，不能者止"，辜鸿铭译为"Let those who can stand the fight fall into the ranks, and let those who cannot, retire"，"让那些能够经得起战斗的人排入队列，让那些不能的人，退出"。其中，"力"指经得起战斗的能力；"列"指队列。这是用战斗能力来比喻做事能力。

"危而不持，颠而不扶，则将焉用彼相矣？"辜鸿铭译为"What is the use of a guide to a blind man if, when he is in danger, the guide does not help him and, when he falls, the guide does not lift him up?"，"如果一个盲人处于危险中，而他的向导不帮助他，当他跌倒时，他的向导也不把他扶起，那么这个向导对于这位盲人来说又有什么用呢"。其中，"危"指处于危险之中；"持"指帮助；"颠"指跌倒；"扶"指扶起；"相"指盲人的向导。这句话是继续批评冉有、季路没有起到应有的作用。

"虎兕出于柙，龟玉毁于椟中"，辜鸿铭译为"when a tiger or a wild animal escapes from its cage, or when a tortoise-shell or a valuable gem gets broken in its casket"，"当一只老虎或一头野生动物从它的笼子里逃了出来，或者，当一片龟甲或一颗珍贵的宝石在匣子里坏

掉"。其中，"虎兕"译为"a tiger or a wild animal"，"一只老虎或一头野生动物"；"柙"译为"cage"，"笼子"；"龟玉"译为"a tortoise-shell or a valuable gem"，"一片龟甲或一颗珍贵的宝石"；"椟"译为"casket"，"小盒子、匣子"。这句仍然是孔子通过比喻来批评冉有和季路。

冉有继续辩驳说，"今夫颛臾，固而近于费。今不取，后世必为子孙忧"。辜鸿铭的翻译是："固而近于费"译为"this principality is very strongly fortified and is within easy reach of our most important town"，"那个公国在非常强有力地设防，很容易就会延伸到我们最重要的城镇"，指军事力量强大引起的周边恐慌。到此，冉有终于不再推脱，而承认自己与季氏有一样的想法，即支持季氏征伐颛臾。

于是，孔子说"君子疾夫舍曰欲之，而必为之辞"。辜鸿铭译为"A good man hates to make excuses when he ought to say simply 'I want it.'"，"一个良善的人，当他应该简单地说'我想这样'时，他会厌恶去找借口的"。其中，"疾"是厌恶之意；"欲之"是"我想这样"之意；"为之辞"是找借口之意，指作为一个"君子"，一般情况下当问到自己的行为原因时，应该真诚地直接作答，而不应闪烁其词寻找借口。

下面孔子进一步谈应如何去治理一个国家，以及维护一个国家的稳定。

"有国有家者，不患寡而患不均，不患贫而患不安。盖均无贫，和无寡，安无倾。"辜鸿铭的翻译是："有国有家者"译为"those who have kingdoms and possessions"，"那些拥有王国与财产的人"，指掌握国家权力与财力的人；"不患寡而患不均"译为"should not be concerned that they have not enough possessions, but should be concerned that possessions are not equally distributed"，"不应担心他们不具备足够的财产，而应该担心财产没有平均地分配"；"不患贫而患不安"译为"should not be concerned that they are poor, but should be concerned that the people are not contented"，"不应担心他们匮乏，而应该担心人民不满意"。"均无贫，和无寡，安无倾"译为"For with equal distribution there will be no poverty; with mutual good will, there will be no want; and with contentment among the people, there can be no downfall and dissolution"，"平均分配，就会没有贫穷；相互友善，就会没有匮乏；人民满意，就不会衰落与消亡"。值得注意的是，辜鸿铭把"安"理解为"人民满意"。

"故远人不服，则修文德以来之。既来之，则安之"。辜鸿铭的翻译是："远人"译为"the people outside the country"，"国外的人民"，指鲁国以外的人；"不服"译为"do not submit"，"不顺服"；"修文德以来之"译为"a ruler should improve the moral education at home in order to attract them"，"为了吸引他们，统治者应该改善国内的道德教育"，"修文德"即改善道德教育；"安之"译为"the ruler should make them happy and contented"，"统治者应该让他们快乐并感到满意"。即用良好的社会环境吸引他们过来之后，就要让他们生活得快乐。

然后，孔子分析季氏当时的政治表现。"远人不服，而不能来也"，辜鸿铭仍译为

"people from outside"，指无法吸引外面的人民。"邦分崩离析，而不能守也"，辜鸿铭的翻译是："分崩离析"译为 "the country is internally torn by factions, dissensions, outbreaks and dissolutions"，"国家被各种派系、纠纷、暴动以及衰败而导致内部分裂"；"不能守"译为 "you are doing nothing to prevent them"，"你们没有做出任何事情去阻止它们"，"守"，即阻止"分崩离析"的发生。

最后，孔子就季氏的安危作出判断，"吾恐季孙之忧，不在颛臾，而在萧墙之内也"。"忧"译为 "the danger in future to the stability"，"未来影响稳固的危险"；"萧墙之内"译为 "within the walls of your master's own palace"，"你们主人自己宫殿的高墙内部"，即指季氏自己的家中。

2. 本节，辜鸿铭注释说，孔子在此描述的是"寡头政治"与"民主政治"的政治形态，都不会长久。他说：

> 孔子要表达的意思，首先是欧洲所谓的"寡头政治"(an oligarchy)，其次是"民主政治"(democracy)：通过此处的段落，它们两者都绝不会是一个国家里真正长久稳固的政治形态。在古代中国，统治阶层或者贵族阶层相当于罗斯金先生所说的英国的地主或乡绅。

3. 这一节，辜鸿铭认为是孔子谈论的当时鲁国的政治状态，是对当下现实的描述。

4. 文中，"益者三友，损者三友"，辜鸿铭译为 "there are three kinds of friendship which are beneficial and three kinds which are injurious"，"有三种友谊是有益处的，有三种是有害处的"。其中，"友"即友谊之意；"益"指对人有益处；"损"指对人有害处。有益处的是"友直，友谅，友多闻"。辜鸿铭的翻译是："直"译为 "upright men"，"正直的人"；"谅"译为 "faithful men"，"忠实、忠贞的人"；"多闻"译为 "men of much information"，"有学问的人"。有害处的是"友便辟，友善柔，友便佞"。辜鸿铭的翻译是："便辟"译为 "plausible men"，"花言巧语的、自我辩护的人"。与第一章第3节"巧言令色"一句中"巧言"的翻译相同。"善柔"译为 "insinuating manners"，"有谄媚态度的人"，与"令色"翻译相近。在第一章第3节，"令色"译为 "fine manners"。"便佞"译为 "glib-tongued men"，"油腔滑调、油嘴滑舌、口齿伶俐的人"。

5. 文中，"乐"，译为 "pleasures"，"快乐，或快乐的事"。这一节谈的是，什么样的快乐有益，什么样的快乐有害。

6. 文中，"侍于君子有三愆"，辜鸿铭译为 "There are three kinds of errors to which men are liable when in the presence of their superiors"，"人们在他们的长者面前，容易犯三种错误"。其中，"君子"译为 "their superiors"，"长者、长辈、上级"等意思；"愆"译为 "errors"，"错误、过失"等意。这一节讲的是人经常会犯的三种错误。

7. 文中，"君子有三戒"，辜鸿铭译为 "There are three things which a man should beware of in the three stages of his life"，"一个人在他人生的三个阶段应该谨防三件事情"。其中，"君子"译为 "a man" 泛指一般人；"三戒"指"人生的三个阶段应谨防三件事"，即每一个年龄阶段，应该注意什么事；"戒"是谨防、留意、小心的意思。

8. 文中，"君子有三畏：畏天命，畏大人，畏圣人之言"一句，"三畏"，辜鸿铭译为 "three things which a wise and good man holds in awe"，"对三件事情保持敬畏"；"天命"，译为 "the Laws of God"，"上帝的律法"。对此，辜鸿铭添加注释认为，"上帝的律法"包含在全部事物之中：

> 字面意思是"上帝的律法"。在其他地方，我们已经把这些字翻译为宗教。我们认为，就是在欧洲所谓的宗教。那并不是摩西、吕库古、基督或孔子的律法，因为这些律法只是对上帝戒律的诠释。上帝的律法包含全部，从简单的二加二等于四，姜对于嘴的感觉是辣的，律法支配着太阳、月亮以及群星的轨迹，最后，关于是与非的最高的律法在人的心中。"噢，是我的命运的力量指引着我在思与行的神圣的纯粹之路上行走，这条路是令人敬畏的各种律法注定的，各种律法源自最高的天上，上帝强大的力量在里面，并且生长永不衰老。"

9. 这一节，孔子按"天生智力"或"天赋"的不同程度，把"有智慧"的人分为四类：即"生而知之"、"学而知之"、"困而学之"和"困而不学"。辜鸿铭译"智慧"为 "understanding"，"理解力"。

10. 文中，"君子有九思"，辜鸿铭译为 "there are nine objects which a wise man aims at"，"一个明智的人会旨在达到九个目标"。"思"，即追求目标之意。这一节讲的是作为一个"君子"应该追求的九个德行目标。

11. "见善如不及，见不善如探汤"一句，"见善如不及"辜鸿铭译为 "when they see what is good and honest, try to act up to it"，"看到优秀与正直时试着去遵守它"。"善"指优秀与正直的事情或行为；"及"指遵守之意。"见不善如探汤"，译为 "when they see what

is bad and dishonest try to avoid it as if avoiding scalding water"，"看到恶劣与不正直时试着去躲避它，就像躲避滚烫的开水"。"探汤"，比喻像躲避滚烫的开水那样，躲避恶劣与不正直。"吾见其人矣，吾闻其语矣"，译为 "such men I have known and the expressions of such principles I have heard"，"这样的人我看到过，这种行为准则的表述我也听说过"。其中，"闻其语"指听说过类似的行为准则。指上面所说的人，孔子是听说过并见过的。"隐居以求其志，行义以达其道。吾闻其语矣，未见其人也"，指这样的人孔子只听说过但没见过。"隐居以求其志"，译为 "live in retirement in order to study their aims"，"为了研究他们的目标而隐居"；"行义以达其道"译为 "practise righteousness in order to carry out their principles"，"为了实现他们的原则而依义行事的人"。

12. 朱熹认为，这节开头缺漏了"孔子曰"（《四书章句集注》，第173页），辜鸿铭从之。最后的诗歌是辜鸿铭所加，是对第十二章第10节中"诚不以富，亦只以异"的翻译，该诗出自《诗经·小雅·我行其野》。朱熹认为这句诗应该放在此节"其斯之谓与？"一句上（《四书章句集注》，第173页），辜鸿铭从之。

13. "子亦有异闻乎"，辜鸿铭译为 "Have you had any special lesson from your father"，"你从你父亲那里学到特殊的课程了吗"。"异闻"指特殊的课程。指别人怀疑孔子是否对自己的儿子的教育，与其他人不同。"不学诗，无以言"，译为 "if you do not study poetry, you cannot make yourself agreeable in conversation"，"如果你不研究诗，在谈话时就不会令人愉快"。"诗"指文学体裁诗歌；"言"指"谈话时让自己变得令人愉快"，即使自己的谈话很有艺术。"不学礼，无以立"，译为 "if you do not study the arts, you will lack judgment and taste"，"如果你不研究艺术，你就会缺乏判断力与鉴赏力"。其中，"立"指判断力与鉴赏力，指通过对艺术的研究与学习，能提升人的人文素养，形成较高的判断力与鉴赏力。以上两句是伯鱼听到的孔子对他格外教诲的仅有的两句话，还是偶然遇到的。"君子之远其子也"，译为 "a wise and good man does not treat even his own son with familiarity"，"一个明智而良善的人即使是对待自己的儿子也不会过分亲近"。"远"指不会过分亲近、不狎昵之意。

14. 这一节说的是当时对国君之妻在不同场合下的不同称呼。辜鸿铭没有按照读音进行名称翻译，而是用了意译。

CHAPTER XVII
阳货第十七

1. An influential officer, who was in the service of a powerful family of nobles in Confucius' native State, on one occasion expressed a wish to see Confucius, but Confucius would not go to see him. The officer then sent Confucius a present of a pig. Confucius thereupon timing his visit when the officer was not at home, called on him to tender his thanks. On returning, however, he met the officer on the way.

   "Come now," said the officer to Confucius, "I want to speak to you. Now I would ask you whether he is a good man who hides the treasures of his knowledge and leaves his country to go astray? " "No," replied Confucius, "he is not." "Is he a man of understanding," asked the officer again, "who is anxious to be employed and yet misses every chance that comes to him of being employed?" "No," replied Confucius, "He is not."

   "Then," said the officer, "you ought to know that days and months are passing away and time waits not for us." "Yes," replied Confucius, "I will enter the public service."

2. Confucius remarked, "Men, in their nature, are alike; but by practice they become widely different."

3. Confucius then went on to say, "It is only men of the highest understanding and men of the grossest dullness, who do not change."

4. When Confucius on one occasion came to a small town where one of his disciples was chief Magistrate, he heard the sounds of music and singing among the people. He then, with a mischievous smile in his look, remarked, "To kill a chicken why use a knife used for

1. 阳货欲见孔子,孔子不见,归孔子豚。孔子时其亡也,而往拜之,遇诸途。谓孔子曰:"来! 予与尔言。"曰:"怀其宝而迷其邦,可谓仁乎?"曰:"不可。""好从事而亟失时,可谓知乎?"曰:"不可。""日月逝矣,岁不我与。"孔子曰:"诺。吾将仕矣。"

   一位有很大影响力的官员,在孔子故国的一个有权势的贵族家族中服务,有一次表达了去看望孔子的愿望,但孔子不愿见他。那位官员就送给孔子一头猪作为礼物。于是,孔子把他的拜访时间安排在那位官员不在家的时候,去看望他表达自己的谢意。然而,返回的途中,他在路上遇到了那位官员。

   "过来,"那位官员对孔子说,"我想对你说几句话。我想问你,如果一个人隐藏了自己的学问的宝藏,而任由他的国家步入迷途,他是否是一个良善的人?""不,"孔子回答说,"他不是。""他是一个有智慧的人吗,"那位官员又问,"尽管他渴望被聘用,却错过了每次来到他面前的被聘用的机会?""不,"孔子回答说,"他不是。"

   "那么,"那位官员说,"你应该知道,岁月正在流逝,时间并不会等着我们。""是啊,"孔子回答说,"我将会参加公职。"

2. 子曰:"性相近也,习相远也。"

   孔子说:"人们在本性上是相似的,但经过实践后变得非常不同。"

3. 子曰:"唯上知与下愚不移。"

   孔子又接着说:"只有最高智慧的人与最迟钝愚蠢的人,才不会改变。"

4. 子之武城,闻弦歌之声。夫子莞尔而笑,曰:"割鸡焉用牛刀?"子游对曰:"昔者偃也闻诸夫子曰:'君子学道则爱人,小人学道则易使也。'"子曰:"二三子! 偃之言是也。前言戏之耳。"

   有一次,当孔子来到了一座他的一位学生担任主要治安官的小城镇

slaughtering an ox?"

"Sir," replied the disciple who was chief Magistrate of the town, "I have heard you say at one time that when the gentlemen of a country are highly educated, it makes them sympathize with the people; and when the people are educated, it makes them easily amenable to government."

"Yes," answered Confucius, turning to his other disciples who were present, "He is right: what I said just now was only spoken in jest."

5. One one occasion a noble in Confucius' native State who held possession of an important town and was in an attitude of rebellion, invited Confucius to see him. Confucius was inclined to go. At this, Confucius' disciple, the intrepid Chung Yu, was vexed. He said, "Indeed you cannot go! Why should you think of going to see such a man?"

"It cannot be for nothing," replied Confucius, "that he has invited me to see him. If anyone would employ me, I would establish a new empire here in the East."

6. A disciple of Confucius enquired what constituted a moral life. Confucius answered, "A man who can carry out five things wherever he may be is a moral man." "What five things?" asked the disciple.

"They are," replied Confucius, "Earnestness, consideration for others, trustworthiness, diligence, and generosity. If you are earnest, you will never meet with want of respect. If you are considerate to others, you will win the hearts of the people. If you are trustworthy, men will trust you. If you are diligent, you will be successful in your undertakings. If you are generous, you will find plenty of men who are willing to serve you."

时，听到百姓们奏乐与歌唱的声音。于是他脸上掠过一丝顽皮的笑容，说："杀一只鸡，为什么要用宰牛的刀呢？"

"先生，"那位担任该城镇主要治安官的学生回答说，"我听您有一次说过，当一个国家的绅士们受过高度的教育，就会体恤百姓；当人民受过教育，就会很容易地甘愿服从政府。"

"是的，"孔子转向现场的其他学生，回答说，"他说得对：我刚才只是开玩笑。"

5. 公山弗扰以费畔，召，子欲往。子路不说，曰："末之也已，何必公山氏之之也？"子曰："夫召我者而岂徒哉？ 如有用我者吾其为东周乎？"

有一次，孔子故国的一位占据着一座重要城镇并有叛乱倾向的贵族，邀请孔子前去看望他。孔子想去。孔子的学生，那位刚勇的仲由对此十分恼火。他说："你确实不能去！ 为什么要考虑去看望这样一个人呢？"

"他邀请我去看他，"孔子回答说，"不可能是没有缘故的。如果有人聘用我，我会在这东部建立一个新的帝国。"

6. 子张问仁于孔子。孔子曰："能行五者于天下，为仁矣。"请问之。曰："恭、宽、信、敏、惠。恭则不侮，宽则得众，信则人任焉，敏则有功，惠则足以使人。"

孔子的一个学生问怎样才算是一种道德的生活。孔子回答说："一个无论在什么地方实现五件事情的人，就可以说是一个有德之人。""哪五件事情？"那位学生问。

"它们是，"孔子回答，"真诚，体贴他人，可信赖，勤奋，以及慷慨大度。如果你真诚，你就永远不会遇到不敬。如果你关心他人，你就会赢得民心。如果你可信赖，人们就会信任你。如果你勤奋，你的事业就会取得成功。如果你慷慨大度，你会发现有大批愿意为你服务的人。"

7. On one occasion a noble of a certain State having rebelled against the legitimate authority, invited Confucius to see him. Confucius was inclined to go, but Confucius's disciple, the intrepid Chung Yu, said to Confucius: "Sir, I have heard you say at one time that a wise and good man will not associate even with those persons who are nearly related to him, when such persons have been found guilty of evil-doing. Now this man is holding a town in actual rebellion against authority. How is it that you can think of going to see him?"

"Yes," replied Confucius, "I have said that. But is it not also said that if a thing is really hard you may pound it and yet it will not crack; if a thing a really white, you may smirch it, and yet it will not become black. And am I, after all, only a bitter gourd to be hung up and not eaten at all? "

8. Confucius once remarked to a disciple, saying: "Have you ever heard of the six virtues and their failures? " "No," replied the disciple. "Sit down then," said Confucius, "and I will tell you.

"First there is the mere love of morality: that alone, without culture, degenerates into fatuity. Secondly, there is the mere love of knowledge: that alone, without culture, tends to dilettantism. Thirdly, there is mere love of honesty: that alone, without culture, produces heartlessness. Fourthly, there is the mere love of uprightness: that alone, without culture, leads to tyranny. Fifthly, there is the mere love of courage: that alone, without culture, produces recklessness. Sixthly, there is the mere love of strength of character: that alone, without culture, produces eccentricity."

7. 佛肸召，子欲往。子路曰："昔者由也闻诸夫子曰：'亲于其身为不善者，君子不入也。'佛肸以中牟畔，子之往也，如之何！"子曰："然。有是言也。不曰坚乎，磨而不磷；不曰白乎，涅而不缁。吾岂匏瓜也哉？焉能系而不食？"

有一次，某个国家的一个反抗法定当局的贵族，邀请孔子去看望他。孔子想去，但孔子的学生，那位刚勇的仲由，对孔子说："先生，我曾听你有一次说过，一个明智而良善的人将不会与那些被发现因恶劣行径而有罪的人交往，即使是他的至亲。如今，这个人占据着一座城镇实际上在反抗官方，你竟然考虑去看望他，是怎么回事呢？"

"是的，"孔子回答说，"我是这样说过。不是也有话说，如果一个东西非常坚硬，你可以敲打它，它却不破碎；如果一个东西非常的白，你可以弄脏它，但它却不会变成黑色。毕竟，难道我只是个苦瓜，被悬挂起来而不被吃掉吗？"

8. 子曰："由也，女闻六言六蔽矣乎？"对曰："未也。""居！吾语女。好仁不好学，其蔽也愚；好知不好学，其蔽也荡；好信不好学，其蔽也贼；好直不好学，其蔽也绞；好勇不好学，其蔽也乱；好刚不好学，其蔽也狂。"

有一次，孔子对一个学生说："你听说过六种美德以及它们的不足吗？""没有。"那位学生回答。"那么坐下，"孔子说，"我来告诉你。

"第一，如果只热爱道德：仅仅如此，而没有修养，就会堕落为愚昧。第二，如果只热爱学问：仅仅如此，而没有修养，就易于成为浅涉文艺的业余爱好者。第三，如果只热爱诚实守信：仅仅如此，而没有修养，就会导致冷酷无情。第四，如果只热爱正直：仅仅如此，而没有修养，就会导致专横。第五，如果只热爱勇气：仅仅如此，而没有修养，就会导致鲁莽轻率。第六，如果只热爱道德力量：仅仅如此，而没有修养，就会导致行为古怪。"

9. Confucius on one occasion remarked to his disciples, "My young friends, why do you not study poetry? Poetry calls out the sentiment. It stimulates observation. It enlarges the sympathies and moderates the resentment felt against injustice. Poetry, in fact, while it has lessons for the duties of social life, at the same time makes us acquainted with the animate and inanimate objects in nature."

10. Confucius once said to his son, "You should give yourself to the study of the first two books in the Book of Ballads, Songs and Psalms. A man who has not studied those books will be out of his element wherever he goes."

11. Confucius was once heard to say, "Men speak about Art! Art! Do you really think that merely means painting and sculpture? Men speak about music! Music! Do you think that means merely bells, drums, and musical instruments? "

12. Confucius remarked, "A man who is austere in his look, but a weakling and a coward at heart — is he not like one of your small, mean people; yea, is he not like a sneaking thief or a cowardly pickpocket? "

13. Confucius remarked, "Your meek men of respectability in a place, are they who unmercifully destroy all sense of moral sentiment in man."

9. 子曰："小子！何莫学夫诗？诗，可以兴，可以观，可以群，可以怨。迩之事父，远之事君。多识于鸟兽草木之名。"

　　有一次，孔子对他的学生们说："我年轻的朋友们，你们为什么不研究诗呢？诗会唤起情感。它激发观察力。它扩大怜悯之心，而且会节制对非正义的不满。实际上，诗在教导社会生活的责任的同时，也会让我们了解自然界中的有生命与无生命的事物。"

10. 子谓伯鱼曰："女为《周南》《召南》矣乎？人而不为《周南》《召南》，其犹正墙面而立也与？"

　　有一次，孔子对他的儿子说："你应该致力于学习那部有关诸多民谣、诗歌和赞美诗的文学典籍中的前两篇。一个没有学习过这些篇章的人，无论他去哪里都会感到不适应。"

11. 子曰："礼云礼云，玉帛云乎哉？乐云乐云，钟鼓云乎哉？"

　　孔子有一次被听到说："人们谈论艺术！艺术！你真的认为仅仅指的是绘画与雕刻吗？人们谈论音乐！音乐！你认为仅仅指铃、鼓和乐器吗？"

12. 子曰："色厉而内荏，譬诸小人，其犹穿窬之盗也与？"

　　孔子说："一个表情上严峻，但内心却软弱而胆怯的人——难道他不像一个微不足道的卑劣自私的人吗，而且，难道他不像个卑怯的贼或胆怯的扒手吗？"

13. 子曰："乡原，德之贼也。"

　　孔子说："那些在一个地方懦弱谦恭却又有名望的人，是他们残酷地破坏了人心中对道德情感的所有观念。"

14. Confucius remarked, "To preach in the public streets the commonplaces which you have picked up on the way is to throw away all your finer feelings."

15. Confucius, speaking of the public men of his time, remarked: "These despicable men! How is it possible to serve the interests of the country in company with such men? Before they gain their position, their only anxiety is how to obtain it; and after they have obtained the position, their sole anxiety is lest they should lose it. In their anxiety lest they should lose their position, there is nothing which they would not do."

16. Confucius remarked, "In old times men had three kinds of imperfections in their characters, which perhaps now are not to be found. Passionate, impetuous men in old times loved independence; but passionate impetuosity nowadays shows itself in wild licence. Proud men in old times were modest and reserved, but pride nowadays shows itself in touchiness and vulgar bad-temper. Simple men in old times were artless and straightforward, but simplicity nowadays hides cunning."

17. Confucius remarked, "With plausible speech and fine manners will seldom be found moral character."

18. Confucius remarked, "I hate the way in which scarlet dims the perception for vermilion. I hate the way in which the modern popular airs are liable to spoil the taste for good music. Finally, I hate the way in which smartness of speech in men is liable to destroy kingdoms and ruin families."

14. 子曰:"道听而途说,德之弃也。"

孔子说:"在公共街道上宣扬那些你偶然在路上听到的陈词滥调,就相当于丢弃你所有美好的情感。"

15. 子曰:"鄙夫可与事君也与哉?其未得之也,患得之;既得之,患失之。苟患失之,无所不至矣。"

孔子谈论他那个时代的公务人员,说:"这些卑劣的人!怎么可能与这样的人一道为国家的利益服务呢?在他们得到他们的职位之前,他们唯一的焦虑就是如何得到它,而在他们得到了职位之后,他们唯一的焦虑就是防止失去它。在他们防止失去职位的焦虑下,没有什么事情是他们不会去做的。"

16. 子曰:"古者民有三疾,今也或是之亡也。古之狂也肆,今之狂也荡;古之矜也廉,今之矜也忿戾;古之愚也直,今之愚也诈而已矣。"

孔子说:"古时候,人们在他们的性格中有三种缺点,或许今天已经找不到了。古时候狂热、冲动的人热爱独立,但今天的狂热冲动却表现为疯狂的放荡。古时候骄傲的人是适度并有所保留的,但今天的骄傲却表现为敏感易怒与粗野的坏脾气。古时候愚蠢无知的人是单纯而率直的,但今天的愚蠢无知却隐藏着诡诈。"

17. 子曰:"巧言令色,鲜矣仁。"

孔子说:"具有貌似合理的言语又有良好的态度,很少会被发现具备道德品质。"

18. 子曰:"恶紫之夺朱也,恶郑声之乱雅乐也,恶利口之覆邦家者。"

孔子说:"我憎恨猩红色模糊了人们对朱红色的认识。我憎恨当今流行的曲调易于破坏人们对好音乐的鉴赏力。最后,我憎恨人们机敏的言语易于毁灭王国并破坏家庭。"

19. Confucius was once heard to say, "I would rather not speak at all."

"But if you do not speak, sir," asked a disciple, "What shall we, your disciples, learn from you to be taught to others? "

"Look at the Heaven there," answered Confucius, "Does it speak? And yet the seasons run their appointed courses and all things in nature grow up in their time. Look at the Heaven there: does it speak? "

20. A man who wanted to see Confucius called on him. Confucius, not wishing to see him, sent to say he was sick. When the servant with the message went to the door, Confucius took up his musical instrument and sang aloud purposely to let the visitor hear it and know that he was not really sick.

21. A disciple of Confucius enquired about the period of three years' mourning for parents, remarking that one year was long enough.

"For," said he, "if a gentleman neglects the Arts and usages of life for three years, he will lose his knowledge of them; and if he put aside music for three years, he will entirely forget it. Again, even in the ordinary course of nature, in one year the old corn is mown away to give place to new corn which springs up, and in one year we burn through all the different kinds of wood produced in all the seasons. I believe, therefore, that after the completion of one year, mourning may cease."

Confucius answered, "If, after one year's mourning, you were to eat good food and wear fine clothes, would you feel at ease? "

"I should," replied the disciple. "Then," answered Confucius, "if

19. 子曰：“予欲无言。”子贡曰：“子如不言，则小子何述焉？”子曰：“天何言哉？四时行焉，百物生焉，天何言哉？”

有一次，有人听到孔子说：“我宁愿一点都不说话。”

“但是如果您不说话，先生，”一位学生问，“我们，您的学生们，能够从您那里获取什么来传授给别人呢？”

“看看那天空，”孔子回答说，“它说话了吗？然而，四季仍会按照预定的正常秩序而运行，而且，自然界的万物会在它们合适的时机而生长。看看那天空：它说话了吗？”

20. 孺悲欲见孔子，孔子辞以疾。将命者出户，取瑟而歌。使之闻之。

一个想见孔子的人拜访他。孔子不想见他，称自己生病了。当那位传话的仆人走到门口时，孔子开始弹奏他的乐器并高声唱歌，以便让来访者听到并且知道他并没有生病。

21. 宰我问：“三年之丧，期已久矣。君子三年不为礼，礼必坏；三年不为乐，乐必崩。旧谷既没，新谷既升，钻燧改火，期可已矣。”子曰：“食夫稻，衣夫锦，于女安乎？”曰：“安。”“女安则为之！夫君子之居丧，食旨不甘，闻乐不乐，居处不安，故不为也。今女安，则为之！”宰我出。子曰：“予之不仁也！子生三年，然后免于父母之怀。夫三年之丧，天下之通丧也。予也有三年之爱于其父母乎？”

孔子的一个学生询问关于为父母而守的三年丧期，认为一年就足够长了。

“因为，”他说，“如果一个绅士疏忽艺术及生活习俗三年，他就会丧失掉与之相关的学问。如果他扔下音乐三年，他就会全部忘记。再说，就算是在大自然的普遍的正常秩序中，一年之内陈旧的谷物就会被割掉，为迅速生长起来的新谷物让出位置，一年之内我们会烧遍各个季节

you can feel at ease, do it. But a good man during the whole period of three years' mourning, does not enjoy good food when he eats it, and derives no pleasure from music when he hears it; when he is lodged in comfort, he does not feel at ease: therefore, he does not do anything of those things. You, however, since you feel at ease, can, of course, do them."

Afterwards, when the disciple had left, Confucius remarked, "What a man without moral feeling he is? It is only three years after his birth that a child is able to leave the arms of his parents. Now the period of three years' mourning for parents is universally observed throughout the Empire. As to that man, — I wonder if he was one who did not enjoy the affection of his parents when he was a child!"

22. Confucius remarked, "It is really a bad case when a man simply eats his full meals without applying his mind to anything at all during the whole day. Are there not such things as gambling and games of skill? To do one of those things even is better than to do nothing at all."

23. A disciple of Confucius, the intrepid Chung Yu, enquired: "Is not valour a quality important to a gentleman? "

"A gentleman," answered Confucius, "esteems what is right as of the highest importance. A gentleman who has valour, but is without a knowledge and love of what is right, is likely to commit a crime. A man of the people who has courage, but is without the knowledge and love of what is right, is likely to become a robber."

生长的各种各样的木柴。因此,我认为,一年结束之后,悲痛也会结束。"

孔子回答说:"一年的悲痛之后,如果你要去吃美味的食物与穿华丽的衣服,你会觉得舒适安逸吗?"

"我会的。"那个学生回答说。"那么,"孔子回答,"如果你能够感到安逸舒适,就那样做吧。但是一个良善的人在整个三年的丧期之内,在吃美味的食物时不会以此而感到愉悦,听到音乐时也不会从中获得快乐,当他处在舒适的条件下,他也不会感到舒适安逸:因此,他不会做任何这类的事情。然而,既然你会感到舒适安逸,当然,你就能够去做这些事。"

然后,当那个学生离开后,孔子说:"他是一个多么没有道德情感的人啊! 一个孩子只有在出生三年之后,才能够离开他父母的怀抱。现在,为父母的三年丧期在整个帝国都在被普遍地遵循着。至于那个人——我想知道在他是个孩子的时候,他是不是没有享受到父母的爱!"

22. 子曰:"饱食终日,无所用心,难矣哉! 不有博弈者乎,为之犹贤乎已。"

孔子说:"一个人在一整天内仅仅是餐餐吃得饱,却没有把心思才智用于任何事情,真是一件糟糕的事。不是有那些诸如赌博、技巧游戏之类的事情吗? 即使是做做这种事情,也比什么都不做要好一些。"

23. 子路曰:"君子尚勇乎?"子曰:"君子义以为上。君子有勇而无义为乱,小人有勇而无义为盗。"

孔子的一个学生,那位刚勇的仲由,问:"勇气对于一位绅士来说不是一种很重要的品质吗?"

"一位绅士,"孔子回答说,"把正义视为首要品质。一位有勇气的绅士,如果没有学问与对正义的热爱,就很可能会犯罪。一个有勇气的普通人,如果没有学问与对正义的热爱,就很可能会成为一个强盗。"

24. A disciple of Confucius enquired, "Has a wise and good man also his hatreds? "

"Yes," answered Confucius, "He has his hatreds. He hates those who love to expatiate on the evil doings of others. He hates those who, themselves living low, disreputable lives, try to detract those who are trying to live a higher life. He hates those who are valourous, but without judgment and manners. He hates those who are energetic and bold, but narrow-minded and selfish. "

"And you," continued Confucius, addressing the disciple, "have you also your hatreds? "

"Yes," replied the disciple, "I hate those who are censorious and believe themselves to be clever. I hate those who are presumptuous and believe themselves to be brave. I hate those who ransack out the secret misdoings of others in other to proclaim them, and believe themselves to be upright. "

25. Confucius remarked, "Of all people in the world, young women and servants are the most difficult to keep in the house. If you are familiar with them, they forget their position. But if you keep them at a distance, they are discontented."

26. Confucius remarked, "If a man after forty is an object of dislike to men, he will continue to be so to the ends of his days."

24. 子贡曰:"君子亦有恶乎?"子曰:"有恶:恶称人之恶者,恶居下流而讪上者,恶勇而无礼者,恶果敢而窒者。"曰:"赐也亦有恶乎?""恶徼以为知者,恶不孙以为勇者,恶讦以为直者。"

　　孔子的一位学生问:"一个明智和良善的人也会有所厌恶吗?"

　　"是的,"孔子回答说,"他有他所厌恶的东西。他厌恶那些喜欢讲述别人恶行的人。他厌恶那些自身过着低俗、声名狼藉的生活,却一心想着去诋毁那些试着过更高尚生活的人。他厌恶那些英勇但缺乏判断力与礼貌的人。他厌恶那些积极而勇敢,却又心胸狭隘与自私的人。"

　　"你呢?"孔子继续向他的学生说,"你也有你所厌恶的东西吗?"

　　"是的,"那位学生回答,"我厌恶那些吹毛求疵而自以为聪明的人。我厌恶那些专横冒失却自以为勇敢的人。我厌恶那些为了公开揭发别人而搜集他们的恶行,却自认为正直的人。"

25. 子曰:"唯女子与小人为难养也,近之则不孙,远之则怨。"

　　孔子说:"在世界上所有人中,年轻女子与佣人在家中是最难对待的。如果你对他们友好亲密,他们就会忘记自己的身份。但如果你疏远他们,他们就会心怀不满。"

26. 子曰:"年四十而见恶焉,其终也已。"

　　孔子说:"如果一个人在四十岁以后还是个令人厌恶的人,他就会一直这样,直到他死的那一天。"

【评述】

1. 文中,"归孔子豚",辜鸿铭译为 "the officer then sent Confucius a present of a pig","那位官员就送给孔子一头猪作为礼物"。"归"为赠送之意,"豚"是猪的意思,指阳货见不到孔子,给孔子赠送了礼物。"孔子时其亡也,而往拜之",译为"Confucius thereupon timing his visit when the officer was not at home, called on him to tender his thanks","孔子把他的拜访时间安排在那位官员不在家的时候,去看望他表达自己的谢意",指孔子回访他,但要避免遇到他。在路上遇到之后,阳货与孔子对话。"怀其宝而迷其邦,可谓仁乎"。"怀其宝而迷其邦",译为 "hides the treasures of his knowledge and leaves his country to go astray","隐藏了自己的学问的宝藏,而任由他的国家步入迷途"。其中,"宝"指学问。"迷"指国家步入迷途。"好从事而亟失时",译为 "is anxious to be employed and yet misses every chance that comes to him of being employed","尽管渴望被聘用,却错过了每次来到他面前的被聘用的机会"。其中,"从事"即被聘用之意;"失时"指失去时机之意。孔子最后感叹"吾将仕矣"。

2. 文中,"性",辜鸿铭译为 "nature",指人的本性、天性;"近",译为 "alike","相似";"习",译为 "practice","实践,笃行";"远",译为 "widely different","大大的不同,非常不同",指生活实践使本性相似的人变得不同。

3. 文中,"上知"译为 "men of the highest understanding","最高智慧的人";"下愚"译为 "men of the grossest dullness","最迟钝愚蠢的人";"移"译为 "change","改变",指只有这两种极端的人,才不会有所改变。

4. 文中,子游说:"君子学道则爱人,小人学道则易使也。""君子",辜鸿铭译为 "the gentlemen of a country,""一个国家的绅士";"学道"译为 "are highly educated","受过高度的教育"。"爱人"译为 "sympathize with the people","体恤百姓"。"小人学道"译为 "the people are educated","人民受过教育。"此处 "小人"指人民。

5. 文中,"以费畔","费"是鲁国地名。辜鸿铭译为 "held possession of an important town and was in an attitude of rebellion","占据着一个重要城镇并有叛乱倾向"。其中,"费"译为 "一个重要城镇";"畔"指叛乱。子路质问孔子 "何必公山氏之之也",辜鸿铭译为 "why should you think of going to see such a man","为什么要考虑去看望这样一个人呢"。后一个 "之"应为前去看望之意。孔子回答 "夫召我者,而岂徒哉",译为 "it cannot be for nothing that he has invited me to see him","他邀请我去看他不可能是没有缘故的"。"如有用我者,吾其为东周乎",译为 "if anyone would employ me, I would

establish a new empire here in the East"，"如果有人聘用我，我会在这东部建立一个新的帝国"。其中，"东周"指在东方建立新的帝国（此处，帝国应该指的是周的文明）。辜鸿铭在此注释说：

即中国的东部。那时，帝国的领域在中国的西部。

6. 文中，"恭、宽、信、敏、惠"。辜鸿铭的翻译是："恭"译为"earnestness"，"真诚，诚挚"之意；"宽"译为"consideration for others"，"关心、体贴、体恤他人"之意；"信"译为"trustworthiness"，"可信任，可信赖"之意；"敏"译为"diligence"，"勤奋，勤勉"之意；"惠"译为"generosity"，"慷慨大度"之意。这是达到"仁"所应具备的五种德性。

7. 文中，"亲于其身为不善者，君子不入也"一句中，"亲于其身"辜鸿铭译为"those persons who are nearly related to him"，"他的至亲"；"为不善者"译为"have been found guilty of evil-doing"，"因恶劣行径而有罪的人"；"不入"译为"will not associate with"，"不与之交往"，指一个"君子"不会与品德恶劣的人交往，即使是自己的至亲。"佛肸以中牟畔"，译为"the man is holding a town in actual rebellion against authority"，"占据着一座城镇实际上在反抗官方"照例省略了佛肸的名字。意思是，佛肸是个反叛国家的人。子路反问孔子，为何要与佛肸这位叛国者交往。

孔子回答"不曰坚乎，磨而不磷；不曰白乎，涅而不缁"。"不曰坚乎，磨而不磷"译为"if a thing is really hard you may pound it and yet it will not crack"，"如果一个东西非常坚硬，你可以敲打它，它却不破碎"。其中，"磨"指敲打；"磷"指破碎之意；"不曰白乎，涅而不缁"，"if a thing a really white, you may smirch it, and yet it will not become black"，"如果一个东西非常的白，你可以弄脏它，但它却不会变成黑色"。其中，"涅"指弄脏；"缁"指变黑。"吾岂匏瓜也哉？焉能系而不食？""匏瓜"，历来多认为是一种瓜名，味苦不能食用。辜鸿铭译为"am I, after all, only a bitter gourd to be hung up and not eaten at all?"，"难道我只是个苦瓜，被悬挂起来而不被吃掉吗？"其中，"匏瓜"译为"bitter gourd"，"苦味的葫芦，苦瓜"之意。

8. 文中，"好直不好学，其蔽也绞"。"好直不好学"译为"there is the mere love of uprightness: that alone, without culture"，"如果只热爱正直：仅仅如此，而没有修养"；"其蔽也绞"译为"leads to tyranny"，"导致专横"，"绞"是专横之意。对此，辜鸿铭注释说：

最残酷无情的人，也许是一位诚实的官僚，而最专横的人，也许是一个正直的教士，尤其是反对基督教的新教徒。而现在，那种正直的教士已经没有了，如赫伯

特·斯宾塞的学生。(《当代洛希夫谷》)

9. "诗",多认为指《诗经》,辜鸿铭译为 "poetry",泛指诗歌。这一节孔子是谈论学习诗歌的意义。"可以兴",辜鸿铭译为 "calls out the sentiment","诗会唤起情感"。"诗"指诗歌这种文学形式;"兴"指唤起、激发情感;"可以观",译为 "it stimulates observation","激发观察力";"可以群,可以怨",辜鸿铭译为一句:"it enlarges the sympathies and moderates the resentment felt against injustice","它扩大怜悯之心,而且会节制对非正义的不满"。"迩之事父,远之事君;多识于鸟兽草木之名"一句,"迩之事父,远之事君"辜鸿铭译为一句:"it has lessons for the duties of social life","教导社会生活的责任"。"多识于鸟兽草木之名"译为 "makes us acquainted with the animate and inanimate objects in nature","让我们了解自然界中的有生命与无生命的事物"。"鸟兽草木"代指自然界所有的事物。最后,辜鸿铭引用华兹华斯的话来对本节加以注释,说明诗歌的作用,他在第八章第8节的注释中也引用了(见本书第174页的评述)。他引华兹华斯注释说,诗歌应该是这样的:

> 在她的成长中滋养想象,
> 并给她领悟能力的思想;
> 凭此,她可以迅速去认识,
> 道德的本质与万物的范畴。

10. 文中,"女为《周南》《召南》矣乎"一句,"《周南》《召南》"均《诗经》篇名。这句话辜鸿铭译为 "you should give yourself to the study of the first two books in the Book of Ballads, Songs and Psalms","你应该致力于学习那部有关诸多民谣、诗歌和赞美诗的文学典籍中的前两篇"。辜鸿铭对《诗经》名称的翻译,见第二章第2节的说明,"为"是致力于学习之意。"正墙面而立也",辜鸿铭译为 "be out of his element wherever he goes","无论去哪里都不适应环境"。这一节指这两篇诗对于人的社会生活而言,具有普遍的指导意义。

11. 文中,"礼",辜鸿铭译为 'art',"艺术"。"玉帛云乎哉",译为 "do you really think that merely means painting and sculpture","你真的认为仅仅指的是绘画与雕刻吗"。其中,"玉帛"指绘画与雕刻;"乐"译为 "music","音乐"。"钟鼓云乎哉"译为 "do you think that means merely bells, drums, and musical instruments","你认为仅仅指铃、鼓和乐器吗"。

12. 文中,"色厉而内荏",辜鸿铭译为 "austere in his look, but a weakling and a coward

400

at heart", "表情上严峻, 但内心却软弱而胆怯"; "小人", 辜鸿铭译为 "one of your small, mean people", "一个微不足道的卑劣自私的人"; "穿窬之盗", 译为 "a sneaking thief or a cowardly pickpocket", "卑怯的贼或者胆怯的扒手"。这一节指外表坚强、严厉, 内心软弱, 就像一个胆怯的贼。

13. "乡原", 辜鸿铭译为 "your meek men of respectability in a place", "在一个地方懦弱谦恭却又有名望的人", 即道德并非真正的高尚, 却获得了与之不相称的较高的名望; "德之贼", 译为 "unmercifully destroy all sense of moral sentiment in man", "残酷地破坏了人心中对道德情感的所有观念"。

14. 文中, "道听而途说", 译为 "to preach in the public streets the commonplaces which you have picked up on the way", "在公共街道上宣扬那些你偶然在路上听到的陈词滥调"。"道听" 指偶然在路上听到的陈词滥调; "途说" 指在公共街道上宣扬。"德之弃", 辜鸿铭译为 "throw away all your finer feelings", "相当于丢弃你所有美好的情感"。"德" 指美好的情感。

15. 文中, "鄙夫", 辜鸿铭译为 "despicable men", "卑劣的人"。"与事君", 译为 "serve the interests of the country in company with such men", "与这样的人一道为国家的利益服务"。"其未得之也, 患得之。既得之, 患失之" 一句, "其未得之也, 患得之", 译为 "before they gain their position, their only anxiety is how to obtain it", "在他们得到他们的职位之前, 他们唯一的焦虑就是如何得到它"; "既得之, 患失之", 译为 "after they have obtained the position, their sole anxiety is lest they should lose it", "在他们得到了职位之后, 他们唯一的焦虑就是防止失去它"。"苟患失之, 无所不至矣", 译为 "In their anxiety lest they should lose their position, there is nothing which they would not do", "在他们防止失去职位的焦虑下, 没有什么事情是他们不会去做的"。"无所不至", 即未达目的不择手段之意。

16. 文中, "古者民有三疾, 今也或是之亡也" 一句, 辜鸿铭译为 "in old times men had three kinds of imperfections in their characters, which perhaps now are not to be found", "古时候, 人们在他们的性格中有三种缺点, 或许今天已经找不到了"。"疾", 指性格缺点。下面的文字是对古今之人的对比。

17. 该节与第一章第3节完全重复。

18. 文中, "恶紫之夺朱也", 辜鸿铭译为 "I hate the way in which scarlet dims the perception for vermilion", "我憎恨猩红色模糊了人们对朱红色的认识"。其中, 他把 "紫"

译为"scarlet"，"猩红色"，该词有负面意味；"朱"译为"vermilion"，"朱红色"；"夺"，译为"dims the perception"，"模糊认识"，即混淆了别人对"紫"与"朱"两种颜色的认知。

"恶郑声之乱雅乐也"，译为"I hate the way in which the modern popular airs are liable to spoil the taste for good music"，"我憎恨当今流行的曲调易于破坏人们对好音乐的鉴赏力"。其中，"郑声"指时下的流行曲调；"雅乐"译为"good music"，"好的音乐"；"乱"指破坏艺术鉴赏力。这一句指流行曲调能够破坏人对何为真正的好音乐的艺术鉴赏力。

"恶利口之覆邦家者"，译为"I hate the way in which smartness of speech in men is liable to destroy kingdoms and ruin families"，"我憎恨人们机敏的言语易于毁灭王国并破坏家庭"。其中，"利口"译为"smartness of speech in men"，"人们机敏的言语"；"覆"译为"liable to destroy … and ruin"，指易于毁灭、摧毁某事物'；"邦家"分别译为"kingdoms"与"families"，指国家与家庭。这一句指对于一个国家或家庭来说，不谨慎的言语有时能够带来祸事。

19. 文中，"天何言哉？四时行焉，百物生焉"一句，"天"辜鸿铭译为"Heaven"，"天空"。在其他地方，辜鸿铭多将"天"译为"God"，"上帝"之意，此处指自然的天空。"四时行焉"译为"the seasons run their appointed courses"，"四季仍会按照预定的正常秩序而运行"，"行"指四季正常运行。"百物生焉"译为"all things in nature grow up in their time"，"自然界的万物会在它们合适的时机而生长"，"生"指万物正常生长。

20. 文中，"孺悲欲见孔子，孔子辞以疾"一句。辜鸿铭略去了"孺悲"的名字。"孔子辞以疾"，译为"Confucius, not wishing to see him, sent to say he was sick"，"孔子不想见他，称自己生病了"。其中，"辞"是托词、推托之意。"将命者出户，取瑟而歌，使之闻之"一句，"将命者出户"，译为"when the servant with the message went to the door"，"当那位传话的仆人走到门口时"。其中，"将命者"指给孔子传话的仆人；"使之闻之"，译为"purposely to let the visitor hear it and know that he was not really sick"，"以便让来访者听到并且知道他并没有生病"。

21. "三年之丧，期已久矣"是宰我提出的看法，辜鸿铭译为"the period of three years's mourning for parents, remarking that one year was long enough"，"关于为父母的三年丧期，认为一年就足够长了"。其中，"期"指一年时间；"久"指足够长。下面，宰我还提出了自己的理由。

"君子三年不为礼，礼必坏；三年不为乐，乐必崩"一句，辜鸿铭的翻译是："君子三年不为礼，礼必坏"译为"if a gentleman neglects the Arts and usages of life for three years, he will lose his knowledge of them"，"如果一个绅士疏忽艺术及生活习俗三年，他就会丧失掉与之相关的学问"。其中，"君子"译为"绅士"，指单个的道德个体；"不为礼"译为

"neglects the Arts and usages of life","疏忽艺术及生活习俗","礼"泛指艺术与生活习俗；"坏"译为"lose his knowledge of","丧失……的学问"。"三年不为乐，乐必崩"，译为"if he put aside music for three years, he will entirely forget it","如果他扔下音乐三年，他就会全部忘记"。其中，"崩"指忘记。

"旧谷既没，新谷既升，钻燧改火，期可已矣"。辜鸿铭的翻译是："旧谷既没，新谷既升"译为"in one year the old corn is mown away to give place to new corn which springs up"，"一年之内陈旧的谷物就会被割掉，为迅速生长起来的新谷物让出位置"；"钻燧改火"译为"in one year we burn through all the different kinds of wood produced in all the seasons"，"一年之内我们会烧遍各个季节生长的各种各样的木柴"，指各个季节用不同的木材取火；"期可已矣"译为"after the completion of one year, mourning may cease","一年结束之后，悲痛也会结束"。

对此，孔子阐释了三年之丧的原因。"子生三年，然后免于父母之怀"，辜鸿铭译为"it is only three years after his birth that a child is able to leave the arms of his parents","一个孩子只有在出生三年之后，才能够离开他父母的怀抱"。"夫三年之丧，天下之通丧也"，译为"now the period of three years' mourning for parents is universally observed throughout the Empire","现在，为父母的三年丧期在整个帝国都在被普遍地遵循着"。"通丧"即普遍遵循的丧制。

22. 文中，"饱食终日，无所用心，难矣哉！"一句，辜鸿铭译为"simply eats his full meals without applying his mind to anything at all during the whole day","在一整天内仅仅是餐餐吃得饱，却没有把心思才智用于任何事情，真是一件糟糕的事"。"用心"，即把心智用于某事，而不是闲着耗时间；"难矣哉"译为"it is really a bad case","真是一件糟糕的事"。后面一句中，"博弈"，译为"such things as gambling and games of skill","诸如赌博、技巧游戏之类的事情"，这里的意思指即使做类似这样的事情，也比无所事事好一些。

23. 子路问孔子"君子尚勇乎"，辜鸿铭译为"is not valour a quality important to a gentleman","勇气对于一位绅士来说不是一种很重要的品质吗"，"君子"译为"绅士"（a gentleman）。孔子回答"君子义以为上"，译为"a gentleman esteems what is right as of the highest importance","一位绅士把正义视为首要品质"，并作出了后面的解释。

24. "君子亦有恶乎"，辜鸿铭译为"has a wise and good man also his hatreds","一个明智和良善的人也会有所厌恶吗"。其中，"君子"译为"一个明智和良善的人"；"恶"，指厌恶某物。本节讨论的是"君子"厌恶怎样的事情。

25. 文中，"小人"，辜鸿铭译为"servants"，"仆人、佣人"；"难养"，译为"the most difficult to keep in the house"，"在家中是最难对待的"。其中，"养"包含"养活，雇佣，藏蓄"等含义，即统一为"对待"之意。

26. 文中，"见恶"，辜鸿铭译为"is an object of dislike to men"，"是人们令人厌恶的对象"；"其终也已"，译为"continue to be so to the ends of his days"，"一直如此直到死的那一天"。这一节指人在四十岁之后，道德品性很难发生实质性改变。

CHAPTER XVIII
微子第十八

1. At the time of the downfall of the Imperial Yin dynasty (the one preceding that under which Confucius lived) of the three members of the Imperial family, one left the country; one became a court jester; and one, who spoke the truth to the Emperor, was put to death.

   Confucius, remarking on the above, said, "The House of Yin in their last days had three men of moral character."

2. Confucius remarked of a well-known worthy of the time: "As Minister of Justice, he was three times dismissed from office. People then said to him, 'Is it not time for you to leave the country?' But he answered, 'If I honestly do my duty, where shall I go to serve men without being liable to be dismissed in the same way? If I am willing to sacrifice my sense of duty, it is not necessary for me to leave my native country to find employment.' "

3. The reigning prince of a certain State on one occasion wished to employ Confucius, remarking, however, "I cannot make him a Minister of State, but I will make him a privy Councillor."

   The prince further remarked, "I am old now. I shall not be able to use his advice."

   When Confucius heard what the prince said, he immediately took his departure from the country.

4. The Prime Minister who held the power of government in Confucius' native state, after Confucius had risen to be Minister of State (Minister of Justice), having on one occasion received a troupe of actresses from another State was so occupied with them that there was no meeting of ministers at the Palace for three days. Confucius thereupon resigned, and left his own country.

1. 微子去之，箕子为之奴，比干谏而死。孔子曰："殷有三仁焉。"

　　殷代（孔子所生活朝代之前的朝代）衰落时期的三位帝国统治家族的成员，一位离开了他的国家；一位成了朝廷的弄臣；而对帝王说出真相的那一位，被处死了。

　　孔子谈到上面的人，说："在最后的日子里，殷王室有三位具有道德品质的人。"

2. 柳下惠为士师，三黜。人曰："子未可以去乎？"曰："直道而事人，焉往而不三黜？枉道而事人，何必去父母之邦？"

　　孔子谈论那时的一位著名的杰出人物："作为法务大臣，他三次被免除官职。于是人们对他说：'这难道不是你离开国家的时候了吗？'但他回答说：'如果我正直地履行我的职责，我到哪里去为人服务而不会被以同样的方式免职呢？如果我愿意牺牲我的责任感，对我来说就没必要离开我的故国而去寻找职业了。'"

3. 齐景公待孔子，曰："若季氏则吾不能，以季、孟之间待之。"曰："吾老矣，不能用也。"孔子行。

　　有一次，某个国家的执政国君想聘用孔子，但是，又说："我不能让他做一个国家的大臣，但我会让他做一个私人顾问。"

　　那位国君又进一步说："我现在老了。我也许不能够采用他的意见。"

　　当孔子听说了国君说的这些话之后，他马上动身离开了那个国家。

4. 齐人归女乐，季桓子受之。三日不朝，孔子行。

　　手握孔子故国的政治权力的首要大臣，在孔子被晋升为国家的大臣（法务大臣）之后，有一次从另一个国家那里收到了一队女演员，他如此沉迷于她们，以至于三天都没有在官殿与大臣们见面。于是孔子辞了职，并离开了他自己的国家。

5. When Confucius was on his travels, an eccentric person once passing by him, sang aloud —

O Phoenix bird! O Phoenix bird,
Where is the glory of your prime?
The past, —'t is useless now to change,
Care for the future yet is time.
Renounce! give up your chase in vain;
For those who serve in Court and State
Dire peril follows in their train.

Confucius then alighted and wished to speak with him; but the eccentric man hastened away so that Confucius had no chance of speaking with him.

6. On another occasion, Confucius on his travels saw two men working in the fields. He sent a disciple, the intrepid Chung Yu, to enquire for the ford.

When Chung Yu came up to the men, one of them said to him:

"Who is he that is holding the reins in the carriage there?" Chung Yu answered, "It is Confucius." "Is it not Confucius of Lu," asked the man. "Yes," replied Chung Yu. "Then," rejoined the other, "he knows the ford."

Chung Yu then turned to the other of the two men, who said to him: "Who are you, sir?" "I am Chung Yu," replied Confucius' disciple. "Are you not a disciple of Confucius?" asked the man. "Yes," replied Chung Yu. Then the man said: "All men in the world are now in a hopeless drift: who can do anything to change

5. 楚狂接舆歌而过孔子曰:"凤兮! 凤兮! 何德之衰? 往者不可谏,来者犹可追。已而,已而! 今之从政者殆而!"孔子下,欲与之言。趋而辟之,不得与之言。

　　孔子正在旅途中行进,有一次,一个怪异的人走过他,高声唱道:

　　　　噢! 凤凰! 噢! 凤凰,

　　　　你本来的荣耀在哪儿?

　　　　过去的——如今去改变是没用的,

　　　　是时候考虑未来了。

　　　　抛弃吧! 放弃你徒劳的追求;

　　　　因为那些在朝堂上服务的人儿,

　　　　可怕的危险必会尾随而来。

　　孔子有所悟,想与他说话。但那个怪异的人赶紧离开了,为的是让孔子没机会与他说话。

6. 长沮、桀溺耦而耕,孔子过之,使子路问津焉。长沮曰:"夫执舆者为谁?"子路曰:"为孔丘。"曰:"是鲁孔丘与?"曰:"是也。"曰:"是知津矣。"问于桀溺,桀溺曰:"子为谁?"曰:"为仲由。"曰:"是鲁孔丘之徒与?"对曰:"然。"曰:"滔滔者天下皆是也,而谁以易之? 且而与其从辟人之士也,岂若从辟世之士哉?"耰而不辍。子路行以告。夫子怃然曰:"鸟兽不可与同群,吾非斯人之徒与而谁与? 天下有道,丘不与易也。"

　　另一次,孔子在旅途中看到两个人在田地里干活。他派一个学生,那位刚勇的仲由,去询问河的渡口在哪儿。

　　当仲由来到那两个人近旁,其中一个对他说:"在马车里抓着缰绳的人是谁?"仲由回答说:"是孔夫子。""那不是鲁国的孔夫子吗?"那人问。"是的,"仲由回答。"那么,"那人回答说,"他知道渡口在哪儿。"

　　仲由于是转向两个人中的另一个,那人对他说:"你是谁? 先生。"

it? Nevertheless, it is better to follow those who renounce the world altogether than to run after those who only run from one prince to another." After saying that, the man went on with his work on the field without stopping again to take any notice of Chung Yu's question.

When Chung Yu returned and reported what the man said, Confucius heaved a heavy sign, and said, "I cannot live with the beasts of the field and birds of the air. If I do not live and associate with mankind, with whom shall I go to live? Besides, if the world was in order, there would then be no need for one to do anything to change it."

7. On another occasion when Confucius was on his travels, a disciple, the intrepid Chung Yu, got separated from the party. Chung Yu met an old man carrying across his shoulders, on a staff, a basket for weeds. Chung Yu said to him, "Have you seen the Teacher Sir?" The old man looked at him and replied gruffly, "Your body has never known toil and you cannot tell the difference between the five kinds of grain: who is your Teacher?" With that, the old man planted his staff on the ground and fell to his work, weeding the ground. Chung Yu, however, laid his hands across his breast and respectfully waited.

Afterwards, the old man took Chung Yu to his home and made him pass a night in his house, killing a fowl and making millet pudding for him to eat. The old man also presented his two sons to Chung Yu.

The next day Chung Yu went on his way and, on rejoining Confucius, reported his adventure. "He is a hermit," said Confucius, and sent Chung Yu back to see him, but when Chung Yu got to the place the old man was nowhere to be found.

"我是仲由。"孔子的学生回答。"你不是孔夫子的学生吗?"那人问。"是的。"仲由回答。那个人然后说:"现在世上的所有人都在无希望地随波逐流:谁能够做点什么事情去改变它呢? 不过,跟随那些一起抛弃社会的人,总比追随那些仅仅从一个国君又跑到另一个国君那里的人好。"说完这些,那人继续他在田地里的活计,而不再停下来搭理仲由的问题。

仲由回来汇报了那人说的话,孔子发出沉重的叹息,说:"我不能与野外的野兽与天空的鸟一起生活,如果我不与人类一起生活、交往,我应该与谁去一起生活呢? 另外,如果社会是有秩序的,就不需要有人去改变它了。"

7. 子路从而后,遇丈人,以杖荷蓧。子路问曰:"子见夫子乎?"丈人曰:"四体不勤,五谷不分。孰为夫子?"植其杖而芸。子路拱而立。止子路宿,杀鸡为黍而食之,见其二子焉。明日,子路行以告。子曰:"隐者也。"使子路反见之。至则行矣。子路曰:"不仕无义。长幼之节,不可废也;君臣之义,如之何其废之? 欲洁其身,而乱大伦。君子之仕也,行其义也。道之不行,已知之矣。"

另外一次,当孔子行进在他的旅途中时,一个学生,那位刚勇的仲由,与队伍走散了。仲由遇到了一位老人正用一条手杖挑着一个装杂草的竹筐。仲由对他说:"您见到过老师阁下吗?"那位老人看着他,粗暴地回答:"从没听说过你曾长期辛苦地工作,你也说不出那五种谷类之间的区别:谁是你老师?"说着,那位老人把手杖插到地上,开始干活,给地面除草。不过,仲由把手交叉地放在胸前恭敬地等着。

过后,那位老人把仲由领到了自己的家中,并让他在家里留宿了一夜,又杀了一只鸡并做了小米糕点给他吃。那位老人还向仲由介绍了他的两个儿子。

When Chung Yu again returned, Confucius said, "It is not right to refuse to enter the public service. For if it is wrong to ignore the duties arising out of the relations between the members of a family, how is it right to ignore the duties a man owes to his sovereign and country. A man who withdraws himself from the world for no other reason than to show his personal purity of motive, is one who breaks up one of the greatest ties in the foundation of society. A good and wise man, on the other hand, who enters the public service, tries to carry out what he thinks to be right. As to the failure of right principles to make progress, he is well aware of that."

8. Confucius, speaking of six worthies, famous in ancient times as men who withdrew themselves from the world, remarked of two of them, Po Yi and Shuhts'i, that they withdrew from the world because they would not give up their high aims, and, in that way, had not to put up with dishonour to their persons; of two others who finally also withdrew from the world, Confucius remarked that they gave up high aims and put up with dishonour to their persons, but in whatever they said were found reasonable and, in whatever they did, were found commendable; finally, of the last two of the six worthies, Confucius remarked that they lived strictly as recluses and refused altogether to hold communication with the world, but they were pure in their lives and so, entirely secluding themselves from the world, they rightly used their discretion.

"As for myself," said Confucius, finally, "I act differently from those men I have mentioned above, I have no course for which I am predetermined, and no course against which I am predetermined."

第二天，仲由继续赶路，与孔子会合后，汇报了自己的奇遇。"他是一位隐士。"孔子说，并让仲由再回去看望他，但当仲由到达那个地方时，那位老人已经不见了。

仲由再次返回后，孔子说："拒绝参与公务服务是不道义的啊。如果说，无视那源自家人关系的责任是错误的，那么，一个人无视那源自他的君主与国家的责任怎么会是对的呢？一个只是因为要表现自己目的的纯净而脱离社会的人，他就是在瓦解维系社会的基石。另一方面，一个参与公务服务的良善而明智的人，他就是在试着去实现他所认为的正义之事。至于正义原则无法取得进展，他是非常清楚的。"

8. 逸民：伯夷、叔齐、虞仲、夷逸、朱张、柳下惠、少连。子曰："不降其志，不辱其身，伯夷、叔齐与！"

谓："柳下惠、少连，降志辱身矣，言中伦，行中虑，其斯而已矣。"谓："虞仲、夷逸，隐居放言。身中清，废中权。我则异于是，无可无不可。"

孔子谈起在古代因放弃社会而闻名的六位杰出人物，认为其中两位，伯夷和叔齐，他们放弃社会是因为他们不想放弃高远的目标，而且，通过这样的方式，他们可以不必忍受耻辱。还有两位最后也放弃了社会，孔子认为他们放弃了高远的目标，并忍受了耻辱，但他们所说的任何话都是合乎情理的，而他们所做的任何事情都是值得称赞的。最后，六位杰出人士中的最后两位，孔子认为他们作为隐士而严格地生活着，并一起拒绝与社会交流，但他们在生活中是纯洁的，并且使他们自己完全与社会隔绝，他们正确地运用了判断力。

"至于我自己，"孔子最后说，"我与上面提到的那些人做法不同，我没有预先设定的行为方式，也没有预先反对的行为方式。"

9. [This section merely gives the names of the famous musicians and great artists of the time who, falling on a time of decay of art and failure of art patronage, had to wander scattered about from one State to another; one, it is said, went out over sea, — perhaps to Japan!]^①

10. The original Founder of the reigning house of Confucius' native State, who was known as our Lord of Chou, in his advice to his son and successor said: "A ruler should never neglect his near relations. He should never give his great ministers cause to complain that their advice is not taken. Without some great reason, he should never discard his old connections. He should never expect from a man that he will be able to do everything."

11. [This section merely gives the names of eight famous gentlemen of the time.]

---

① 方括号中的文字是辜鸿铭的解读,但他没有对经文做进一步翻译。第11节情况相同。

9. 大师挚适齐,亚饭干适楚,三饭缭适蔡,四饭缺适秦。鼓方叔入于河,播鼗武入于汉,少师阳、击磬襄入于海。

　　〔这一段只是介绍了那个时代的一些著名的音乐家与艺术家的名字,他们落入一个艺术衰败及艺术失去保护的年代,不得不分散地从一个国家漫游到另一个。其中一个,据说,漂洋过海——也许到了日本！〕

10. 周公谓鲁公曰:"君子不施其亲,不使大臣怨乎不以。故旧无大故,则不弃也。无求备于一人。"

　　孔子故国的执政王室的最初创始人,作为我们的周公而被熟知,他在对他的儿子也即他的继承者的忠告里说:"一个统治者不应该对他的近亲疏于照看。他不应该让他的重要的大臣们因意见不被采纳而抱怨。没有重大的原因,他不应该抛弃他的旧亲故友。他不应期望一个人能够做所有的事情。"

11. 周有八士:伯达、伯适、仲突、仲忽、叔夜、叔夏、季随、季骒。
　　〔这一段只是介绍了那个时代的八位著名的绅士。〕

【评述】

1. 第一句是辜鸿铭补充的对本节的介绍，即这一节讲的是"殷代（孔子所生活朝代之前的朝代）衰落时期的三位帝国家族的成员"的事迹。同时，该句也大体指出了"微子"、"箕子"、"比干"的身份，即商纣的亲属。后面，辜鸿铭翻译时省略了他们的名字，对微子，他注释说：

> 他是孔子的一位远祖。

2. "柳下惠"，辜鸿铭翻译中称之为"a well-known worthy"，"一位著名的杰出人物"。下面讲的是柳下惠如何杰出。

3. 文中，第一句话，辜鸿铭即介绍了背景："The reigning prince of a certain State on one occasion wished to employ Confucius"，"有一次，某个国家的执政国君想聘用孔子"。"若季氏则吾不能；以季、孟之间待之"，辜鸿铭译为"I cannot make him a Minister of State, but I will make him a privy Councillor"，"我不能让他做一个国家的大臣，但我会让他做一个私人顾问"。这里的"季氏"代指国家大臣，而"季、孟之间"代指私人顾问。"吾老矣，不能用也"。这是齐景公对孔子的职务问题的附加说明，即可能会对他的建议不予采用。辜鸿铭译为"I am old now. I shall not be able to use his advice"，"我现在老了。我也许不能够采用他的意见"。"孔子行"，译为"When Confucius heard what the prince said, he immediately took his departure from the country"，"当孔子听说了国君说的这些话之后，他马上动身离开了那个国家"。

4. 翻译中，辜鸿铭首先特意介绍了该段故事发生的背景，即"after Confucius had risen to be Minister of State (Minister of Justice)"，"孔子被晋升为国家的大臣（法务大臣）之后"。季氏专权，但孔子也担任政府要职。在这样的背景下，"齐人归女乐，季桓子受之。三日不朝"。"齐人归女乐，季桓子受之"译为"The Prime Minister who held the power of government in Confucius' native state, having on one occasion received a troupe of actresses from another State"，指"手握孔子故国的政治权力的首要大臣，从另一个国家那里收到了一队女演员"；"三日不朝"，译为"was so occupied with them that there was no meeting of ministers at the Palace for three days"，"如此沉迷于她们，以至于三天都没有在宫殿与大臣们见面"。这里的"孔子行"，辜鸿铭译为"Confucius thereupon resigned, and left his own country"，"于是孔子辞了职，并离开了他自己的国家"。

5. "楚狂接舆"，传统学者多认为是一位楚国的隐士高人，辜鸿铭译为"an eccentric

person","一个怪异的人"。

"凤兮！凤兮！何德之衰？"接舆诗的前两句，辜鸿铭译为"O Phoenix bird! O Phoenix bird/Where is the glory of your prime?"，"噢！凤凰！噢！凤凰/你本来的荣耀在哪儿？""德之衰"即凤凰失去了以往的荣耀。"往者不可谏，来者犹可追"，辜鸿铭译为"The past，—'t is useless now to change/ Care for the future yet is time"，"过去的——如今去改变是没用的/是时候考虑未来了"。据此，接舆是让孔子"考虑未来"，即劝他改掉过去"知其不可而为之"的性格，及时归隐。"已而，已而！今之从政者殆而"，辜鸿铭译为"Renounce! give up your chase in vain/ For those who serve in Court and State/ Dire peril follows in their train"，"抛弃吧！放弃你徒劳的追求；/因为那些在朝堂上服务的人儿/可怕的危险必会尾随而来"。据此，接舆是在明确地劝孔子归隐，并警告他，危险将会到来。

6. 文中，"问津"，辜鸿铭译为"enquire for the ford"，"询问河的渡口在哪儿"，指孔子让子路去问路旁两位耕作的农人。

"夫执舆者为谁"，辜鸿铭译为"Who is he that is holding the reins in the carriage there"，"在马车里抓着缰绳的人是谁"。子路去问农夫，农夫反而问车上人的身份。

另一个农夫说，"滔滔者天下皆是也，而谁以易之"，辜鸿铭译为"All men in the world are now in a hopeless drift: who can do anything to change it"，"现在世上的所有人都在无希望地随波逐流：谁能够做点什么事情去改变它呢"。其中，"滔滔"指人们随波逐流的现状。"且而与其从辟人之士也，岂若从辟世之士哉？"译为"it is better to follow those who renounce the world altogether than to run after those who only run from one prince to another"，"跟随那些一起抛弃社会的人，总比追随那些仅仅从一个国君又跑到另一个国君那里的人好"。据此，"辟人"指"仅仅从一个国君又跑到另一个国君那里的人"；"辟世"指"抛弃社会的人"。

对此，孔子说"鸟兽不可与同群，吾非斯人之徒与而谁与？"辜鸿铭译为"I cannot live with the beasts of the field and birds of the air. If I do not live and associate with mankind, with whom shall I go to live?""我不能与野外的野兽与天空的鸟一起生活，如果我不与人类一起生活、交往，我应该与谁去一起生活呢？"其中，"与同群"指一起生活、交往之意；"斯人之徒"指人类。

"天下有道，丘不与易也"，辜鸿铭译为"if the world was in order, there would then be no need for one to do anything to change it"，"如果社会是有秩序的，就不需要有人去改变它了"。"有道"指社会井然有序；"易"指改变。

在《中国人的精神（在北京东方学会上所宣讲的论文）》一文中，辜鸿铭认为，在孔子的时代，老子、庄子一类人抛弃了文明，而孔子则坚持拯救文明："在重建秩序和文明的过程中，二千五百年前的中国人也发生了心灵与头脑的冲突。……老子和庄子（后者为老子

417

的得意门生）就告诉中国人应该抛弃所有文明。老子对中国人说：'放弃你所有的一切，跟随我到山中去当隐士，过一种真正的生活———一种心灵的生活、不朽的生活。'然而，同样是看到了社会与文明造成的苦难和牺牲，孔子却认为错误不在于社会与文明本身，而在于这个社会与文明的发展方向上，在于人们为这个社会与文明打下了错误的基础。孔子告诉中国人不要抛弃他们的文明——在一个有着真实基础的社会与文明中，人们同样能够过上真正的生活、过着心灵的生活。实际上孔子毕生都致力于为社会和文明规定一个正确的发展方向，给它一个真实的基础，并阻止文明的毁灭。"（夏丹等选编，《辜鸿铭作品精选·中国人的精神》，第37页）

7."从而后"，辜鸿铭译为"got separated from the party"，"与队伍走散"。这是子路掉队之后的一次奇遇。

"遇丈人，以杖荷蓧"，译为"Chung Yu met an old man carrying across his shoulders, on a staff, a basket for weeds"，"仲由遇到了一位老人正用一条手杖挑着一个装杂草用的竹筐"。其中，"丈人"是老人之意；"荷"是肩挑之意；"蓧"指装杂草的竹筐。

老人说子路"四体不勤，五谷不分，孰为夫子"。"四体不勤，五谷不分"译为"your body has never known toil and you cannot tell the difference between the five kinds of grain"，"从没听说有过你的身体曾长期辛苦地工作，你也说不出那五种谷类之间的区别"。

"植其杖而芸"，译为"the old man planted his staff on the ground and fell to his work, weeding the ground"，"那位老人把手杖插到地上，开始干活，给地面除草"。"植"指插在地上，即竖立之意；"芸"指除草。

子路"拱而立"，译为"laid his hands across his breast and respectfully waited"，"把手交叉地放在胸前恭敬地等着"，"拱"指把手交叉地放在胸前。这是子路在遭到质疑之后的表现，彬彬有礼，非常有教养。

老人最终"止子路宿，杀鸡为黍而食之，见其二子焉"。"杀鸡为黍"，译为"killing a fowl and millet pudding"，"杀了一只鸡并做了小米糕点"，指老人对子路的款待。

孔子称老人"隐者也"，译为"He is a hermit"，"他是一位隐士、遁世者"。"至，则行矣"，译为"when Chung Yu got to the place the old man was nowhere to be found"，"当仲由到达那个地方时，那位老人已经不见了"。

"不仕无义"是孔子得知子路遭遇后，对那位老人的评价，辜鸿铭译为"It is not right to refuse to enter the public service"，"拒绝参与公务服务是不道义的啊"。"无义"指不道义、不对。下面是孔子的解释。

"长幼之节，不可废也；君臣之义，如之何其废之？"辜鸿铭的翻译是："长幼之节，不可废也"译为"it is wrong to ignore the duties arising out of the relations between the members of a family"，"无视那源自家人关系的责任是错误的"。"长幼之节"指的是家庭责任；

"废"是无视、否认之意。"君臣之义,如之何其废之","how is it right to ignore the duties a man owes to his sovereign and country","无视那源自他的君主与国家的责任怎么会是对的呢"。"君臣之义"指他对君主与国家的责任。同样是不可无视的。

"欲洁其身,而乱大伦"一句,"洁其身"译为"withdraws himself from the world for no other reason than to show his personal purity of motive","只是因为要表现自己目的的纯净而脱离社会";"乱大伦"译为"breaks up one of the greatest ties in the foundation of society","瓦解维系社会的基石"。其中,"大伦"指维系社会的基石。"乱"指瓦解、分裂、破坏。

"君子之仕也,行其义也",译为"A good and wise man, on the other hand, who enters the public service, tries to carry out what he thinks to be right","一个参与公务服务的良善而明智的人,他就是在试着去实现他所认为的正义"。"行其义"指实现他所认为的正义。

"道之不行,已知之矣",译为"As to the failure of right principles to make progress, he is well aware of that","至于正义原则无法取得进展,他是非常清楚的"。"道",指正义原则;"知之"指老人自己知道。前面孔子批评老人"不义",最后认为老人肯定感到了正义的难以实现,才选择了归隐。

8. "逸民:伯夷、叔齐、虞仲、夷逸、朱张、柳下惠、少连",辜鸿铭译为"six worthies, famous in ancient times as men who withdrew themselves from the world","在古代因放弃社会而闻名的六位杰出人物"。他理解为六位人物,即下文孔子说话中提到的伯夷、叔齐、柳下惠、少连、虞仲、夷逸,不包括"朱张"。"逸民"指放弃社会的人,即遁世隐居的人。

"不降其志,不辱其身",译为"they withdrew from the world because they would not give up their high high aims, and, in that way, had not to put up with dishonour to their persons","放弃社会是因为他们不想放弃高远的目标,而且,通过这样的方式,他们可以不必忍受耻辱"。其中,"降志"指放弃高远目标;"辱身"指忍受耻辱或受到羞辱。这句话是说,伯夷、叔齐为了坚持自己的理想而放弃社会,同时,也躲过了被羞辱的可能。

"降志辱身矣,言中伦,行中虑,其斯而已矣"。"降志辱身"译为"gave up high aims and put up with dishonour to their persons","放弃了高远的目标,并忍受了耻辱"。"言中伦,行中虑",译为"in whatever they said were found reasonable and, in whatever they did, were found commendable","他们所说的任何话都是合乎情理的,而他们所做的任何事情都是值得称赞的"。"中伦"指合乎情理;"中虑"指值得称赞。柳下惠、少连放弃了自己的理想,但他们还是保持了言行的合理。

"隐居放言。身中清,废中权。""隐居放言"译为"lived strictly as recluses and refused altogether to hold communication with the world","作为隐士而严格地生活着,并一起拒绝与社会交流";"放言"指拒绝与社会交流。完全与社会隔绝;"身中清"译为"they were pure in their lives","他们在生活中是纯净的","清"指心灵纯净;"废中权"译为"entirely secluding themselves from the world, they rightly used their discretion", "使他们自己完全地与社会隔绝,他们正确地运用了判断力"。虞仲、夷逸这样做是经过正确判断的,也即合理的。

孔子说自己"我则异于是,无可无不可",辜鸿铭译为"I have no course for which I am predetermined, and no course against which I am predetermined", "我与上面提到的那些人做法不同,我没有预先设定的行为方式,也没有预先反对的行为方式"。

9. 文中"大师挚"、"亚饭干"、"三饭缭"、"四饭缺"、"鼓方叔"、"播鼗武"、"少师阳"、"击磬襄",这些人物传统学者多解释为古代各种乐师。辜鸿铭译为"the famous musicians and great artists of the time who, falling on a time of decay of art and failure of art patronage", "那个时代的一些著名的音乐家与艺术家的名字,他们落入一个艺术衰败及艺术失去保护的年代"。这一节讲的就是他们在那个时代的遭遇。

"适齐"、"适楚"、"适蔡"、"适秦"、"入于河"、"入于汉"、"入于海",辜鸿铭译为"had to wander scattered about from one State to another", "不得不分散地从一个国家漫游到另一个"。即流落四方,颠沛流离。最后一句,辜鸿铭是个猜测:"one, it is said, went out over sea, — perhaps to Japan!", "其中一个,据说,漂洋过海——也许到了日本!"应该指的是"少师阳、击磬襄入于海",但中文里说的是两个人。

10. 文中,"周公谓鲁公",辜鸿铭译为"The original Founder of the reigning house of Confucius' native State, who was known as our Lord of Chou, in his advice to his son and successor", "孔子故国的执政王室的最初创始人,作为我们的周公而被熟知,对他的儿子也即他的继承者忠告"。"君子不施其亲",译为"A ruler should never neglect his near relations", "一个统治者不应该对他的近亲疏于照看"。这里,"君子"指国家统治者;"亲"指近亲;"施"指疏于照看。"不使大臣怨乎不以",译为"He should never give his great ministers cause to complain that their advice is not taken", "他不应该让他的重要的大臣们因意见不被采纳而抱怨"。"不以"指意见不被采纳。"故旧无大故,则不弃也",译为"Without some great reason, he should never discard his old connections", "没有重大的原因,他不应该抛弃他的旧亲故友"。"故旧",应该包括老朋友、老亲戚等长期以来关系很好的人。"无求备于一人",译为"He should never expect from a man that he will be able to do everything", "他不应期望一个人能够做所有的事情"。"备"指一个人能够做所有的事情。

11. 文中列举"八士","士",辜鸿铭译为"famous gentlemen", "著名的绅士"。他略去了所有人的姓名,也未作解释。

CHAPTER XIX
子张第十九

1. A disciple of Confucius remarked, "A gentleman in presence of danger should be ready to give up his life; in view of personal advantage, he should think of what is right; in worship, he should be devout and serious; in mourning, he should show heartfelt grief: the above is about the sum of the duties of a gentleman."

2. The same disciple remarked, "If a man holds fast to godliness without enlarging his mind; if a man believes in truth, but is not steadfast in holding to his principles — such a man may as well leave such things alone."

3. The same disciple was on one occasion asked about friendship by the pupils of one of his fellow disciples. He answered by asking the pupils, "What did your teacher say on the subject? " "Our teacher," replied the pupils, "said, 'Those whom you find good, make friends with; those whom you find not good, turn your back upon.' "

   "That," replied Confucius' disciple who was asked, "is different from what I have been taught. A wise and good man honours worthy men and is tolerant to all men. He knows how to commend those who excel in anything and make allowance for those who are ignorant. Now, if we ourselves are really worthy, we should be tolerant to all men; but if we ourselves are not worthy, men will turn their backs upon us. How can we turn our backs upon them? "

1. 子张曰："士见危致命，见得思义，祭思敬，丧思哀，其可已矣。"

　　孔子的一个学生说："一个绅士在危险面前应该准备好舍弃生命；见到私利，应该想到正义；祭拜时，应该虔诚而庄重；服丧时，应该表示出由衷的悲痛：上面这些大约就是一个绅士的全部义务。"

2. 子张曰："执德不弘，信道不笃，焉能为有？焉能为亡？"

　　那同一位学生说："如果一个人坚持虔诚之心，却不能扩充自己的思想；如果一个人信仰真理，却坚持他的原则时不够坚定——这样的一个人，还是远离这样的事情为好。"

3. 子夏之门人问交于子张。子张曰："子夏云何？"对曰："子夏曰：'可者与之，其不可者拒之。'"子张曰："异乎吾所闻：君子尊贤而容众，嘉善而矜不能。我之大贤与，于人何所不容？我之不贤与，人将拒我，如之何其拒人也？"

　　有一次，那同一位学生被他一个同学的弟子问到友谊的问题。他先问那些弟子："你们的老师对这个问题是怎么表述的？""我们的老师，"那些弟子回答说，"说：'那些你们发现好的人，与他们建立友谊；那些你们发现不好的人，置之不理。'"

　　"这个，"被问到的那位孔子的学生回答说，"与我所学到的不同。一个明智而良善的人尊敬那些高尚的人并能够容忍所有的人。他知道如何去称赞那些不管在任何领域能够有所擅长的人，并且能够体谅那些愚昧无知的人。那么，如果我们自身是真正高尚的，我们就应该容忍所有的人；但如果我们自身是不高尚的，人们就会对我们置之不理。我们怎么能够对他们置之不理呢？"

4. A disciple of Confucius remarked, "Even in any small and unimportant branch of an art or accomplishment, there is always something worthy of consideration; but if the attention to it is pushed too far, it is liable to degenerate into a hobby; for that reason a wise man never occupies himself with it."

5. The same disciple of Confucius remarked, "A man who from day to day knows exactly what he has yet to learn and from month to month does not forget what he has learnt, will surely become a man of culture."

6. The same disciple remarked, "If you study extensively and are steadfast in your aim, investigate carefully what you learn, and apply it to your own personal conduct; in that way, you cannot fail in attaining a moral life."

7. The same disciple remarked, "As workmen work in their workshops to learn their trade, so a scholar gives himself to study in order to get wisdom."

8. The same disciple remarked, "A fool always has an excuse ready when he does wrong."

9. The same disciple remarked, "A good and wise man appears different from three points of view. When you look at him from a distance he appears severe; when you approach him he is gracious; when you hear him speak, he is serious."

4. 子夏曰：“虽小道，必有可观者焉；致远恐泥，是以君子不为也。”

　　孔子的一个学生说：“即使是在一种艺术或专长中的，任何微小而不重要的一项，都会有一些是值得考虑的东西。但如果对它的关注是过分强迫的，它就易于堕落为一种业余的嗜好，因此，一个明智的人决不让自己只是埋首专注于它。”

5. 子夏曰：“日知其所亡，月无忘其所能，可谓好学也已矣。”

　　孔子的同一位学生说：“一个日复一日都明确地知道他还必须要学什么，而且月复一月都不会忘记他已学到的东西的人，就必定会成为一个有教养的人。”

6. 子夏曰：“博学而笃志，切问而近思，仁在其中矣。”

　　同一位学生说：“如果你广泛地学习并坚定你的目标，仔细谨慎地研究你所学到的东西，并将之运用于你自身的言行举止之中，这样，你自然就会过上一种道德的生活。”

7. 子夏曰：“百工居肆以成其事，君子学以致其道。”

　　同一位学生说：“就像工匠在作坊中工作学得手艺一样，一位学者致力于研究是为了获得智慧。”

8. 子夏曰：“小人之过也必文。”

　　同一位学生说：“一个蠢人在犯错时，总是事先准备好借口。”

9. 子夏曰：“君子有三变：望之俨然，即之也温，听其言也厉。”

　　同一位学生说：“一个良善而明智的人从三个视角来看会显得不同。当你从远处看他时，他显得严厉苛刻；当你接近他时，他和蔼亲切；当你听他说话时，他严肃庄重。”

10. The same disciple remarked, "A wise man, as a ruler, first obtains the confidence of the people before he puts them to hard work — which otherwise would be regarded by the people as oppression. A wise man, as a public servant, first obtains the confidence of those whom he serves before he ventures to point out their errors; otherwise his superiors will only regard what he says as prompted by a desire to find fault."

11. The same disciple remarked, "When a man can keep himself strictly within bounds where the major points of the principles of morality are concerned, he may be allowed to use his discretion in the minor points."

12. A disciple of Confucius, speaking of the pupils of another disciple, remarked, "Those young gentlemen are well enough in matters of manners and deportment, which are mere minor matters; but as regards the foundation of a true education, they are as yet nowhere."

When the disciple whose pupils were thus animadverted upon, heard the remark, he said to the other disciple: "There you are wrong. In teaching men, what are the things which a good and wise man should consider it of first importance that he should teach; and what are the things which he should consider of secondary importance, and which he may allow himself to neglect? As in dealing with plants, so one must deal with pupils and class them according to their capabilities. A good and wise man in teaching, should not befool his students. For it is only the most holy men who can at once grasp the beginning and end of principles. "

10. 子夏曰:"君子信而后劳其民,未信则以为厉己也;信而后谏,未信则以为谤己也。"

同一位学生说:"一个明智的人,作为统治者,在他让人民从事繁重的工作之前,首先要获得人民的信任——否则,那将会被人民视为压迫。一个明智的人,作为公务人员,在他冒险指出他所服务的人的错误时,首先要获得他的信任,否则,他的上级只会认为他在挑剔找茬。"

11. 子夏曰:"大德不逾闲,小德出入可也。"

同一位学生说:"当一个人能够让自己严格地保持在与道德原则主要要点相关的范围之内,他可以在一些次要要点上酌情决定。"

12. 子游曰:"子夏之门人小子,当洒扫、应对、进退,则可矣。抑末也,本之则无。如之何?"子夏闻之曰:"噫!言游过矣!君子之道,孰先传焉?孰后倦焉?譬诸草木,区以别矣。君子之道,焉可诬也?有始有卒者,其惟圣人乎!"

孔子的一个学生谈论到另一个学生的弟子们,说:"那些年轻的绅士们在规矩礼仪与行为举止这些事情上已经足够好了,但这只是些次要的事情,至于真正教育的本质,他们到目前为止还离之甚远。"

当那位其弟子受到如此非难的学生听到这些话后,对那位学生说:"你错了。在对人们的教育中,什么是一个良善而明智的人应该视为首要而应该教授的东西,什么又是他应该视为次要而可以允许自己去忽略的东西呢?就像植物一样,一个人对他的弟子,也要根据他们的资质而分为不同的级别。一个良善而明智的人,在教学中不应该愚弄学生。因为只有最为神圣的人可以马上从始至终地领悟掌握那些原则。"

13. A disciple of Confucius remarked, "An officer who has exceptional abilities, more than sufficient to carry out his duties, should devote himself to study. A student who has exceptional abilities, more than sufficient to carry on his studies, should enter the public service. "

14. A disciple of Confucius remarked, "In mourning, the only thing indispensable is heart-felt grief."

15. The same disciple, speaking of another disciple, remarked, "My friend can do things which nobody else can do, but he is not quite perfect in his moral character. "

16. Another disciple of Confucius, speaking of the same disciple alluded to above, remarked, "What a style that man carries about with him! It is really difficult to live out a moral life along with such a man! "

17. The same disciple remarked, "I have heard the Master say, 'Men often do not themselves know what is really in them until they have to mourn the death of their parents.' "

18. The same disciple remarked, "I have heard the Master, speaking of the filial piety of a nobleman, say, 'What other things he did on the occasion of the death of his father, other men can do. But what he did in keeping the old servants of his father, and in following out the policy of his father, men will find it difficult to do.' "

13. 子夏曰:"仕而优则学,学而优则仕。"

  孔子的一个学生说:"一个拥有超过履行其职责之外的优秀天资的官员,应该致身于学习。一个拥有超过从事其学业之外的优秀天资的学生,应该参加公务服务。"

14. 子游曰:"丧致乎哀而止。"

  孔子的一个学生说:"服丧时,唯一必不可少的事情,就是由衷而发的悲痛。"

15. 子游曰:"吾友张也,为难能也。然而未仁。"

  同一个学生,谈到另一个学生,说:"我的朋友能够做别人所不能做的事情,但他的道德品质并不十分完善。"

16. 曾子曰:"堂堂乎张也,难与并为仁矣。"

  孔子的另一个学生,谈及上面提到的同一个学生,说:"他是一个多么奢华的人啊! 和这样的人在一起真的很难过一种道德的生活。"

17. 曾子曰:"吾闻诸夫子:人未有自致者也,必也亲丧乎!"

  同一位学生说:"我曾听老师讲:'人们并不总是了解自己的本性,直到他们不得不为他们父母的死而哀痛。'"

18. 曾子曰:"吾闻诸夫子:孟庄子之孝也,其他可能也;其不改父之臣,与父之政,是难能也。"

  同一位学生说:"我曾听见老师谈到一位贵族的孝道,说:'他父亲死的时候,他所做的其他事情,别人也能做。但他在养活他父亲的老仆人以及贯彻执行他父亲的政策方面,人们会发现很难做到。'"

19. The Prime Minister in Confucius' native State having on one occasion appointed an officer to be Chief Criminal Judge, the officer came to a disciple of Confucius for advice. The disciple then said to the officer: "Rulers have long failed in their duties, and the people have long lived in a state of disorganisation. If you should discover enough evidence to convict a man, feel pity and be merciful to him; do not feel glad at your discovery."

20. A disciple of Confucius, speaking of an infamous emperor and tyrant of ancient times, remarked: "His wickedness was, after all, not so bad as tradition reports. Therefore a wise man will not persist in a low, disreputable life in defiance of what men may say: for otherwise, people will give him credit for all the wickednesses that are in the world. "

21. The same disciple remarked, "The failings of a great man are eclipses of the sun and moon. When he fails, all men see it; but, when he recovers from his failing, all men look up to him as before."

22. An officer of the Court in a certain State asked a disciple of Confucius, "From whom did Confucius learn the principles he taught? "

The disciple answered, "The principles of religion and morality held by the ancients have not all disappeared. Even now among men, those who are wise and worthy understand the great principles of the system, and those who are not wise, and even unworthy men,

19. 孟氏使阳肤为士师，问于曾子。曾子曰："上失其道，民散久矣。如得其情，则哀矜而勿喜。"

　　孔子故国的首要大臣有一次任命一位官员为主要刑事法官，那位官员向孔子的一个学生询问意见。那位学生于是对那位官员说："统治者们已经很长时间疏忽于他们的义务了，而人民也很长时间生活于混乱的状态之中。如果你发现了足够的证据来宣判一个人有罪，要感到怜悯并对他仁慈，不要为你的发现而高兴。"

20. 子贡曰："纣之不善，不如是之甚也。是以君子恶居下流，天下之恶皆归焉。"

　　孔子的一个学生，谈起古时候的一个臭名昭著的帝王与暴君，说："毕竟，他的邪恶没有传说的那么坏。因此，一个明智的人将不会保持在一种低俗、声名狼藉的生活中而无视人们可能会说什么：因为否则的话，人们将相信他拥有这个世界上所有的邪恶。"

21. 子贡曰："君子之过也，如日月之食焉：过也，人皆见之；更也，人皆仰之。"

　　同一位学生说："伟人的过失就像日食与月食。当他犯错误时，所有的人都看得见；但当他挽回错误时，所有的人又会像以前那样敬仰他。"

22. 卫公孙朝问于子贡曰："仲尼焉学？" 子贡曰："文武之道，未坠于地，在人。贤者识其大者，不贤者识其小者。莫不有文武之道焉。夫子焉不学？而亦何常师之有？"

　　某国朝廷的一个官员问孔子的一个学生："孔夫子是从谁那里学到他所教授的那些原理的？"

　　那位学生回答说："古人坚信的那些宗教与道德的原理并没有全部消失。即使在今天的人们中，那些明智而高尚的人是懂得这一体系中

understand the lesser principles. As to our Teacher, he had no need to learn; and even if he had to learn, why should he necessarily have had one special teacher?"

23. An officer of the Court in Confucius' native State, expressing admiration for a disciple of Confucius, remarked in presence of the other Court officers: "In my opinion this disciple of Confucius is superior to Confucius himself."

Afterwards, when somebody reported what the officer had said to the disciple above referred to, the latter said: "Let me use the comparison of two buildings. The wall of my building only reaches to the shoulders; one has only to look over and he can see all that is valuable in the apartments. But the wall of the Master's building is hundreds of feet high. If one does not find the door to enter by, he can never see the treasures of art and the glory of the men that are in the holy temple. Perhaps, however, there are few men who have found the door. I do not therefore wonder that the officer spoke as he did."

24. The same Court officer was once heard to abuse the character of Confucius. The same disciple on hearing of it, said: "It is no use for him to do that. Confucius can never be abused. The moral and intellectual endowments of other men as compared with those of Confucius are as hillocks and mounds which you may climb over. But Confucius is like the sun and moon. You can never jump over them. You may break your neck in trying to do it, but the sun and moon will remain as they are. In trying to do that, you only show your want of sense in not knowing what you can do."

的伟大原理的,而那些不明智,并且甚至是不高尚的人,也懂得那些次要的原理。至于我们的老师,他不必去学,即使他不得不学,为什么必定要有一个专门的老师呢?"

23. 叔孙武叔语大夫于朝,曰:"子贡贤于仲尼。"子服景伯以告子贡。子贡曰:"譬之宫墙,赐之墙也及肩,窥见室家之好。夫子之墙数仞,不得其门而入,不见宗庙之美,百官之富。得其门者或寡矣。夫子之云,不亦宜乎!"

　　孔子故国的一位朝廷官员,在其他朝廷官员面前赞美孔子的一位学生,说:"在我看来,孔夫子的这位学生要胜于孔夫子本人。"

　　过后,有人把那位官员的话告诉给了上面提到的那位学生,后者说:"让我来用两个建筑物打比喻吧。我的房屋的墙只达到肩膀这么高,一个人只要放眼一看,就能看到房间里所有珍贵的东西。但老师房屋的墙有数百英尺高。如果一个人没有找到门走进去,他就永远不会看到圣殿里的艺术的宝藏和那里的人们的华丽壮观。然而,或许很少有人找到了门。因此,那位官员那么说我并不感到惊讶。"

24. 叔孙武叔毁仲尼。子贡曰:"无以为也,仲尼不可毁也。他人之贤者,丘陵也,犹可逾也;仲尼,日月也,无得而逾焉。人虽欲自绝,其何伤于日月乎? 多见其不知量也!"

　　那同一个朝廷官员有一次曾被听到毁谤孔子的品格。那同一位学生听到了它,说:"他这样做是没有用的。孔子永远不能被毁谤。其他人的道德与才智的天赋与孔子相比就像小丘和土堆,你可以翻越过去,但孔子就像是太阳与月亮,你绝不可能越过它们。你可以拼命地试着去这样做,但太阳和月亮将依然保持原样。试着那样做时,你只会表现出你不知道自己能做点什么的理性的匮乏。"

25. Another man on another occasion said to the same disciple, "But you are too earnest and conscientious. How can Confucius be superior to you? "

"For one word", replied the disciple, "an educated man is held to be a man of understanding, and for one word he is held to be foolish. You should therefore be careful indeed in what you say. Now Confucius cannot be equalled, just as no man can climb up to the sky. If Confucius, our Master, had been born an emperor or a prince, he would then have done those things told of the holy kings of old:'What he lays down becomes law; what he orders is carried out; whither he beckons, the people follow; wherever his influence is felt, there is peace; while he lives, he lives honoured by the whole world; when he dies he is mourned for by the whole world.' How is it possible for a man to equal Confucius, our Master! "

25. 陈子禽谓子贡曰:"子为恭也,仲尼岂贤于子乎?" 子贡曰:"君子一言以为知,一言以为不知,言不可不慎也。夫子之不可及也,犹天之不可阶而升也。夫子之得邦家者,所谓立之斯立,道之斯行,绥之斯来,动之斯和。其生也荣,其死也哀,如之何其可及也。"

又有一次,另外一个人对同一个学生说:"但你是如此真诚而且有良知,孔夫子怎么能够胜过你呢?"

"根据一句话,"那位学生回答说,"一个有教养的人就会被认为是个有智慧的人;根据一句话,他也会被认为是愚蠢的。因此,你确实应该在说话方面仔细小心。孔子无法超越,就像没人可以爬上天空。如果孔子,我们的老师,生来是一位帝王或者国君,他就已经完成古代神圣的国王们所讲述的这些事情了:'他所规定的成为律法;他所命令的得到实施;无论他向何处召唤,人民就会跟随;无论哪里感受到他的影响力,那里就会和平;他活着时,受到整个世界的尊敬;当他死时,整个世界都为他悲痛。'一个人怎么可能去超越孔子,我们的师父呢!"

【评述】

1. 文中，"见危致命"，辜鸿铭译为"in presence of danger should be ready to give up his life"，"在危险面前应该准备好舍弃生命"。"见得思义"，译为"in view of personal advantage, he should think of what is right"，"见到私利，应该想到正义"，"得"指私利，"义"指正义、道义。"祭思敬"，译为"in worship, he should be devout and serious"，"祭拜时，应该虔诚而庄重"，"敬"指虔诚庄重。"丧思哀"，译为"in mourning, he should show heartfelt grief"，"服丧时，应该表示出由衷的悲痛"，"哀"指由衷的、发自内心的悲痛。"其可已矣"，译为"the above is about the sum of the duties of a gentleman"，"上面这些大约就是一个绅士的全部义务"。

2. 文中，"执德不弘"，辜鸿铭译为"holds fast to godliness without enlarging his mind"，"坚持虔诚之心，却不能扩充自己的思想"。其中，"德"译为"godliness"，指虔敬之心；"弘"译为"enlarging his mind"，扩充思想之意。"信道不笃"，译为"a man believes in truth, but is not steadfast in holding to his principles"，"信仰真理，却坚持他的原则时不够坚定"。其中，"道"指真理；"笃"指坚定。"焉能为有？焉能为亡？"辜鸿铭译为"such a man may as well leave such things alone"，"这样的一个人，还是远离这样的事情为好"，指这样的人还不如避免"执德"与"信道"两种行为的好。

3. 文中，"子夏之门人问交于子张"一句。"交"，辜鸿铭译为"friendship"，"友谊"。本节是子张与同学子夏的学生之间关于友谊的对话。

4. 文中，"虽小道，必有可观者焉"一句，辜鸿铭译为"even in any small and unimportant branch of an art or accomplishment, there is always something worthy of consideration"，"即使是在一种艺术或专长中的，任何微小而不重要的一项，都会有一些是值得考虑的东西"。其中，"小道"指在一种艺术或专长中微小而不重要的东西；"可观"指值得考虑。"致远恐泥，是以君子不为也"，辜鸿铭译为"if the attention to it is pushed too far, it is liable to degenerate into a hobby; for that reason a wise man never occupies himself with it"，"如果对它的关注是过分强迫的，它就易于堕落为一种业余的嗜好，因此，一个明智的人决不让自己只是埋首专注于它"。其中，"致远"指被迫过分关注，而不是由衷地热爱；"泥"指堕落为业余嗜好。

5. 文中，"日知其所亡，月无忘其所能"一句，辜鸿铭译为"day to day knows exactly what he has yet to learn and from month to month does not forget what he has learnt"，"日复一日都明确地知道他还必须要学什么，而且月复一月都不会忘记他已学到的东西"。其

中，"所亡"指必须要学习什么；"所能"指已学到的东西；"好学"译为"of culture"，有教养的。

6. "博学而笃志"，辜鸿铭译为"study extensively and are steadfast in your aim"，"广泛地学习并坚定你的目标"，"志"，指目标、志向。"切问而近思"，译为"investigate carefully what you learn and apply it to your own personal conduct"，"仔细谨慎地研究你所学到的东西，并将之运用于你自身的言行举止之中"。这里的"仁"，辜鸿铭译为"moral life"，道德的生活。

7. 文中，"百工居肆以成其事"一句，辜鸿铭译为"workmen work in their workshops to learn their trade"，"工匠在作坊中工作学得手艺"，"肆"指作坊。"君子学以致其道"译为"a scholar gives himself to study in order to get wisdom"，"一位学者致身于研究是为了获得智慧"，此处"君子"特指学者，"道"指智慧。两句之间，辜鸿铭用了"as ... so"进行连接，为比喻关系。

8. 这里的"文"，辜鸿铭译为"has an excuse ready"，"准备好借口"，指"小人"在犯错误时，总会为自己准备好借口辩护。朱熹注释："文，饰之也。小人惮于改过，而不惮于自欺，故必文以重其过。"（《四书章句集注》，第189页）

9. 文中，"三变"，辜鸿铭译为"appears different from three points of view"，"从三个视角来看会显得不同"，即"君子"常有的不同侧面，"俨然"（severe）是远观，"温"（gracious）是近观，"厉"（serious）是说话的样子。

10. 文中，"君子信而后劳其民；未信则以为厉己也"一句中，"君子"译为"a ruler"，"统治者"；"信而后劳其民"译为"first obtains the confidence of the people before he puts them to hard work"，"在他让人民从事繁重的工作之前，首先要获得人民的信任"，"信"指获得人民信任；"以为厉己"译为"be regarded by the people as oppression"，"被人民视为压迫"。这句话的意思是，如果政府得不到人民的信任却使其艰苦劳作，人民会将之视为压迫。"信而后谏，未信则以为谤己也"。"信而后谏"译为"first obtains the confidence of those whom he serves before he ventures to point out their errors"，"在他冒险指出他所服务的人的错误时，首先要获得他的信任"。其中，"谏"译为"point out their errors"，指出某人的错误；"信"指获得被服务者的信任；"以为谤己"译为"his superiors will only regard what he says as prompted by a desire to find fault"，"他的上级只会认为他在挑剔找茬"。

11. 文中，"大德不逾闲"，辜鸿铭译为 "keep himself strictly within bounds where the major points of the principles of morality are concerned"，"让自己严格地保持在与道德原则主要要点相关的范围之内"。其中，"大德" 译为 "the major points of the principles of morality"，道德原则的主要要点；"闲" 译为 "bounds"，界限、范围之意。"小德出入" 译为 "use his discretion in the minor points"，"在一些次要点上酌情决定"。其中，"小德" 译为 "the minor points"，即道德原则的次要要点；"出入" 译为 "use his discretion"，"使用酌情决定、自由决定的权利"，即酌情决定。

12. 在教育问题上，子游说子夏的学生 "当洒扫、应对、进退，则可矣。抑末也，本之则无，如之何"。辜鸿铭译 "洒扫应对进退" 为 "matters of manners and deportment"，"规矩礼仪与行为举止"，指的是礼仪的外在要求。"末" 译为 "mere minor matters"，"仅仅是次要、琐碎的事情"；"本之则无，如之何"，辜鸿铭译为 "as regards the foundation of a true education, they are as yet nowhere"，"至于真正教育的本质，他们到目前为止还离之甚远"，"本" 指真正教育的本质或基础。

对此，子夏反驳说 "君子之道，孰先传焉? 孰后倦焉?" 这里的 "道"，辜鸿铭译为 "in teaching men"，"在对人们的教育中"。这句话针对子游提到的 "本末" 的问题，问在教育中什么是重要和次要呢?

"譬诸草木，区以别矣"，辜鸿铭译为 "as in dealing with plants, so one must deal with pupils and class them according to their capabilities"，"就像管理植物一样，一个人也要管理他的弟子，并且根据他们的资质而分为不同的级别"。其中，"草木" 泛指植物；"区以别" 指按学生的资质分为不同级别，也即区分对待之意。

"君子之道，焉可诬也"，是子夏再次强调自己的观点。"诬"，辜鸿铭译为 "befool"，愚弄、欺骗之意。这一句的意思是，如果老师不认真地对学生们进行合理地教育，比如因材施教，帮助学生进行最理想的、最适合自己的发展，就是对学生的愚弄和欺骗。

子夏最后提出，只有 "圣人" 可以做到对 "君子之道" 的完全领悟，辜鸿铭译 "圣人" 为 "the most holy men"，"最神圣的人"。

13. 文中，"仕而优则学"，辜鸿铭译为 "An officer who has exceptional abilities, more than sufficient to carry out his duties, should devote himself to study"，"一个拥有超过履行其职责之外的优秀天资的官员，应该致身于学习"。其中，"仕" 指官员；"优" 译为 "has exceptional abilities, more than sufficient to carry out his duties"，"拥有能够超过履行他的职责之外的优秀天资"。"学而优则仕"，译为 "A student who has exceptional abilities, more than sufficient to carry on his studies, should enter the public service"，"一个拥有超过从事其学业之外的优秀天资的学生，应该参加公务服务"。其中，"学" 指学生；"优" 译为 "has

exceptional abilities, more than sufficient to carry on his studies","拥有超过从事其学业之外的优秀天资",也即"行有余力"之意;"仕"指参加公务服务,也即出仕为官。

14. 文中,"丧致乎哀而止",辜鸿铭译为"In mourning, the only thing indispensable is heart-felt grief","服丧时,唯一必不可少的事情,就是由衷而发的悲痛"。其中,"哀",指由衷而发的悲痛,真正的悲痛;"止",指唯一必不可少的事情。

15. 文中,"为难能",辜鸿铭译为"can do things which nobody else can do","能够做别人所不能做的事情",指能力格外突出。"未仁",译为"he is not quite perfect in his moral character","他的道德品质并不十分完善"。

16. 文中,"堂堂乎张也",辜鸿铭译为"what a style that man carries about with him","他是一个多么奢华的人啊"。"堂堂"译为"style",奢华、作风气派之意。"难与并为仁矣"译为"it is really difficult to live out a moral life along with such a man","和这样的人在一起真的很难过一种的道德生活"。"并为仁"指与他一起过道德的生活。

17. 文中,"人未有自致者也,必也亲丧乎"一句,辜鸿铭译为"Men often do not themselves know what is really in them until they have to mourn the death of their parents","人们经常并不了解自己的本性,直到他们不得不为他们父母的死而哀痛"。其中,"自致"指人们了解自己的本性。

18. 文中,"孟庄子之孝",辜鸿铭译为"the filial piety of a nobleman","一位贵族的孝道"。略去了"孟庄子"的称呼。"孝",辜鸿铭第一次译为专属性比较强的词"filial piety",字面意思指来自子女的虔敬之情,即"孝"之意。以往"孝"做形容词时,他都以"good son"等词来代指。

19. 文中,"孟氏使阳肤为士师,问于曾子"一句。按传统学者解释,阳肤为曾子的弟子,孟氏想任命他为自己家的狱官,他来请教自己的老师曾子。辜鸿铭的翻译是:"使阳肤为士师"译为"appointed an officer to be Chief Criminal Judge","任命一位官员为主要刑事法官";"问于曾子"译为"the officer came to a disciple of Confucius for advice","那位官员向孔子的一个学生询问意见"。下面曾子对阳肤的答复:"上失其道,民散久矣。如得其情,则哀矜而勿喜。"辜鸿铭译"失其道"为"fail in their duties","统治者疏忽他们的义务。"

对于本节表达的"哀矜而勿喜"的思想,辜鸿铭最后注释说:

人类要想达到他们懂得如何仁慈地对待作恶者、体谅违法者,并人道地对待那些无人性的人这一阶段,必须要走多长的路啊!那些首先传授这个道理,以及那些为了使它可能实现,并因促进它实现而献出生命的人,是真正有神性的人。(歌德,《威廉·麦斯特》)

人们现在谈论"发展"(Progress,发展,进步)。发展,根据歌德,是指人类应该向着越来越人道的方向"发展"。由此判断,中国在两千年以前,看来已经在文明上取得真正的发展了。

20. 文中,"纣之不善,不如是之甚也"一句,"纣",略去了名字,译为"an infamous emperor and tyrant of ancient times","古时候一个臭名昭著的帝王与暴君";"不如是之甚"译为"his wickedness was, after all, not so bad as tradition reports","他的邪恶并没有传说的那么坏"。"是以君子恶居下流,天下之恶皆归焉"。"君子恶居下流"译为"a wise man will not persist in a low, disreputable life in defiance of what men may say","一个明智的人将不会保持在一种低俗、声名狼藉的生活中而无视人们可能会说什么"。其中,"下流"指低俗、声名狼藉的生活状态;"天下之恶皆归焉"译为"people will give him credit for all the wickednesses that are in the world","人们将相信他拥有这个世界上所有的邪恶",即聚集世界上所有的恶名。

21. 文中,"君子之过也,如日月之食焉"一句,辜鸿铭译为"the failings of a great man are eclipses of the sun and moon","伟人的缺陷就像日食与月食"。"君子之过"译为"the failings of a great man",指伟人的缺陷、不足。"过也,人皆见之;更也,人皆仰之",辜鸿铭译为"when he fails, all men see it; but, when he recovers from his failing, all men look up to him as before","当他表现出缺陷时,所有的人都看得见;但当他从缺陷中恢复过来时,所有的人又会像以前那样敬仰他"。其中,"更"指从缺陷中恢复过来;"仰"指像从前那样敬仰他。

22. "仲尼焉学?"辜鸿铭译为"From whom did Confucius learn the principles he taught?","孔夫子是从谁那里学到他所教授的那些原理的?"这一节,卫公孙朝问子贡孔子的学问与思想的来源。"文武之道,未坠于地",辜鸿铭译为"The principles of religion and morality held by the ancients have not all disappeared","古人坚信的那些宗教与道德的原理并没有全部消失"。其中,"文武之道"指古代的宗教与道德原理;"坠于地"指全部消失。"在人,贤者识其大者,不贤者识其小者",辜鸿铭译为"Even now among men, those who are wise and worthy understand the great principles of the system, and those who are not wise, and even unworthy men, understand the lesser principles","那些明智而高尚的人懂得这一体系中的伟大原理,而那些并不明智,即使是并不高尚的人,也懂得那些次要的原

理"。其中,"大者"指"文武之道"中的重大原理,"小者"指次要的原理。这句话指"文武之道"(即古代的宗教与道德原理)还被人们(贤者与不贤者)所传承。

23. "譬之宫墙,赐之墙也及肩,窥见室家之好"是当别人指出子贡优于孔子时,子贡拿"宫墙"作为比喻,来形容自己与孔子的差距。并且,子贡不仅强调了孔子"宫墙"之高,而且强调了里面的"富"和"美"。"夫子之墙数仞,不得其门而入,不见宗庙之美,百官之富"。其中,"数仞",译为"hundreds of feet high","数百英尺之高"。为了便于西方读者阅读,他将"仞"翻译成了"英尺"这一西方计量单位。

24. "叔孙武叔毁仲尼",辜鸿铭译为"The same Court officer was once heard to abuse the character of Confucius","那同一个朝廷官员有一次曾被听到毁谤孔子的品格"。略去了"叔孙武叔"的名字。"毁"译为"abuse","毁谤,侮辱"。下面是子贡对此辩护,并称毁谤孔子的人"不知量",辜鸿铭译为"want of sense","理性的匮乏"。

25. "子为恭也",辜鸿铭译为"you are too earnest and conscientious","你是如此真诚而且有良知",指陈子禽称赞子贡"真诚且有良知",认为比孔子更优。下面子贡对他进行了驳斥。其中,"夫子之不可及也,犹天之不可阶而升也",译为"Now Confucius cannot be equalled, just as no man can climb up to the sky","孔子无法超越,就像没人可以爬上天空"。其中,"及"译为"equal","相比";"天",译为"sky","天空"。这是辜鸿铭继"God"、"heaven"后的第三种译法。"夫子之得邦家者",辜鸿铭译为"If Confucius, our Master, had been born an emperor or a prince","如果孔子生来是一位帝王或者国君"。"所谓立之斯立,道之斯行,绥之斯来,动之斯和,其生也荣,其死也哀",辜鸿铭翻译时首先在这十六字排比句前加了一句"he would then have done those things told of the holy kings of old","他就已经完成古代神圣的国王们所讲述的这些事情了",指如果孔子生来是位帝王或诸侯国君,那么,他早已完成历史以来帝王们就在追求的成功了。十六字排比句,辜鸿铭认为是一句古代成语。"立之斯立,道之斯行,绥之斯来,动之斯和,其生也荣,其死也哀",译为"What he lays down becomes law; what he orders is carried out; whither he beckons, the people follow; wherever his influence is felt, there is peace; while he lives, he lives honoured by the whole world; when he dies he is mourned for by the whole world","他所规定的成为律法;他所命令的得到实施;无论他向何处召唤,人民就会跟随;无论哪里感受到他的影响力,那里就会和平;他活着时,受到整个世界的尊敬;当他死时,整个世界都为他悲痛"。其中,"立"指做出规定、成为律法;"道"指命令;"行"指实施;"绥"指召唤人民;"来"指人民的跟随;"动"指某地受其影响;"和"指和平;"荣"指受到尊敬;"哀"指世界为他而悲痛。

CHAPTER XX
尧曰第二十

1. The ancient Emperor Yao, when in his old age he abdicated the throne in favour of his successor, Shun, thus gave him charge: "Hail to thee, O Shun! The God-ordained order of succession now rests upon thy person. Hold fast with thy heart and soul to the true middle course of right. If there shall be distress and want among the people within the Empire, the title and honour which God has given to thee will be taken away from thee for ever. "

Afterwards the Emperor Shun, when he abdicated in favour of his successor, the great Yü, used the same language in giving him charge.

The Emperor T'ang, when he ascended the Imperial throne, thus offered up his prayer to God: "I, Li, who am one of thy children, do here take upon me to offer up to thee in sacrifice this black heifer, and to announce to Thee, O supreme and sovereign God, that sinners I shall not dare to pardon; and, in the choice of Thy servants, I pray Thee, O God, that thou wilt let me know Thy will and pleasure. If I do sin against Thee, let not the people suffer for my sin. But if the people shall sin against Thee, let me alone bear the penalty of their iniquities."

With the inauguration of the Chou dynasty, the country was greatly prosperous; but only the good were rich.

The Emperors guided themselves by the principle contained in these words: "Although there are men attached and related to our person, yet we do not consider them equal in value to men of moral character. If the people fail in their conduct, it is we alone who are to blame."

The Emperors set themselves to adjust and enforce uniformity in the use of weights and measures; to organise the administration and laws; to re-establish disused offices: in this way the administration throughout the Empire was well carried out. They restored extinct

444

1. 尧曰："咨！尔舜！天之历数在尔躬。允执其中。四海困穷，天禄永终。"舜亦以命禹。曰："予小子履，敢用玄牡，敢昭告于皇皇后帝：有罪不敢赦。帝臣不蔽，简在帝心。朕躬有罪，无以万方；万方有罪，罪在朕躬。"周有大赉，善人是富。"虽有周亲，不如仁人。百姓有过，在予一人。"谨权量，审法度，修废官，四方之政行焉。兴灭国，继绝世，举逸民，天下之民归心焉。所重：民、食、丧、祭。宽则得众，信则民任焉，敏则有功，公则说。

那位古代帝王尧，在他年老时把帝位让给了他的继承者舜，并这样给他训示："我向你致敬，噢，舜！对来自上帝旨意的指令的继承，现在就依靠你本人了。要用你的心与灵魂牢牢坚持住那真正正义的折中方针。如果帝国的人民之中会有痛苦穷困，上帝所赋予你的职权与荣耀将会永远地从你手里被拿走。"

后来，那位帝王舜，在他把帝位让给他的继承者，那位伟大的禹时，训示了他同样的话。

那位帝王汤，在他登上帝位时，他这样向上帝祷告："我，履，您的子女之一，在此向您献上这头黑色的小母牛，并向您宣告，噢，地位至高与权力至上的上帝，罪人我不敢赦免；在您的仆人的选择上，我祈求您，噢，上帝，您要让我知道您的意志与愿望。如果我得罪了您，不要让人民为我的罪恶受苦。但如果人民得罪了您，让我独自忍受对他们的罪恶的惩罚。"

周王朝开创后，国家非常繁荣昌盛，但只有那些良善的人才是富有的。

帝王们通过包含如下几句话的原则来指导他们自身："尽管有人依附并亲近于我们本身，但我们不会把他们与有道德品质的人在价值上视为是相等的。如果人民在行为中有失误，只谴责我们就好。"

帝王们致力于调整并实施重量与长度度量单位的统一使用；致力于组织行政与制定法律；致力于重建被废弃的公共机构：这样，整个帝国的政令得以畅通。他们接续覆灭贵族的传承；任命那些有美德与学问

families of nobles; called to office retired men of virtue and learning: thus the people throughout the Empire gladly acknowledged their authority. What they paid serious attention to were food for the people, rituals and mourning for the dead, and religious services. By considerateness, they won the heart of the people; by good faith, they caused the people to have confidence in them; by diligence in business, what they undertook prospered; by their fair and impartial dealing, the people were contented.

2. A disciple of Confucius enquired of him, "What should be done in order to conduct the government of a country? "

Confucius answered, "In the conduct of government there are five good principles to be kept in mind and respected, and there are four bad principles to be avoided. "

"What are the five good principles to be respect? "asked the disciple. Confucius replied, "First, to benefit the people without wasting the resources of the country; Secondly, to encourage labour without giving cause for complaint; Thirdly, to desire for the enjoyments of life without being covetous; Fourthly, to be dignified without being supercilious; Fifthly, to inspire awe without being severe."

"But," again asked the disciple, "What do you mean by 'To benefit the people without wasting the resources of the country'?"

"It is," replied Confucius, "to encourage the people to undertake such profitable labour as will best benefit them, without its being necessary to give them any assistance out of the public revenue; that is what is mean by, 'To benefit the people without wasting the resources of the country'."

的隐退的人为官：这样，整个帝国的人民欣然地承认他们的权威。他们所重点关注的事情是人民的食物、为死者举行典礼与丧事，以及宗教礼仪。凭着体谅关怀，他们赢得了民心；凭着好的信义，他们让人民信任他们；凭着做事勤勉，他们所从事的事情得到了成功兴旺；凭着他们的公平与公正的行为，人民感到满意。

2. 子张问于孔子曰："何如斯可以从政矣？"子曰："尊五美，屏四恶，斯可以从政矣。"子张曰："何谓五美？"子曰："君子惠而不费，劳而不怨，欲而不贪，泰而不骄，威而不猛。"子张曰："何谓惠而不费？"子曰："因民之所利而利之，斯不亦惠而不费乎？择可劳而劳之，又谁怨？欲仁而得仁，又焉贪？君子无众寡，无小大，无敢慢，斯不亦泰而不骄乎？君子正其衣冠，尊其瞻视，俨然人望而畏之，斯不亦威而不猛乎？"子张曰："何谓四恶？"子曰："不教而杀谓之虐；不戒视成谓之暴；慢令致期谓之贼；犹之与人也，出纳之吝，谓之有司。"

　　孔子的一个学生问他："管理一个国家的政治应该做哪些事？"

　　孔子回答说："在政治的管理中，有五种好的原则要记住并遵守，还有四种坏的原则要避免。"

　　"哪五种好的原则要去遵守？"那个学生问。

　　孔子回答说："第一，让人民受益而不要浪费国家的财力；第二，鼓励工作但不要引起不满；第三，渴望生活的乐趣而不贪婪；第四，高贵而不傲慢；第五，令人敬畏但不过分苛刻。"

　　"但是，"那个学生又问，"你说'让人民受益而不要浪费国家的资源'是什么意思？"

Confucius then went on to say, "In the employment of the people in forced labour on works for the public good, if you select those who are most able to bear it, who will have any cause for complaint? Make it your aim to wish for moral well-being and you will never be liable to be covetous. A wise and good man, whether dealing with a few people or with many, with great matters or with small, is never presumptuous and never regards anything as beneath his notice or as unworthy of serious and careful attention: that is what is meant by being dignified without being supercilious. And, finally, to inspire awe without being severe, a wise and good man has only to watch over every minute detail connected with his daily life, not only of conduct and bearing, but even in minor details of dress, so as to produce an effect upon the public mind, which, without these influences, could only have been produced by fear."

"Now I understand," said the disciple, "But what do you mean by the four bad principles of which you have spoken? "

"First," replied Confucius, "is cruelty; that is, the undue punishment of crimes committed through ignorance arising out of a neglected education. Secondly, tyranny of that kind which renders people liable to punishment for offences without first clearly giving public notice. Thirdly, heartlessness; which means to leave orders in abeyance and uncertainty, and suddenly to enforce their performance by punishment. And lastly, meanness; to treat your subordinates as if bartering with them exactly and meanly: that is called behaving like professional men and not like gentlemen. "

"它是指，"孔子回答说，"鼓励人民从事诸如不必从政府收入中为他们提供援助就能够让他们最受益的有利工作，这就是'让人民受益而不要浪费国家的资源'的意思。"

孔子然后接着说："使役人民为公众的利益而进行艰苦工作时，如果你挑选那些最能够承受它的人，谁还有理由不满呢？将希望得到道德的安宁作为你的目标，你就永远不会容易变得贪婪。一个明智而良善的人，不管是对待少数人还是许多人，不管是重大的事情还是细微的事情，从不应专横冒失，从不将任何事情视为是不够引起他注意，或者不值得严肃对待和慎重处理的：这就是高贵而不傲慢的意思。最后，要令人敬畏而不过分苛刻，一个明智而良善的人必须管理好与生活有关的每分钟的细节，不仅仅是举止行为与姿态，甚至包括衣着方面的次要细节，以便于对公众的思想产生影响，如果没有这些因素的话，那么影响只能产生于畏惧。"

"现在我明白了，"那位学生说，"但你所说的四种坏原则是指什么？"

"第一，"孔子回答说，"是残忍，它是指，过分地惩罚因教育的忽视导致无知而引起的罪过。第二，是暴政，它表现为人民因为没有事先明确的公告而容易违法并受到惩罚。第三，冷酷无情，它是指让命令暂时搁置并变化不定，却突然通过惩罚的措施来强制执行。最后，吝啬卑劣，对待你的下属就像交易货物一样严密与吝啬：这被称作行为像官僚而不像绅士。"

3. Confucius remarked, "Without religion a man cannot be a good and wise man; without knowledge of the arts and of the principles of art, a man cannot form his judgement; without the knowledge of the use of language, a man cannot judge of and know the character of men."

[This last chapter sums up the teaching of Confucius: the 1st section shows the grand and high principle of responsibility in the rules towards God as the foundation of government, and gives also the important function necessary for the carrying out of good government; The 2nd section gives what principles a ruler must constantly guide himself by and what principles he must avoid; the last section sums up the three things necessary for the education and formation of the character of a gentleman: three things, namely, Religion, a Knowledge of the Arts, and Literature.][1]

---

① 方括号内的文字是辜鸿铭对第二十章的总结。

3. 子曰："不知命，无以为君子也。不知礼，无以立也。不知言，无以知人也。"

　　孔子说："离开宗教，一个人就不能够成为良善而明智的人；没有关于艺术及艺术原则的学问，一个人就不能够形成他的判断力；没有关于如何使用语言的学问，一个人就不能够评价与了解人们的品质。"

　　[最后的这一章概括了孔子的学说：第1节说明了在统治中对上帝的重大责任与高级原则，而对于实现好的政治来说，也有重要的作用；第2节规定了一个统治者应该坚定地用什么样的原则来指导自己，以及什么样的原则他应该避免；最后一节概括了对于绅士道德品质的教育与形成来说十分必要的三件事：即宗教、关于艺术的学问，以及文学。]

【评述】

1. 第一段，辜鸿铭认为是尧把帝王让给了他的继承者舜时对他的训示。"天之历数在尔躬"，辜鸿铭译为 "The God-ordained order of succession now rests upon thy person"，"对来自上帝旨意的指令的继承，现在就依靠你本人了"。其中，"天之历数"指上帝的旨意，"天"辜鸿铭再次译为 "God"，"上帝"。

"允执其中"，辜鸿铭译为 "Hold fast with thy heart and soul to the true middle course of right"，"要用你的心与灵魂牢牢坚持住那真正正义的折中方针"。"执"指坚持；"中"指正义的折中方针。

"四海困穷，天禄永终"，译为 "If there shall be distress and want among the people within the Empire, the title and honour which God has given to thee will be taken away from thee for ever"，"如果帝国的人民之中会有痛苦穷困，上帝所赋予你的职权与荣耀将会永远地从你手里被拿走"。其中，"四海"指帝国之内；"困穷"译为 "there shall be distress"，有痛苦穷困之意；"天禄"译为 "the title and honour which God has given to thee"，"上帝所赋予的职权与荣耀"；"永终"指永远被夺走。这句话是尧对舜的一个告诫。

"予小子履，敢用玄牡，敢昭告于皇皇后帝：有罪不敢赦。帝臣不蔽，简在帝心"。辜鸿铭在句前加了一句："The Emperor T'ang, when he ascended the Imperial throne, thus offered up his prayer to God"，"那位帝王汤，在他登上帝位时，他这样向上帝祷告"。辜鸿铭认为，这段话是汤的祷辞，句中的"履"，即商汤的名字。

"予小子履，敢用玄牡，敢昭告于皇皇后帝"译为 "I, Li, who am one of thy children, do here take upon me to offer up to thee in sacrifice this black heifer, and to announce to Thee, O supreme and sovereign God"，"我，履，您的子女之一，在此向您献上这头黑色的小母牛，并向您宣告，噢，地位至高与权力至上的上帝"。其中，"玄牡"译为 "black heifer"，"黑色的小母牛"，传统学者一般解释为黑色公牛；"昭告"译为 "to announce"，"宣告、宣布"；"皇皇后帝"译为 "supreme and sovereign God"，"地位至高与权力至上的上帝"。

"有罪不敢赦"译为 "sinners I shall not dare to pardon"，"罪人我不敢赦免"。"帝臣不蔽，简在帝心"译为 "in the choice of Thy servants, I pray Thee, O God, that thou wilt let me know Thy will and pleasure"，"在您的仆人的选择上，我祈求您，噢，上帝，您要让我知道您的意志与愿望"。其中，"帝臣"指上帝的仆人；"不蔽"与"帝心"结合起来，指 "let me know Thy will and pleasure"，"要让我知道上帝的意志与愿望"。

"朕躬有罪，无以万方；万方有罪，罪在朕躬"，辜鸿铭译为 "If I do sin against Thee, let not the people suffer for my sin. But if the people shall sin against Thee, let me alone bear the penalty of their iniquities"，"如果我得罪了您，不要让人民为我的罪恶受苦。但如果人民得罪了您，让我独自忍受对他们的罪恶的惩罚"。其中，"罪"译为 "sin against Thee"，指得罪上帝；"以"指殃及、连累之意；"万方"指人民。

"周有大赉,善人是富",辜鸿铭译为"With the inauguration of the Chou dynasty, the country was greatly prosperous; but only the good were rich","周王朝开创后,国家非常繁荣昌盛,但只有那些良善的人才是富有的"。此处,"大赉"应是"greatly prosperous",非常繁荣昌盛之意。

"虽有周亲,不如仁人。百姓有过,在予一人。"辜鸿铭翻译时在这两句话前加了一句说明:"the Emperors guided themselves by the principle contained in these words","帝王们通过包含如下几句话的原则来指导他们自身"。也就是说,这两句话是古代帝王们共同遵守的原则。"虽有周亲,不如仁人"译为"Although there are men attached and related to our person, yet we do not consider them equal in value to men of moral character","尽管有人依附并亲近于我们本身,但我们不会把他们与有道德品质的人在价值上视为是相等的"。"周亲",指依附并亲近帝王们的人;"仁人"指有道德品质的人;"不如"译为"do not consider them equal in value to …","不会把他们在价值上视为相等"之意。这一句的意思是,尊贤,要超过亲亲。"百姓有过,在予一人",译为"If the people fail in their conduct, it is we alone who are to blame","如果人民在行为中有失误,只谴责我们就好"。指帝王们如果治理国家不善,即受上帝的谴责。

"谨权量,审法度,修废官,四方之政行焉"一句,"谨权量"译为"to adjust and enforce uniformity in the use of weights and measures","调整并实施度量衡的统一使用"。其中,"谨"指统一使用之意;"权量"译为"weights and measures","重量与长度的度量单位";也有人译为"度量衡";"审法度"译为"to organise the administration and laws","组织行政与制定法律";"修废官"译为"to re-establish disused offices","重建被废弃的公共机构";"四方之政行焉"译为"in this way the administration throughout the Empire was well carried out","这样,整个帝国的政令得以畅通"。这段话说的是古代帝王对国家具体的行政管理。

"兴灭国,继绝世,举逸民,天下之民归心焉"一句,"兴灭国,继绝世"译为"they restored extinct families of nobles","他们接续覆灭贵族的传承"。"举逸民"译为"called to office retired men of virtue and learning","任命那些有美德与学问的隐退的人为官","逸民"指有美德和学问的退隐的人;"天下之民归心焉"译为"the people throughout the Empire gladly acknowledged their authority","整个帝国的人民欣然地承认他们的权威",指承认帝王们的权威或权力。

"所重:民、食、丧、祭"一句,辜鸿铭的翻译是:"重"译为"paid serious attention to","所重点关注的事情"。"民、食、丧、祭"译为"food for the people, rituals and mourning for the dead, and religious services","人民的食物、为死者举行典礼与丧事,以及宗教礼仪"。他是把"民食"连读,即人民的食物。"祭"译为"religious services","宗教仪式",指古代帝王们关注民生与人民的精神信仰。

"宽则得众，信则民任焉，敏则有功，公则说"。辜鸿铭的翻译是："宽则得众"译为"by considerateness, they won the heart of the people"，"凭着体谅关怀，他们赢得了民心"；"信则民任焉"译为"by good faith, they caused the people to have confidence in them"，"凭着好的信义，他们让人民信任他们"；"敏则有功"译为"by diligence in business, what they undertook prospered"，"凭着做事勤勉，他们所从事的事情得到了成功兴旺"，"敏"指做事勤勉，"有功"指所做的事情成功兴旺；"公则说"译为"by their fair and impartial dealing, the people were contented"，"凭着他们的公平与公正的行为，人民感到满意"，"公"指公平、公正，"说"指人民满意。这句话说的是古代帝王们的现实行为特征与执政成效。

2. 子张问从政，孔子提出了"五美"、"四恶"的概念。"尊五美，屏四恶，斯可以从政矣"，辜鸿铭译为"in the conduct of government there are five good principles to be kept in mind and respected, and there are four bad principles to be avoided"，"在政治的管理中，有五种好的原则要记住并遵守，还有四种坏的原则要避免"。其中，"五美"指五种好的原则；"四恶"指四种坏的原则。下面的文字是孔子的具体阐述。其中，"欲仁而得仁，又焉贪"中的"仁"，辜鸿铭译为"moral well-being"，"道德的安宁"。

3. 文中，"不知命，无以为君子也"，辜鸿铭译为"Without religion a man cannot be a good and wise man"，"离开宗教，一个人就不能够成为良善而明智的人"。他把"命"解释为宗教，可见第二章第4节的评述（本书第39页）。"不知礼，无以立也"，译为"without knowledge of the arts and of the principles of art, a man cannot form his judgement"，"没有关于艺术及艺术原则的学问，一个人就不能够形成他的判断力"。其中，"礼"指关于艺术与艺术原则的学问。通过全书来看，把"礼"译为艺术，是他最常见的翻译。"立"指判断力，这也是他对"立"最常见的翻译。"不知言，无以知人也"，译为"without the knowledge of the use of language, a man cannot judge of and know the character of men"，"没有关于如何使用语言的学问，一个人就不能够对人们的品质进行评价与了解"。"知言"指掌握使用语言的学问，即懂得如何运用语言；"知人"指了解别人的品质。

后　记

辜鸿铭的英译《论语》是本很奇特的书，最令人着迷之处在于——它不仅是本《论语》，更是一本直接体现辜鸿铭独特思想、并以儒家经典为承载的读本。众所周知，辜鸿铭是近代一位享誉国际的思想家，很多人视之为东方文化及中国文化的代表，英国作家毛姆称之为"孔子学说的最大权威"，然而，其特殊的教育背景与思想特征，又使其哲学思想及学术结论颇具争议性。那么，通过此《论语》，我们可以窥见他对儒家经典的最直接理解。所以，从"思想"角度去探索这本书，而非从"翻译"角度去做专业研究，是我译述本书的初衷。

而挖掘并展现《论语》的精神价值，也确实是辜鸿铭所极力在做的。为此，他甚至不惜删去了书中绝大部分人名、物名、地名等固有名称，只将对话内容展示给读者，以让他们免于受到古代繁琐名称的困扰，影响到对本书精神内涵的把握。而且，因他把英译的读者主要设定为西方人，所以，为了让西方人更易读懂，他还在书中对诸多中西人物及事件进行了大量类比。这在很大程度上也带来了另一重意义，即扩大了《论语》中某些概念的外延，给我们了解《论语》的精神价值提供了更广阔的视野。从这个意义上讲，他通过翻译实则把《论语》的精神价值进行了最大化。当然，从翻译角度来讲，他对书中某些概念翻译的准确度仍具争议，但这对于整本书来讲无疑"瑕不掩瑜"。

辜鸿铭是第一位向西方译介儒家经典的中国人，但迄今为止，他的译本仍是公认的最具文采的一本，有人甚至认为，他的英译《论语》本身就是一本生动的文学作品。我想，当你翻开此书时，并不难发现这一点，甚至会很容易被其书所具有的强烈的现场感而带入情境之中，似乎能直接与孔子等人对话，生动的形象呼之欲出。这也构成了本书的魅力之一。我想，对于这一点，可能也是读者所最期待的吧。

从2005年产生译述本书的想法算，迄今已十年了，期间也经历过多番修改润色。然而，囿于我自身的浅见寡识，至今仍无法令本书达至最理想的状态，书中仍存有诸多不足，惟有以惶恐之心望请各位方家不吝指正，并尤盼与对本书萌生兴趣的诸师友可以在思想层面交流互进。

最后，感谢所有对本书的写作，以及在此期间对本人的工作与生活提供过帮助与关爱的人，我将铭记于心。

是为记。

王京涛，于北京
写于2015年5月11日晨
改于2016年2月1日夜及3月12日晨